Godhunter

Godhunter

Isobel Lynn

Paperback ISBN: 979-8-9885306-0-2

Ebook ISBN: 979-8-9885306-1-9

For Jack and Sophie

Chapter One

There must come a moment in every girl's life when she looks back over her bevy of mistakes and ill-advised decisions and questions which it was that brought her to this. Surely, the feeling is universal. At least that's what Bryony assumed as she stood over the body of a young man racked with seizures—in full view of some fifty of her most devout followers—and wondered whether it might be kinder to just let the boy die.

How did she get here? What could she have done differently? Where exactly did she turn left when she was meant to go right?

The healing tent was thick with life—perspiration, tears, the electrified breath of those who sang Bryony's praises. The sick boy had been carried to the stage by his parents, laid across a stone altar assembled just for this purpose, and left to Bryony's tender ministrations. He couldn't have been more than sixteen years of age. His muscles tensed and twisted as his body reacted to a fever no one could break. His chest had been bared in anticipation of the healing touch of his god, or rather his parents' god if Bryony was honest. She had no idea whether the boy was a devotee of hers, though he probably was. Very few in the community rejected her. Why would they? All she ever did was heal them. And she asked nothing in return other than life's basic necessities and a little love perhaps. She was as benevolent a god as she could be. Still . . .

How had it all come to this?

Bryony Moss wasn't born a god, and she hadn't set out to become one either. She'd been a quiet child with few friends and fewer acquaintances, content to play by herself in the little grove of plum trees behind her family's old farmhouse. She'd loved the spring when the grove would flower and rain pink confetti onto her hair and shoulders. She recalled being some version of happy, even with the background noise of fear and paranoia that permeated her world.

Then her mother got sick, followed by her little brother and her father. And like most people who found themselves in the grip of disease post-apocalypse, they quickly died.

It was easy to blame the angels. They'd taken so much, decades before Bryony was even born. Every guardian angel turned out to be somewhat less of a guardian than people had assumed. They were more like assassins, dutifully awaiting their orders, and when the orders came down, they were devastating. Every person of scientific learning—every doctor, chemist, biologist, and physicist—was exterminated. All media referencing such knowledge was destroyed upon discovery. Technological advancement came to a standstill as planned obsolescence quickly ate away at humanity's twenty-first century gains.

Mortals could no longer be trusted to rule themselves. War, corruption, and environmental destruction were evidence of that. So the angels generously offered to rule instead. Ignorance, being such a valuable tool for encouraging submission in notoriously rebellious creatures, was achieved in the most brutal, traumatic way possible. But what was the sacrifice of a few lives in the grand scheme of things? Surely the ends justified the means. Now there was no such thing as war, the environment was positively teeming with life, and no one ever questioned whether the sacrifice was necessary. No one dared.

Yes, it was easy to blame the angels, but honestly, it wasn't their fault. How many children had suffered the after-effects of the same massacre, grown up in the same superstitious world, and yet hadn't become gods? They didn't all find themselves the heads of small but devout congregations. They didn't welcome worship the way Bryony did. So she couldn't hand all the responsibility for her choices to angels.

Perhaps it came down to the loss of her family. After all, that was the birth of her unusual relationship with death. When her little brother took sick, Bryony began wearing her dead mother's costume dresses around the house to amuse him. Her favorite was a beautiful, formal gown from a performance of *The Unsinkable Molly Brown*. For her brother's funeral, she dyed it black, and it felt like a second skin to her. So she dyed all her mother's old costume dresses black and wore them out like it was the fashion of the day.

She had watched everyone she loved suffer and suffer until death became a gentle relief, and she'd learned to be grateful for it. Life was a struggle, not just for survival but for meaning and identity. Death, instead, offered its assurance: *You belong here in my arms, in the earth, in the wind and sea. Your meaning is rest, and quiet, and new life. You are the grass, the trees, and little, scurrying feet.*

Bryony frequently visited the graveyard where her family was buried. She felt at home among the crumbling headstones and marble monuments. She was a ghost among ghosts, a citizen of their country. She spoke their language, heard their music, read their poetry. It wasn't that she was anxious to die. She just knew one day she would, and she was perfectly comfortable with the idea. If life was an exhausting journey abroad, death was the creaking front door of her childhood home.

It had been the loss of her first family that led Bryony to seek out a second one in the graveyard. And the graveyard had provided.

"Please, Mistress." A quiet voice from the congregation brought her back to the present. It was a woman in the front row. The boy's mother? Grandmother? "Please, save him."

Bryony tilted her head and squinted at the woman. The black veil she always wore obscured her vision a little, but it was worth the anonymity it provided. No one could see her face, her questions, her doubt. She performed miracles dressed as a shadow, and no one ever bothered her outside the tent.

She glanced down at the boy on the stone slab, his body only just quieted from his most recent seizure. He panted and wheezed, sweating and tossing in abject misery. Bryony pinched her lips closed and twisted the ring she wore on the middle finger of her left hand. "But . . . is that what he wants?"

The woman in the front row frowned, her brow furrowed in confusion. "Mistress, he is dying."

"I know." Bryony was surprising herself. She didn't usually address her congregation. She preferred to play her part quietly, soak up the love and gratitude offered in exchange for healing, and then retreat. It felt wonderful, receiving that love, but was it right? Why did she try so hard to convince herself she was worthy? Something in her protested too much.

If only she could ask Shakespeare. He would have a reasonable answer like he always did. She imagined him standing before her now, cocking his black head, wiping his beak on the body of the boy, irreverent as always. Of course, irreverent was all he would ever be. He was a bird, a crow to be precise, and he neither knew nor acknowledged any god but himself.

Just heal the boy, Shakespeare would say. *Get on with it, so we can eat.*

But what if he prefers to die? she would ask.

And Shakespeare would pause his grooming long enough to say, *He can kill himself later if he wants.*

But suicide is forbidden.

And Shakespeare would shake his head at her. *If he doesn't want to take matters into his own hands, he can go insult an angel, and they'll happily oblige him. Just heal the boy, Bryony. Appease your followers, and let's get dinner.*

"I will heal him," Bryony said aloud. Her congregation responded with a collective sigh of relief. The woman in the front row burst into grateful tears, and behind the stone altar, Bryony turned her ring again. It was an unusual piece. A silver hummingbird's skull was mounted where a gemstone would normally be. Bryony never took it off.

The boy on the table shifted, and Bryony leaned over his body. She laid her head on his chest and listened to his slowing heartbeat through her veil. If she did nothing, he would die within hours. Death might have been exactly what he wanted, but she had no way of asking him.

She began to hum, a misdirection in anticipation of a little sleight of hand. She murmured a chant and placed both her palms on the boy's chest. Everything happened under her veil. Those watching saw a mere shadow of her movements. No one noticed the way she curled her left hand into a fist and scratched the surface of the boy's skin with the beak of her ring. It was nothing, the pinprick of a kitten's claw. The mark would heal before anyone even noticed it was there.

And already the boy's heartbeat was strengthened, his color returned. Already his breath became measured, and he sank into the comfort of true rest, his infection eradicated, his fever broken.

Bryony straightened and lifted her gaze to heaven. She held out her hands and spread her fingers as if releasing the illness into the ether. Then she announced, "He is well."

The crowd erupted. His mother wept. Bryony's devotees began to sing a ballad of her praises. She bowed like a performer, a circus magician—which was what she was, really—and backed out of the tent.

The ring was the trick, the lie, the con. The congregation believed that Bryony herself had the power to heal, that she laid her hands on the bodies of the sick and her holy touch drove the illness from them. It wasn't true at all.

Wherever she went, Bryony wore her little treasure. She'd found it ten years ago, the same day she met Shakespeare. He'd been standing over it in a graveyard—though it didn't look like a ring at the time—not far from her family's burial plots. He'd pecked at the ground as if to say, *Look at this. Isn't it something?*

Innocent curiosity led her to this. That's what was to blame in the end. Well, that and her ridiculous desire for a fairy-tale life. She'd been nourished on her own fantasies, and she half believed they were possible. The idea of a crow in a graveyard leading her to a fated, magical item was irresistible. So, even though it was stupid, impossible, childish, she heeded the crow.

As she approached, the bird retreated. It flew onto an adjacent, crumbling, stone angel and cawed three times in an almost comical display of displeasure. Bryony chuckled, but her eye was immediately drawn to the item the crow had been plucking at. It was silver, half buried, yet it gleamed as though it had just been polished. She brushed the earth and dead leaves away from what appeared to be a kind of sword hilt. Two serpents with emerald eyes wound their way up the handle, through which she could easily slip her hand, and she did.

The crow shook the dust from its feathers, and Bryony laughed at herself even as she daydreamed about a young King Arthur, pulling his prophetic sword from the stone. It figured hers would be buried in a graveyard. As she lifted the hilt, she felt the weight of the weapon. It was heavier than she expected, but it felt good in her hand. This was no actor's prop. It was beautiful. Even on such an overcast day, it caught and reflected the light like a diamond.

She considered keeping it. It made no sense to bury it again. And she was drawn to the idea that some cosmic power or other had just handed her an extraordinary destiny. The second she made her decision, the sword began to transform in her hands. It shrank and twisted as though the metal were being re-forged in an invisible fire. She almost dropped the object—it no longer resembled a sword—but she couldn't bear the thought of giving up her new, fairy-tale life.

In the smoothest of shifts, the sword in her hand became a ring. Where the bulk of it had gone, Bryony couldn't say. It was small, delicate, and perfectly suited to her. The band was scaled, reminiscent of the serpents that once made up the hilt of the sword. But instead of the emerald eyes of a snake, the defining feature of the new object was the skull of a hummingbird. It was tiny and had a long, silver beak. Bryony hesitated only a moment before slipping it onto the middle finger of her left hand. She wore the beak pointed toward the tip of her finger and found that it barely extended past her knuckle. It was perfect, as though it had been made for her.

"Very attractive," a voice commented.

Bryony jumped. Someone was watching. She gulped and looked around, but no one was there.

"It suits you, I mean," said whoever it was. It was a masculine voice but soft and airy. "They always reshape themselves to suit those who keep them—the swords. And you've given this one an attractive form."

No, there was no denying it now. The speaker was definitely the only other living thing in the graveyard. The crow.

Bryony's first thought was that she had somehow gone afoul of a lesser angel, and it had chosen this pretense as a kind of lesson or test. She glanced down at the ring and back up again, fighting a powerful urge to scream and run. *Never show an angel you're afraid,* she reminded herself. Angels hated fear almost as much as they hated indifference. "Is it yours?"

The crow cocked its head and lifted its wings in an awkward kind of shrug. "I had thought to use it in a nest if it became small enough when I took it, but I couldn't seem to get it out of the ground. It glitters nicely, don't you think?"

Bryony agreed. "Do you still want it?" she asked, secretly hoping the answer was no but resolving to return the ring if the crow requested it. If this was a test, Bryony was not going to fail.

But the crow shook its head and blinked its beady, black eyes. "I'd rather see what else it can do."

"Aside from changing shape, you mean?"

"I mean aside from giving me the power of speech. They all change shape."

Bryony held her hand out in front of her and spread her fingers wide, examining the ring. So this trinket had somehow given a crow the power of human speech. The bird was not an angel after all. "Who did it belong to?" she wondered aloud.

The crow answered, "Whichever angel could commune with beasts, I assume. But he has either abandoned his sword intentionally or been killed. Now it belongs to you."

"Angels can't be killed." Bryony let her hand fall back to her side. "Everyone knows that."

The crow chuckled at her and hopped closer, speaking in a low, conspiratorial tone. "They can indeed. You just need the right weapon."

So Bryony kept the sword that was now a ring. And she kept her crow companion too, whom she named Shakespeare, and whom she allowed to accompany her almost everywhere. But he never came into the healing tent, and Bryony still wasn't sure why.

CHAPTER TWO

As usual, Shakespeare waited outside the tent. When Bryony left, he followed, hopping from branch to branch until they reached her childhood home. Then he slipped into an open, upstairs window like it was the most common thing for a crow to do. By the time Bryony unlocked her front door, he was already standing on the newel post at the base of the main staircase.

He cocked his head and spoke. "Dinner?"

"Good to see your one-track mind hasn't derailed." She grinned. It was nice to come home to someone, and Shakespeare had become a kind of family to her. *Family*, she figured, was whomever you saw every day or the people with whom you cohabited. It was the only way she cared to define the word because defined any other way meant she had no family, and she couldn't bear the thought of that.

Shakespeare flew to her shoulder and let her carry him upstairs. "I've a craving for raw liver."

"We're fresh out, I'm afraid." Bryony ascended the staircase, trailing her hand along the banister. She knew every creak before it sounded. That was what made a place *home*—knowing all its creaks and drafts and moldy corners, knowing where each secret passage and attic spider and old photo album kept itself. Maybe that's what made someone *family* too. Maybe Shakespeare had become her family, not just because they cohabited, but because Bryony knew, for example, exactly what he would say next.

"Then we're going out, aren't we?" He flew from her shoulder to her mother's vanity as soon as she entered the master bedroom. "I'll accept my liver fried, but I won't accept none at all. I won't."

The vanity mirror's yellowing corners and dark gray flecks only accentuated the years that had passed since Bryony's mother was last reflected within its frame. It was an antique piece of furniture, small and delicate, with carved flowers on the drawers and silver butterfly handles. Bryony sat before the mirror and lifted her veil. Her face was still flushed from the healing tent, still glistening with sweat. She dipped a washcloth into a full basin and began to dab at her cheeks and throat.

"I've been thinking," she began, "about how I got here, what choices I made, and whether this is really the best I could have done."

Shakespeare ignored her. "Let's go to Martha's Café. She's never stingy. I bet she gives us a small portion of liver for free. After that boy you saved? Surely, she'll spare a few bites for your poor, hungry crow."

Bryony carefully unpinned the veil from her head and unwound her long, dark hair. "I've been thinking about the day I met you and found the sword. And about the day I learned what it could do."

That day had been unusually warm, and Shakespeare had suggested she cut through the forest on her way home to take advantage of the shade. She recalled the way the sun had shimmered on the aspen leaves, as though the forest were a dancer with hundreds of legs, twisting around in torn, white stockings and a gold-sequined gown. And she recalled the rat she'd seen pulling itself along the forest floor with only its front paws, half paralyzed.

She had stood over it and watched it a while. Its struggle was familiar, like the nightmares she had in which terror overtook her but she could not run. The creature's eyes were black and surprisingly expressive. Its ear had been torn once and healed—a little scar, the story behind which only the rat could know. Its milk-chocolate fur looked so velvety, she had to fight the urge to stroke it.

Shakespeare had landed on her shoulder and looked down with one eye at the poor creature. "An owl probably dropped it. Broke its spine. Never came back for it because, if it can't run, what fun is hunting it? Owls are assholes that way."

Bryony squatted for a closer look. "And crows aren't?"

"We eat dead things mostly. I've never half-killed anything. That's an owl thing, I'm telling you. Owls and house cats." Shakespeare sighed, a sound that always endeared him to Bryony. It had a high pitch and reminded her how small he was despite his big personality. "It would be kindest to kill it now rather than allow it to starve to death or get toyed with further by some heartless kitten."

The rat continued its struggle to escape, but it wasn't making progress. "I don't want to kill it," Bryony said. "It wants to live."

"That's because it doesn't understand its own predicament."

"Doesn't it? Maybe we should help it."

Shakespeare hopped off her shoulder and stood next to the rat, which worked even harder to escape the new threat but got nowhere just as fast. "You'll only frighten it more," he said. "Look, just pick up that rock and bring it down on the head. Aim true and hit hard. It's easy. The rat won't even know what happened. I could eat it after so it doesn't go to waste. Or . . ." The crow paused, lost in an idea he couldn't seem to verbalize straight away.

"Shakespeare?"

"Or you could test the sword on it." He hopped back to Bryony, suddenly excited. "Just to see what it does. It's perfect. What's the worst that could happen? If the rat dies, it would be the kindest thing. If it doesn't . . ."

Bryony glared down at her eager companion. "And what if it's a torture sword?"

"It's not a torture sword."

"It could be. You don't know."

"If it is, we use the rock quick as we can, and it's all over." He shrugged his wings. "It's the same ending either way."

"And what if it's a live-forever, torture sword?"

Shakespeare opened his beak to speak but closed it again, unsure quite how to counter Bryony's unusual flair for creative problem-building. "It's not a live-forever, torture sword."

"You don't know that." Bryony looked down at the rat. It had stopped pawing the ground, too exhausted to keep up its futile struggle. She carefully reached out and touched its lifeless tail. "Do you want to try something crazy?" she whispered to the poor creature. It seemed right to include it in the decision.

The rat turned its head toward her, its whiskers twitching. It reached out and just managed to touch the tip of her middle finger with its nose. Curious. Unafraid. Resigned. Bryony took it as a *yes*.

She scooped the little rodent from the pile of dead leaves. Its body was warmer than she expected and far softer. It trembled in her hand, its ribcage still expanding and collapsing automatically, willing the poor creature to go on until the very last. Shakespeare was right. It did seem unreasonably cruel to leave it.

"Prick it with your ring," Shakespeare said, leaping to the top of her head. "That's all it should take. Maybe it will be able to talk after. Then you can ask it whether it wants to live or die." His wiry claws curled into her hair, but she didn't mind. She was already used to the weight of him.

It all seemed so reasonable. Just one little scratch. She balled her left hand into a fist and turned the hummingbird skull toward the rat. She brought the beak down through its fur and punctured the skin of its back. It didn't jump or scream. It couldn't feel anything at all. It was truly paralyzed. After several seconds of waiting, nothing happened, and Bryony lowered the rat back onto its bed of dry leaves. "I'm sorry," she said. "I guess it doesn't do much of anything."

She sat on her heels, quite unable to leave the creature, not ready to do what needed to be done. She glanced at the rock and frowned. Death would come one way or another. But did she have to be its harbinger? "I don't think I can kill it."

"Suit yourself." Shakespeare shook his feathers and hopped down to her knee. "I suppose you could fashion it a tiny wheelchair." He laughed.

She shrugged. "I mean why not?"

"Because you can't save everything, that's why. You can't turn your house into a rehabilitation center for disabled rodents. Honestly, I'll never understand why humans don't seem to know their own limitations. I've never taken it upon myself to care for something that wasn't my responsibility. If you can't kill the rat, then leave it. Nature will do the deed for you, although not as quickly and far more painfully. Also, I won't get to eat it, which I may never forgive."

Deep in contemplation, Bryony sat before her mother's mirror, wearing her mother's dress, and combed her hair until it clung with static. "It's funny," she said. "In my imagination today, you were insisting I heal the boy. But the rat, I remember, you wanted me to kill."

"Rats are delicious." Shakespeare's reflection seemed to move very little. "I'm not completely heartless, just hungry. If you kept me better fed, I might show mercy more often."

"Didn't you ever have to feed yourself, you spoiled bird?" She chuckled and tied her hair into a ponytail at the base of her neck.

"I did stop you from killing that creature in the end if you recall." The crow was indignant. "You wouldn't even have noticed had I said nothing. So maybe your subconscious version of me isn't entirely off. Maybe I'm a kind, hopeful crow, who only wishes to feast on that which has already passed from this world . . ."

He went on, but Bryony wasn't listening. He was right, of course. She'd lifted the rock over her head and closed her eyes. And then Shakespeare had told her to stop. *Look.* And she did. The rat's tail had begun to twitch. Then a foot. Two feet. And there, in the speckled, golden light of the aspen grove, the rat stood, tested its joints with an almost imperceptible weight shift, and bolted. The sound of its flight scattering the leaves of the forest floor had been sheer music to the girl who'd saved it.

Shakespeare finished his rant. "I went to bed hungry that night. And that's why I'm saying, today, let's go to Martha's. I just know she'll give me some liver with a few noodles to accompany. Her service is always superb and so generous, don't you think?" He hopped onto her shoulder and pecked gently at her earlobe. "Don't you? Don't you?"

Bryony sighed and replaced her veil. "How can I say no to you?" She reached out and ruffled the feathers on his head with her fingernails. "Let's go."

Shakespeare rode on Bryony's head and sang an invented song as they walked down the country lane into town.

> *At dawn, the sun sips color from the sea,*
> *And spits it back across the sky,*
> *Like a babe refusing peas,*
> *Mushed and floating where I fly . . .*

"Very alliterative," she said, laughing. "But not your best. You should practice more."

"And you should get a car. Time is precious—your time doubly so."

But the lane was beautiful this time of year, and Bryony never regretted her walks into town. Summer grasses grew tall on either side of the road and in one long strip down the middle where tires hadn't quite managed to kill them. Rows of trees reached long, leaf-heavy branches in an arch overhead. The walk was quiet, secluded, and Bryony thought it a much-needed respite from her public life.

It wasn't that she didn't appreciate her congregation. In fact, she loved them. They were a crowd, sure, but they respected her. They never grabbed at her or demanded healing. They merely asked and thanked, and thanked, and thanked. How could she not adore them? They were good people who only wanted to live their lives free from the ever-present fear of disease and infection. It cost Bryony nothing to give that to them. And in turn, they gave her something priceless. They gave her their undying affection. Their worship was more than love, and Bryony had begun to crave it as much as the air she breathed.

Maybe that was why she didn't hesitate or worry when the RV pulled alongside her and slowed, rolling only as fast as she walked. The crunch of its tires was a slow, chewing sound, as though the beast of a vehicle enjoyed the lane as much as Bryony but in a different way.

As the RV moved alongside her, the door opened and a woman called to her. "You're the one who can heal, aren't you? It must be you."

Bryony looked up and nodded.

"Oh, thank you! Thank you, god! I've been searching everywhere. They told me you sometimes went this way into town." The woman had a marvelous Eastern European accent that indicated she'd not been in the country long. And she was not a congregant. Bryony knew her worshipers well, and none of them would approach her on the road like this. They always waited for the weekly tent meetings, or if they had need of an unscheduled healing, a meeting would be called. But for some reason, it seemed her congregants had sent this woman to find her.

"What do you need?" Bryony asked, trying to sound less generous than she felt. Keeping up appearances was important.

"I'm so sorry to bother you, Your . . . uh . . . Majesty?"

Bryony smiled. "*Bryony* is fine."

The woman smiled back, and her RV stopped. The man who'd been driving poked his head out alongside his companion.

"I just don't think she'll last the night," the woman said. "I don't know what else to do. Please . . ."

Bryony stepped closer. Shakespeare hopped off her head and onto her shoulder. "Be careful," he whispered.

"She's in the back." The woman stepped out of her RV to make room for Bryony. "In our bed."

Shakespeare muttered, "You don't know them, Bryony. They're strangers."

"In a strange land," Bryony added, and she stepped into the RV.

The first sensation that struck her upon climbing into the vehicle was a blast of cold, stale air. The couple had been running the air conditioning, though the weather outside was mild. The RV looked clean but lived-in. Their travels had been going on some time.

The woman led Bryony and Shakespeare past a dated, orange sofa, a fake-wood paneled kitchen, through a narrow hall, and into a tight bedroom. "She took sick just yesterday," she explained, wringing her hands. "But already she can hardly breathe." She moved out of the way to reveal a figure sprawled on a flower-print quilt.

It was a dog, and a small one at that. Long, white fur moved like feathers in the draft from the air conditioning. The dog's bulging eyes were fixed on the wall as it struggled to take in each gasp of air.

The woman stifled a sob. "It must have been something she ate. I don't know." She spoke quickly, tripping over her English in an attempt to outrun her panic. "She can't stand. She doesn't bark. Her nose is hot. I don't know what to do. Please, they said you could talk to animals. At least tell me what's wrong with her. I know she's just a dog. I know, but . . ." Her voice broke, and she finally wept.

Her companion stood in the doorway and finished her thought for her. "She isn't just a dog to us," he said. "She's our family. She's all we have."

That hit Bryony harder than she expected it to. She reached up and laid the tips of her fingers on Shakespeare's toes. "I understand. I have a small family too." She leaned over to examine the dog. Its people weren't wrong. It was quite close to death, but Bryony couldn't tell what had caused it. She tilted her head over the dog as though listening, and she let her black veil fall around the poor thing's tired and overheated body. "Your dog says she was bitten by something." It was a lie but a harmless one. The truth was Bryony couldn't talk to animals. She was just better than most people at paying attention to their body language. And of course there was Shakespeare, although her congregants assumed he was merely a talented mimic, and she preferred it that way.

Gently, Bryony turned the little dog over in her hands as though searching for the bite. She kept its body under her veil and bent her knuckles toward its rising and falling stomach. Then she punctured its skin with the beak on her ring. "There!" she said as though the discovery had surprised even her. "There is the mark. It must have been a venomous insect or spider." She lifted the little dog in her arms and let her veil slide off its body, showing the tiny puncture wound to the couple.

The woman moaned, the man gulped, and they both took a step back. "Can anything be done?" the man asked, his eyes glistening with the guilt of someone who has failed to protect a life in their care.

Bryony kept her expression stern. People believed a grim expression more than a smile in such situations, and it was important that these people believed her. "I am already drawing the venom from her body."

Both travelers' mouths dropped open at the same time. She could see the gratitude welling in them even before the dog showed improvement. She could see them hold back their immediate adoration. She had to stop herself from grinning.

"It was not your fault," Bryony continued. "She wants you to know that. Even she did not see the creature that bit her."

Slowly, the dog began to stir. Its breathing grew easier. The pink returned to its skin and gums, and it panted in the residual heat of its fever. Bryony set it on the foot of the bed, and it sat, glancing around the room, its tail tentatively wagging.

The woman burst into fresh tears, and the man fell to his knees. Bryony opened her arms to receive them. The man took one of her hands and kissed it in an act that was almost automatic. He seemed ashamed after he'd done it, like he wasn't sure it was the right thing, but Bryony squeezed his hand and gave him her most benevolent smile.

"Oh, thank you, thank you!" The woman rubbed tears from her red, swollen eyelids. "Please, what can we give you?" She reached into a purse she'd been carrying like a satchel and pulled out a canvas wallet.

Bryony loved moments like this, when she could show them more grace than they expected, when she could prove there were good gods in the world. She reached out and squeezed the woman's shoulder, pulling her in slightly, hinting at an intimacy the woman immediately accepted. She stepped into Bryony's welcoming arms and wept tears of relief and joy.

Bryony drank it in like a fine cordial. "I need nothing from you, my traveling friend. Your little family is safe. Take good care of them." She let the woman hold her a moment longer and then stepped back. The woman smiled brilliantly. Bryony recognized the expression on her face. It was more than love. It was worship, and Bryony needed it like an addict needs their drug of choice. She soaked it in, the adoration, the devotion. She let it wash over her and strengthen her, and suddenly, she did not feel hungry anymore.

CHAPTER THREE

Bryony watched the RV disappear down the lane in a crippling, euphoric haze. She could see every ray of sunlight that pierced the foliage and lit the ground around her in irregular patterns. Tiny insects danced at the tips of every blade of grass like dust motes in an attic window. Her arms, legs, and scalp tingled as though she could feel the minute growth of every hair in her skin.

"Now you've done it," Shakespeare said, having resumed his place atop her head.

Speak, she told herself. *Answer. Move your mouth, your tongue, and speak.* "What?"

"You've created missionaries."

His words registered too slowly. "Only a couple," she said, but it didn't matter. She knew he was right, though she couldn't quite parse why. She and Shakespeare had decided early on to keep her congregation small, discreet, and now she had converted travelers. But what could be wrong with gaining a couple missionaries when it felt so unequivocally right? This feeling . . . This was why the gods of old demanded converts. There was nothing like the love of a new worshiper. Nothing.

Shakespeare spent the entire walk to his favorite restaurant lecturing Bryony, but she didn't hear a word he said. She was dazed and grinning to herself. The air smelled sweet and musky, and she couldn't get enough of it. Her feet still tingled with every step, though the sensation had begun to creep away from her hands. Her belly was still warm and sated as she sat down to eat.

When, at last, Bryony regained her ability to focus, she found herself in her usual private booth, and Martha had parted the curtains to take her order. It was always Martha herself who insisted on serving the god and her crow. And it was always the same corner booth she sat them in, as though she saved it for Bryony and no one else. The restaurant had dark, elegant décor, and the private booths with their heavy, velvet curtains pleased both Bryony and Shakespeare, who liked to chat while he ate but did not appreciate the attention it attracted.

"What can I get you today, Mistress?"

Bryony flushed. She did not like being called *Mistress*, but there seemed to be no way around it. Her congregants were not comfortable using her name, and she wanted them to be comfortable around her. Martha was a particular favorite. She was a tall, thin woman with bright red hair and eyes that crinkled in the corners when she smiled. She had the air of someone who tolerated no nonsense unless it amused her. Amusing nonsense, she would tolerate to the end of the world and back.

Shakespeare puffed himself up and shook his feathers impatiently. This was clearly not the first time they had been asked. "You know what?" he said, after another meaningful sigh. "I'll have a bowl of liver, jerky, cooked barley, and four spiral noodles."

Martha's eyes grew wide when Shakespeare ordered, but she did not skip a beat. "Anything else?"

"She'll have a club sandwich and a Riesling," he said. Then he added, "Thank you so much," as an afterthought. While Martha scribbled his order on her notepad, Shakespeare continued to rant. "I mean why bother keeping up appearances, right? I can talk, as you know, but not only that. I can also carry on intelligent conversation, which seems to be more than my companion is capable of at the moment." He tilted his head toward Bryony. "We're ruined anyway, so why hide it anymore?

Why bother hiding anything? Hordes of lepers are probably already on their way."

Martha nodded and tapped her notepad with her pen. "Would you care for any blueberries this time around then?"

Shakespeare paused, astounded by the restaurateur's unflappability. "I . . . I'm feeling raspberries today, thank you."

"Fantastic." Martha scribbled an abbreviated note and smiled. "I'll be right back with your Riesling, Mistress."

As soon as Martha left, Bryony let out a giggle she'd already swallowed twice. If anyone could throw Shakespeare off his game, it was Martha, and there was nothing Bryony loved so well as seeing that bird thrown off his game.

The crow began to pace the length of the booth, eyeballing the place where the wine-dark curtains came together, their gold fringe giving them just a hint of gaudiness. The table was covered in old pennies and a clear lacquer that reflected the incandescent lights, giving the booth a warm, coppery glow. If any place other than the farmhouse could feel like home to Bryony, it was Martha's Café.

"I am serious, you know," Shakespeare whispered. "You really may have gotten us into trouble this time."

Bryony leaned on her elbow and smiled. "It's cute when you worry about me."

"Look, I know you're drunk on converts right now, and that wine I ordered for you isn't going to help matters, but can you please try to care about your own survival? Just this once?" He stopped pacing and turned one eye to her, which was his way of giving a stern look. It only made her giggle. "This isn't a joke," he hissed. "How many gods do you suppose there are in the surrounding area?"

"Only one or two." Bryony leaned back and tried to focus.

"And how many do you think have actual powers like yours?"

She squinted at him. "None?"

"Damn right, none." He began to pace again. "So far, you've succeeded in keeping your congregation small. You live outside the city, and that's helped. But now you've created missionaries, out-of-towners. Word of mouth travels fast in these times, Bryony. How quickly do you think they'll flock to you, people who find out a real healing god lives in this little town? They throw themselves so easily at the feet of charlatans and hacks. How quickly do you think they'll shift their devotion to you, the real thing?"

Something, some fraction of what the crow said, hit Bryony like a weight to the chest. She was no longer floating. Now she could barely keep from slumping in her seat. "How much time do you think I have before they come?"

"You mean before your congregation quadruples?"

She felt the weight in her face now, in the apples of her cheeks, drawing every part of her expression down. But somewhere in the back of her mind, she was already making plans to create new converts. She chided herself for it, but still she considered it. Just one more couldn't hurt. Much.

Shakespeare went on ruthlessly. "They'll come more quickly than you can conceive. And right behind them, the Black Armada."

A gasp broke the illusion of private conversation. Martha stood in the parted curtain with a tray, upon which she'd balanced a generous glass of white wine and a small plate of four identical croutons. "No," she muttered. The blood drained from her face, causing her freckles to stand out more than usual, and her hands began to shake. She quickly set the wine in front of Bryony and the croutons at Shakespeare's feet.

"Sit down, Martha." Shakespeare hopped to the back of the booth and made room for their host. "Take a breather."

She did, but breathing seemed easier said than done. "This can't be happening," she said. "Not now. Not the armada. Mistress, I heard they were close." She gripped the edge of the table with whitened knuckles.

It was the sight of Martha, the stalwart owner of the best and oldest café in town, trembling like a frightened child in her own booth that finally broke Bryony's already tenuous hold on her high.

The Black Armada. Bryony had heard stories of it when she was a child. If the famous fleet of black ships with black sails flying were ever to make port anywhere near your town, you could consider your local gods as good as gone. Some people claimed it was coincidence, but Bryony never believed that. Coincidences with such perfect regularity were rarely real coincidences. And it seemed Martha felt the same. She slumped next to Shakespeare, lost in her own despair. Bryony was certain she had never seen the woman actually sit for so long.

"You should run," Martha said at last. "You should get out of here while you can. If the armada comes for you . . ."

Shakespeare pecked at one of the croutons. "And go where?"

"Anywhere." Martha leaned in, her cheeks flushed with fear and the thrill of escape. "Take my van. Head further inland and find an angel. Tell them you're a god. They'll protect you. They like gods."

It was true. The angels did favor the presence of gods in their brave, new society, especially along the coasts, though no one really knew why. Still Bryony's stomach turned at the thought of working with angels. Their massacre was only the beginning of the damage they had done. The deaths in her own family had been entirely preventable, as she understood it. An all but eradicated disease had taken them along with so many others—a disease now running rampant in the angels' ongoing war on science.

"I won't turn to angels," she muttered. "I'd rather die."

Martha reached across the table and patted Bryony's hand in an almost motherly way. "Please don't say that, Mistress."

Shakespeare dipped his crouton into Bryony's water and then swallowed it whole. "The angels can't help you anyway. If they could, don't you think they would have stopped the armada by now? No, they're afraid of the black sails, same as you and me. And I think I know why."

Now that the bird had the attention of everyone at the table, he became fully engrossed in his croutons. One was not the right shape, apparently, so he held it down with a foot and began pecking off the corners. His diligence was so intense that Martha spoke next in a near whisper, as though afraid to break his concentration. "The croutons are meant as an apology for . . . for treating you like a pet all this time."

Shakespeare lifted his head. "It's no nevermind to me, Martha. I expect to be treated in accordance with my behavior." He wagged his tail and cocked his head, the smile apparent in his voice. "I could never be angry with you."

"Thank you," Martha murmured. She was still unsure, still wringing her hands.

Bryony took a deep breath and massaged her brow. Shakespeare would keep them waiting until he tired of the game, and she didn't have the patience for it just now. "Why are the angels afraid of the Black Armada, Shakespeare?"

"Oh!" The crow hopped back. "I thought it was obvious." His feigned surprise was not remotely convincing. "There's a godhunter aboard."

That stopped the breath of everyone at the table. *A godhunter.* It was all Bryony could do to keep from bolting in a blind panic. Godhunters were legendary but fiction, she'd assumed. Gods were either born immortal, like many in the ancient pantheons, or had achieved immortality through worship. As long as a single worshiper remained, their god went on living. A godhunter would have to massacre every member of a god's congregation, every last true believer, to kill one god.

"There's no such thing as godhunters," Bryony muttered, but she wasn't so sure. Gods had gone missing—it was true—disappeared from their homes, their communities. And always, always the Black Armada was rumored to have come in the night.

"I believe there's at least one," Shakespeare said. He'd stopped fiddling with his croutons. He was dead serious. "Not only that, I believe this godhunter can destroy immortality without touching a single congregant. And if he's doing it the way I think he is, he can kill angels just as easily."

Bryony mouthed the word *how.*

Shakespeare cleared his throat. "Martha, would you mind bringing our mistress her dinner?"

Martha took the hint. She rose, bowed, and left them alone.

Shakespeare flew across the table and landed on Bryony's shoulder. He spoke softly into her ear, and she had never heard him more somber in all the years she'd known him. "Remember I told you, when we met, that an angel can be killed. It takes a special weapon, one that invites death wherever it pierces, one that renders mortality impossible to resist."

She knew where he was going with this, but she couldn't bring herself to finish his thought for him as she normally would. She couldn't bring herself to say the words aloud. She could barely even bring herself to think them.

He whispered, "The Angel of Death had a sword, too, you know."

Death. Years ago, Bryony might have welcomed it, even if it had come in the shape of an angel. Her family gone, her future destroyed, her isolation insurmountable. But now she was a god. She had a congregation, responsibilities. People needed her, and she could not fathom what they would do without her. Becoming a god, accepting the kind of love that had no equal—the kind of love that could make a person immortal—had its downside, it seemed.

"Wh . . . what . . ." she breathed. "What can I do?"

"It's simple really." Shakespeare came so close the whisker-like feathers at the corners of his beak brushed against her ear. "The godhunter will come for you as soon as your new missionaries get the word out. All you have to do is find him before that happens. Steal his sword and kill him first."

Chapter Four

Even as a child, Bryony wore melancholy like a favorite, knitted shawl. She draped it around her neck, nuzzled in the warmth of unprovoked sadness, breathed in the perfume of her own tears. She wandered at night, marveling at the magic of the stars, talking to ghosts, and creating elaborate fantasies out of her own dreams. She felt too deeply for everyone who suffered, cried real tears for complete strangers. But she never knew anyone really.

Bryony sat in Martha's parked, rusty van—having driven through the night and into the next morning—and gripped the steering wheel far too tightly. As she gazed out the dirty windshield, across the beach to the fleet of shadowy ships on the horizon, she realized she had only ever loved melancholy because it distracted her from her loneliness. Leaving her congregation was perhaps the hardest thing she had ever done. For the first time in her life, she knew her place in the world. People loved her. And to be loved . . . To be loved was more than everything.

Martha would explain to the congregation, without too many details, why their god had abandoned them so suddenly. Surely they'd understand that the approach of the Black Armada and a possible godhunter made Bryony's flight necessary. She would be back just as soon as she could. Martha would promise on Bryony's behalf, and it was a promise Bryony had every intention of keeping. If she survived.

The wind picked up, and all the ships shifted in unison. Bryony shivered. "What if I get seasick?"

Shakespeare perched on the headrest of the passenger seat and absentmindedly pulled at the loose threads he found there. "You'll bear it out. You're tough."

"I used to be." Bryony sighed. Did the ships have to be quite so sinister? "I don't like getting myself into situations where there's no possible escape."

"You can swim, can't you?"

Bryony glared hard at the crow.

He cleared his throat. "Well, you're already in one of those situations, wouldn't you say? You can't escape the godhunter for long. The bigger your religion gets, the easier you are to find. You can tell your congregation to be hush-hush all you want. Someone will spill the beans. And that's not even taking into account your new propensity for making missionaries. Think of the Black Armada as your means of escape."

"More like a mouse knowingly waltzing into the lion's mouth."

"Nah, it's subterfuge." He pulled a particularly long thread from the seatback and tossed it over his shoulder. "You'll do great. I know you will. Just make yourself useful to them. Be someone they'll want to have on their side. You're clever. You'll figure it out." He puffed up, round and proud. "I believe in you."

Bryony blushed. She never did feel worthy of Shakespeare's compliments. His opinion of her was extraordinary. She'd never live up to it. As much as she feared the godhunter, she also feared letting Shakespeare down.

The bird's black eyes glittered in the afternoon light. "I know you can do this," he said. His voice was soft and sure, indistinguishable from a man's. He was a strange kind of parent to Bryony, someone she desperately wanted to please despite his diminutive size. She nodded, and he hopped closer to her. "The Black Armada rarely leaves this late. We were lucky to catch them. We don't know where they're headed next, so you've got to channel your inner performer. Put on a show. Go on, make 'em love you. You're good at that."

Bryony opened the van's door and held it for Shakespeare. She slung an enormous duffle bag over one shoulder and offered the other to the crow. He would be with her, and that was a comfort. But he'd be mute most of the time, relegated to a pet.

As she drew closer to the crew on the beach, she began to play a kind of game—guess who's the godhunter. There was a broad-shouldered man with a buzz cut and a blond beard. Perhaps it was him. Beside him was a smaller, younger man, who had delicate features and an oversized coat. Perhaps it was him. They were both heaving boxes into boats, preparing to take whatever they'd obtained with them to their ships.

And then Bryony noticed the rest of the crew. To her amazement, most of them were women. She hadn't even considered the possibility that the godhunter might be a woman, but why not? The tallest was an older, white woman with her hair in a knotted, gray bun; and the shortest was a muscular, Asian woman whose ponytail was flush with curls. Among them were all manner of race and style and culture. The only thing they seemed to have in common was an almost robotic, rhythmic efficiency as they loaded box after box into their boats.

Bryony came as close as she dared and stood watching them. Either they didn't notice she was there or they didn't really care. Not one of them addressed her, threatened her, or even glanced at her. She stood frozen with anxiety as they passed and packed and readied their boats.

Then Shakespeare cawed, and all their eyes simultaneously turned to her.

The only two men in the group marched toward her, and she got a better look at them. The leaner one had tattoos climbing his neck from beneath his collar, licking his chin like fire. The bigger one wore boots that sank in the sand and then kicked it up again where it caught in the hem of his cotton, pressed pants. Bryony took two involuntary steps backward.

"What do you mean by approaching us like this?" the big one shouted at her. "What do you want? Do you know who we are? Do you know the danger you've put yourself in? Who are you? Where do you come from?"

Bryony had opened her mouth to answer several times but snapped it shut again as the intimidating questions continued. She cowered inside but reminded herself to square her shoulders, stand tall, and make eye contact. *Never show them you're afraid,* she told herself. *Perform for them. Make them love you.*

"Please." She spoke in a small voice. "I'm only . . . I'm only looking for work." She felt obscenely out of her depth in the clothes she was forced to wear. Gone were her favorite black costume dresses. Gone was her veil, her beads, and her laced ankle boots. Instead, she wore blue jeans, a black blouse with gathered sleeves that covered her hands to the knuckle, and sensible, canvas shoes. She resisted the urge to bow her head and hide her face with her hair.

"Work?" the big man repeated, laughing. "What kind of work do you think you could get with the Black Armada?"

"I . . . I . . ." She gulped. Shakespeare dug his claws into her shoulder and she straightened up. "I'm good with medicine. I have tinctures." She opened her duffle bag and withdrew a small briefcase she had stuffed inside. Then she opened the briefcase to reveal rows and rows of tiny bottles, carefully packed and labeled. "I'm a heal—" She coughed and corrected herself when Shakespeare dug his claws in deeper. "I have medical training."

"And where did you get that kind of training?" The big man narrowed his eyes.

"You know I can't reveal my sources." She took a chance they would appreciate that, being anti-angel and anti-god. Solidarity. She smiled a half-hearted, awkward smile. The big man glared at her.

The smaller, tattooed man chewed his cheek. "Andy, do ya think we should consider—"

The big man whirled on his companion. "Consider what?"

"The commodore."

"You think this . . . this *quack* can help the commodore?"

The tattooed man shrugged. "Not convinced she's a quack. And I think anything's better than nothing at this point."

"And if she can't help?"

With another shrug of his shoulders, the tattooed man spoke and sent a shiver down Bryony's spine. "Then we kill her."

Bryony looked up to see the short, muscular woman marching toward them, her hands on her hips and her feet plowing through the sand with purpose. "What's the meaning of all this, fellas? Why aren't you sending this little spy back to her angels?"

At that, Bryony found her tongue. "Angels! I would never—not in my life, not in a million years! The angels killed my family!" She felt heat creep past her collar. She was indignant, and she realized, as she fumed, her anger was exactly what her interrogators wanted to see. She closed her eyes and forced herself to remember her family—warm meals, cocoa by the fire, how good it felt to sink into her mother's arms whenever she was afraid. "Angels took everything from me." Her eyes stung from the tears she held back, though she knew she should have let them fall for effect. They were real tears, and real vulnerability terrified her. She abandoned her attempt at sincerity and thrust her box of supplies at the woman who had joined them. "I have tinctures," she repeated. Her voice cracked, and she swallowed her own weakness like bile.

The woman chuckled. "Gotcha. Come along." She turned away and waved for them to follow.

Bryony had to remind herself to breathe. She'd done it. She was in. Shakespeare ruffled his feathers, obviously pleased with her performance. But it wasn't a performance, and he knew it as well as she did. How much more belly would she have to show to win the Black Armada's trust?

The tattooed man walked beside her while the bigger man followed behind. "That's Dara." He gestured to the woman who led them. "She came from Cambodia with her father. Been in the armada going on ten years now. Behind us is Andrew—California boy, newish, protective. And my name's Jesús, but everyone calls me Chuy. Been here since before I could walk. How 'bout you?"

Bryony tried to smile back and felt her failure keenly. "I'm Bryony." She saw no reason to use a pseudonym. No one would have heard of her. Many of her congregants didn't even know her given name, and it would be easier to answer to a name already familiar to her. "I'm new to boats."

Chuy laughed. "You're in for a lovely time then." She noted his sarcasm. "What made ya want to join the Black Armada, Bryony?"

"I want to fight the angels." It wasn't really a lie. She did want to fight them. Though her primary objective was self-preservation, the idea of getting a little of her own back was icing on a cake she'd been craving since her brother died. "My whole family died of influenza within weeks of each other. I heard they vaccinated people against it before the angels outlawed vaccinations. I heard it used to be more of a nuisance than a plague, that in the old days you just . . . took off work and went to a doctor."

Chuy laid a hand on her shoulder. "That what inspired you to learn medicine?"

"Maybe." She might have considered it had the ring not given her healing powers that put medicine to shame.

"And the crow?"

Ah, she'd almost forgotten the unusually silent bird was still on her shoulder. She reached up and patted his toes. "I call him Shakespeare. He's a pet—more than a pet really. I never go anywhere without him. He's all the family I have left."

"He'll stick around? Even on a ship?"

Bryony nodded. "He won't leave me."

"Smart bird." Chuy reached out to Shakespeare who gave him a warning peck.

"He doesn't like strangers," she said, apologizing on her ornery bird's behalf.

"Even smarter." Chuy smiled, and his smile was warm and welcoming. Despite her first impression, Bryony didn't believe she would find an ounce of duplicity in him. He had medium-length, dark hair, sharp features, and hazel eyes that came to life whenever he spoke. She noticed he had more tattoos peeking out from under his sleeves, which led her to conclude they probably covered his entire torso.

"Why are you being so nice to me?" Bryony couldn't help but ask.

"Maybe I'm just a nice guy. Or maybe I keep my enemies close." He laughed again, and Bryony couldn't help smiling at him. "It's probably more of the former, but there's enough paranoia among the crew to make up for the lack of mine."

When they arrived at the ships' boats, Bryony noted that many were already on their way to their respective ships. They were all painted black like the rest of the fleet, which she imagined allowed the armada to keep well hidden in the night.

She was just beginning to feel a touch optimistic about her chances when Chuy patted her shoulder and said, "Well, here's where we part ways. Good to meet you. Hope to see you ashore soon."

"But I thought . . ." Bryony gulped. "I mean I assumed you were . . ."

"Coming with you? Nah, my friend, you're luckier than that. My ship's an unimpressive, little cutter. You get to board the flagship." He pointed at the largest ship in the fleet. "She's a brigantine and a beauty. You won't be disappointed." He grinned and trotted off toward another boat, kicking up wet sand as he went. "Heal our commodore, Bryony with the tinctures! I know you can!"

Just like that he was gone, and Bryony was left to board a boat with Andrew and Dara, both of whom seemed comparatively taciturn. "I thought he was coming with us," she muttered.

"He can't," Dara said, rearranging the boxes to make room for Bryony. "He's a captain."

"Oh."

"You'll sit here on these boxes. Stay on the center line and keep still. We don't want to capsize with cargo."

Bryony did as she was told, holding her duffle bag tight to her stomach, rarely taking a breath. Perhaps she was overcautious, but the last thing she wanted to do was upset any crew in the Black Armada. She did not want them on guard. If she was honest, she didn't want them to hate her either, even though it would be unavoidable in the end. Andrew seemed to have gotten a head start. The way he looked at her as he rowed, all narrowed eyes and tight lips. He didn't trust her, and he was right not to. But Bryony wanted to belong, even if it was only temporary, and part of her wanted even more than that. She wanted to be loved, needed, adored.

She shook off her craving and squeezed the handles of her bag. "I won't let you down," she said, but whether she was speaking to Shakespeare or Dara and Andrew, she couldn't have honestly said.

It was Andrew who answered. "You'd best not. The commodore is not known for leniency." He sat before her while Dara sat behind, and Bryony avoided making eye contact with him. Instead, she looked at the two little braids he wore on either side of his beard. Then she watched his big arms drag the oars through the waves like it was his job to churn the whole sea into butter. He was not someone she wanted to disappoint, and Bryony couldn't help but imagine that his commanding officer, their commodore, would be a hundred times more intimidating.

The closer they drew to the flagship, the milder the breakers became, until their little boat was lifted and lowered on gentle swells. Bryony closed her eyes and offered Shakespeare a scratch on the head, more for her own comfort than his.

You can't fail, she reminded herself. *You're a healer—it's what you do.*

She only opened her eyes again when she felt Shakespeare lift off her shoulder and heard the flap of his wings as he flew toward the ship. The brigantine towered before her, a dark castle on the sea. Its two masts were the trunks of alien trees, and the portholes that lined the hull were windows to another world. She took a deep, shuddering breath as a ladder was lowered by more crew. They all looked like dark specters above her with the sun directly behind them. She could just make out her crow perching on the rigging overhead.

She breathed shallow, anxiety wringing her lungs like a dish cloth. Dara and Andrew caught two lines and secured their boat. Then, well before Bryony was ready, Dara took hold of the ladder and held it taut. "Up you go."

Bryony latched on to the first excuse she could think of to delay. "But . . . my bag."

Dara held out her hand and took the duffle bag. "I'll handle it. Go on. Up and over the bulwarks now. There's no time to waste."

Chapter Five

The ladder Bryony had to climb made her feel like an absolute fool. It was two long ropes with wooden rungs strung between them, which was not the best design for someone unaccustomed to climbing any ladder at all let alone one that appeared to have been constructed from scrap. All the fiction she'd consumed wherein the hero would swing on a rope from one place to another or scale a sheer rock wall with gusto had not prepared her for her own lack of upper-body strength. And the way the ladder hugged the hull, the way it swayed whenever she shifted her weight . . . She gritted her teeth and cursed her sedentary lifestyle.

When she finally reached the deck and failed to swing her legs over the bulwarks, a woman she had not yet seen hoisted her aboard by her underarms. Bryony blushed and brushed invisible dust from her blouse.

The woman held out her hand in greeting, and Bryony took it instinctively. She was an older woman with short, gray hair and a strong grip. "The name's Rose," she said.

"Bryony." Bryony wasn't sure whether she should smile or imitate a more aggressive persona. The result was a kind of half-smile that felt forced and ridiculous. She'd never realized how much she relied on her veil to help hide her expressions.

Rose leaned over the rail to holler. "Care to explain?"

"Ask Chuy!" Dara called back up. "He's the one who decided to take in a stray!"

"She has tinctures!" Andrew shouted, and Bryony did not appreciate his sarcasm.

Rose righted herself and leaned back against the bulwarks. "Tinctures, huh?"

Bryony grimaced. They were making fun of her, and she deserved it. She was a fraud—she always had been. In fact, this was the first time since she'd found the angel's sword that anyone treated her exactly as they ought. "I have medical training," she muttered, suddenly feeling less sure of her own con.

"Take her to the commodore!" Dara hollered up again. "We'll deal with the cargo!"

Rose rolled her eyes and threw a line down to her fellow crew. They hauled Bryony's duffle bag first with Andrew following close behind. Bryony marveled at how he maneuvered up the ladder as though he had never done anything less thrilling in his life. When he reached the top, he threw his leg over the rail like he was mounting a horse, untied Bryony's bag, and handed it to her. "Do your thing, Tinctures."

Fantastic. She'd already earned a nickname.

I'm not here to make friends, she reminded herself. But she couldn't help turning to Andrew as she slung the bag over her shoulder. "I will save your commodore. I promise."

"Do it, and I'll give my night's ration of brandy to you."

A challenge. Much better than mockery. Bryony held out her hand and gave Andrew one firm shake. Then she followed Rose to a hatch and yet another ladder, descending into the depths of the ship. To her dismay, Shakespeare did not follow.

Belowdecks aboard the Black Armada's impressive flagship was not nearly as cramped as Bryony expected it to be. It was small, to be sure, with passageways and doors more compact than those in the farmhouse she'd grown up in. But they were more generous than those on the RV her first missionaries had traveled in. Perhaps staying aboard this ship would not be so horrifying after all. She could get used to it, she assured herself.

The passageways were dark and moody, the only light streaming in from round portholes along the hull. Everything below was made of wood, and Bryony found herself marveling at the craftsmanship of the vessel moments before her guide ducked into a doorway and invited her to follow.

The small room was lit with electric lamps and an open porthole. There was a counter along the far wall with a tiny sink and a mess of medical supplies, some of which were already bloody. In the center of the room was an examination table which was currently occupied by a woman. She was lean with very dark skin, sharp eyes, and a head full of braids that she wore tied at the base of her neck.

So this was the commodore. Bryony felt a chill run down her arms. The woman on the table before her was the leader of the most dangerous organization in the known world. She looked the part with her tall black boots, fitted pants, and lightweight blouse. But the commodore shook with fever, and an ever-darkening blood stain spread across her abdomen. Bryony stepped closer, and the commodore's gaze shifted uncomfortably to the intruder.

"This woman claims to have medical training," Rose explained. "She's going to try to help you if you allow it."

The sweat gathering on the commodore's brow glistened as she nodded. "At dis point, what 'arm could come of it?" Her voice was low in pitch, and Bryony noted an accent she couldn't place at first. "Wah yuh name, stranger?"

It reminded her of a Jamaican character she had once heard in a radio show. Although, she now realized the actor might have been putting on the accent since it didn't match this one very well. "I'm Bryony." She held out her hand, but the commodore didn't take it. "Sorry." She withdrew her hand and dropped her duffle bag to the floor. "Let's get started." Here was where Bryony knew she could shine. As soon as she brought out her box of props, she felt renewed confidence. "You have an injury. May I get a closer look?"

The commodore narrowed her eyes but lifted her hands from her stomach all the same.

"I'll have to unbutton your blouse." Bryony laid her box of supplies on the counter.

The commodore showed her palms in surrender, and Bryony began gently releasing the buttons on the lower half of the woman's shirt. When she'd finished all but the top few, she peeled the shirt from the commodore's stomach and saw an injury that sent her reeling. It had been treated, but it was not responding to treatment. Someone had washed and dressed it, but the wound had soaked the dressing and festered beneath it. The swelling was bad. The color was worse. And when Bryony finally peeled away the dressing, the smell sent her running back to her supply box to hide her nausea.

"It's infected," she said, swallowing her disgust.

"Obviously," Rose replied, unimpressed.

"I can wash and disinfect it." Bryony quickly found fresh bandages and pulled her briefcase from her bag. "With medicine, it should heal." That was a lie. The commodore had a date with death, and soon. Her bowels had likely been pierced, and the kind of medicine Bryony had at her disposal would do little for her. Magic, on the other hand . . . "How did this happen?" Bryony asked, mostly to keep Rose from focusing too much on what she was doing.

But it was the commodore who answered. "Vigilantes," she said. "All a dem dead now, including di one who cut me."

"You're very brave," Bryony said. It was an attempt at flattery, but she meant it.

The commodore chuckled and winced from the pain. "I accept yuh compliment."

"I'll need a sterile bowl for mixing." Bryony turned to Rose, who began fishing around in the lockers. She came out with a glass bowl and a silver spoon.

"How sterile do you need it exactly?" Rose asked.

Bryony raised an eyebrow. "That'll do in a pinch." She brought it under the tap and filled it halfway. Then she withdrew a brown bottle from her briefcase and carefully measured out three capfuls to add to the water. "This will disinfect the wound and reduce scarring."

It would not in fact. It was all theater. The tincture she added to the water was more water with a little purple food coloring for effect. She suddenly felt like a fraud and wondered why. Had she not been a fraud all along? What had changed? Was it because now she was imitating real medicine? It was easier to steal power from an angel and pretend to be a god. Pretending to be a doctor was just . . . corrupt.

She dropped a cloth in the bowl and brought it to the commodore, still struggling not to gag from the smell of infection. *It will be gone soon*, she reminded herself, *in minutes in fact*. She just had to get through this performance first. "This is going to hurt. I'm sorry."

The commodore smiled weakly. "Do wah yuh do, girl. Neva mind me."

Bryony wrung water over the commodore's wound. Then she dabbed around the edges as gently as she could manage and marveled at the woman's fortitude. The commodore should have been writhing in pain, but her expression barely changed. She was stoic, strong, fearless. Bryony hoped she wasn't the godhunter.

"Done with the hard part." Bryony gathered bandages and fished in her case for another tincture, this one scented with eucalyptus oil and colored green. "This is for the pain." She returned to the commodore's side and held the small bottle over her body. With an overabundance of caution, Bryony allowed exactly four drops to fall into the commodore's raw wound. "That will take effect in a few minutes," she said. "You should not feel the pain again after that."

Rose crossed her arms over her chest. "I've never heard of a painkiller lasting that long."

"This one does." Bryony set the bottle aside and helped the commodore to sit. "It's a trade secret." She grinned, hoping they would not press her further.

The commodore kept her fevered tremor under remarkable control as she held up the bottom half of her shirt. Bryony wrapped the wound tightly, and as she tied the bandage in its final knot, she sealed her performance with one last ingredient—a scratch from the angel's sword around her finger.

The commodore flinched and frowned. "Dat is a sharp piece yuh 'ave."

"Oh, I'm sorry." Bryony touched her ring and feigned embarrassment. "I never take it off. It's . . . a lucky charm." She chuckled. "Anyway, you should start feeling the effects of the painkiller soon, but remember your injury. Go easy on yourself. And don't take the bandage off for at least a week or the infection could return." She hoped beyond hope the commodore was the type to follow instructions, otherwise her gig was sure to be up.

As Bryony began returning her bottles to her little bag of tricks, she heard the commodore moving around behind her.

"It feels better already," the woman said, her accent faded to a mere sliver. "I can hardly believe it."

"It's fantastic medicine, isn't it?" Bryony closed her briefcase. "My grandmother taught me how to make it before she died. It's an ancient family recipe, herbal medicine from the old days." Improvisation was not her strong suit, but sometimes one had to make do.

Out of the corner of her eye, Bryony caught a dubious look from Rose, but then she turned to see the commodore standing on her feet, the beads of sweat already evaporating from her brow. "You do know what you're doing, don't you?" She smiled and offered a hand. "I'm Raeni, your new commodore."

Bryony failed to stifle her excitement. "I got the job?"

Raeni laughed. "Of course you did. And you should be more confident, talented as you clearly are." She strode to a bunk in one corner of the room and slid a belt out from under the blankets piled there. Attached was a sheath for what looked like an antique machete.

No. Bryony pouted. Raeni couldn't be—not the commodore. Why not Andrew instead? He seemed entirely unlikeable. "That's an interesting weapon." Bryony tried her best to sound indifferent. "Or is it a tool?"

The commodore buckled her belt and smiled the most mischievous half-smile Bryony had ever seen. "It's a lucky charm," she said. "I never take it off."

Damn.

"Rose, show our new medic to her quarters, will you?"

Rose arched an eyebrow. "But there are no more bunks, Commodore."

"I'm aware of that, which is why she'll have to bunk in the captain's quarters."

Bryony didn't understand. "Will I room with you, Commodore?"

Raeni laughed, and her laughter was so musical Bryony would have been happy to listen to it all day. "I sleep with the crew. You'll be bunking with Michael in the captain's quarters." She laid a hand on Bryony's shoulder. "It's an unusual arrangement, to be sure. But you'll see why it is the way it is. And don't fret about Michael. He won't lay a hand on you. He's a celibate."

With that bombshell dropped, the commodore waltzed out of the room as though she hadn't been lying on a table alongside the Grim Reaper only moments before.

Rose wasted no time. "Follow me," she said coolly. They walked back down the hall and climbed the companionway into the light, Bryony keenly aware that this would be home from now on. "You'll sail aboard *Dragonfly* with us. There are nine other ships in our fleet with which you should familiarize yourself as you'll be medic to them all."

Bryony shielded her eyes from the light when she emerged. "What's Chuy's ship called?"

"*Papillon.*"

"Oh!" She hadn't expected the deadliest fleet in the world to have such innocuous names. "Cute."

Rose whirled around and narrowed her eyes, which Bryony could now see were a shade of gray that almost perfectly matched her hair. "His ship is our fastest and scouts our course. It should not be underestimated."

"I wouldn't dare." Bryony forced a smile. "It's just . . . he was so kind and welcoming. I'm glad his ship is named for butterflies. I always liked them. Are all the ships named for insects?"

"It helps to have a theme."

"Is there a *Cicada*? Please tell me there's a *Cicada*."

"There is." Rose's expression softened at that. "It's my sister's ship."

Bryony couldn't help bouncing on the balls of her feet. She was elated to be part of this adventure, to have a real change in her life—one that didn't revolve around death. It was travel. It was new horizons, blue and eternal. The idea that she would have to kill a godhunter in the end buzzed around her head like a bothersome fly. She shook it off.

Rose led Bryony across the main deck, aft toward the captain's quarters. They approached twin staircases curving up to a deck above, and Rose knocked twice on the ornately carved, wooden door nestled between them.

An impressive, deep voice answered, "Come in." Rose opened the door, and Bryony's newfound courage slithered away like a den of disturbed garter snakes. It was dark inside, and all she could see was a silhouette sitting against a row of tall windows at the back.

"Commodore says you get a bunkmate, lucky."

The voice grunted. "Why?"

"She's a medic. We need a medic, and we're out of bunks. I guess the commodore didn't want to throw any crew overboard. Sacrifices had to be made—by you, it seems." She laughed, and the shadow did not laugh back. "I'll leave you two to make your own introductions."

And then Rose was gone, and Bryony was left alone with the stranger occupying the captain's quarters. The entire crew were strangers to her, she realized, but this felt . . . different. Something about the threshold to the captain's quarters repelled her. The air inside seemed thick with shadows. Bryony scanned the sky for Shakespeare but caught no sight of the elusive crow. She missed him immensely. They were supposed to be in this together.

"I'm Bryony," she said from the doorway, still hesitant to cross the threshold.

"Come in, Bryony. Make yourself at home." Michael's voice thrummed low like a massive engine.

Bryony wished she could stop her own hands from trembling, but it was no use. She gulped. She gritted her teeth. She stepped into the cabin and closed the door behind her.

Chapter Six

Bryony held on to her duffle bag like it was a flotation device and she was about to walk the plank. She couldn't see a thing. The bright light from the windows turned everything inside to shadow. The silhouette bowed his head and did not address her again.

As her eyes slowly adjusted, Bryony began to make out her surroundings. The room was every bit as decadent as she expected the captain's quarters to be. The wood was rich and dark with pillars carved into the shapes of Chinese dragons. The windows were hung with draperies the color of midnight and all of it fringed in black. There was a long table at the center, bolted to the floor, and that was strewn with papers and maps, looking far less organized than Bryony felt it should. The back bench stretched all along the row of windows. It appeared to have been modified into an overlong bunk and piled high with comforters and pillows. It was here the silhouette sat and read a small paperback, which Bryony now realized he'd been doing all along.

She dropped her duffle bag onto the floor alongside a smaller, albeit far more elegant bunk built into an alcove against the hull. Then she approached the silhouette, and as she did, she realized the book he was reading wasn't nearly as small as she'd first assumed. It was an average sized paperback. His hands were just . . .

He set his book face down and stood to greet her. And Bryony found herself tilting her head further and further back as he rose. He was enormous. Had she looked at him straight on, she would have been staring at his stomach. She took several steps back to avoid straining her neck. So this was why he had the captain's quarters. The man was a giant—a real, honest-to-god giant. He had to bow his head to avoid hitting it on the support beams. He held out his hand to her, and she took it, feeling downright miniature beside him. She swam in his shadow. Her hand disappeared inside his.

"I'm Michael," he said, withdrawing his hand when Bryony failed to withdraw hers. "I suppose we get to room together."

He wasn't unattractive at all. His body was well proportioned, his features angular but soft. His hair curled gently around his ears and at the base of his neck. And he had a broad, expressive mouth. Aside from his height, what struck Bryony as most unusual about him was his complexion. He had fair skin, very fair, but charcoal eyes—they were so dark she could not tell his pupil from his iris—and his lips were naturally rosy. That, combined with his pitch-black hair, made him the picture of contrast.

Michael shifted uneasily, and Bryony realized she'd been staring at him. *Say something,* she advised herself, but her tongue took its time getting the message. "Ah . . . I uh . . . Can I just ask . . ."

He tilted his face down to her. "More than seven, less than eight," he said. "I think. I haven't measured in a while."

Bryony chewed her lower lip. "What?"

"In feet. You were going to ask my height, yes?"

"Oh!" She laughed. He had gotten it wrong. She was glad he had gotten it wrong. Though she couldn't have entirely explained why, just now, she wanted to be someone who surprised him. "I was going to ask what you were reading."

And suddenly, without any warning whatsoever, the giant smiled. His smile crept up on her like an ember from a bonfire, and she stood entirely disarmed. It was warm, sincere, and it dimpled on one side.

More than anything else about him, she found it was his smile that left her breathless.

He reached behind himself and handed her the book. She took it from him, careful not to lose his place, unable to avoid touching his hand again in the process. When she turned the paperback over, she was more baffled than ever. She had expected something scholarly, perhaps some poetry, but no. There on the cover was a man, unabashedly shirtless, holding a woman in his arms. The woman wore a Victorian gown whose bodice unraveled at the back for no discernible reason, and the two of them were kneeling together on an enormous, canopied bed.

"Is this a romance?" *Stupid question.*

Michael laughed, and Bryony almost dropped the book in shame. Instead, she handed it back like it was too hot to hold any longer.

"I enjoy romance," he said, placing it back on his oversized bunk. "I've been reading the genre since I was a child. It holds a certain nostalgia for me. But honestly, what's not to love?"

Bryony shrugged. She preferred gothic horror to romance, but she wasn't about to admit it. Not now anyway.

"I apologize if it isn't to your taste," he said. "Unfortunately, it's all I have on hand at the moment. But you're welcome to read any of my books as often as you like." He smiled again, and Bryony thought perhaps she really should take another look at the genre. "Let's get you settled in before we set sail."

He went about the cabin like it was second nature, gathering bedding, pillows, and blankets. He must have been living aboard *Dragonfly* a long time. She wondered how many years he'd been with the crew. How long had the alcoved bunk in the captain's quarters been unoccupied?

Then she had a most unpleasant thought. If he was the godhunter . . . She scanned the cabin for anything sharp, any kind of weapon, but found nothing. Good. She couldn't stand the thought of killing him, especially now, as she watched him crouch down to make her bed for her. She wanted to stop him, apologize and make her own bed, but the way he managed it fascinated her.

"I hope you stay warm enough through the night," he said.

He was far chattier than Bryony would have guessed based on his appearance. He talked about the weather, the crew, the ships. He asked what Bryony had done to get the job and was overjoyed when she told him she had healed the commodore.

"There's only one Raeni." He tucked the bedding under the mattress and stood. "No one else could do what she does."

Bryony remembered, with a frown, the machete the commodore carried at her hip. It seemed reasonable to assume the godhunter would be aboard the flagship. Whoever it was, they had to defend the entire fleet against angels.

Michael returned to his bunk and sat, his knees rising well above the mattress. "So you met Rose. She's our cook. You would do well to stay on her good side. And who else?"

"I met Chuy on the beach."

"Lucky you. He's been here so long, he's practically family."

"And Dara."

Michael nodded. "Her father is the captain of *Ladybird*. She'll take over when he retires."

Another captain. Bryony would have to remember who the captains were. "I also met Andrew."

"Ah, yes. Our newest recruit next to you."

Bryony scowled at that. She could rule out Andrew in that case. The godhunter had been with the fleet for many years.

"I take it you didn't hit it off."

"He doesn't like me," she said.

"Don't mind him. He's had it rough. Doesn't trust so easily. He'll come around to you in no time, especially after he hears what you did for the commodore."

Andrew would be mistaken if he did come around, but Bryony just smiled. Why did the crew of the nightmare-inducing Black Armada have to be so . . . so normal? How was she going to betray them without hating herself in the end? She tried to remind herself of how they traveled the world hunting down gods just like her, mercilessly executing them. No trial. No evaluation. Just death. She shivered and suddenly felt lonely for Shakespeare.

Michael picked up his book and made himself comfortable. "Have you ever been aboard a ship like this, Bryony?"

She shook her head. "Never."

"Then you should watch the crew set sail. You'll enjoy it. Just try to stay out of the way, and hang on to something. And let me know if there's anything you need, bunkmate." He grinned.

Bryony stuffed her duffle bag behind her pillows. She could only hope Michael didn't have the tendency to taste test unknown tinctures, or he would quickly discover that most of them were just water. He didn't seem the suspicious type. Anyway, she would have to learn to trust at least some of the crew if she ever expected to be trusted in return. His intimidating size aside, Michael seemed relatively harmless. Perhaps his loose tongue would even be a boon to her. She would think of questions to ask him about the rest of the crew later.

She left Michael to his book and pushed open the tightly fitted door of the captain's quarters. Sunlight hit her eyes, and she shielded them with her hands. The ship had come alive with activity.

Crew were up and down the deck, and climbing the masts like a colony of ants. The commodore stood atop the captain's quarters, commanding her crew. Raeni had her eye on everything, and in no time, she was shouting down to Bryony. "Medic! Join me on the quarterdeck!"

Bryony climbed one of the two stairways that flanked the door to the captain's quarters. When she finally reached the commodore's side and turned forward, she had to remind herself to close her mouth. The ship stretched out below her, alive and swarming, and beyond it was the sky and sea. The shore was at her back, and before her she saw only blue on blue, distant whitecaps, and the glitter of the sun on the waves. The wind hit her face and tugged at the sleeves of her blouse like an insistent puppy.

"You already love the sea, don't you?" Raeni laid a hand on her shoulder. "It has its own angel, you know, though he's been dead for ages. They call him Rahab. He'll charm you for a while. Then he'll take your trust and crush it under his heel. Not one of us aboard worships any god, but we've all caught ourselves praying from time to time. Don't be ashamed when it happens to you. Now pay attention. You'll need to learn the ropes, literally." She laughed a laugh that was half mirth, half wickedness.

There was a warning in the commodore's speech, Bryony realized, but it wasn't what she would have expected. It was not a prescription for toughness or bravery. All Bryony heard was sympathy, commiseration. *You will be humiliated,* it said. *You are not as strong as you think you are, but neither were we. We have all been through what you will suffer.*

Bryony raised her chin to the sky, closed her eyes, and drank in the smell of the sea. When she opened her eyes again, she saw a crow circling the masts, making a nuisance of himself. "Shakespeare!" she called, and the crow flew down to her. He made himself comfortable on her shoulder and nuzzled against her cheek.

"You have a pet?" Raeni looked down at the crow with one eyebrow arched.

"He's family. He goes where I go."

"Will he be all right underway?"

Bryony smiled her most reassuring smile. "He's smart. He'll be fine." There was no chance she was going to let Shakespeare off the hook for a plan he himself concocted.

"Well, that's all good then." The commodore turned her attention to her ship and began calling out orders. "Haul anchor, and let's be off! We're heading south!" The crew cheered and began tugging vigorously on the lines around them. "They love it when we head south." Raeni's smile was broad and warm. She looked fantastic, as though she had never been injured at all. She stood tall, the heels of her boots keeping time to a song only she could hear. She had tied a brightly colored bandana around her head, and her braids fell long over one shoulder.

Bryony wondered how long she would pass as a mere medic when she couldn't help but perform miracles every time.

"Keep an eye on them, girl," the commodore said. "Consider this your first lesson. Ah, there's our main now."

The black mainsail rose above Bryony's head, pull by pull. It was an intimidating, massive pall. A number of crew on the line responded simultaneously to one person's rhythmic song as the great sail wavered and whipped in the wind. It was like an animal, fighting the lines the crew used to control it. It was a living, breathing thing.

Raeni called for more sails to be unfurled, and the crew on the masts obeyed, dropping the black, canvas standards one by one. Each sail had a name, and Bryony tried to memorize them but, in her excitement, failed. Her mind was too fixed on the wind that billowed each square sail, caught the broad belly of the mainsail, and slowly, slowly brought their beast of a ship to motion.

Dragonfly had spread its wings.

Bryony ran to the bulwarks to watch each of the other ships raise their sails and catch the wind. She was so engrossed she almost didn't notice Raeni lean her elbows on the rail beside her. "I hear you took a liking to Chuy," the commodore said, crossing her ankles behind her. "There's his ship, already pulling out ahead." She pointed to a boat with three triangular sails. It was smaller than *Dragonfly* but much faster. Bryony wondered how many crew it took to sail.

Alongside *Dragonfly*, she noticed another ship—one that stood out from the others. It was medium-sized, not more than sixty feet, with two tall masts. Its sails were striped with battens and shaped like a dragon's wings. "What ship is that?" She pointed.

"*Cicada*. She's a Chinese junk. Pretty, isn't she?"

"Rose's sister." Bryony loved the ship immediately.

"Daisy is its captain, yes. Already keeping track, are you?"

Bryony caught a whiff of suspicion in that. She worried that Raeni was already skeptical of her newfound medic. But then Bryony remembered something Shakespeare had told her years ago. *You only make your deception more obvious if you worry too much about getting caught.* She willed herself to take the commodore at her word, think of her as a friend, as someone who owed Bryony her life, which she was. Bryony allowed her excitement to overwrite her fears and sincerely smiled. "You've got to start somewhere, right?"

Raeni clapped her on the back. "Good initiative." And she proceeded to point out ship after ship, naming and explaining them until Bryony's head was too full of insects and rigging. Then Raeni turned her to face their own *Dragonfly* and began naming the decks and sheets and shrouds. "Down there is the main deck." She pointed to the level where Bryony had first boarded the ship. "The forward, raised deck is the forecastle, but you'll hear us pronounce it *fo'c'sle.* Beneath is where the rest of the crew sleeps. It's cramped. You're lucky you're not bunking with us. Thank me later." She winked.

Bryony noticed most of the new words she learned were pronounced clipped and casual. The word *sail* was almost invariably shortened to a quick suffix: *mains'l, fores'l, tops'l.* She muttered them all to herself, well aware she would sound like an outsider if she got any of them wrong.

Shakespeare hopped off Bryony's shoulder and perched on the rail, ruffling his feathers in the wind, listening just as much as Bryony was. He had always been a curious bird.

"Dara!" The commodore called out, and Dara was there, quick as a rabbit. "Give our new medic the tour, will you? And then bring her to mess."

Dara nodded and took Bryony by the wrist.

"And, Dara." The commodore's mouth turned down as she stood statuesque before them. "I know how heavy it must have been for you, weighing caution against my welfare. I want to thank you for taking that risk for me."

Dara bobbed her head in deference. "Yes, Commodore."

Raeni waved them along, and her smile returned, bright as the sun on the waves. "Just don't do it again."

Though the commodore laughed, Bryony felt the gravity behind her words, and Dara must have too. The quiet Cambodian tensed and dropped her head as they made their way belowdecks. She mumbled curses at Chuy for getting her into this situation and squeezed Bryony's wrist until it began to ache. Shakespeare rattled a threat deep in his throat and hopped down Bryony's arm toward Dara, who let go and glared at the bird.

"He's not always friendly," Bryony said by way of an apology.

To Bryony's shock, Dara turned and said, "He's loyal. It's admirable. You're lucky to have such a loyal friend."

And Bryony sank under the dark realization that she was finding it far too easy to like the crew of the Black Armada, and increasingly difficult to think about killing any one of them.

Chapter Seven

"You've always been too tenderhearted for your own good." Shakespeare perched on Bryony's shoulder and murmured into her ear. They waited together in the mess hall, which Bryony had learned was just a ridiculous word for the place where sailors ate. What was so wrong with *dining room*? Still it was amusing to learn new names for everyday things. The bathrooms were called *heads* for some god-only-knows reason, and the kitchen was a *galley*.

The tour had been shorter than expected. Most of the ship was reserved for berths and cargo, which was carefully boxed and hidden from view. Bryony made it an immediate goal to discover what the Black Armada was moving, its primary purpose being a mystery to most of the world. But Dara was the conversational opposite of Michael. Quiet, concise, no nonsense. When the tour ended early, Dara sat Bryony on a long, wooden bench at a long, wooden table and simply said, "Wait here."

Bryony was grateful for a moment alone with Shakespeare. She wanted to argue with him about her tenderheartedness, but she couldn't. He was right. She was too soft, and perhaps it would be the death of her in the end. Instead she said, "Where were you anyway?"

"Checking out the other ships. You can only be on this one. Who's to say the godhunter isn't holed up on a smaller ship?" Shakespeare hopped off her shoulder and onto the table. "It would be smart for a godhunter to keep a low profile, don't you think?"

. Bryony shrugged. "I don't know. I think whoever she is, she'll be on the flagship. It holds most of the cargo and should be protected in case of angels."

"So you've already decided it's a woman aboard the flagship, have you?"

"That's statistically the most likely answer."

"You just don't want it to be the young man who took you in. What was his name?"

"Chuy." Bryony frowned. "He's been with the armada long enough to play the role. But the only person I've seen carrying a weapon is the commodore."

Shakespeare lifted a foot and stepped down as heavily as a crow could on the back of Bryony's ring finger. "You don't carry a weapon either, remember?"

Bryony shook him off. "It's still sharp. I think whatever shape the death sword takes, it will have to be sharp. Otherwise, how will it puncture?"

"Good *point.*" He laughed at his own pun.

"Well, there are needles in the ship's hospital."

"And knives in the galley."

Bryony groaned. "God it could be as small as a hairpin. How will I ever find it?"

"Subterfuge." Shakespeare quickly scratched his head with his middle toe, and Bryony reached out to help him. He always appreciated a good scratch. "Win their trust, and get them to tell you where it is."

"I don't know." She sighed. "What if I'm no good at subterfuge?"

"You've been doing it most of the years I've known you."

"But only so people would trust me to heal them. Not to get information from them. Not to kill—"

"Shh!" Shakespeare hissed.

Bryony leaned in to whisper. "I mean what if it is Chuy, or Raeni, or Dara? They seem like genuinely good people. What will I do if it's one of them?"

"You'll remember who you are and that no godhunter will hesitate to kill you as soon as they know *what* you are. And you'll remember your congregation. Who will heal them when you're gone?" Shakespeare paused and bowed his head, but Bryony understood he was not asking for a scratch this time. "And I hope you'll remember me. I've abandoned my old life to follow you. What will I do without you?" He paused. "What will I do without the only family I know?"

Bryony bowed her head over him, mirroring his gesture. She could smell the distinctive, indescribable scent of his feathers, his breath. He was so precious to her, this little crow. And the fact that he had called her family . . . "I swear I won't let you down," she said.

He brought his head up until it bumped against Bryony's chin. "Just survive this. Promise me you'll survive."

"I love you, Shakespeare," she whispered. Shakespeare didn't respond at all, but she thought he understood. She had never really spoken it aloud before, and perhaps he was just taken aback. Or perhaps he was quiet because he'd heard footsteps moments before Bryony did.

She glanced up to see Rose setting places at the table. There was a lip all around to keep things from sliding off, but it didn't keep them from sliding back and forth with the rolling of the sea.

"What does your bird like to eat?" Rose asked.

"He'll eat anything, but he likes meat best, organs. Also grains and the occasional fruit treat. Mostly he eats what's in front of him."

Rose grinned. "I'll bring him a little plate of goodies then."

"Oh, you don't need to—"

"Shush! I want to. He's adorable. It's been a long time since we've had a pet aboard. I'm a fool if I don't spoil the hell out of him."

"Thank you." Bryony was genuinely pleased to hear that someone else would be looking after Shakespeare too. And the bird would surely grow to like Rose. The way to his heart was most definitely through his stomach. "His name is Shakespeare. Once he warms up to you, he'll be a friend for life."

"Good." Rose finished setting the table and brought out various plates of food that slid back and forth in time with everything else.

"I suppose you don't often serve soup," Bryony mused.

Rose laughed. "Soup night is serve-yourself and hold-on-to-your-bowl night. Unless we're in the doldrums. Then it's a smorgasbord."

The rest of the crew trickled into the mess hall as the hour wore on. They sat and chatted, some of them asking to feed Shakespeare a little piece of roll or a strip of chicken. Shakespeare reveled in the attention, putting on his best adorable-bird act, hopping and bobbing his head. Partway through the meal, some of the crew left and were replaced with others who had been on watch. All in all, the atmosphere was pleasant and friendly. Even Andrew offered a quick, tentative smile from across the way. But Bryony noticed someone was conspicuously absent.

"Where's Michael?" she asked. "Doesn't he eat with us?"

It was Rose who answered first. "Does it look like he could fit comfortably at this table?"

Bryony blushed. It was easy to forget that the world wasn't built with Michael in mind. Still it must be terribly isolating, taking his meals alone while everyone else took them together. "Does anyone ever eat with him?"

The table went silent at that, and she wondered why. Was it an awkward question, or was it just that no one had really thought about it? Raeni sighed. "It's not that no one wants to, girl. Michael is just . . . his own man. He doesn't choose to spend time with us, and we leave him to himself."

Bryony found that hard to believe, but she didn't push the subject. Perhaps her first impression of the giant in the captain's quarters had been wrong, but he'd seemed deeply personable at first blush. She had considered him an easy source of information. He was so eager for conversation. Why would he impose isolation on himself if he didn't prefer it? Maybe he just didn't fit in. Bryony could understand that. She had an entire adoring congregation, but she'd never felt like one of them. She was their beating heart, but she was also an outsider.

She was deep in thought when Andrew passed by and tipped his brandy into her empty glass. She hadn't planned on having a drink that night, but the man nodded to her and mumbled, "I don't renege," so she felt a kind of obligation. Truly, she hadn't even finished her meal. She was tired, and all she wanted to do was lie down and sleep. She sipped at the drink and watched as the others carried their empty plates into the galley.

Once again, Bryony sat alone at the table. Rose stared down at her plate, hands on her hips. "Not hungry, eh?" Her voice was relaxed with a touch of Southern drawl. "If your appetite's left you, don't force it. You're probably just feeling the sea."

Bryony finished off Andrews's brandy and appreciated the way the room spun a little more slowly. "I think I'd like to lie down for a bit." She thanked Rose for the meal and climbed the companionway to the main deck. Shakespeare stayed behind, probably in the hopes of getting more scraps, which was fine by Bryony.

When she approached the door to the captain's quarters, she paused and then decided to knock. What if Michael was changing? She wasn't sure how shy he was or how sharing a room with him was even going to work. When no answer came, she opened the door and found the cabin empty. Michael must have gone out for some reason. Come to think of it, she wasn't sure exactly what it was he did on the ship.

Then she noticed the difference in the cabin. Stretched across the opening to her bunk, there was now a brass curtain rod and new, cream-colored curtains. They were perfect—cotton, she thought. They let the light through but offered her privacy. How Michael had managed to remedy a problem she had yet to voice baffled her, but she was grateful all the same. And she didn't feel much like thinking anymore. Her head was heavy. She just wanted the dizziness to stop. She crawled into her new little sanctuary, curled up, and fell into an easy sleep.

Once or twice, Bryony woke to find the light had changed. She knew she was sleeping too much, but every time she opened her eyes, all she wanted to do was close them again. A monumental headache crept up on her, and she felt it more keenly with every passing hour. The final time she woke, her head and stomach conspired to keep her from sleeping again.

A warm light filtered through her cotton wall, and she pushed it aside to see Michael sitting at the table in the middle of the room, poring over charts and notebooks. An oil lamp hung over his head and was secured in three directions so it wouldn't swing too much. He held a pencil in his mouth and took it out to make calculations. Then he measured, walking a tool like an artist's compass across a chart, and drew a line with a ruler. So that answered the question of what he did.

"You're the navigator," she guessed aloud.

He lifted his head and smiled. "That I am. How was your rest?"

"Good." She noticed he was not seated at a chair but sitting instead on his heels, which put him at the right height to use the table. Of course he didn't want to eat in the mess hall. She felt stupid for even having asked. "Although, I think I'm feeling a little . . . off." She didn't want to say *seasick*. That was admitting weakness—admitting she'd maybe made a mistake in thinking she could be some kind of sailor like the rest of them. But the longer she tried to deny the thing, the more she became convinced her dinner would make a reappearance.

Michael looked up after making another mark on the chart. "You do look pale—well, paler than you were when we first met. You may need to get some air. It helps. Inside is the worst place to be on a ship."

"Yeah, maybe I will." At least then she could lean over the side if she had to be sick. Less mess, slightly less humiliation. "By the way, thank you for the curtains."

He nodded. "I thought you'd like a little privacy."

"They're perfect. And you know, if you ever want any—privacy, that is—just tell me. I'll go, I promise. I feel bad you got stuck with me."

"I don't." He smiled his enormous, disarming smile, and Bryony had to remind herself to smile back. Why anyone would think he was "his own man" was beyond her. He positively radiated charm.

Stop staring, she scolded herself. *He's going to think you're one of those people who stares at anything out of the ordinary.*

But that was just it, wasn't it? He was out of the ordinary. Not just his height. No, it was something else—something that made her chest tighten and her palms sweat. She wiped them on her pants and laughed nervously. "Thanks I guess. I'll go out now." She waved and left, mentally flogging herself for behaving like an awkward teenager.

Outside, the night air was cool and refreshing. Bryony breathed deep and luxuriated in the feel of the breeze on her flushed skin. The wind whistled through the rigging, but it wasn't a harsh wind. She looked up to see the towering masts and shadowy sails above, and just to add to the otherworldly feel of the night, Bryony was certain she could hear music.

Somewhere above her, a fiddle played. Its song was soft and sweet. As she listened, she realized it came from the quarterdeck, and she climbed the stairs, careful not to disturb the player. Whoever it was, she was grateful. The music distracted her from her churning stomach. But when she reached the topmost stair, she froze. The player was not who she'd expected. Andrew sat with his back to the bulwarks, a fiddle nestled between his beard and shoulder, and produced perhaps the most beautiful lullaby Bryony had ever heard.

Before she could abort and back down the stairs, he glanced up. "Howdy, Tinctures. What're you doing up at this hour?"

She sighed and continued up the stairs. "Michael suggested I go outside. I've been feeling a little . . ."

"Seasick?" He finished for her, though not in the way she would have liked.

She glowered at him.

He just laughed. "Ah. Well, physician, heal thyself."

Of course. Why hadn't she thought of it? Surreptitiously, she pressed her ring into her hand and scraped the surface of her skin. She winced at the sting of it, and then she waited. Nothing. Maybe she hadn't quite broken her skin. She tried again, digging deeper until she felt the sick, little pop of the sharp beak breaking through. A bead of blood formed on her palm, and she pressed her thumb to it. Surely, that would be enough. But it wasn't. And she couldn't figure out why.

"I don't think I can heal myself of this," she said to Andrew. "I don't have a tincture for seasickness." Self-deprecating humor was worth a try.

Then Andrew solved her puzzle for her. "Probably because you're not really sick. Your body is acting exactly as it should under the circumstances." He patted the deck beside him, and Bryony hesitated. Was he being friendly? Could she trust him not to throw her overboard? He was the only crew member she'd actually ruled out as the possible godhunter. And he had given her his brandy as promised. She puffed up her chest and forced herself to be sociable.

When she settled in beside him, he leaned back and gazed up at the stars, casually plucking at his fiddle. "It's because your body thinks you've been poisoned. That's what I learned anyway. It feels like you're moving because you are, but when you look around, everything's stationary. Your signals are conflicting. So your brain tells your stomach you must've eaten something off, and your stomach tries to eject it. That's why going outside helps. When you see the horizon, the signals match up better." He turned to look at her, and she noticed for the first time how pale blue his eyes were. "But you probably already knew all that."

"I didn't actually." She shrugged. "I've never treated people on a boat before. But where on earth did you learn about it?"

"I read about it. The watch gets dull sometimes, so I go below and grab a book from the cargo hold. I was sick as a dog my first few days aboard, so I found an essay on motion sickness."

"There are books?"

He squinted at her as though he were trying to read an essay written on her forehead. "You mean you don't know? I would've thought that was your whole reason for joining the Black Armada."

"I honestly have no idea what you're talking about."

"The books. All the books in the cargo hold. A lot of them are forbidden medical texts. I just assumed you wanted at them. To further your training or to steal them or whatever."

"Books?" Bryony's mouth dropped open. "That's what the armada traffics in? Just books?"

"It's not *just books*. Oh my god, look." Andrew turned to face her, and Bryony realized she'd frustrated him again. That didn't take long. "The whole point of the armada is to circulate forbidden texts, scientific texts. We're educating people. The angels can't keep an educated population down forever. Why do you think they've been so careful to stifle scientific curiosity? They know it as well as we do. The armada is single-handedly preserving the knowledge the angels tried to wipe out. Nothing could be more important. *Just books?*" He scoffed. "I'd have thought you of all people would appreciate what we're trying to do here."

"Oh, I do!" She meant it. "I'm just trying to wrap my head around it. The Black Armada traffics in books. All this time, I thought it was weapons or something."

"Pfft! What good would weapons do against angels?"

That was a point she couldn't argue with. So she just nodded and tried not to throw up at the movement.

"Well, you should check some of them out sometime," he said. "No one will stop you. You're our medic now, and I'm sure they'll want you to learn as much as you can."

"I will." Bryony closed her eyes and leaned back. It was taking all her concentration to keep her dinner down.

Andrew grew quiet for a moment. Then he said, "So if it wasn't to get at the books, why did you join the Black Armada?"

There was a question she couldn't answer honestly—not really. So she kept her lie brief. "Revenge." A half-truth. "Against the angels."

"Ah-ha." With that, Andrew resumed his playing.

Bryony listened a while, drifting in and out of a pleasant doze. The quiet folk song he played lulled her and soothed her headache. Finally, she found the courage to ask, "How did you get over your seasickness?"

Andrew lowered his fiddle. "Three days. Wait it out for three days. The commodore won't give you any duty until you find your sea legs. Once your body is used to the motion, you won't feel sick anymore."

Three days. She could do that. Maybe. She lowered her head onto her arm and closed her eyes. As the music continued, the sea grew still, and Bryony fell asleep beside the man who trusted her least of all.

Chapter Eight

Bryony woke to the sensation of a cool breeze chilling the dew that had gathered on her skin. She cursed under her breath and propped herself up on her elbow. The sky was a grayish purple, the horizon a ghost on the sea. It was dawn or nearly dawn. She had slept through the night outside on the quarterdeck. She sat up and dried her face with her sleeves. And she noticed at once she was not alone.

Crouched at the bulwarks, staring through the strangest looking spyglass she'd ever seen, was her roommate. He made adjustments on the device, tilting it this way and that before he was satisfied. Then he crouched even lower, glanced at an open wooden box at his feet, and quickly wrote in a notebook. He studied the spyglass and wrote down more information. Then he closed the little box and slipped the spyglass into a soft bag with a drawstring. When he finally looked up, he paused.

"You're awake," he said. "My apologies if I woke you."

"You didn't," she assured him. "It was the chill."

"In that case . . ." He marched toward her, his footfalls surprisingly light on the wooden deck, probably because he wasn't wearing shoes. She wondered briefly whether he'd removed them to avoid waking her. He slipped his jacket from his shoulders, knelt down, and offered it to her.

She thanked him and took it, realizing it was far more blanket than coat on her. "What was that you were doing just now?"

"Oh, this?" He removed the spyglass from the drawstring bag and handed it to her.

It was heavier than she'd expected, though its component parts were delicate, intricate. It swung on an axis with knobs and mirrors she couldn't begin to make sense of. "What is it?" she asked.

"A sextant. With that I can measure the stars and calculate exactly where we are."

She turned it over in her hands reverently. "And what was in the box?"

He offered it to her and took the sextant back. It was strange asking him questions outright. It would have felt more natural to sneak around his cabin and rifle through his things. But this was nice. She opened the lid and saw what looked like a beautiful, brass clock suspended in the box.

"It's a chronometer," Michael explained, "so I can record the exact time I took each measurement. When I'm finished, I'll return to our quarters and make the appropriate adjustments. Then I can pinpoint our position on the chart. It sounds romantic, but it's mostly just math." He laughed.

"It's amazing."

"Before the massacre, people used a system they called GPS, but the angels destroyed every satellite in the sky, so it doesn't work anymore. This is a much older technique, but it doesn't rely on artificial satellites. And as much as they may want to, the angels can't destroy the stars."

"Which stars are you measuring?" Bryony glanced up at the sky. Though it was dawn, the stars still shone bright, some glittering, some steady and true. She couldn't have told anyone which was which.

Michael pointed. "From here, I measure the North Star. There."

She leaned in and followed the line of his arm to a star—just an ordinary star. She couldn't see anything special about it.

"It's the only star that doesn't appear to shift in the sky." Michael answered the question she hadn't gotten around to asking. "So you can always rely on it to show you the way. It's trustworthy, steady."

"That sounds like my father." Bryony hadn't thought much about what she'd said. It was just an offhand utterance, a little memory, the camera flash of an image—her father, sitting on the porch, shucking corn and singing his favorite songs. But Michael stared down at her as though she had just spoken the most profound words he'd ever heard. He went unusually quiet. His ever-animated mouth slumped into a crooked line. His eyes were . . . She stiffened. Was that grief?

"I'm sorry," she said. "I didn't mean to . . ."

He snapped out of it and shook his head. "No, no. It's nothing, it's nothing. Listen, I've got to adjust this reading, and you'll probably want to get ready for the day. You've got a couple hours before breakfast. Everyone will be wondering how your first night aboard went." He heaved himself to his full height, and she handed him his chronometer so he wouldn't have to crouch again. "Thank you," he said.

Before he could turn away, Bryony found her courage and her tongue. "Michael, I was wondering." He waited, and she cleared her throat a few too many times before she went on. "Well, would you like to take breakfast with me? It's just I noticed you weren't there at dinner, and I thought maybe you'd like . . . a little company . . ."

Her voice petered out. She had to stop talking because he was positively beaming down at her, and she found herself catching her breath at the sight of it. The ghost of his grief evaporated. His dimple returned. His eyes glittered like the stars he measured. She felt so unbelievably good that she'd been able to make someone that happy without the use of the healing sword. All it took was breakfast.

"I usually eat meals in our quarters," he said through his smile. "I mean I would love some company. Of course I would."

Of course he would. Of course. Of course.

Bryony was lost in the refrain as she readied herself for the day. She showered and dressed in the captain's private head, located at the fore end of the captain's quarters. It was far roomier than she'd expected, with brass fittings, a brass sink, and a shower Michael could easily make use of. She wondered how much of the room had been modified to suit him and how much was just the luxury captains were afforded when *Dragonfly* was a legal merchant vessel.

During her tour, Dara had shown Bryony how to use the shower and explained that it was plumbed for seawater because they had to conserve the fresh for drinking. Bryony didn't mind the salty film left on her skin. Her mood was high and could not be brought down. *Of course he would,* was a song stuck in her head as she brushed her teeth, buttoned a clean shirt—light gray, this time, with lace accents on the collar—and put the same jeans back on. She tied her hair back with a purple ribbon and straightened her bangs until she was satisfied with her appearance. She could get used to this style. Perhaps the veil and beads were unnecessary after all.

From the quarterdeck, she watched the crew trim the sails until she could stand it no more, and then she went early to mess. Rose was already there, so Bryony asked her about *Dragonfly*'s books.

"They're below. Way below." Rose pointed straight down. "Head down, and you'll see 'em in the cargo hold. They're in boxes labeled according to topic. You are, of course, welcome to read any of them. Just put them back when you're done."

Of course.

And why hadn't anyone thought to ask Michael whether he would like company? Why was he so set apart from the rest of the crew? Was there some aspect of his personality he was hiding from Bryony? A temper perhaps? That seemed unlikely. Was it his celibacy? But why on earth should that make a difference? It was as though he was part of the crew but not. He was a calculator, an amusement, a curiosity. He was useful and docile. No one spoke ill of him, but no one spoke well of him either.

Rose was still talking. "I believe the medical texts are aft if that's what you're looking for. The commodore will be pleased to learn you're furthering your training."

Bryony smiled, fairly certain she'd heard the important parts. "Thank you so much. I'll take a look at them today. Oh, and by the way, I plan to take breakfast with Michael this morning."

Rose's mouth snapped shut, and she looked momentarily confused. "I see," she said at last, apparently having come to terms with the abnormality. "Well, then you can save me some time by taking his meal to him."

"Of course."

Bryony's frequent failure to anticipate what would seem to be obvious issues relating to Michael's stature astounded her. This time, it was the size of his meal. He needed to take in more food than most people, and his plate reflected that—a fact Rose found amusing. Bryony didn't mind. It was good to be given a task, even if it was a simple one.

As she opened the hatch to climb onto the main deck, she saw Shakespeare waiting for her. "Please tell me that plate is for me." He hopped onto her shoulder and tilted one eye down at Michael's breakfast. "I'll roll around in it and call it a day."

In an answer, she passed him a corner of her own toast. "You know, if you were around more, I'd be able to feed you more."

He swallowed the crust and shook out his wings. "I've been spending time aboard *Ladybird*. It is *such* a party boat. They're constantly dropping crumbs."

"You don't like *Papillon*?" she asked.

"The cutter?" He groaned. "It's so damned wholesome. I can't tolerate it, not even for meat. Better bread in a brothel."

Bryony took the hint and offered Shakespeare some of her egg.

The bird could not have tasted it as quickly as it disappeared down his gullet. "You don't eat much, do you?" he said, eyeing her comparatively small breakfast of one fried egg on toast.

"I've been sick," she explained. "Gotta take it easy."

"And why are you waiting on the giant in the captain's quarters?"

"I'm not waiting on him. I'm eating with him. He doesn't fit at the mess hall table, and he could use the company."

Shakespeare shook his head. "Don't spend all your time with one person, even if he is more sequoia than man."

"Quit it, bird. Go be cruel somewhere else. Anyway, Michael's a talker and the ship's navigator. I could find out where we're headed if I work on him a bit. He and Andrew are turning out to be good sources." She told him what she'd learned about the Black Armada's primary purpose.

"Books!" Shakespeare cawed. "I would not have guessed. I honestly figured they were just out to kill as many angels and gods as they could."

"Me too. So you see? It's good to have sources."

"Well, you've had better luck than I have anyway. No one seems to talk about the godhunter—and I mean at all."

"Keep trying, my faithful familiar." Bryony chuckled, and Shakespeare stole a sausage off Michael's plate just to show her. Then he took off over the sea to eat it on one of the other ships.

"Bad bird!" She watched to see which ship he landed on. It was the Chinese junk, *Cicada.*

Then she noticed the fleet's formation. All the smaller ships sailed in a wide circle surrounding the flagship. Each of them had to adjust their course to match *Dragonfly.* They felt like sentinels guarding their queen, and Bryony thought the idea couldn't be far from the truth. Certainly, if an angel were to take *Dragonfly,* the Black Armada would be lost, most of its cargo destroyed forever. Surely, the angels knew that. So why didn't they attack?

They were afraid of the death sword. That was the only answer. It was as though the further one got from death—the smaller the role it played in one's life—the more terrifying it became. Those who saw death all around them tended to treat the end of life as a milestone. And those who rarely witnessed the dead and dying were horrified by the mere idea of a corpse. The angels, being functionally immortal, gave death the widest possible berth.

Yes, the godhunter had to be aboard the flagship. The smaller vessels were just eyes on the sea. *Let Shakespeare waste his time*, Bryony thought.

A little voice in her head seemed to whisper, *You're getting warmer . . . warmer.* And as she stepped into the captain's quarters, she began to devise ways to wring information from the Black Armada's most essential crew member.

Chapter Nine

The navigator of *Dragonfly* handled everything with enormous delicacy, as though he were afraid to break whatever he touched. His gentleness was almost unnatural. Bryony tried not to stare as he ate, instead forcing herself to finish off her toast and egg.

"Did you make your adjustments?" she asked.

He nodded. "Would you like to see where we are?"

She set her plate down and approached him. Michael sat cross-legged with his back against his bunk, but he rose up on his knees to point out their location. "Here," he said.

She leaned in to look. According to the chart, *Dragonfly* was just a little black dot on a vast blue ocean, but they knew exactly where they were and where they were going. There was something beautiful about that. *If only nautical navigation could be applied to the rest of life*, Bryony thought. *It's easier to climb a mountain when you know something good is waiting on the other side.*

"We're following the coast now," Michael said. "Tomorrow, we'll change tack and make for the harbor. We should arrive in the evening, make our trades under cover of darkness, and leave again before dawn."

"Are we trading books?"

"Yes." Unlike Andrew, Michael seemed surprised she already knew as much as she did. At least *he* hadn't assumed she was a petty thief.

"Do we trade books for more books?"

"We usually trade for provisions: food, water, fuel, canvas." He sat back against his bunk and left the chart for Bryony to examine. "People who give us books do so for the love of the books. They know if they keep them, the angels will not only find and destroy the books but execute their owners. So we take the books and promise to distribute them to those who need them. On our next run, we'll often get those same books back. We basically circulate them."

"Like a floating library." She traced their path on the chart before her.

"Exactly."

"It's funny," she said. "When I was a kid, I heard stories about the Black Armada. I imagined it more like a military fleet or pirate ships, firing cannons and swinging swords around. Terrifying heroes—that's what I thought. I rooted for you in secret but hoped to never meet you in my lifetime. Then my parents died and my baby brother with them, and everything changed. When I joined the armada, I thought maybe I'd die fighting. All that mattered was giving everything to resist the angels." She looked up, hoping he could read her emphasis. "But the closest thing I've seen to a weapon since I joined is the commodore's lucky machete."

Michael chewed his lower lip in thought. What would he tell her? How much? He just smiled and said, "Don't underestimate the commodore's machete. You do so at your own peril." He said it like it was a joke, but was it? Bryony couldn't tell.

Well, at least she had broached the subject. That would do for now. No need to appear too eager. He knew she was curious, and he would talk when he wanted to, maybe after he trusted her a little more.

Bryony slipped away after breakfast to find some books on medicine. She figured it would be better to treat non-life-threatening injuries with more conventional medicine and save the healing sword for occasions when nothing else would work. That way she'd better keep her cover as a regular, scientifically trained medic. Cuts would heal in the right amount of time. Bruises would fade slowly.

The cargo hold was dark and cool. Inside, several dehumidifiers ran on a generator. Their hum provided a strange comfort for Bryony, like a constant, ghostly whisper in her ear. She was glad for it, honestly, because the cargo hold was a lonely labyrinth of boxes and blackness. Ghosts would have been a welcome addition.

Rose had told her how to find the lamps hanging at the entrance, which were plastic, battery powered, and worked well enough. Bryony held one out before her as she wove her way around cedar boxes. Each of them was labeled in dark paint: *History of the Sahara, Romanic Languages, Calculus.* She pushed as far aft as she could and found all the medical texts she could ever want to read. She took four, which was as much as she thought she could easily carry. They were not light reading by any stretch. One was on infectious diseases, one was basic first aid, and one was a well-illustrated tome on anatomy.

The last book she chose she tucked between the others, keeping the spine pressed to her stomach. It was a history of human growth abnormalities, and she could not resist taking it as soon as she saw it. But she didn't want to offend Michael or for him to believe she thought him broken or wrong in any way. She just wanted to understand him better.

As soon as she climbed through the companionway, she spotted him on the quarterdeck, looking once more through his queer, little spyglass. She smiled to herself and watched him a moment. The way the rest of the crew moved around him unnerved her. They were like a school of fish avoiding a boulder. They laughed and chatted with each other, but no one said a word to Michael. No one joked with him or slapped him on the back as they passed.

He was recording another reading, and Bryony couldn't stand to see him so alone despite being surrounded by his shipmates. She clutched her books tight to her chest and called up to him. "Michael! What star are you measuring now?" She meant it as a joke. Obviously, there were no stars out at high noon.

But Michael pointed straight up. "That one, of course."

He was pointing at the sun. Bryony stood stunned, her thoughts shifting through several phases of confusion. Realization crept up on her slowly. When she grasped the meaning behind his answer at last, she felt such a rush of elation, she couldn't help shouting it out, no matter how ignorant it made her look. "The sun is a star?"

Michael's smile broadened. "A very close one."

"It's a star!" She nearly dropped her books. "The sun is a star! Why did no one ever tell me before?"

Every other sailor on deck stopped what they were doing and stared at her, their faces expressing everything from horrified disbelief to amusement. She didn't care.

Only Michael was delighted by her outburst.

"It's a star. I'll be damned." She looked up again, shielded her eyes, and laughed at herself. It seemed so obvious now that she knew. Her mind reeled with the added understanding that every other star in the sky was also that bright, that powerful. And then she began to feel how truly far away the distant stars must be.

She was in awe of the universe for the first time in her life, astounded by how small and unimportant she was. How could she worry so much about something as insignificant as her own little role in the world? She wanted to burst into tears at the thought of everything she didn't know, everything she hadn't been taught. She hurried into the captain's quarters before she embarrassed herself further by crying in front of a healthy chunk of the Black Armada.

Once she was safely behind her curtains, Bryony rubbed her eyes with her sleeves and placed the three innocuous books in the corner of her bunk. Her secret research, though, she stuffed into the bottom of her duffle bag and covered with everything she had yet to unpack, including her clean underwear, certain her roommate wouldn't dare go digging that far if he went digging at all.

Then she sat down to read. Once she had a rudimentary grasp of medicine, she promised herself, she would find a book on the stars. And that was the moment it began to dawn on her that she didn't really want to find the godhunter at all. She didn't want to be a god anymore. She wanted to stay aboard *Dragonfly*, glut herself on knowledge, and work as an illicit librarian for the rest of her natural life.

Bryony slept through most of the next day. She would wake and read, collect her headache like raindrops in a jar, and then sleep until the pain ebbed again. She knew better than to read while in motion, but she couldn't help it. And whenever Michael was asleep or out of the cabin, she pulled out the book on human growth abnormalities and read as much as she could in his absence.

Gigantism was a rare condition, it turned out, but not unheard of. And it was treatable. In the old days, they might have performed surgery on Michael, which could have stopped his growth, but there were no real surgeons anymore. They had all met a terrible end in the massacre, and no one wanted to take up the practice after that. Still, a treatable condition would respond to the healing sword. Bryony considered healing Michael, but how would she do it without blowing her cover? She couldn't fake a surgery, could she? And, somehow, healing him without his knowledge or consent seemed wrong.

She resolved to wait. Once she completed her task and was safe, she would tell him everything and offer to heal him. His life was not in immediate danger. He seemed healthy enough. Perhaps, when the time came, he would even forgive her for all her lies.

Perhaps but not likely. She cringed. Inevitably, her charade would come to an end, and all the new people she'd met, all the friends she'd made in her short time aboard *Dragonfly*, would hate her. She would have killed one of their own. She would deserve their hatred and more besides. She groaned and forced herself up. Her own thoughts were just taking her in miserable, little circles. Time to get some air.

Outside, the sun was just beginning to set. Bryony leaned her elbows on the rail and gazed down at the water below. She heard wings on the wind before she felt Shakespeare land directly on the top of her head.

"Where have you been?" He pecked her gently. "What on earth have you been doing?"

She rested her chin on the backs of her hands. "Sleeping. Reading. Not throwing up. Thanks for asking."

"You're supposed to be searching for the death sword."

"I am actually. How do you think I'm going to find it if no one trusts me enough to tell me where it is? I've got to be a better medic."

"The word is *mimic*. You've got to be a better *mimic*." The crow hopped off Bryony's head and sat beside her on the rail. "It's all smoke and mirrors. You don't need to know the particulars. Don't overburden yourself with them." He inched closer and cocked one eye up at her face. "And search for the death sword. You don't need them to tell you where it is. Just pick up every object that could be a weapon and decide to keep it. If it's the sword, it'll transform for you."

She stood up straight. Of course. Why hadn't she thought of it? It was so much easier than she'd imagined. "I hate when you're smarter than me."

"That's an awful lot of hate to feel in one lifetime."

She was about to chide him for his impudence when the crow gave out a loud, uncharacteristic, "Caw caw caw!" He flapped his wings and pointed his beak at something behind her.

When she turned, she saw the commodore standing atop the forecastle with binoculars. Raeni's energy was palpable. "Land, ho!" she called, and the flurry of shouts and activity that followed left Bryony feeling even more excited for the harbor than she already was. She salivated at the mere thought of standing on solid ground.

Raeni descended the steps to the main deck and approached Bryony, who did her best not to stare at the machete hanging from the commodore's belt. Somehow, she would have to get her hands on that blade and claim it. But not now.

"Your first anchorage, medic." The commodore slapped Bryony on the shoulder. "How are you faring?"

"Excited to feel solid earth under my feet, Commodore," Bryony answered.

"Perish the thought, girl—you won't set foot off this ship for months." Raeni continued to grin as though disappointing her new recruit was the most amusing thing she'd done all week. She even seemed a bit disheartened when Bryony did not laugh along.

"But why?" Bryony sounded like a punished child, even to her own ears.

"No one steps off the ship until they've earned our trust. You've only just joined us. You've yet to prove yourself."

Bryony stared down at their feet, at her own sad sneakers beside Raeni's tall, leather boots. The woman always put her to shame. "How does one earn your trust, Commodore?"

"Just a matter of time and your good work. We can't allow strangers to join our ranks and then go parading around on land with all our secrets, can we?"

"And if I never earn your trust?"

The commodore's grin didn't even waver as she said, "We send you weighted to the depths, of course. But I've faith you'll be in our good graces in no time. You should've known when you joined up this was no summer job. When you're in, you're in for life." She gave Bryony another slap on the shoulder. "For life!" She laughed, and there was both infectious mirth and cruelty in that laugh. Then she said, "A so di ting set," and marched off to holler orders at the rest of her crew.

Shakespeare hopped onto Bryony's shoulder and nuzzled against her throat. She could feel him tremble as he hissed, "Find that sword."

Chapter Ten

Two thirds of *Dragonfly*'s crew went ashore that night. Bryony watched as they lowered their boats—using tiny cranes called davits, she learned—into the water and tried not to think about Raeni's not-so-subtle threat. Shakespeare was right. Bryony needed to keep her eyes on the prize. Getting distracted could cost her life.

She offered to help Rose in the galley "to pass the time," she said. She did as much of the cleaning and prep as she dared, careful to handle as many knives as she could. She held each one in her hand, let the weight of it balance on her fingers, and thought about keeping it for herself. Nothing transformed.

They chatted about the harbor. Rose had gone ashore here before. It was an old logging town with a modest community of self-sufficient folk. A small faction among them traded with the armada and often distributed the books they got further inland.

Once again, Bryony found herself growing fond and mentally kicking herself for it. But how was she supposed to help it? The entire Black Armada was magnificent, impressive. Even the stories Rose told about her younger sister, Daisy—how hard she'd fought to become a captain and how proud Rose was the day her sister finally won the position—made Bryony fond of a woman she had yet to meet.

When they were finished, Rose wiped her hands on her apron. "You know, kid, if you ever want a second job, I wouldn't turn you down as an assistant. You're a hard worker and pleasant company. Everyone's got more than one job aboard, so give it a thought, will you?"

"I will." Bryony smiled, pleased to have been asked. She would love to work alongside Rose. Cleaning, cooking, gossiping about the entire armada. The woman loved to talk, and Bryony loved to listen. It would be a perfect match. And there was no way Rose was the godhunter. Bryony decided this as she left the galley and climbed the companionway to the main deck. She couldn't even imagine the elder cook battling gods and angels in her spare time.

Outside, Dara leaned on the rail and stared at the faint outline of the town with its twinkling, orange lights and unnatural quiet.

"How long do they usually stay ashore?" Bryony asked.

"Until the wee hours. Sometimes longer," Dara answered. "If I were you, I'd get some sleep."

"It seems like all I've been doing lately is sleeping."

"That's just seasickness. Makes you tired. You'll get past it."

Bryony sighed. "One more day. That's what Andrew said. I just have to bear it one more day."

"He's not a liar, Andrew."

Waves lapped at the side of *Dragonfly*'s hull in a steady rhythm. It was good to just be with someone rather than feeling the need to fill the quiet with trivial chatter. Standing alongside Dara, listening to the sea, Bryony felt a kind of peace. But Raeni's threat kept niggling at her. Did anyone ever leave the Black Armada alive?

"Which boat does your father captain?" Bryony asked.

Dara pointed to a beautiful boat with two wooden masts. "That sixty-foot schooner there."

"Michael told me you'll take over as captain when your father retires."

Dara scoffed at that. "*Retire.* Interesting choice of words." Bryony just stared at her, allowing all her questions to hover unspoken in the moment. Dara answered them anyway. "When he's too old to captain, he'll be demoted. He'll do some menial task, and someone else will be appointed captain. I hear his replacement will likely be me. Then it'll be my job to determine when he's too old to be of any use. When that happens, he'll be cast out."

"How? Will they just leave him ashore one day? Who will take care of him after that?"

Silence punctuated Bryony's question along with a withering look from Dara that told her she'd grossly misunderstood. "*Cast out*," Dara said, "means cast out literally. They will throw his body overboard."

Bryony failed to hide her horror. Before she could stop herself, the words, "But that's barbaric!" escaped her lips. She clapped her hand over her mouth, but she needn't have bothered. If the smile on Dara's face was any indication, Bryony had said exactly what she wanted to hear.

"No one ever said the Black Armada was a compassionate enterprise," Dara conceded. Then her expression darkened. "But I'll be damned if I let anyone else put my father down. When the time comes, I've a bullet saved for him. He knows it, and I know it. No one else knows it." She turned to look hard into Bryony's eyes. "Do you understand?"

Bryony nodded, mute with renewed horror.

Dara went on. "My father and no one else will decide the day of his death. His daughter and no one else will be his executioner. Let this be my little test of your trustworthiness. If you tell a soul about my plan or my weapon, I won't hesitate to use it on you." She tapped a finger against the middle of Bryony's forehead.

Bryony shivered at her touch. "I understand." She crossed her arms and held her own elbows like she was afraid to lose them. "I think I'll try to get some sleep after all."

"You do that. And enjoy the stillness while you can. Our next stretch at sea is a long one."

Bryony told herself she should be grateful as she tossed and turned in her bunk. Raeni and Dara had both demonstrated why the Black Armada was dangerous, how brutal and ruthless it was at its core. They showed her the true face of the fleet, not the kind, friendly mask Rose and Michael had shown her. She needed to remember the sharp side of the blade too. It was becoming increasingly clear that the godhunter wasn't the only member of the Black Armada who would attack her if they knew what she really was.

But Bryony didn't want to believe it. If it was true, then she really would have to kill someone. She couldn't imagine killing anyone. She hadn't even been able to mercy-kill a rat. Her heart was just not in this plan, but the more time she spent aboard *Dragonfly*, the more she understood there would be no other way out. She would have to strike. She would have to kill.

Alone in the dark, Bryony finally allowed herself to cry. She was frustrated and alone. She missed her congregation. She missed the warmth and love that had surrounded her for years. The Black Armada was not her home, no kind of family, and far from a friend. And she was only just beginning to realize that life as she knew it would never go back to the way it was. Even if she accomplished her objective, something would be dead inside her. Something would be lost forever.

She slept fitfully and woke to a commotion outside. In the dark, she rose and made her way toward the door. Michael lay stretched out on his bunk, fast asleep. He must have snuck in sometime in the night. Bryony was both grateful that he hadn't woken her and mortified that he might have heard her sniffling. If he had, he hadn't let on, which was a kindness in itself. Nothing seemed to stir him now. The draw and release of his breath was a slow, steady rhythm, and Bryony was tempted to keep listening to it. But curiosity overcame her, and she snuck out, hoping to be as quiet as he had been.

The entire crew was gathered on the forecastle, lanterns high over their heads, arguing over something. The anchor. It was fouled, apparently, which meant they could not haul it up. One of them, a man she hadn't yet been introduced to, finally noticed Bryony watching.

"Tinctures!" It wasn't Andrew, but it seemed his nickname for her had spread. "Go get your bunkmate, will you?"

"He's asleep." Bryony shrugged.

"Are you kidding? Wake him up! We need him."

Damn. Bryony's stomach turned, and she groaned. The thought of waking the giant she'd been sharing a cabin with for the last three days gave her the kind of anxiety she usually only experienced right before entering the healing tent. She cursed her own curiosity as she made her way back to the captain's quarters.

Once inside, she approached Michael and stared down at him. He slept so peacefully—no fitful breathing, no tossing and turning the way she did. She hoped he would just open his eyes suddenly, look up at her and ask what she needed, but he didn't. She took a deep breath and laid a hand on his shoulder. He was warm, quite warm, and the sheer size of his shoulder overwhelmed her for a moment. She rested her hand there, hoping again that was all it would take. No such luck. She shook him gently. Nothing. She shook him again.

"Michael," she whispered. Then a little louder. "Michael, please wake up." She was almost pleading with him now. She shook him one more time, far more vigorously than she was comfortable with, and he stirred. Cool moonlight streamed in through the row of windows behind him and lit his face just enough that she could see his eyes fly open. His body jolted in shock.

She leapt back. "I'm sorry, I'm so sorry."

He sat up. "Bryony?"

"Yes. I didn't mean to startle you." She couldn't stop wringing her hands. "I really didn't want to wake you, but they told me they needed you. The anchor is . . . It's stuck."

And there in the dark, she was once again graced with the outline of his smile. "Please don't apologize. I'm glad they sent you. Usually, they just hammer the door with an oar." He stood and touched her shoulder.

Perhaps it was her imagination, but she got the distinct impression he did so only to quell her discomfort at having had to touch him the same way.

He left her there. She took a moment to breathe before following him out. She had felt the color rush to her cheeks, and she wasn't in a hurry to display her embarrassment to the rest of the crew. Michael still disarmed her, no matter how thoroughly she'd been armed by the threats she received the previous night. He seemed to genuinely like her. And the way he appreciated all the little nothings she did—as though her ordinary courtesies were rare generosities—made her want to treat him to true generosity, but she couldn't think of how. Anyway, if Shakespeare knew she was letting herself get swept up in a friendship with the enemy, he would flatten his feathers and peck her. She resolved to be stronger.

But when she made her way to the forecastle and saw Michael standing shirtless with a light strapped to his head, she lost all her resolve to stop caring about him. "What is he doing?" she asked, but it wasn't a question really. She sounded more like a schoolteacher, demanding an answer of bullies caught in the act.

Raeni responded from somewhere behind Bryony. "He's going to dive down and free our anchor."

It was all Bryony could do to keep her voice from going up an octave now that she knew this plan had been sanctioned by the commodore. "But it's the middle of the night."

"He has a light," Raeni said. "We're in less than fifty feet, give or take—"

"*Give or take?*"

"He can do it, girl. He's done it many times before."

Andrew spoke next. "It's this or get a new anchor."

Bryony fumed. "So get a new anchor." She was running too fast down this hill and finding it difficult to skid to a stop. "You can't send him down there without a lifeline or any support. What if he loses consciousness? Who's going down after him? Who could pull him out?"

Someone laughed, and it only made her angrier. "People drown all the time, even when they're doing stunts they've done a hundred times before." She didn't know this was true for sure, but it sounded true enough. "I can't help a drowned man."

Bryony heard someone mutter the word *stunt* derisively, and she clenched her own teeth to stop herself from screaming at them.

Finally, the commodore stepped in. "All right, children, the medic has a point. Let's get a line 'round his waist, so we can haul him out if something goes wrong. After three minutes, we'll start heaving." She turned to Bryony. "Does that sound satisfactory, medic?"

Michael lifted his arms and allowed Andrew to secure a line around him before he finally spoke. "Five minutes will be fine." He turned back a moment and smiled a small smile that seemed so utterly unlike him, Bryony almost cried. Then he dove into the inky water. The light on his headlamp was visible only a few seconds before it, too, faded into the depths.

CHAPTER ELEVEN

When Bryony was seven, her mother gave birth to her baby brother. The labor was hard and took far too long. Every hour, Bryony's panic grew. She feared for her mother's life, knowing full well, even at seven, that childbirth was a dangerous business. She continually asked her father whether it was over, and why wasn't it over, and when was it going to be over, and then, finally, whether her mother was still alive.

That same feeling, that impotent panic, surged in her now. Every minute Michael was underwater felt like an hour. She leaned over the bulwarks and gripped the rail so hard she was surprised it didn't crumble in her hands. She tried to hold her breath along with him and found herself gasping for air again and again. And finally, to her utter shame, she couldn't help repeatedly asking the commodore how long it had been, thinking maybe Raeni had forgotten to check her watch.

When Raeni answered, "Three minutes, fifty-eight seconds," Bryony begged them to pull him up.

"He said five, we give him five." Raeni continued staring at her pocket watch, and Bryony returned to her post over the water. She thought about jumping in herself. She was itching to do *something*. It killed her to just stand there, waiting. But she also knew she could never pull the giant up, not with all her strength and then some. She didn't even think she could dive down as far as he had gone to retrieve him.

Just as Bryony began to seriously consider darting in to steal the commodore's machete and holding her hostage until the crew hauled Michael back up, a dark head breached the waves. Michael gave a weak thumbs up, and the crew cheered. They dropped a ladder for him and then immediately went to work hauling the anchor and setting the sails.

Only Raeni stayed behind to ensure Michael made it up the ladder safely. As soon as he swung a leg over the bulwarks, she said, "Well done," and turned to join the rest of the crew.

Michael was left alone, dripping and shivering. He sat against the rail and breathed heavily.

Bryony gritted her teeth and ran to retrieve his shirt, which had been left in a heap on the forecastle. Now she understood why he over-appreciated the little courtesies she performed. No one else even thanked him, not even when he risked his own safety to spare them from having to buy a new anchor. He had gone down with no gear, no breathing apparatus, no partner—just a line knotted around his waist.

There was something cruel about the way they treated him, though they never abused him. They just ignored him until they needed him. Bryony watched him struggle with the knot, his fingers still trembling. A little river of blood flowed down his arm and formed a watercolor delta on the back of his hand.

Enough. She didn't care if Shakespeare chided her for favoritism. She'd counter the bird's concerns with his obvious preference for *Ladybird* over the other ships. *No doubt, that's where he is now, collecting crumbs and begging for scraps.*

"Can I try?" she asked. Michael dropped his arms, exhausted, as Bryony unraveled the knot at his waist. He was powerfully built, with broad shoulders and a deep chest. That was likely why they had sent him down. He was probably the only crew member strong enough to lift the anchor on his own.

She let the loosened line fall around his bare feet and handed him his shirt. "I wish I could give you my coat," she said, recalling the kindness he had shown her that first morning. He took his shirt back but didn't put it on. "You've cut yourself. I can patch it."

He held out his arm and examined the gash. "I see." His voice was weak and rasping. Bryony hardly recognized it. "Cold water makes it bleed more. It's not as bad as it looks."

"Nonsense. What else am I here for? Come on." She led him back to their quarters and sat him down on his bunk. "Stay right there."

Bryony hurried to the ship's hospital and ransacked the place looking for gauze and tape. She found gauze but no tape. She would have to make do with a wrap. In her search, she ran across quite a few sharp objects she would need to hold and test later, though she doubted any godhunter would just keep a death sword lying around unsupervised. Still, no stone unturned. She threw the gauze and wrap into a clean bowl and thanked herself for being smart enough to read the first aid book early on.

When she returned to the captain's quarters, Bryony saw that Michael had recovered enough to light the lamps. She made him sit again and looked at the gash on his forearm. He was right. It wasn't as bad as it looked. She filled the bowl with fresh water from their private sink and gathered soap and a washcloth from her own things.

"The best way to prevent infection is to keep the wound clean." She recited the first aid book like a proper student as she sat beside him and began to work. She thought about applying one of her tinctures, but she didn't want to be false. Right now, she wanted to practice real medicine, even if it was just a wash and a bandage.

At last, she tied the wrap around his forearm and sat back to examine her good work. "That'll do." She nodded. "Although I wish I'd had tape." She handed him a stack of sterile gauze. "Change the dressing every day, and do *not* go swimming until it's healed." She wanted to add, *or ever again*, but resisted.

"Thank you." He smiled.

She dismissed his gratitude with a wave of her hand. "It's my job. You don't have to thank me for doing my job."

Then it occurred to her. Perhaps that was why the crew hadn't thanked him. He was just doing his job. She wanted to believe they hadn't been so callous, but the more she recalled their behavior, the more she felt there was no real explanation. At the very least, they should have included him in their celebratory whoops and high fives. But they'd just left him there, shivering. Only Raeni had thanked him in her way, and even that was terse.

Michael looked better. His color had improved anyway. Naturally, he didn't have much blush to his cheeks, but his lips had been almost as white as the rest of his skin when he'd emerged from the sea. Now they were looking closer to their usual shade.

Bryony headed back to the hospital to sterilize the bowl she'd used and put things away. On her way, Raeni glided past.

"Medic," the commodore said. Bryony stopped and turned to face her. "You seem to have taken quite a liking to our navigator."

Bryony shrugged. "I do share a room with him, and he's been kind to me so far."

"Good. Then you won't mind shadowing him for the rest of the day." The commodore grinned, and Bryony couldn't tell whether it was cruel or delighted. Or both.

"No problem." It was almost a question the way Bryony said it. She was confused. Raeni seemed to expect her to beg for mercy, as though shadowing Michael were an obvious penalty, though Bryony didn't think it would be unpleasant at all.

Raeni planted her hands on her hips and narrowed her eyes, apparently dissatisfied with Bryony's reaction. "You'll keep watch with him tonight as well."

Is that supposed to make it worse? Bryony wanted to argue, but she already seemed to be in trouble for something, so she bit her tongue. "Yes, Commodore."

Raeni gave one nod of acknowledgement and continued on her way.

Bryony took her frustration out on the ship's hospital. She sanitized the bowl aggressively and put it away with a slam of the locker door. Then she proceeded to pick up every sharp object she could find and mutter, "This is mine now." Scissors, scalpels, tweezers. It didn't matter. All of it was hers. But nothing transformed, and she was forced to leave the hospital with no new baubles to speak of.

When Bryony finally returned to the captain's quarters, she found Michael sitting on his heels at the table, studying charts. She threw herself onto her bunk and screamed into her pillow.

Michael looked up from his work, his brow creased in bewilderment. "Are you all right?"

"Fine, fine." She sat up and held her pillow in her lap. "I just met our commodore on the way to the hospital. She says I'm to shadow you today and tonight."

He cocked his head. "But why? Surely she doesn't intend you to navigate this early on."

"That's just the thing, *why*!" Bryony stood and began to pace, dragging her much abused pillow after her. "Because she said it like it was . . . like it was some kind of punishment or something, I don't know. And the way the crew treated you when you came out of the water, like all they cared about was their precious anchor, like *you* were expendable. And the way they look past you every day like you're not even there. The way they looked at me when I asked where you were at dinner. I mean what the hell is going on? They seemed like nice people at first. Am I just in the middle of some ship-wide prank I'm not in on? Is that what this is? Why am I rooming with you if they didn't think I was going to like you? Is this supposed to be a Black Armada hazing, me getting 'stuck' with you?" She paused her pacing to put air quotes around the word *stuck*. "Is it? Because it's stupid, Michael! You're frankly the best roommate anyone could ask for. You're friendly and considerate. You've been far more welcoming than anyone else on this ship, and you're . . . you're . . ."

She stopped, not because she'd finished and not because she real-ized how unhinged she sounded, but because, as her tirade went on, Michael's expression began to change. He started off confused, and then he looked sad, wounded even. Then he smiled, and his smile grew broad as she fumed, and she suddenly found she couldn't think of any more words in the English language. She slumped back down in her bunk, mute but still hot with rage.

"It's not a hazing." Michael's voice was soft and reassuring. "And it's not a joke. You're rooming with me because no one else wanted to, all the bunks in the forecastle were occupied, and the commodore didn't want to eliminate any of her crew." He shrugged. "She's got a soft heart at her core. She doesn't like executions. And I imagine you're being punished mostly with my watch tonight, which happens to be midnight to four in the morning."

Bryony took a deep breath and considered it. "But why am I being punished at all? What did I do wrong?"

"You questioned the commodore. She hasn't always been the com-modore, and she's still establishing her authority. Maybe she didn't like the new medic taking her on in front of her crew. Now she has to show some teeth and make an example of you."

That made sense. Bryony never was one to bow to authority. She would have to remember to hold her tongue in the future, at least until she found the godhunter. Still she couldn't help muttering, "But that doesn't explain the way they treat you."

Michael closed his eyes for a moment and allowed silence to fill the cabin. He breathed slowly, and Bryony was sure she heard him swallow a knot in his throat. So it did hurt him, this isolation. She felt ashamed for having brought it up at all. "They don't mean to be cruel," he said at last. "They're just uncomfortable around me because I'm different."

Bryony refused to accept that. "You're not, though. You're just . . . tall."

He chuckled and scooted back from the table until he could rest against the base of his bunk. "But *you* are," he said. "Different I mean."

She looked up.

"I've never met anyone like you."

She blushed and scoffed to hide it. "Says the giant who reads romance novels and freedives like a maniac."

His dimple made another appearance, and Bryony looked down at her lap to keep herself from turning any redder. "Well," he said, "if you're stuck shadowing me all day, we should make the most of it. Would you like to learn to use a sextant?"

Shadowing Michael was hardly the chore the commodore made it out to be. He was pleased with the company, eager to share stories of trading ports, man-overboard drills gone awry, and whales breaching far too close for comfort.

At noon, he taught Bryony to use the sextant, how she would need to look through the little spyglass and line the mirrored horizons up. He showed her how to adjust the dials until the sun in the spyglass appeared to sink and kiss the sea. She kept checking to see that the real sun was still high in the sky, that she hadn't somehow pulled the closest star down with magic.

After Michael took down the time and measurements Bryony had acquired, he thanked her for her help, as though he ever really needed it. Somehow, though, she got the impression he meant every word. He was grateful for her help, not because it made the task easier, but because it made the task more pleasant.

Back in the captain's quarters, Michael showed her how he made his adjustments. He wrote each calculation in detail, for her sake, and plotted their position on a chart. Bryony paid close attention, though she was sure she would not remember much of it.

Then they both sat down to read—he a romance and she a textbook on infectious diseases—before catching some sleep.

Later that night, Bryony carried both their dinners back to the cabin, which was a boon to Rose, who was once again happy to be relieved of the chore. As they ate, a loud caw sounded outside their door. Then another and another.

"What on earth?" Michael said.

"That's just my crow." Bryony suddenly realized she hadn't told Michael about the bird at all. "He's a pet. Do you mind if I let him in?"

"Please do." Michael put down his plate and leaned in. "I've never met a crow before."

"You haven't?"

"Well, I've never been formally introduced."

Bryony laughed and opened the door. Shakespeare hopped in like he already owned the room. He was quick to find the chart table and eyeball the maps. Then he dropped the intelligent-crow act and went straight for Michael's plate.

Bryony shouted, "Shakespeare, no! That's not yours."

"It's all right. I don't mind sharing." Michael offered his plate to Shakespeare, no doubt immediately endearing himself to the bird.

Shakespeare pulled an entire slice of ham and half a potato onto the floor and began making a complete mess of himself as he tore into them. Before he had quite finished what he'd stolen, he went back begging for more, and Michael handed him a crust of bread.

"He'll take all of it if you let him," Bryony warned. "And what he can't eat, he'll stash somewhere for later."

Shakespeare gave her a quick, one-eyed scowl.

"I don't mind," Michael said. "He's cute. Smart too. I like him." Then he turned to the crow. "You can have as much as you want, Shakespeare. I've had plenty." He handed Shakespeare a green bean.

"You'll mind when you find rotten food stuffed under your mattress and between your floorboards." She laughed.

After Bryony put a stop to Shakespeare's good fortune, the crow hopped back to the door in a huff and pecked it several times in quick succession. Bryony let him hop onto her arm and showed him out.

Once they were outside, Shakespeare fluffed his feathers at her. "Don't get attached," he said in a low, husky voice. "Remember why you're here."

"I'm not getting attached," Bryony lied. "I'm using subterfuge like you said I should. And I haven't forgotten why I'm here." She tilted her head close to the bird. "I have a job for you in fact. The deckhand Dara—she has a gun hidden somewhere. I need you to find it and tell me where it is. I can't get into the forecastle without looking suspicious, but you can."

Shakespeare cocked his head. "I can?"

"Just be adorable and charming. You know, beg for treats, search the bunks. Act like you're looking for crumbs. Just make yourself a regular presence in their quarters. Let me know when you find it so I can test it."

"Yes, Mistress."

Bryony noted his sarcasm but gave him a scratch on the head anyway.

"I'll find you the gun and its ammunition," he said. "Test the weapon and every bullet with it. It'll be a flesh-piercing component that's the sword, don't forget."

"I won't." She lifted her arm and let him fly up to the highest yard, so he could scan the boats for which one he wanted to visit that night. Then she muttered, "If only I could," before making her way back to her quarters.

Chapter Twelve

At midnight, Bryony shadowed Michael on her first official watch. He brought two cups of coffee. He recalled that she took hers with sugar only, and he had only cream.

"Did you go below for these?" she asked, wide-eyed at the idea of him bent at the waist, making his way to the galley.

He laughed and nearly choked on his drink. "Partway. I did get help."

"That's good." She blew on the surface of her coffee and took a tentative sip. "I don't imagine you enjoy going below much. How high are the ceilings down there? Six feet?"

"It's not so bad for a short time."

That wasn't the impression Bryony got at all. She thought it would be extraordinarily uncomfortable for him, not only because of the ceiling height and the narrow companionways, but because he would be forced to move in close proximity with people who avoided him on a regular basis. She clutched her cup tight. It hadn't been easy—she knew that much. "Well, next time it's my turn. Deal?"

He grinned and propped himself against the rail.

They were on the forecastle, and they were the only ones there. Two more people kept watch on the quarterdeck, taking turns at the helm, and someone on the main deck walked back and forth with a covered lantern. Both Bryony and Michael had a lantern too, as did the people on the quarterdeck. Every fifteen minutes, they lifted their lanterns high to let their distant comrades know where they were. All the ships did this simultaneously, so every fifteen minutes, the entire Black Armada looked like a forest of synchronous fireflies. The rest of the time, they were all under cover of darkness. This was an unusual and risky way to sail, Bryony had learned, but the armada made a science of it, and it worked like a perfectly choreographed dance.

"Thirty seconds," Michael said, and Bryony set down her coffee and picked up her lantern. She took it to the port side of the ship and waited until she saw his go up. Then she followed suit. Seeing all the ships around them lift their lanterns high gave her a warm feeling. So much loneliness was dispelled with just a little light. The darkness made it feel like they were the only ship on the ocean, but they weren't. Friends were all around, sailing in that same darkness, ready to come to their aid should they need it.

Loneliness is an illusion, Bryony told herself, and she tried to believe it was true. Perhaps, in her own isolated world, she would soon see a dance of lights around her—evidence of people walking the same path with her, asking the same questions, feeling the same uncertainty. She would give almost anything for that little moment of proof that she wasn't remotely as alone as she thought she was. Even if it was just one light—one floating lantern in the distance—she would never ask for another.

She returned to Michael's side, feeling more hopeful than she had in years.

"Where's your crow, by the way?" he asked.

"Oh, probably he's gone to whichever ship he's taken to sleeping on. He's made his rounds the last few days. I call him a pet, but that's not entirely true. He's a wild crow, and we became friends I guess. Now he follows me around, and I feed him." She hesitated but decided to be honest. "He's basically family, which probably sounds weird."

Michael smiled and let his cup rest on the rail. "Not at all. I would be proud to be adopted by a crow. They know who is kind and who is cruel. You must be very kind to have gained his trust like you did."

"Well, he seemed to like you too."

Bryony took in Michael's attention the way she used to take in her followers' worship. It was the smoke of incense, the breath of a bonfire, the familiar sound of many voices brought together in song. Yes, she still had the worship from her congregation—distant worship that kept her warm and alert—but the hit of it was too soft, the high too faint. It was just enough, and now she realized she was relying on something else to feel truly alive. Someone else.

She smiled and tried to act casual. "So we're on watch. What are we watching for exactly?"

Michael shrugged. "Other ships, for the most part. Any strange lights on the horizon, weather, and flares, of course."

"Flares?"

"We use them to communicate." He took a sip of coffee and stared out to sea. "Green is for other ships, yellow is for storms, red is an SOS, and white . . . See if you can guess."

Bryony blew her bangs out of her eyes and thought. What else would the armada be on the lookout for? What could come for them over the sea and pose a threat? "Angels?"

"You got it."

Here was an opening. She would ask a question that led to a mention of the godhunter. Then she would ask who it was, and Michael, being Michael, would tell her. "What do we do if we see a white flare?"

"We haven't seen a white flare in over twenty years, so you don't have to worry about that. Or were you hoping to get your hands on an angel?" He chuckled, but she frowned.

"I'm not sure I'd have much hope of killing one, but I wouldn't mind trying. I'd risk my life in a heartbeat if I thought I stood a chance."

Michael glanced down at her, his expression unusually solemn. "Don't think like that, Bryony. Life is so valuable, and you only have the one. Don't throw it away on an angel. Cling to life. Change the world instead." He sipped his coffee and turned back to the sea.

Change the world instead.

What more could she say to him? How could she push the subject now? She was short of breath, overcome with doubt. Was she doing the right thing, hunting a hunter just to save herself? Could there be another way? She didn't want to throw her life away—not really—but she didn't want to throw away anyone else's either. Could she change the world instead? Was it possible for a small-town healing god to effect that kind of revolution? She wasn't special to anyone other than her little congregation. If she hadn't found the angel's sword, who would she even be? Just Bryony. Just some bizarre woman who liked black dresses and graveyards and hung around with birds.

She slid down with her back to the bulwarks, drew her knees to her chest, and clutched her cup tightly. Her coffee was gone, but she didn't want to let go of the mug yet. It had been a warm and mundane token in her otherwise outlandish life.

A steady wind blew her hair over her eyes and blocked the stars from view. Bryony squinted through the strands, imagining herself a fish caught in a net. She was trapped in this life, this scheme. As far as she knew, she had two choices—accept her inevitable assassination or kill the godhunter—but Michael had presented a third, impossible option that Bryony was desperate to believe in.

Change the world instead.

Despite the coffee sitting warm in her belly, Bryony felt drowsy. The slow, pitching motion of the ship sent her into an almost hypnotic trance, and she was grateful for it. She didn't want to think anymore. Life had become too constricted, her path too narrow. She wanted to believe in choice.

She let her gaze wander down the length of the ship and saw three lanterns lift into the air. Michael hadn't given her a warning. He probably thought she'd drifted off and didn't want to wake her. She felt simultaneous gratitude and shame. She had failed her first watch.

Fine. Whatever. She hadn't joined the Black Armada to learn to sail. She'd joined to find and kill a monster.

She let her head sink onto her chest and felt the weight of every decision she'd made until now. They seemed to be universally bad. But she'd done her best, hadn't she? She'd done her best with the information she had at the time.

The sea finally lulled her into dreams of sharp objects—jewelry, scissors, syringes, and knives—and her reluctance to touch them. They piled up around her, and no matter how she tried to avoid them, they kept sliding down that pile, its base creeping ever closer to her feet. And the brick wall behind her wouldn't give an inch. It was only a matter of time.

She woke to a touch. A heavy hand squeezed her shoulder and a low, now familiar voice said, "Wake up, Bryony. You're going to want to see this."

She stirred. The film of salt on her skin seemed thicker than usual, like a sugar glaze. The wind was cool and gentle. She breathed deep and stretched her arms and legs before wearily pushing herself to her feet. Nothing out of the ordinary caught her eye. "What is it?" she said, unable to quite mask the irritation she felt at being woken, even though she knew she wasn't supposed to be sleeping in the first place.

Michael just pointed down over the side. Bryony turned and followed his gesture to the place where *Dragonfly*'s hull met the sea.

At first, she thought she was seeing things. Perhaps she hadn't awoken completely, and the dreams still clinging to her consciousness made her see this . . . this light. It was a soft green color, like mint candy or the dusty peacock feathers she used to see on some of her mother's costumes. It seemed artificial, and the way it glowed was even more unbelievable. Everywhere *Dragonfly* carved out its path, the sea glowed. Each time the ship was lifted by a wave and crashed into the next one, there were swirls and splatters of the fluid, green light. It sprang to life suddenly and gradually faded.

Bryony's heart raced. No, this wasn't the ghost of a dream. This was real. The sea glowed all around them, and *Dragonfly* brought it to life.

Michael pointed aft, and Bryony looked to see their lighted path, swirling and fading behind them. *Dragonfly* left little lingering trace, but where it was now and where it had just been was alive with fairy lights.

"What is it?" Bryony asked, breathless.

"Bioluminescence," Michael answered. "I thought you might like it."

She leaned so far over the bulwarks her toes lifted off the deck. "But how?"

Michael joined her, leaning on his hands. "It's usually algae or tiny sea creatures that give off light when they're disturbed."

"It's alive?" She couldn't believe it. She had never seen anything so magical. This was better than a transforming sword, more impressive than a talking crow. "Like fireflies."

He nodded. By the breadth of his smile, Bryony could see once more how he delighted in her wonder. She should have been embarrassed by her own naiveté, but she didn't care. She'd never imagined anything like this. She straightened up to catch her breath and leaned back over the bulwarks to see the light unveiled a second time. She stretched her body further over the rail and shifted her hands to better balance herself.

And then she froze.

She hadn't been paying attention. She hadn't been careful. Instead of the wooden rail she expected to feel under her right hand, there was warmth—there was flesh. She'd laid her hand over the top of Michael's. It was an accident, a stupid mistake. But she was high on the magic of her new discovery, and she did not readjust her position. She rationalized. If she quickly pulled her hand away, what would that communicate to him? That he disgusted her? That she couldn't stand the idea of touching him? No, she chose to act as though she'd meant to take his hand all along, and she curled her fingers around his.

It was only a friendly gesture, right? It was just a thank-you squeeze. It seemed like something people did anyway—people who weren't a god and her congregation. Michael was celibate, so if he felt this was more than a friendly gesture, he would surely pull his hand away, and she wouldn't be offended at all.

But he didn't.

And he didn't.

And he didn't.

He closed his thumb over her fingers and gently stroked her knuckles. His touch was as tender as she expected it to be. And she realized the fact that she even had an expectation meant she had already imagined it—his touch. As the seconds wore on, she grew dizzy, the whole world seemed to pulse with her heart, and her cheeks burned with a feverish exhilaration.

What was this? She hesitated to answer her own question, but when she allowed herself to be honest, she had to admit she seemed to have developed a bit of a crush. How ordinary. How human. How wonderful.

It was a safe crush. Nothing would come of it. Michael would not let it progress and neither would she. There was no need to alert Shakespeare at all. She would still continue her search for the godhunter—of course she would.

But the sea was glowing and living and singing its song, and Michael was still holding her hand. Out of the corner of her eye, she saw her own little fingers cradled between his thumb and the palm of his hand. It was a kind of intimacy she'd never known, nor had she expected to experience it in her lifetime. These days, gods didn't fall in love, date, or marry. They just took in worship, like energy from a battery, and put out the illusion of safety in an otherwise merciless universe.

Still Michael held her hand. She let her eye travel past his wrist, up his arm, over his broad shoulders. She let herself appreciate the way his black hair curled at the cut ends, the strength of his jaw, the crease at the corner of his mouth that deepened when he smiled. His cheeks were flushed, and she wondered whether it was the chill or if he was feeling the same way she was. His eyelashes were dark and long. She hadn't noticed them before now.

He glanced down at her, and she quickly looked away. She cleared her throat. "So . . . what did you say this was called?"

He took a moment too long to answer. She heard him swallow and take a breath first. "Bioluminescence."

"Oh, *bio* means life." She remembered it from one of the textbooks she had taken.

He nodded and turned his charcoal eyes back to the sea. "And *lumin* is light."

Still he held her hand. She had no idea what she was supposed to say, whether she was supposed to say anything at all. "That's a good name for a boat, I think."

"It is."

She held perfectly still, careful not to move a single muscle in her hand, as though this moment was a wild rabbit, ready to dart away at the slightest provocation. The last thing she wanted to do was remind him he was holding her hand. The last thing she wanted him to do was let go.

Then, in a hushed, hoarse voice, Michael said, "Thirty seconds." And when he slipped his hand out from under hers, something huge, bright, and wonderful inside her deflated.

She took her lantern and held it high, and she did not touch his hand again that night. She did not fall asleep again either. She watched the bioluminescence crest around the hull and swirl in the dark behind them. She lifted her lantern every fifteen minutes along with the rest of the crew on watch. And she tried to make small talk with Michael, whose uncharacteristic reticence unnerved her more than she cared to admit.

Chapter Thirteen

B ryony ate her breakfast in the mess hall that morning. The timid, withdrawn presence that Michael had become was something she couldn't bear to see. It was her fault—she knew that at least. She had assumed his celibacy was due to a simple lack of desire, not a religious or moral conviction. He was the navigator of the Black Armada, for crying out loud. Wasn't that the antithesis of religiosity? But what if it wasn't? What if he had a faith that demanded celibacy, one she was unfamiliar with? Had she violated that faith somehow? Had she pressured him, tempted him, made him uneasy and uncomfortable?

She was ashamed of her own thoughtlessness, and seeing Michael move around their cabin, silent as a penitent monk, delivered that shame straight to her heart. She hated the feeling, so she avoided it. There was no way to undo what she had done, but she couldn't forgive herself either.

Of course she would ruin the only good thing to come out of her crisis. Of course she would break the only man aboard *Dragonfly* who'd befriended her. And why? What for? Simple curiosity. She just wanted to know what it was like to feel that rush of happiness, that sensation of endless possibility she knew would never really be hers. She had become a god, and a god was worshiped. A god was adored. A god wasn't kissed and caressed in the dark. A god could never belong to one person that way. Bryony belonged to her entire congregation, and none of them could love her intimately, so that all of them could love her devotedly.

After breakfast, she had an opportunity to sleep, but she didn't take it. She just stood on the main deck and stared at the door to the captain's quarters like it was on fire. She couldn't go in—not with him there, not while he read his romances which she knew she had also somehow ruined for him. He would leaf through his novels and feel ashamed that he'd allowed himself a little flirtation outside them. They would remind him of his failure. He would put his book down without saving his place and stare out his windows in dispirited silence.

"Medic!" The commodore's voice cut into Bryony's miserable fantasy. "Still seasick?"

Bryony shook her head.

"Good. Time to train. First thing, you climb up the foremast on the ratlines."

"The what now?"

Raeni gestured with a flourish to the net-like ladders that stretched from the hull to the top of the foremast.

"How . . ." Bryony caught her breath. "How high?"

"The whole length of it." She let that sink in a moment before shouting across the main deck. "Andrew! Get her in a harness! Go up with her! I don't trust the girl to stay conscious!" She turned back to Bryony, grinning like she had when she'd ordered her to shadow Michael. "Five times up and down every day." Then she slapped Bryony on the back and walked away.

The mast rose above Bryony like a towering evergreen. She let her eye follow the path of it until she saw the pinprick peak, and she had to remind herself to close her mouth. Andrew shuffled toward her with two harnesses in his hands.

"The commodore is trying to kill me," Bryony muttered.

Andrew chuckled. It was friendly, but she missed Michael's warm laugh. *You broke that too,* she thought. The longer she considered it, the more she decided she deserved this new, meaningless task. Maybe she would go up and down the mast ten times over, just to be sure she felt it the next day.

The California Viking held a harness while Bryony stepped into it. Then he brought the straps over her shoulders and clipped a carabiner to her. "You should know she doesn't push you if she doesn't like you," he said.

Bryony followed him to where the ratlines met the hull. "So how do I get on her bad side?"

It was meant as a joke, but Andrew shrugged and answered, "Harm her crew. She'll personally bisect anyone who threatens or abuses any one of us." Bryony shivered at the thought of the commodore's machete cutting through her torso, catching on her spine. Andrew grinned and pulled his fingers through his sandy-blond beard. "*One of us* also means you, you know."

In any other situation, that would have been something Bryony craved to hear. She'd always wanted to be part of a real family. And how much more like a family could you get than the crew of the Black Armada? It was everything she'd ever wished for, everything her congregation could not give her. And that made the fact that she had lied and cheated to get in even more ugly to her.

Andrew climbed onto the bulwarks, gripped the ratlines, and leaned back, stretching his arms. "Up we go," he said. "You first. I'll follow."

"Aren't you going to give me a lesson, some tips or something?"

"Tips, eh?" He counted them off on his fingers. "One, don't let go. Two, don't pass out. Three, do look down. A lot. It's beautiful up there."

Several deep breaths later, Bryony clung like the worst spider in the world to the widest part of the ratlines. Andrew leaned in and clipped her carabiner to the lines. "This is your lifeline," he said. "Move it as you go. Eventually, you'll only need it at the tricky bits."

Tricky bits? Bryony groaned. She recalled climbing the hanging ladder to board the ship on her first day, how utterly weak she'd felt. If only someone had warned her that she would one day be required to regularly climb what amounted to vertical netting on a rocking ship, she might have begun a routine of pull-ups ahead of time. Of course, that was probably the purpose of this exercise—to strengthen her arms and get her used to climbing.

She placed her feet on the lower boards, gripped the lines, and took a deep breath. *Focus.*

Her ascension was clumsy at first. Her feet couldn't find the lines, and she had to pause to see where they had gone wrong. From below, she could hear Andrew's impatient sighs. She chose not to acknowledge them. Served him right for rattling her nerves on her first day. She climbed a few feet at a time, linking her elbow through the lines whenever she had to move her carabiner.

Just as she began to think she was getting the hang of it, she came to the first platform. "Up and over!" Andrew shouted.

But how? The lines met the mast under the platform, and she couldn't even see over it.

"You can do it," Andrew said, though he sounded more per-turbed than encouraging. "Clip your carabiner to the lines above."

She took his advice. Then she dragged herself over the edge, her belly and thighs scraping against it as she did. Once on the platform, she crawled inward and clung to the mast. Andrew hauled himself up like it was nothing, and she hated him just a little for it.

"What'd you stop for?" he asked.

She glared at him. Strands of her hair had slipped out of her tie and tickled her face in the wind. It annoyed her more than she thought it should.

"Let's go," he urged.

The ratlines narrowed as she climbed, and where the highest sail hung from its yard, two short beams provided a tenuous spot for someone to stand. Bryony heaved herself over the beams, clung to the mast, and panted. She did not unclip her carabiner here, but she stood, holding the ratlines in one hand while her other arm wrapped around the mast.

"Take a load off." Andrew joined her and sat on the beams. He was so casual she half expected him to pull a sandwich out of his pocket and start eating.

She shook her head. "Don't we have to go back down?"

Andrew kicked his feet like a boy in the branch of a tree. "Nah. The commodore said you had to go up and down five times, yeah? But she didn't say how quickly you had to do it as long as it gets done today. So have a seat. Enjoy the view."

Bryony inched her way to sitting, hugging the mast all the while. Each swell that rocked the boat swung them in an exaggerated arc. It felt as though the ship itself was trying to shake her off. But as soon as she took in the expanse of the sea around her, Bryony noticed nothing else. It was a shade of blue she'd never seen in her life. It looked as though someone had dumped the entire world's supply of blue food coloring into the ocean. It was a liquid jewel that rippled in the wind like silk.

She caught her breath and muttered, "Wow."

"Pretty, isn't it?" Andrew said, his own gaze held by the same ocean.

"Yeah." She was almost speechless. Tiny whitecaps formed at the crests of the waves below. It was a playful sea that begged her to forget her worries and join the game. She felt good, proud even, to have made it this far.

After a long rest, Andrew said, "Let's get back down. We'll be up here again in no time."

"You're going again?"

He nodded. "Sure, I'll join you a few more times. I don't mind. It reminds me of my own training. Good memories."

Andrew joined Bryony up the mast two more times, and then she told him she was comfortable going alone. It was a partial truth. She was panting from the effort, and it only comforted her a little to see that he, too, had broken a sweat.

By her fifth climb, Bryony had to stop to rest every few feet, curling her elbows around the lines so she could relax her tired fingers. And when she finally stood on the highest beams for the last time, she took in the expanse again. It was magnificent. The wind cooled her face, and she tilted her head back to appreciate the sensation. *This is as close as I will ever get to flight*, she thought, and she momentarily envied Shakespeare.

She watched the world unseen for a while. The crew below moved about the decks without taking note of her. The sun was high in the sky, and she realized it was noon when she saw Michael's long form climb the stairway to the quarterdeck and kneel at the bulwarks. All her calm and pride melted away, and she wrapped both arms around the mast, more to hide than for fear of falling.

His movements were familiar to her. Now he looked through the sextant. Now he adjusted the dials. Now he checked the chronometer and wrote it all down in his notebook. He was methodical and precise. No one would suspect he struggled with any great moral failing. Maybe he didn't. Maybe it was all in Bryony's admittedly overactive imagination. What if he felt nothing for her and had simply held her hand so as not to embarrass or reject her? Perhaps he was only doing for her what she told herself she was doing for him.

When he stood, he turned his face up and shielded his eyes from the sun to see Bryony perched at the top of the foremast, staring down at him.

"Shit." She squirmed. There went her hiding place. Now it was more like a stage from which she could not exit, at least not quickly, not unless she threw herself off the mast and overboard. She briefly considered it.

Michael lifted his hand in greeting, and she waved back automatically. She felt foolish. As soon as he left the deck, she started back down the ratlines.

Bryony spent the rest of the day browsing through books in the cargo hold and nursing her aching arms. At dinner, she ate spaghetti with the crew and listened to them regale her with tales, half of which she was certain were embellished. Then they started talking about the raid and the commodore and the vigilantes, and Bryony knew they were telling the truth. She'd seen and smelled the evidence of it herself.

"You should have been there!" The man now speaking was the same one who had called Bryony "Tinctures" during the anchor incident, so she assumed he was friendly with Andrew. He was a large man in bone and belly with rosy cheeks, a curly head of hair, and a full beard. In the course of conversation, she learned that his name was Dylan and that he had come from Alaska. He seemed pleasant and lively. He also drank a lot of beer.

"We saw the green flare go up, and we sounded the alarm. Their ship plowed through our fleet like we were nothing. There's no way they could have known we had no cannons. They didn't care. They had a death wish. We found out later they were worshipers. They thought we'd killed their god—heard a rumor we had a godhunter in our midst." He paused to take a gulp of beer.

Bryony tried to hide her shock. This was the first time a crew member had spoken the word *godhunter*, the first acknowledgement that the Black Armada might do more than just traffic in books. She pushed her food around her plate and laughed. "But there's no such thing as a godhunter."

Prove me wrong, Dylan. Prove me wrong by telling me who it is. But Dylan didn't get a chance.

Raeni interjected. "That's right, there's no such thing. Rumors are evil and should not be heeded. Now you see how many people had to die because of a rumor."

Someone laughed. "You mean how many people *you* had to kill because of it!" It was a woman whose name Bryony had failed to memorize. She was drunk, even more so than Dylan. And her tone was far from accusatory. It was proud.

With that opening, Bryony was subjected to a sudden onslaught of bloodthirst and adrenaline from the rest of the crew. Only Dara stayed quiet, and Bryony wondered why. Perhaps she didn't like the violent culture of the Black Armada. She'd seemed more than a little at odds with the armada's way of "retiring" its crew, and she wasn't shy about saying so, at least not to Bryony.

"They managed to board *Dragonfly*," Dylan was saying. "There were too many of them, and they didn't mind dying. Half of them were the diversion the other half needed to climb aboard. We kicked them back to the sea."

Someone else provided more details. The worshipers who didn't make it aboard were clocked in their faces with the armada's boot heels and left to drown. The rest were not so lucky. Raeni's machete finally made its appearance in the story, and Bryony felt the color drain from her face as she listened. She closed her eyes, but all she could see was that antique blade, whipping through the air so fast no one could follow it, cutting down people like they were brambles. Limbs littered the deck. Heads were tossed overboard separate from their bodies. The commodore was a killing machine, a warrior to be feared. And Bryony feared her—now more than ever.

She thought about her gentle congregation and hoped beyond hope they would never try to avenge her. She uselessly attempted to send a telepathic message to them. *Don't be stupid. Stay where you are. Stay safe, no matter what.* She chided herself for not communicating to them personally before she left. Martha was her only hope. Martha would keep them settled, keep them reasonable. Bryony felt the urge to pray for them, but to whom would she pray? She was their god. She was the one who was supposed to protect them.

Then a crew member said something that pulled Bryony out of her own dark thoughts. "Too bad *the pacifist* didn't make an appearance, eh? The vigilantes probably wouldn't have even had the nerve to board."

It was the woman whose name Bryony could not remember, and when she said *the pacifist,* her voice dripped with derision. It meant *coward* when she said it—that much was clear.

Bryony looked up. "Who's the pacifist?"

Dylan answered. "You can't guess? I thought you were quicker than that. You're rooming with him after all."

Michael.

The woman sneered. "He's the strongest among us. He could've spared the commodore her injury without breaking a sweat, but"—she rolled her eyes and spoke in a mocking tone—"he doesn't kill people." Then, directly to Bryony, she said, "He's better than the rest of us, didn't you know?"

Bryony decided then and there that she didn't like this woman, and she didn't feel at all bad for having forgotten her name.

Raeni put a stop to the verbal assassination before it could go any further. "Enough. I won't tolerate disrespect for one of our own, no matter who it is. He's crew, and we're a team. We forget that at our peril."

"Sure, we're a team," the woman said. "Some of us just spend more time on the bench than everyone else."

Raeni sighed. "See, now you're on scouring duty. At dawn, and not a minute later, you'll scour the galley, the heads, and the bilge. I want to eat off the floors. Do you understand?"

The woman took another shot of liquor and muttered, "Worth it," before pushing off the table and stalking away.

Chapter Fourteen

Bryony spent the next several days occupied by her new routine. She would wake, take breakfast with the crew, and then climb the mast repeatedly until noon. At noon every day, she watched Michael take his readings. He no longer looked up to see her. After her physical training, she would shower and change and spend the rest of the afternoon in study, interrupted only by those with superficial injuries—a rash, a cut, a pulled muscle.

Day by day, Bryony began to find her place in the Black Armada. The crew began to trust her and tell her more about themselves. She listened attentively, but no one ever mentioned a godhunter again. Their stories were not without charm, though, and Bryony didn't mind hearing them for their own sake. The vast majority of adventures the crew shared were not so violent as the raid that felled the commodore. Still Bryony could never forget the tale of that slaughter, how it made her skin crawl and how Michael refused to participate.

She missed him. She couldn't have honestly said whether she insisted on climbing the mast beyond what was required of her because she wanted to become stronger, or so she would be sure to be aloft at noon when Michael took his measurements. She wanted to watch him from a harmless place. Here, she was not tempted to touch him, and he would not feel her presence or the shame she imagined it brought him.

In fact, the first platform on the foremast had become Bryony's favorite place to sit and think. She was even able to make herself useful from time to time when a crew member would shout to her to loose a sail or furl it. She was happy to save them the trouble.

The first time Shakespeare found her on the *foretop*—as she learned it was called—he laughed and laughed. "All right, all right, I'll make you an honorary bird already. You can stop hinting."

She held out her arm for him, and he happily alighted there. "Any news?" she asked.

"Not as such. I can tell you where the gun isn't. It's nowhere in the forecastle. I spent endless hours clowning around the bunks for the amusement of the entire crew, and I haven't seen hide nor hair of the damned thing." He shook his head vigorously. "All that humiliation, and for what?"

"Oh, you poor, poor little birdy." Bryony scratched his head, and he pecked at her hand playfully. "Like you had any pride to begin with. You'd have done all that and more for an ounce of cuttlefish, and you know it."

He fluffed his wings, and all his feathers rose up in unison. "Point taken. Any news on your end?"

She heaved a frustrated sigh. "Well, they mentioned the rumor of a godhunter once, and then the commodore denied the existence of godhunters altogether. I mean what if there really isn't one? Did I abandon my congregation for nothing?"

"There's a godhunter in the armada. I know there is." Shakespeare's voice was low and deadly serious. "Do you think I would have suggested you risk your life like this on a hunch? You're my best friend. I feared for you because the godhunter is real. I've done my homework. Every time a god went missing in the last ten years, the Black Armada was close by. The coast has been losing gods at an unprecedented rate while their congregants are still alive. That's impossible without a weapon that can destroy immortality itself. The only other way to kill a god is to eliminate its worshipers first. This *has* to be a godhunter, it *has* to be the death sword, and the most likely mode of travel is this very fleet."

Bryony let her head and arm drop a little, and Shakespeare flew to her shoulder. He scooted close until his warm, feathered body was pressed against her skin. "I'm sorry," he murmured. "I know you didn't want it to be true."

"It's not that." She drew her knees to her chest, and Shakespeare hopped onto their summit. "I just . . . don't want to kill anyone."

"I know."

She folded her arms around her knees, hugging herself and the bird in a roundabout way. The frightened girl in her wanted to go home, to feel safe again. But that was impossible. "I wish I'd never become a god."

"Don't say that. Think of all the lives you've saved, all those people who'd be dead if not for you. Think of the mother of that boy you saved last. And that sweet couple in the RV who can continue their travels without grief because you were magnanimous enough to save their dog. If I could choose anyone else to have the healing sword, I wouldn't." He tugged at a strand of Bryony's hair until she looked up at him. "Think of how many lives you'll be able to save in the future just by ending one. It's one life, Bryony. Take one life in order to save so many more."

She thought of the crew of the Black Armada mercilessly cutting down the vigilantes who boarded their ship. Drowning them. Killing them. But the crew were only defending themselves, weren't they? Was it really so terrible to fight for your own life? And wasn't that all Bryony was doing—fighting for her life? But no one had threatened her yet, not really. It was the preemptive strike that unsettled her. It was killing someone because she thought they *might* kill her.

"What if the godhunter only kills dangerous gods?" She was still thinking of Raeni. She couldn't imagine the nerve it would take to cut the commodore down with her own machete. Then she thought of Dara and of shooting her with her own gun. But the death sword wouldn't look the same once Bryony took possession of it, would it? It would change to suit her. It would become some sharp piece of costume jewelry maybe. She tried to imagine scratching either one of them with a deadly hairpin and groaned. This was not going to be easy. "What if the godhunter lets me live because I've done no harm?"

"Oh, Bryony," Shakespeare said in a quiet, sympathetic voice. "To a godhunter, there's no such thing as a harmless god."

From then on, Bryony dedicated her in-between time to finding Dara's gun. When she wasn't climbing the mast or researching bacterial infections, she searched every locker. Every door that would open, she opened. She was careful not to be witnessed, and when she was, she pretended curiosity. She found rain gear, spare sails, life rafts, food stores, but no gun.

She spent evenings on the quarterdeck watching the sunset. Sometimes she brought a book with her to study in the fresh air. She was secretly glad that Dara had hidden her gun so well, and that the commodore guarded her machete with such vigilance. Bryony wasn't ready to leave the armada. She didn't want to go back to living her life behind a black veil, not yet anyway. Just a few more days.

It was selfish, she knew. Her congregation was surely worried. What if one of them got sick or injured while she was away? But no matter where Bryony went, somewhere, someone beyond her reach was suffering. She could not be in all places at once. The weight of being the sole wielder of the healing sword had hung around her neck for so long, she'd forgotten what it felt like to just be.

Bryony happened to be staring at the evening sky, musing about her new life and analyzing her new problems, when she saw the yellow flare.

It was far ahead of them. She couldn't see the ship the flare had come from, but she knew it would be Chuy's. *Papillon* was the fastest, the scout, the lookout.

Bryony shot up and shouted, "Flare!" She pointed to the still climbing light. "Yellow flare!"

Dylan was at the helm, and he darted forward to ring the alarm bell. What followed was a flurry of activity Bryony only partially understood. Raeni emerged from below and started shouting orders. Among them were orders to furl a number of square sails and reef the main. Crew climbed the masts faster than Bryony had ever seen it done. They all put her daily regimen to shame.

Then the commodore turned to Bryony. "Get inside! Secure your supplies!" Her tone left no room for questions.

Bryony obeyed before she could even think about what she was meant to do. Her actions were automatic, immediate. She went below to the ship's hospital and began shoving things into lockers, anything she could find that was out—cotton containers, glove boxes, disinfectant. As soon as she was satisfied, she closed the door behind her, climbed back through the companionway to the main deck, and rushed to the captain's quarters.

Michael was already there, shuttering the back windows. Bryony shoved all her books into the drawers under her bunk and stowed her toiletries in the head. *Dragonfly* pitched, and she caught herself on the doorframe. The crew were still shouting to each other outside, but she could not make out what they were saying. She finally found tongue enough to ask, "What's happening?"

"A squall, apparently." Michael turned his eyes upward as though he could see through the ceiling to the quarterdeck above. "We've been through these before. It'll pass. Just brace yourself."

She did. She lodged herself into the corner of her bunk, squeezed her eyes shut and repeated a mantra in her head. *It's no big deal. They've been through these before. It's no big deal. It'll pass.* But she couldn't quite make herself believe it.

The more *Dragonfly* lurched, the more her body betrayed her. The swells seemed to be coming from every direction now. They were steep and close together, and *Dragonfly* accommodated them without considering the crew at all. Bryony heard things crashing around below the captain's quarters and knew the sounds came from the galley. Rose would have been prepping the next day's breakfast when the yellow flare went up. Bryony worried for her only a moment before her mind became completely occupied by her own troubles.

She had pressed one palm to the ship's hull and the other to the outside corner of her bunk. And her arms ached. She'd overdone it climbing the mast. She was weak and sore, and she hated herself for not anticipating this exact predicament.

Dragonfly rolled, and Bryony couldn't help crying out. Until now, the ship had taken the largest swells on the nose, but this one hit them broadside and she was nearly thrown from her bunk. As she caught herself, a sharp pain shot through her arms and the muscles in her chest. And a book flew out from under her pillows.

No.

No!

She'd forgotten one book in her haste. She'd forgotten it because she'd hidden it. It was the volume on the history of human growth abnormalities—the only book she did not want Michael to see. And now it was sliding back and forth across the floor in front of him.

Her reaction was stupid, so stupid, and she knew it. She mercilessly berated herself for her own poor instincts, even as she leapt from her bunk and chased the volume across the floor. *Really, incredibly stupid, Bryony. Not only have you just thrown yourself on the mercy of gravity—who is far from a friend right now—but you've drawn even more attention to the object you were hoping to hide.*

Before she could catch the absconding book, Bryony's body was thrown forward. She hit the table and tried to hold on to it as the boat tilted back again. Her arms screamed with pain, and she screamed too. Pulling was so much worse than pushing. Of course it was. She'd been pulling herself up the mast for days now. She fell back, landed on her tailbone, and pushed herself to her feet just in time for the boat to rock the other way. Michael's maps had long since left his table and were traversing the entire floor along with the damned book and Bryony herself.

She fell into the table again, this time without grabbing hold of it. Her hips hit the edge and her torso kept going. She saw her fate a second before it hit. Her poor head careened toward the table, propelled by a force so powerful she couldn't even slow it down. Her eyes closed involuntarily, ready for impact. But when her head hit the surface, it felt soft. And warm.

She opened her eyes to find Michael's oversized palm cradling her forehead. He had stood and caught her before she was knocked unconscious or worse. He was bent at the waist and clinging to the edge of his bunk as he quickly took hold of Bryony's wrist and reeled her in.

In a matter of seconds, he'd pulled her back with him onto his mattress. He positioned himself without letting go of her, one leg braced against the floor while the other acted as a barrier between Bryony and the windows. He clung to a brass handhold with his right hand, and his left arm wrapped around her back to secure her.

The boat rolled again and Bryony was tossed into him, but she caught herself and pushed her body away from his. Both her hands were flat against his ribcage, and she kept them there, pressing her back into his arm though her muscles ached. She refused to violate his personal space again—not intentionally anyway. She was certain this was a violation all on its own. After the storm, he would go quiet again, and she would have to avoid him all the more.

She looked up to see his face. His expression was focused, intense, worried. But when he glanced down and saw her looking up at him, he smiled. "You'll be okay," he said. "I've got you."

Chapter Fifteen

When the sickness hit Bryony's family, her mother was the first to die. She went quick and without too much suffering. But when Bryony's little brother came down with the same fever, his body fought it for weeks. Their father was determined to save him, visiting witch doctors and faith healers alike. Few would come close, and those who did could not help.

Grief overcame Bryony's father long before his son was dead. He was useless, weeping, drinking, and sleeping all day. It was up to Bryony to care for her little brother in his final hours. She brought him water and dabbed it onto his lips. She washed his hands and feet, put fresh clothes on him, and tucked him in at night. She combed his sweat-soaked hair and sang him lullabies she'd learned from their mother. She told him all his favorite stories, over and over again, even when she was no longer sure he could hear them.

And then one day, mercifully, he died. Bryony's father was passed out in the next room when her brother took his last, shuddering breath. The death was a relief to her. She didn't even cry in the moment because the sickness had been so much worse than death. For the first time in weeks, the boy rested peacefully without moaning or tossing or throwing up. The muscles in his face relaxed, and he looked familiar for a change. He looked like the boy who used to sleep so soundly beside Bryony she'd actually envied him.

As she smoothed her brother's hair one last time, tucked the sheet under his chin, and kissed his forehead, she whispered, "Don't worry, baby. I'll be right behind you." And she meant it. She had no reason to believe she would survive her family. Her father coming down with the same illness confirmed it for her. Death was imminent, and Bryony was ready for it. She hoped for a quick end, a sickness that took her all at once and left her at peace soon after.

But death never came for her, no matter how much she embraced it. She dyed her clothes black, wore a veil, and visited the nearby graveyard often. She didn't consort with living people for months because what would be the point? Soon she would join her family in the ground.

A year passed, and she didn't get sick, and she didn't die, but she didn't go back to her old ways either. Embracing death had become a habit Bryony didn't want to break. The thought of being finished, of being allowed to let go at last, comforted her when the loneliness became too much. With her fascination came the melancholy, the music, the poetry of death. And she took her aesthetic with her into godhood, into immortality. She was a gothic healing deity, always chasing after death and fending it off for everyone else.

But eternal rest would never be Bryony's, no matter how much she longed for it. And she had longed for it . . . until now. Now she was afraid to die.

Michael pulled her close, and she pushed away from him. Together, they were an immovable object, and the force of the storm was no match for the tension between them.

After what felt like an hour, her tired arms began to tremble, but she would not stop pushing against him—not even when the swells grew farther apart and she thought she could perhaps brace herself alone. Michael still held on to her, and she could no more demand he let go of her than she could allow herself to sink into his body and rest. Her eyes welled with the struggle, but Michael didn't seem to notice. His eyes were turned upward. He was listening to the storm, she realized, making sure it wasn't just slowing down before a final surge.

By the time he looked down again, Bryony was choking back sobs. The physical pain was too much. And the shame, lest she forget. She had forced him to hold her in his arms as the storm raged on, and all because she didn't want him to see what she'd been reading. She was dishonest and disrespectful. She swallowed the lump in her throat and shook her head. "I'm sorry. I'm so sorry. I didn't mean to . . . It was stupid, all of it. It wasn't on purpose."

Michael let his arms drop. His brow furrowed in a look that was nothing short of utter bewilderment. "What are you talking about?"

"This." She gestured to the space between them. "I know I made a mistake before. I know it was wrong. I didn't mean to hurt you, but here I am doing it again."

He shifted away from her and looked at her like she'd gone off the rails. "Okay, now I have to ask. What's going on with you lately? Why have you been acting like this? I don't understand why you're avoiding me, why you don't talk to me. You can't even stand to look at me anymore. I thought maybe it was something I'd done, but now *you're* apologizing to *me*. Why?"

She squared her shoulders and gathered all her courage. "I shouldn't have avoided you, that's true. I was just afraid to say what I knew I needed to say."

"And what's that?"

"That I crossed a line with you, and I know it. I put my hand down, and I didn't know yours was already there. It seemed rude to move away too quickly, so I didn't. It was an accident at first, but then it wasn't. It was selfish. I just kept on holding your hand because . . . I don't know." She slouched and looked down. "Because it was nice."

Michael took a deep breath and leaned back against the windows. "This line you think you crossed—it was because you held my hand?"

She nodded, slowly becoming aware that she might have overreacted, maybe just a little.

"But why?" He rubbed his forehead like a mathematician trying to solve an especially difficult equation.

"Because . . ." She could feel her cheeks redden. "Because of your celibacy."

His eyes grew wide, and he sat up straight. "My what?"

"They told me you were celibate."

"They told you that?" He was indignant.

Bryony gulped. "Is it . . . not true?"

He threw his hands up. "It's true, but I mean it's a weird way to introduce someone, don't you think? Hi there, new recruit. This is Raeni our commodore, and Rose our cook, and Dara our best deckhand. And oh, this is Michael. He doesn't have sex."

She stifled a laugh. It did seem absurd when she thought about it.

Michael shook his head, but his expression softened when he saw Bryony had relaxed a little. One corner of his mouth turned up, even as he buried his face in his hands. "Just why?"

She shrugged. "I think they wanted me to feel safe with you."

He turned to face her, and she couldn't help noticing the way his shin brushed against her knee as he drew it onto his bunk. "First thing," he said, tilting his face down to her. "You will always be safe with me. I promise you that. Celibacy has nothing to do with it. I would never harm a friend. I'd like to think of you as a friend. May I?"

She nodded, perhaps a little too eagerly.

"Good." He grinned. "Second thing. You held my hand, *and* I held yours because I also thought it was nice."

Now it was her turn to be confused. "But you were so quiet afterwards. I was sure you were upset, and I was afraid to make it worse."

"Ah. Well, the truth is I was feeling a little shy."

"You"—she arched an eyebrow—"are never shy."

He laughed, and there was that crease at the corner of his mouth. Somehow the reappearance of his dimple stitched Bryony back together. Everything was going to be all right. She hadn't broken him after all.

"I wasn't sure what to say," he admitted. "It was a new experience for me." Here Michael held out his hand and waited.

Bryony caught her breath. Did he mean it, or was he teasing her? She reached out tentatively and let the tips of her fingers slide over his. He held still—as still as she had been that night on their watch. Only this time, she was the rabbit. She was the frightened thing. She swallowed her insecurity and let her hand slip further into his until his fingers brushed the inside of her wrist. For a moment, he did not close his hand over hers, and she saw clearly the difference between them. Her entire hand nearly fit within just the palm of his.

When he finally let his fingers close, the movement was so subtle she might not have noticed had she not been acutely aware of every shift in his position. He simply allowed his hand to relax. His fingers curled around her wrist, and his thumb dropped over the back of her knuckles.

"So . . ." The faintness of her own voice surprised her. "So this is okay?"

He nodded.

"And I didn't make things awkward for you?"

He shook his head.

"Not even during the storm?"

His brow creased only a moment before the truth dawned on him. "That's what this is about, isn't it? You were worried because I had to hold you through the squall. You were afraid you'd forced it on me somehow, that you had—how did you put it?—crossed a line."

She hesitated. All her distress, all her dread seemed ridiculous now. "I didn't want to disrespect your boundaries."

"But I was the one who pulled you in."

"Because you had to. Because I got up in the storm, and you had to . . ." She couldn't go on. He was letting go of her hand, and for some reason, it broke her heart a little.

"I see." He took a deep breath and frowned. "I should have said something sooner. I should have asked you what was wrong."

"No."

"Yes." He leaned in. "You worried for days over nothing, and I let you worry. Bryony, you didn't cross any lines." She was dubious, and he sighed. "Right. Let's get something out of the way then."

She wanted to ask him what, but he didn't give her the chance. He moved closer and wrapped his great arms around her shoulders. She froze, terrified. Somehow this was her fault. Somehow. But he was pulling her in, and she didn't want to resist. She wanted to melt, and after a moment of forced rigidity, she did. She wrapped her arms around his ribcage and curled her fingers into the folds of his shirt. It was so easy, holding him this way. It felt familiar. Even though she hadn't hugged anyone since her father last told her goodbye. Even though she'd given up the hope she ever would the day she became a god.

Too long she held him, hyperaware of each breath he took in her arms. Then she sat up on her heels so she could wrap her arms around his shoulders and press her cheek to his neck. His skin was so warm. He took her in his arms again, and she whispered, "Thank you for not laughing at me."

"No." He tightened his embrace. "Never."

"The problem is I like you, but I've never had a real friend before. For years, it's just been Shakespeare and me. With people, I guess, I just don't know the rules."

"Can you keep a secret?" Michael loosened his hold on her. "Neither do I. So I suppose we'll have to make up our own."

She let her arms fall and sat back. He wasn't kidding. He wasn't just placating her either. She'd seen the way the crew treated him first hand. Was it possible the intimidating navigator of the Black Armada had always been as lonely as she was? Was it possible that he, too, had lived his entire life surrounded by people who were family to each other but not to him? She suddenly understood what her friendship might have meant to him and how much her avoiding him might have hurt him.

"Let's start tonight," he said. He smiled, and she made a silent promise not to take that smile from him ever again. "If you like, when you're happy or excited about something, it's okay to hold my hand. In a storm, if you haven't found your footing, I might help to brace you. That's okay too. And if you're ever feeling lonely or afraid, and you need a hug from a friend, I'm here. Just because I'm celibate doesn't mean I'll never feel affection for anyone or want to show it from time to time."

The seas were quiet again, eerily so, and Bryony almost missed the storm. Michael sat opposite her, waiting on her response, and all she wanted to do was spend another hour in his arms. She closed her eyes and let all her built-up worry drift away in one long breath. "I'm glad the commodore made us share a room," was all she could think to say.

Michael seemed to understand. "Me too," he said. Then he rose and began gathering his maps from the floor.

Bryony quieted the buzz of her own excitement and tried to puzzle together everything that had happened in the last hour. She was still confused, but her confusion was far more bearable now. More than anything, she wanted to keep this friendship, even after her inevitable betrayal. Maybe Michael would understand that she only meant to protect herself, that in her everyday life she hated violence as much as he did. Even a pacifist could see she had no choice in the matter. Perhaps he didn't even know there was a godhunter in the Black Armada. She couldn't imagine he would approve if he did.

Bryony's heart had just begun to lighten when Michael picked up the book that had escaped her in the storm. He handed it to her, and she watched in agonizing slow motion as he glanced down to read the title.

All her shame came flooding back. She bowed her head and took the book from him. She didn't want to see his face. She didn't want to read the disappointment in his eyes. She felt his friendship, which she'd just learned to treasure, evaporate in a matter of seconds, all his forgiveness turned to disdain. She held the book in her lap, squeezed her eyes shut, and waited for his anger to finally coalesce into the words he would hurl at her.

Instead, she felt his hand come to rest atop her head. And when he spoke, all he said was, "Curiosity is okay too."

She dropped the book, leapt to her feet, and threw her arms around the giant's waist. A hug was okay, she told herself. A hug was allowed.

He brought one arm around her shoulders and bowed over her. "You really do worry too much." His voice was a low rumble in his chest. *Like thunder,* she thought. *Like a storm.*

Chapter Sixteen

B ryony tended to several minor injuries in the ship's hospital before she was allowed to sleep. In fact, she was glad for it because she didn't think she could have slept if she wanted to. She was giddy, and she had to repeatedly remind herself to rein in her own expressions. Her face wanted to break into inappropriate laughter on a regular basis and without her permission.

One more-than-minor injury she treated was Rose's burned ankle. The cook had been prepping for breakfast, just as Bryony guessed she would be, and hadn't gotten everything put away in time. One boiling pot hadn't even cooled before *Dragonfly* pitched and sent it flying across the galley into Rose's bare ankle.

The injury was bad enough that Bryony had some difficulty settling on whether or not to use the healing sword. On the one hand, the burn was not life threatening and not yet infected. On the other, large blisters had already begun to form, and Rose flinched with every touch. The scar would not be pretty. And Bryony was in a particularly good mood.

"I've got just the thing," she said with a smile, and she opened her briefcase full of potions. From the hospital stores, she retrieved a real soothing ointment and some fresh bandages. She let Rose watch as she put four drops from one of her vials into a bowl with the ointment.

Then she applied her concoction to Rose's wound with sterile gloves to complete the charade.

"Is that the same stuff you gave the commodore?" Rose asked.

"Uh-huh. Just the same."

"Good!" Rose clapped her hands. "I heard her pain went away and never came back. She doesn't even have a scar now."

"That's right." Bryony began to slowly wrap the wound, wincing sympathetically every time Rose let her know how much it hurt. "You'll have to keep the bandage on for a week. Don't take it off or the burn will scar." She continued to wrap Rose's ankle and turned her ring inward as she did. The injury was so bad that Bryony didn't worry about the scratch she would have to deliver. She didn't imagine Rose would notice one little sting over all the rest. "Your pain should start to fade now."

Bryony secured the bandage, and Rose rotated her ankle. "I'll be damned," she said. "That stuff is potent, isn't it?"

"It's the best there is. But remember your injury even though you can't feel it. Go easy on it."

"Oh, I will."

Rose sat and contentedly chatted away while Bryony cleaned up. "Been meaning to ask. I heard you've finally had enough of your roommate. Is it true? They said you barely even acknowledge him anymore. I mean no judgment if it's true." She waved her hands in front of her as though she were actively fending off her own judgment. "A person can only take so much of our rather peculiar navigator. You were just so adorably attached at first. I'm dying to know what he did to lose you. We both know what he *didn't* do, yeah?" She winked. "So what was it?"

Bryony fought the urge to roll her eyes. She had forgotten how much *Dragonfly*'s cook enjoyed gossip. And sure, as an infiltrator, she appreciated Rose's willingness to enlighten her about the rest of the crew's private lives. But Bryony was protective of Michael, so she chose to defend him with as little detail as she could manage. "No, it was nothing like that. We just had a misunderstanding. It's all cleared up now."

Rose leaned her chin on her fist in mock fascination. "A misunderstanding, you say? What about? If it's anything other than fashion, navigation, or trashy novels, I can't imagine he has much to say."

Fashion? Bryony decided not to ask. "It was my fault," she said. "He didn't do anything. I just have an overactive imagination sometimes." She tried to laugh it off, but Rose wasn't about to let go of the juicy morsel she now had clutched between her teeth.

"All right, so what did you *imagine* he had done?" Rose carefully hopped down from the examination table. "Don't leave me with nothing, eh? The galley's been so unbelievably dull without you."

"You just rode out a squall in the galley and had a pot of boiling water chase you across the floor. How on earth is that dull?" Bryony shook her head and closed her briefcase.

Rose shrugged. "Happens all the time. Oh, fine then. You don't want to tell me, you don't have to. I'll just have to make it all up, and it's going to be a doozy, let me tell you."

"Knock yourself out."

"Oh, I will." On her way out the door, she said, "I might even throw in a little romance to spice it up a bit. See who believes me on that one!" Her lighthearted laughter still rang in Bryony's ears long after she had gone.

Bryony could only be glad Rose hadn't seen the way the mere suggestion of a tryst with Michael sent the blood straight to her cheeks. She patched up the last of the squall-related injuries, which were mostly small abrasions and rope burns from the halyards. She was almost certain most of these injuries would never have been seen by a ship's medic, were it not for the crew's curiosity about the reportedly miraculous skill of theirs, and their willingness to use any excuse to witness it for themselves.

Well, they're about to be disappointed, she thought. *All except for Rose.* Bryony even resisted the urge to use her healing sword on herself again. Her own experience with the squall was certain to leave her hips and tailbone a lovely shade of purple, not to mention the muscles she probably pulled in her arms. But bruises were just bruises, and she chose to let them heal the slow way. Her pretense was too important to risk for something so superficial.

As soon as she stepped onto the main deck, Bryony saw Shakespeare circling the masts. A massive relief hit her at the sight of him. She'd been worried, so worried about how he weathered the storm. The crow tilted one eye down at her and made for her immediately. She held out her arm to receive him.

"Where were you?" she said when he landed. She pressed a cheek to his wing.

He hopped onto her shoulder and waited until she was a good distance from everyone else. "I was on *Ladybird.*"

"Of course you were." She laughed.

"But not for the reason you think, I swear. I thought to myself, why would Dara hide her gun anywhere near the commodore? Why wouldn't she hide it closer to someone she trusted, like say, her father perhaps?"

"Oh, that's brilliant!" She tapped his beak affectionately. "You really are a genius bird."

He fluffed his feathers and stood proudly. "I know. So I decided to spend the squall on *Ladybird,* and you'll never believe what I found while they were all busy pumping out their bilge."

"The gun?"

"Even better. The bullets." He paused while some crew passed by, cawing once or twice for good measure. "And here's where the good news gets bad," he said, his voice more hushed now. "I tested the bullets myself. They all think I'm a weird little bird who just likes shiny things."

"You *are* a weird little bird who just likes shiny things."

"Touché, mon amie. But none of the shinies transformed into something I could really use." He scooted closer and huddled in her hair. "So I think we might have to eliminate the gun. I'm certain they've got it aboard, though. I'm working on a plan to get you over there. Even if it isn't the death sword, a gun wouldn't be a bad idea at this point."

Bryony shook her head. "I don't want a gun."

Shakespeare mimicked a clicking tongue at her. "You'll change your mind once you find the godhunter."

"I doubt it." She didn't want to argue the point, so she made her way toward the captain's quarters and knocked on the door. Michael's voice welcomed her in, and she entered with Shakespeare still on her shoulder.

Michael glanced up from his work. "Hello, Shakespeare." He greeted the bird first, which Bryony had to admit was probably the right choice.

Dragonfly's navigator sat on the floor of their cabin, his back to his work table, cross-legged and swimming in black canvas. It was spread out to such a degree that Bryony had trouble deciding where she could step to get to her own bunk. "What's that you're doing?" she asked.

He threaded an oversized needle he'd been holding in his teeth. "Sail repair. A couple of smaller ships had some damage from the squall."

"And they brought their damaged sails to you?"

He nodded. She noticed that he had a leather strap looped around his hand and thumb, and that he used it to push the needle through the canvas. Bryony watched Michael work for a few minutes before Shakespeare began tugging at her collar.

"What?" she said. "What do you want now?"

The crow looked meaningfully at Michael and then back at her.

"I don't think so." She guessed Shakespeare had seen the needle too and had immediately thought of the death sword. She tried to answer in code. "I promise he doesn't have any food for you, bird."

Shakespeare pulled her hair and rattled at her.

"Michael doesn't eat at this hour, silly crow. Ever. So he's not the one you're looking for if it's a snack you want."

Michael looked up just in time to see Shakespeare peck Bryony hard. "I don't have anything. See?" He showed his empty palms to the bird, revealing a raised metal plate sewn into the leather strap at the base of his thumb.

Shakespeare pointed his full, flat-feathered body at Michael, and Bryony could almost hear his gesture say, *The hell you don't.*

"I think he probably needs to go outside." She marched the bird right back out the door.

As soon as they were out on the main deck and a moment after Bryony closed the door behind her, Shakespeare whirled around and flicked his wings to express his displeasure. "I knew this would happen. As soon as I heard they'd sent you to room with just one person, I knew you'd get attached."

Bryony's laugh in response was unconvincing, even to her own ears. "What are you talking about?"

Shakespeare growled. "That . . . man. That man is not your friend."

Now it was Bryony's turn to be indignant. "And why not?"

"Because he's the navigator of the bleeding Black Armada! Honestly, Bryony, you'll get yourself killed. I should have known this would happen. You've always been too tenderhearted, too soft. Don't let your heart get in the way of your fight for survival. Imagine yourself as prey and him as your predator. Can you do that?"

"But he's a pacifist."

Shakespeare puffed himself up. "Of course he is. And what does that mean exactly? Have you asked him?"

"It means he abhors violence and doesn't kill people. I don't have to ask him because the rest of the crew already confirmed it. They told me how the commodore was injured. Vigilantes attacked, and Michael refused to fight them, even after they boarded *Dragonfly.*"

"That's hardly commendable." Shakespeare gripped her arm a little tighter.

"You're missing the point. If he refuses to kill, he can't be a god-hunter. A godhunter, by definition, is a killer." She was angry now. Had she ever been angry at Shakespeare before? She couldn't recall a time. "You just want it to be him because he looks the part. You're just like everyone else."

She could feel her arm tremble with her own repressed rage. She tried to stop it through sheer force of will and failed. It wasn't just Shakespeare fueling her anger. It was the whole crew. She identified with Michael. His isolation was all too familiar, and it infuriated her because it was so unnecessary. He wasn't a god. He didn't need worship. No intimate friendship would destroy his carefully crafted status or identity. He was just . . . Michael.

Shakespeare relaxed his grip and sighed like he was dealing with an over-passionate child. "You're right. I shouldn't judge people I don't know, but neither should you. Don't trust people so easily. It's too dangerous, especially for you. I'm not asking you to shoot the man, just be willing to test him. Okay? Can we agree on that at least, just to rule him out if for no other reason? Test him. For me?"

His voice betrayed his worry, and Bryony felt guilty for being so harsh with him. He was only trying to protect her. He loved her. Maybe he even needed her. Who's to say how he would get along in the wild after having given up his flock for her? She forced herself to calm down and stroked his beak lovingly. "I'm sorry, Shakespeare. Sometimes I forget this isn't just about me."

"It's not just about me either," Shakespeare said. "Think of your congregation. Think of Martha."

"I know, I know. All right, I promise to test him. Now off you go, bird. Try to find exactly where that gun is hidden, and I'll do my best to get a hold of it when I can."

Shakespeare nodded and flew off with a quiet caw. Bryony took a deep, nervous breath and went back to the captain's quarters.

Michael worked without looking up. Bryony gingerly made her way around the massive folds of canvas until she stood just behind him and could watch over his shoulder. He was mending a tear with a black patch and black thread. It wasn't a large tear, but Bryony supposed it was better to mend a small tear before it got bigger.

Curiosity is okay, she reminded herself. He would not be angry at her questions, and she had already established herself as someone who was perhaps a little too curious about things. It wouldn't even seem unusual.

She cleared her throat. "What's that on your hand?"

He looked up and smiled at her. "It's a sailmaker's palm." He lifted his hand and showed her the leather strap up close. It was a few inches at its widest, and it circled his palm and looped around his thumb.

She bent down to examine it more closely. "What's it for?"

"Canvas is difficult to hand stitch. The palm helps secure the needle and thimble so you can apply enough pressure." He demonstrated for her, placing the head of the needle into a thimble divot. Then he secured the needle between two fingers and used his whole palm to push it through the canvas. "This way you don't puncture your hand."

"Can I try?" She hated herself for being even a little false. It felt wrong with Michael, perhaps because she got the distinct impression he was never false with anyone.

He didn't seem to suspect any artifice in her curiosity and cleared a space for her to sit beside him. "It might not fit so well." He chuckled and handed her the sailmaker's palm. She slipped it over her thumb, just as she had seen him wear it, and held it up to examine. It was far, far too big for her, hanging off her hand in an awkward, oversized loop. He then handed her the needle and thread, and shifted the sail so the repair was over her lap.

It was too easy. No one would hand a death sword over so easily. But Bryony had promised to test Michael, and so she would, if only so she could be smug about proving Shakespeare wrong.

Michael showed her how to hold the needle. "Push the thread through here." He pointed to part of the patch where he had already created a pattern of stitches. "Pull it very tight when you're done."

She did as she was shown, and as she pulled the thread tight, she took a moment to think about the needle pinched between her fingers. *This is a good needle*, she thought. *He doesn't need it, though. I think I'll keep it for myself.* And she made herself believe it. The needle didn't change.

Bryony handed Michael back his tools and thanked him for showing her how they worked. "You're right," she said. "That takes a lot of pressure, doesn't it? What do you do if the needle breaks?" How she hated herself.

"Oh, I have spares, of course. I have a whole kit. Do you want to see it?"

Too damned easy. Bryony nodded, and Michael stood to retrieve a large tackle box he'd converted into a sewing kit. He handed it to her and sat back down beside her to continue his work.

The kit was extremely well organized. Bryony wondered how a man who kept his work table so messy could keep a sewing kit this pristine. All the spools of thread were organized according to color, and there were patches and rows of various types of needles. In the kit, she also saw buttons, zippers, and other objects she thought were not appropriate for sail repair.

"Do you fix everyone's clothes too or something?"

He glanced over, and she held up a button. "Oh! Well, not as a rule. I wouldn't say I've never done it before. When they ask nicely." He grinned. "Mostly, I just make my own clothes."

Bryony blushed. *Stupid question.* "Of course you do. You probably can't find a lot of clothes in your size, can you?"

He laughed. "Not a lot, no. Shoes are a particular problem." He wiggled his toes, which were tucked under his knees as he sat cross-legged beside her. And Bryony realized she hadn't ever seen him wearing shoes. He usually went barefoot or wore just his socks around the cabin.

"Do you even have shoes?"

"I do, but I try not to wear them much. I save them for shore excursions. I don't want to wear them out, as I have yet to perfect the art of shoemaking." He grinned again, and Bryony thought he was trying a little too hard to make her feel comfortable. Still she appreciated it. "I'll probably outgrow them soon though," he said, and his smile faded.

So he was still growing. That agreed with everything Bryony had learned about his condition so far. People would just continue to grow until their gigantism was treated, and if they weren't treated, their growth would eventually cut their lives short. She wondered whether there was anyone left alive who knew how to treat Michael's condition. If there was, surely the Black Armada was aware of them and might even have enabled their education. But if that was the case, why hadn't Michael already been treated? Bryony decided not to ask. It was probably a painful question for him, and it wasn't relevant to her search.

Still she remembered the promise she had made to herself. She would offer to heal him as soon as she knew she was safe. She would tell him everything and give him the only gift she had to give. Then, at the very least, he could live his life without the fear of growing too big and dying too young.

One at a time, Bryony held up every needle and several pairs of tiny scissors in Michael's sewing kit. Every time she pinched one between her fingers and decided to keep it, her heart felt a little stab of fear. If any of them transformed, Michael would know, and the two of them would be caught in a standoff. Right now. Not later. Bryony would have the death sword in her hand, and she would have to use it on her friend.

But nothing transformed. Not the long needles nor the ones shaped like crescent-moons. Not the scissors nor the straight pins either. No single sharp object in Michael's sewing kit was any kind of angel's sword. Bryony closed the box with a loud sigh of relief she immediately regretted. She improvised her way out of having to explain it. "I wish I knew how to make my own clothes. I used to love my mother's costume dresses, and once one tore, I had to stop wearing it."

He glanced up. "Costume dresses?"

"I liked a certain style, you know? I was most comfortable in old dresses, black ones. Probably, it made me more comfortable with mortality. Also it looked cool." She shrugged.

Michael laughed again and Bryony did too. It was good to finally relax. Shakespeare was right. Eliminating Michael was important, and it was a tremendous relief to her. She would remember to thank the bird later. For now, she told Michael all about her old wardrobe—her gowns and veils—and he asked what cut she preferred for sleeves.

Suddenly, Bryony realized what Rose had meant when she'd suggested Michael had an interest in fashion. She meant that he knew about clothes because he made them. He knew about style too. His own clothes flattered him well. They were a perfect fit, tailored to suit him. His style was timeless and neat. He wore dark slacks and a white shirt, suspenders sometimes or a leather belt. His coat was neither formal nor casual, and it accentuated his broad shoulders. It was impressive, honestly.

"I wouldn't mind teaching you sometime if you like," he said, pulling the needle through the canvas and tugging it taut. "You should be able to wear what makes you comfortable."

"It's hardly practical for a sailor, though."

"You'll be allowed to go ashore soon. You can wear what you like then."

She imagined herself riding in one of the ship's boats in black taffeta and lace-up boots. The thought made her smile, not only because she missed her old wardrobe, but because to imagine herself going ashore was to imagine herself staying with the armada for a long time.

She offered her hand to Michael and he took it, still wearing his sailmaker's palm. "It's a deal," she said, and they shook on it. Then she failed to let go right away and so did he. And she realized her ill-advised crush might not be quite as unrequited as she'd originally assumed.

Chapter Seventeen

Less than twenty-four hours after the storm, the entire Black Armada dropped anchor in a California bay. Andrew was more than a little excited. They were near his hometown, apparently, and he was going to be allowed to go ashore. He had sisters and an uncle he hadn't seen in years, and he showed off the gifts he'd gotten them from other ports. There was Mexican jewelry for his older sister, an Alaskan winter coat for his younger sister, and a belt he'd gotten from Texas some years prior that he was certain his uncle would adore.

He also had a surfboard, and he helped ready the boats in an uncharacteristic good mood, talking nonstop about the waves he planned to catch that evening.

"You'll do all that in one night?" Bryony asked.

"I'll do my best," he said, loading a crate full of books into a ship's boat.

Bryony leaned against one of the still-upturned boats and smiled. "I can't help feeling a little jealous." She imagined him, braided beard and all, wearing a pair of Bermuda shorts and a flower-print shirt, walking across the beach into the sunset with his surfboard under one arm.

"Aw, don't be jealous, Tinctures." He hoisted another box into the boat. "It'll be you soon enough. The commodore was impressed with how you handled the squall, and Rose can't stop talking about whatever it was you did for her burn."

"I just gave her a salve." Bryony shrugged like it was no miracle when she knew damn well it was.

"Well, whatever you did impressed both of them, and if there's any real second in command on this ship, it's Rose. I'd say you're sitting pretty."

Bryony allowed herself to feel optimistic after that. If Michael and Andrew both thought she'd won the commodore's favor, it must be true. She liked them both, and neither one of them was the godhunter, so it was safe to like them. Shakespeare didn't know what he was talking about. Bryony had begun to feel good about Rose and Dara, as well. She'd tested every knife and fork in the galley, and Dara was one of the few crew members who did not join in the gleeful description of the mass slaughter of worshipers. She seemed to disapprove more than anything, and so Bryony decided she must be a closet pacifist. She liked both of them, too, so she hoped she wouldn't be proven wrong in the near future.

Bryony was watching all the boats go ashore that evening, thinking about what it would be like to step on dry land again, when she noticed one little dinghy moving toward them.

"Ahoy!" someone called up, and the dinghy bumped against *Dragonfly*'s hull. "Ahoy, medic!" Two women Bryony didn't recognize rowed the dinghy, but the man who sat between them with his arms crossed over his chest was more than familiar to her.

She leaned over the bulwarks and shouted, "Chuy!"

Chuy waved and flinched, and Bryony suddenly realized there was something very wrong with him.

"Are you hurt?" she called down.

One of his companions answered. "Broke a rib in the squall. He insisted it was only bruised, but he's over his denial now. Aren't you, Captain?" She elbowed Chuy, who flinched again. Then she called up to Bryony. "The captain insisted we board the flagship. Their medic is the best, he said. Saved the commodore, he said. Tell us there's something you can do. We've got nothing."

"There is something I can do. Wait there!" Bryony went to get help, and Dara was the first person she found who was still aboard.

"Chuy, huh?" Dara seemed surprised. "I thought that guy was made of rubber." She swung the davits over the bulwarks. "We'll haul up the whole boat with the crew in it. That'll save him having to climb with that rib."

"You can do that?"

"It's a small dinghy with no cargo, so I think it should be fine." She instructed the three in the little boat to stay on the centerline, and she called more crew over to help haul them up.

When Chuy was finally able to board, Bryony saw just how much pain he was in. His hair and face were soaked with sweat. He looked like he hadn't slept since the squall.

Bryony flinched every time he cried out. "Oh, Chuy, you should have come sooner."

He groaned but managed a weak smile. "It's not as bad as it looks."

"No, it's worse." She palpated his chest and found the offending rib when he screamed. "Can you help him to the hospital?" she asked Dara.

"I could pick him up like a baby if you needed me to." Dara wasn't lying. Her arms alone looked more powerful than most of the men aboard, and Chuy was just a wisp of a thing.

"I don't doubt it," Bryony said. "But just a body to lean on should be enough."

They left, and Bryony turned back to Chuy's crew, who finally let their worry show now that their captain couldn't see. "How bad is it?" one of them asked.

Bryony leaned over the rail and spoke in a hushed, serious voice. "I promise he'll be fine. I'll fix him."

One of the women reached up and squeezed Bryony's hand. "We're counting on it, medic. We thought he was going to die last night. We think he might have hurt himself worse than he's letting on."

"I will heal him." Bryony finally let herself say what she meant. Not *fix*, not *treat*, but *heal*—truly, honestly heal—like it never even happened. There was no doubt in her mind she would use the healing sword on Chuy. Even if she'd used it on no one else, she would use it on him.

"Bless you," the other woman said, and it felt almost like worship. They loved their captain so much. Bryony thought he was lucky to have such loyal crew. Or maybe he wasn't lucky. Maybe he'd earned their love. That seemed more likely after all.

Down in the ship's hospital, Bryony found Chuy already lying on the examination table. Dara gave him a pillow for his head and made him comfortable with a blanket and some water. Then she left them alone.

Bryony folded down his blanket. "I'll have to remove your shirt," she said by way of asking permission.

He nodded and pushed himself to a seated position, wincing. He lifted his arms, and she helped him pull his shirt over his head. But she paused halfway through the motion and stared, stunned at what lay glistening among the tattoos on his otherwise bare chest. A chain with a cross pendant. The gold cross was made of woven thorns and had an angular, sharp tip. It reminded Bryony of her ring—of her sword in the shape of a ring.

Chuy snapped her out of her daze. "Now, I know I'm not that handsome."

"Sorry." She finished pulling his shirt over his head and slid it off his arms. "Your tattoos are so interesting. I can't help staring at them."

He smiled and pushed his hair out of his face. "You think so, eh? I've got more where those came from." He laughed and winced again. Even his voice sounded weak. His breath was shallow. Bryony could hardly stand it.

"Go ahead and lie back if it's more comfortable."

He did, and the cross he wore slipped to one side. She tried to comfort herself. No one would really wear a death sword, would they? Wouldn't it be too much of a risk? Surely this was just a pendant. Surely. She would prove it to herself right now and get her worries out of the way.

"I have to remove your jewelry," she said as casually as she could manage.

Chuy grabbed the cross and pulled it up and out of the way. "No, you don't."

"It's special to you, is it? Lucky?" She could hardly control the tremor in her voice.

"You could say that."

Bryony turned away to prepare bandages and her counterfeit pain relief. She didn't want him to see her face any longer, certain she was utterly failing at hiding her horror. Chuy was *not* the godhunter. He couldn't be, could he? Deep down, Bryony had wanted it to be someone she didn't know. In vain, she'd hoped it would be crew from another ship, but this was a terrible twist on that wish. Even though it made sense. Even though the scout ship was just as appropriate for the godhunter to be aboard as the flagship.

The fastest ship. The ship out front.

Oh god. Maybe it really is him. She forced the idea out of her head. "I'll give you something for the pain right away." She brought him a small glass of water to which she'd added one of her tinctures. "It's not an open wound, so you'll have to drink it down." He did, and she took the glass back.

Then Chuy held his pendant out of the way, so she could bandage him. She wrapped carefully, slowly, thinking all the while. How could she get the pendant from him without alerting him to her theft? For her own peace of mind, she needed to rule him out. She secured the bandage and turned her knuckles in to tuck the end away. She let her ring scratch into his skin, and he cried out.

"Hey, that's a sharp ring," he said. "Maybe you should take it off before you treat your patients."

"Ditto." Bryony gestured to his pendant.

He laughed. "Oh, teaching me a lesson, were you?" Trust Chuy to come up with her cover story for her.

"That's right." She winked at him, but before she could turn away, he grabbed her wrist. It wasn't an aggressive gesture—it was more playful—but Bryony couldn't ignore the chill that raised all the hairs on her arms. He pulled her hand close and examined her ring.

"What a beautiful piece." He tipped her hand left and right, examining the way the light glinted off the silver hummingbird's skull. It felt like a dance, their little game, only Bryony got the distinct impression it wouldn't end on a good note. "It's perfect for you," Chuy said. "Suits you I mean. Looks like it was made just for you."

Bryony resisted the urge to snatch her hand away. "Thank you."

Chuy looked up at her, his dark eyes full of meaning. "Was it?"

Force a smile. That's right. Act like you're taking all his compliments at face value. "Sort of. It was my mother's," she lied. "I had it sized to fit."

"Never seen anything quite like it."

She decided to use the opportunity to press him. "I was thinking the same thing about your pendant. Looks handmade."

"That's because it was." He glanced down at the cross now resting over his bandages. "I never take it off."

If he was trying to tell her he knew what her ring really was, she wanted to let him know that she, too, would be on guard. "Same here. This ring dates back to pre-massacre. It's the only one of its kind. The artist never made another."

"Too bad." Chuy let her hand go and grinned at her.

She did not smile back. "Well, I think that about does it for now. Keep yourself propped up. You may have punctured a lung."

Chuy sat without assistance. "Already feel much better." He examined his bandages. "You're a miracle worker, aren't ya?"

"I am most definitely not a miracle worker." More lies. She helped him down from the examination table and guided him to the bunk in the corner. There she placed several pillows behind him so he could lean back against them. "It's just the pain relief. You have to go easy even though you don't feel it anymore. Promise me?"

He nodded.

"And I'd be much more comfortable if you stayed aboard *Dragonfly* for a while. Your crew will be all right without you, won't they?"

He chuckled. "They'll be glad to be rid of me."

"Well, we'll tell them not to celebrate too long. You'll be good as new in no time."

She washed her hands and closed her briefcase, but before she could leave, Chuy called her back. "I want to thank you," he said. "And say I'm glad you're here. Knew you were special that day on the beach." He held out his hand, and she took it. "I'd like to formally welcome you to the Black Armada, Bryony. Didn't get the chance before."

Why did he have to be so nice? She was not at all confident in her ability to play cat and mouse with someone she legitimately liked. She'd never been good at that sort of thing anyway. Why did Shakespeare's plan have to involve subterfuge? She would have been much better at stowing away and sneaking around, but then she wouldn't have the access to the crew that she did now. She groaned. That bird was never wrong.

If Chuy was the godhunter, he'd just raised the stakes by suggesting he knew what Bryony was. As far as she was concerned, there were only two ways to interpret his insistence that her ring was special, that *she* was special. Either his comments were straightforward, or he knew the truth about her. If he knew, she was as good as dead unless she got that sword from him. But if he knew, why hadn't he killed her already? Could it be the godhunter was just as hesitant to kill someone he liked as she was? Maybe he hated his position and the expectations placed upon him. She wished she could ask him outright. She hoped, though she knew it was naïve, that she could reason with the godhunter, that she wouldn't have to kill anyone to survive. Chuy would choose compassion over ruthlessness—she just knew it. He was Chuy.

Change the world instead.

Michael's words pulsed through her thoughts like a lighthouse in a sea of darkness. And for the first time since she'd heard them, she began to believe it was really possible. If Chuy was the godhunter, it was more than possible.

Chapter Eighteen

The Black Armada left the harbor at dawn, and thankfully, the anchor left the sea floor without a hitch this time. Bryony wasn't sure she'd be able to tolerate another sanctioned freedive without physically attacking the commodore.

She spent most of the morning dangling her legs off her favorite perch. She had to think, and the foretop was the best place to do it. How would she go about sharing her new conviction with Chuy? She decided she'd still have to get the death sword from him. Once she had it, she would confront him with the truth until he had no choice but to admit what he was. Then she would confess her own truth. Then they would sit down like adults and talk it out.

It made her giddy just thinking about it. She would show Shakespeare that anything was possible. Maybe Chuy and Bryony could even convert other gods and godhunters to their way of thinking. Maybe only the cruel and dangerous gods had to be put down. Or not. Maybe, for the safety of everyone else, the worst gods could just be locked away . . . in god prison. She nearly fell off the foretop laughing. *God prison.*

She started imagining a world in which gods had to be licensed, in which operating a religion without a license would just get you suspended or fined. She imagined what it would take to get such a license and wondered whether she would pass the test. Would there be an age limit, an annual renewal, long lines and tedious paperwork? Wouldn't it be wonderful to wait in line and fill out paperwork and never ever have to kill anyone?

She hadn't felt this hopeful in a long time. Her ribs were sore from laughter when she glanced up to see Shakespeare circling overhead. The crow looked down at her, his suspicion evident. She held out her arm for him, but he landed on her head and pecked her gently.

"What's so funny, eh?" he demanded. "Out with it!"

She gasped and held out a finger, requesting a moment to compose herself. "It's nothing," she said at last, breathless and overjoyed. "I just had a funny thought. It's stupid really." But it wasn't. It wasn't stupid at all. It was beautiful.

Shakespeare didn't buy it. He hung his head upside down over her forehead so she could look into one of his beady, black eyes. "You're not going to tell me? All right then. I won't tell you my exceptional news."

"Yes, you will." She tickled his feet, and he hopped down to perch beside her. "I call your bluff, you motormouth."

"Okay, fine. You win. No jokes for Shakespeare to enjoy. He's just a bird anyway. He wouldn't get it."

But she wouldn't be moved, no matter what the crow tried. She didn't want to hear him tell her it was impossible, that it would inevitably fail. She needed to believe. "Go on, bird. Tell me your news."

He sighed. "Well, I found the gun. They have it hidden in their chain locker, taped to the inside wall. No one would see it unless they knew where to look. I can't pull it off the wall though, and it was too dark to see if there were any sharp bits—"

"It's not the death sword," she interrupted.

He perked up at that. "You know this how?"

"I think I've found it. I'm almost certain."

"Almost?" He cocked his head.

"Yes." She leaned in. "It's Chuy's pendant. It's sharp, unique, and he guards it like a dragon guards its treasure." She left out the part about how Chuy might already know she was a god. She didn't like keeping secrets from her best friend, and she felt a twinge of guilt for it. But she knew it was the right thing to do. The poor bird would only worry.

"So you haven't tested it yet?" he said.

"No. He wouldn't let me touch it."

"Does this mean you've finally managed to rule out the commodore's machete?"

She frowned. "No."

"Then why are you so certain it's him?"

"I have my reasons." *Don't ruin this for me, Shakespeare. Don't you dare ruin this.*

Shakespeare paused to consider. He looked almost comical, one eye to the sky, deep in thought. "So you just have to figure out how to get the pendant off him?"

She nodded.

"Well, that's easy," he said.

"Is it?"

"Knock him out."

The idea was preposterous. "How? You don't expect me to hit him over the head, do you? Wouldn't that blow my cover pretty quickly if it failed?"

Shakespeare shook his head like he couldn't believe how slow his friend was. "That man is the captain of *Papillon*, the worst ever boat for scraps, and parties, and song, and dance. And drink. You get me?"

"He doesn't drink!" She sat up straight as the realization hit her.

"Not as a rule, no. I doubt he's a teetotaler. He'll participate in a toast if it's called for. But I'd bet my weight in gold he can't hold his liquor."

"Ha!" She could have danced for joy. "I just have to get him drunk." This was going to be easier than she thought. It didn't even have to be unpleasant. She just had to spend a celebratory evening with a friend, take his pendant while he was sleeping, and explain the situation as soon as he woke up. It would be painless, absolutely painless. She couldn't believe it. All that worry over nothing. She bent over the crow and kissed his little, black head. "I don't know how I'd do this without you, Shakespeare. You really are the best friend a girl could ask for."

Shakespeare hopped backward in the wake of her overzealous affection. "Of course I am. They say dogs are man's best friend, but corvids prefer women." He took a short bow, lifting his wings just a touch to enhance the theatrics of the gesture. "I must say, I've never been prouder. You've been so hesitant lately, but now that you found the bastard, you seem almost anxious to end this. I knew you would fight for your life when the time came."

She leaned against the mast, turning her back to Shakespeare in the process. "Yeah. I guess I'm just ready to go home. I miss my congregation." It was a partial truth. She did miss her worshipers, especially Martha, but she was far from ready to go home. She wanted her life to keep transforming, one change at a time, until she no longer recognized it. She wanted to move forward always and never allow herself to stagnate again.

That afternoon, Bryony read her book on human growth abnormalities in front of Michael without worry. She didn't even draw her curtain. She lay on her stomach, diagonal across her bunk with her ankles crossed in the air behind her. He lounged in front of the windows at the back of the cabin, a new romance in hand. This one's cover had a man and a woman together on horseback. The woman had swooned in the man's arms because of course she had. Bryony thought it looked ridiculous, but she was in a good mood, and maybe the book was better than the cover suggested.

"What's that one about?" she asked.

Michael looked up, disbelief coloring his expression. "Uh . . . Well, he's a duke and she's a prostitute pretending to be a lady. He falls in love with her right away, but she just wants to steal his fortune. Then she realizes she loves him too, but there's a whole mess of nonsense getting in the way of their relationship."

"What's the horse got to do with it?"

He turned the book over and glanced at the cover as though he had to remind himself what it looked like. "Not a lot."

She laughed. "Maybe I'll read that one when you're done with it."

"Really?" He was excited but tentatively so.

"Sure. I've never read the genre before. I should give it a try." This was good. Small talk was good. Soon she would have the godhunter backed into a corner, and instead of killing each other, they would form an alliance. She wasn't betraying anyone. No one had to get hurt. She could get attached, make friends as much as she wanted.

"What genre do you usually read?" he asked.

She hesitated. He was a pacifist, so maybe he would be put off. But no, she was tired of being false. "Horror mostly."

Much to her surprise, he threw his head back and laughed. "I should have guessed."

"That doesn't mean I like actual violence," she clarified. "Because I don't."

"You don't need to explain that to me," he said. And of course, she didn't. He was a celibate man who read romance and possibly erotic romance to boot. She couldn't quite tell by the covers.

"So why do you like romances? You never really told me before."

He shrugged. "I honestly don't know. Maybe because they're about people falling in love. They always have a happy ending, so no matter what the lovers go through, you know they'll be all right. Maybe I wish that were true of my own life. Maybe I'm living vicariously through fictional characters, but that doesn't seem quite right. It feels more like . . ."

She finished his thought for him. "It feels like coming home."

He smiled his broad, heart-melting smile. "Exactly. Is horror the same for you?"

She nodded. "And it puts my nightmares into perspective."

His smile faded, and he leaned forward. "One of these days, when you're ready, you'll have to tell me more about your life. I suspect we have more in common than either one of us knows."

Bryony was in excellent spirits as she raided the galley for rum. It had to be rum, she'd decided. Rum was sweet, and for a person who did not drink as a habit, sweet was better. She also chose to bring shot glasses because shots were the quickest way to accidentally overdo it. She found an unopened bottle of Bahamian rum and took it along with the glasses. Hopefully, Rose wouldn't mind. Better yet, hopefully, she wouldn't even notice. If she did, Bryony had already decided to play the poor-injured-sailor card on behalf of Chuy.

The sun had long set by the time she made her way to the ship's hospital. Chuy was still awake, reading under the lamp in the hospital bunk. He wore square-rimmed glasses and looked quite fetching in them. Someone had also brought him dinner. The tray still lay on the floor beside him. Bryony moved it out of the way and pulled up a stool.

He removed his glasses and smiled a bewildered smile. "What's all this?"

"I'm here to keep you company." She set the bottle down beside him and handed him a shot glass. He hesitated but took it. "I just thought you and I could have a little toast."

"To what?"

"To my first squall and your first broken rib. It is your first one, isn't it?"

That got him to laugh, and he held out his glass for her to fill. "Doesn't even hurt when I laugh anymore. That stuff you gave me is amazing."

"Isn't it? I don't know why anyone uses anything else, honestly." She tried to keep it casual, keep it fun. "Sometimes I'm tempted to take it for every little headache, but it wouldn't be a good idea. It's pretty potent stuff."

"What is it anyway?" he said, still holding his glass.

"It's an old family secret." She winked, hoping that would be enough to stop his questions. She would explain everything to him soon. Then all the lies could stop. Her stomach turned with the singing of her nerves. This was happening now. She wasn't sure she was ready. It was a good thing she had rum on hand, she thought, and she lifted her glass. "To my first squall."

She swallowed her shot and appreciated the warmth that came with it. And out of the corner of her eye, she saw Chuy swallow his as well. She filled their glasses again. "And to your first broken rib."

Chuy raised his glass first this time and gulped down the shot. "That's good." He grinned. "So Rose has been hoarding the tasty stuff, has she?"

"Not anymore." Bryony laughed conspiratorially and poured their third shots. She decided to wait to drink hers. As much as she wanted Chuy to pass out, she herself needed to stay as sober as she could manage. But Chuy held on to his glass without drinking, following her example.

So he was only participating in obligatory drinking after all. She would simply have to outdrink him. Hopefully, he was as unaccustomed to drink as Shakespeare suggested, or Bryony would be in trouble. She was already feeling the effects of the rum. She decided to start a conversation to pass the time and take his attention away from how much he was drinking. "Are you ever going to tell me how you got all those tattoos?"

The eager expression on his face told her she'd chosen the right topic.

He went into great detail about each tattoo. Here was his first on his arm. He'd gotten that the day he raised his first sail. The one on his ankle was an anchor with the name of his family's hometown in Mexico. This one over his stomach was for his stillborn twin brother. This one was for his grandfather who died in the massacre, and this was for his mother, who was killed on a shore excursion, he suspects by an angel. This one was for his first circumnavigation, and this was for his first time rounding Cape Horn.

He talked for an hour about his tattoos, lifting his pant legs to show her some hidden ones, sipping rum all the while. And the more he drank the more talkative he became. Bryony poured him another shot when he wasn't paying attention, and he just kept on sipping it like it was a fine wine.

"Why tattoos, though?" Bryony asked. This time she wasn't just trying to keep the conversation going. "Why mark every milestone on your body like that?"

He finished his rum, and she poured him another. "They're like scars, you know?"

"Scars? But why would you want more of those?"

His laugh told her he was very drunk. "To remember. 'Cause scars are memories, but you don't get to choose 'em. Tattoos are memories you choose . . . I choose. These're my favorite scars. All people, everything I've done, everything lost. All here." He gestured to his own body. "All I gotta do is look at one, and I'm right back there . . . remembering . . . things . . ." He was stabbing his finger into a tattoo over his heart that was nothing more than a date, and then he finally broke down. He began to cry.

It was awful. Bryony had wanted this to be a celebratory occasion. Chuy was always so pleasant, so upbeat. She didn't imagine he'd been hiding a personal hell behind his smile. He cried and hiccupped and downed another shot.

"I'm so sorry," she said, and she meant it. She was sorry for getting him drunk, sorry for coercing him into revealing his pain like this. It wasn't right, and she knew it. But she told herself it was for the greater good. It was for the survival of both of them.

"'S okay," he slurred. "Happens tuh allus."

She nodded. He was right. Everyone had their tragedies. The angels had created a world in which no one's life was free of trauma.

Bryony decided to wait a while in silence. She didn't know quite what to say, and she didn't want to bring back more painful memories for Chuy. She couldn't stand his tears. She reached out and tentatively patted his forearm. He lay back and closed his eyes. "You're nice girl," he mumbled, and he drifted off to sleep.

CHAPTER NINETEEN

Bryony waited perhaps longer than she should have to begin her test. She felt a rising pang of guilt for having deceived Chuy. His grief was familiar to her. She started to imagine what it would be like to let someone see the darkest parts of her, to make herself that vulnerable only to be tricked by them in the next moment. It felt like the worst kind of lie.

She sat hunched on her stool beside his bed and watched his chest rise and fall in a deep, intoxicated slumber. This man had welcomed her, trusted her, given her a chance when no one else did. She didn't want to see the look in his eyes when he realized she'd been conning him since day one. But fighting the crowd of her worried thoughts was the hope that, with Chuy's help, she might start to change the way her world worked. One day, maybe it would be safe for her, and she wouldn't need to be afraid anymore. She took several deep breaths, stood, and kicked the stool away.

She leaned over Chuy's body and watched him for any signs that he might wake. She touched his shoulder, nudged him. His head tilted back and his mouth fell open. He looked so young when he slept, younger than he was certainly. How was it that such a young man had become a godhunter? Maybe he didn't even want the job. Maybe he would be glad to be rid of it. She told herself all these things to bolster her courage as she carefully lifted the pendant from his bandaged chest.

Gloves would have been a good idea, was her first thought as she held the thorny cross in the palm of her hand. She tried to tell herself she was going to keep it, but the fact that it was still attached to a chain looped around Chuy's neck made that hard to believe. Chuy moaned in his sleep, and Bryony held her breath. She would have to get the chain over his head somehow. Slow or quick? Should she just pull until it broke and run for it? No, she decided to be gentle, careful. She had time after all. He wasn't just asleep. He'd passed out twenty minutes ago, and he was still very drunk.

Bryony leaned over his body, holding the cross in one hand while the other worked at the chain around his neck. It didn't slide smoothly. It caught between the pillow and his hair. She reconsidered her strategy.

Time to rip the bandage off. But she didn't get the chance.

Chuy's hand shot up, quick as a viper, and caught hers before she could pull it away. She was so shocked, at first, she didn't quite realize what had happened. Then she felt the pain in the palm of her hand, and Chuy's eyes snapped open. He tightened his hold on her closed fist, forcing her to grip the cross.

"What are you doing?" he demanded, but Bryony couldn't find the words to answer.

Her eyes were fixed on a drop that formed at the heel of her hand. Blood. She'd been punctured. She couldn't scream. She couldn't move. Poison coursed through her veins. It was the end of her. She wondered how many seconds she had left to live.

Very few thoughts passed through Bryony's head during the moments in which she waited to die. The first was of Shakespeare, of what he would do after she was gone. Would the crew let him live? Would he find someone new to follow and tease? Would he cry? Could he cry? Her second and most surprising thought was of Michael. She hadn't gotten the chance to heal him. Not only that, but her story would now be told by those who survived her. She would never be able to explain herself to him. He would hate her probably. He would be glad she was dead. And he would think their entire friendship was fabricated, that every word she spoke was a lie, even the kind ones.

It took Bryony far too long to realize she'd survived being pierced by the cross. At first, she hyperventilated, and that felt like death. Her heart pounded with a rhythm that better resembled a flickering lightbulb, and that, too, felt like death. Her own veins pulsed in her throat. Her face tingled. Her extremities grew cold. Death, death, death.

But then . . . she was still breathing. She was still bleeding.

A drop of her blood fell to the floor, and another bead began to form. Chuy was a cornered beast, angry and terrifying. She hadn't thought him capable of so much ferocity.

"Please," she begged. "Please let go."

"What are you doing?" He repeated his question, and Bryony had to think fast to come up with a believable lie.

"I . . . I just wanted to check your bandages. I swear. I had to move your pendant out of the way." Every word was a gasping plea. "Please," she begged him again and tugged at her hand. "Please, Chuy."

The sound of his own name seemed to snap him out of it. He blinked and let go of her hand.

"I just had to check your bandages." Bryony repeated her lie as she backed away from him. "Your pendant was in the way. I'm so sorry, Chuy. I'm sorry."

His expression was pained, confused. All Bryony wanted to do was get away from him. She didn't want to explain or hear him question her again. She was humiliated and terrified. Adrenaline still coursed through her veins.

She darted in to grab the bottle of rum and then ran from the ship's hospital, tripping over Chuy's dinner tray as she went. She climbed the companionway aided with only one hand. Her foot slipped, and she caught herself but didn't let go of the bottle. She protected that bottle like it was the only evidence she had to prove her innocence. She couldn't have said why. Perhaps she wanted to give the rest back to

Rose, to minimize the amount of damage she'd done, even if only by a fraction.

Outside, the air was warm but refreshing. The wind dried the beads of sweat fear had drawn from her skin and cooled the heat in her cheeks. And on the wind was music, the cheerful sound of Andrew's fiddle.

The music was a splash of cold water to her face. How she needed something normal just now, something easy, something pretty and inconsequential. She followed the sound of his fiddle like she had the first time she'd heard it. He was on the quarterdeck again, and she ascended the stairway in a lost daze. Two minutes ago, she was as good as dead. Two minutes ago, she had thought her final thoughts.

Andrew saw her approach and nodded a greeting. He did not stop playing, and Bryony was grateful for that. She sat against the starboard bulwarks beside him and closed her eyes.

Just breathe.

Breathe.

It's over.

When she opened her eyes again, she noticed the commodore at the helm. Raeni appeared to scrutinize her with amused suspicion. Well, that was that, Bryony thought. There'd be no hiding her theft now. She stared right back and took a swig of rum straight from the bottle. Then she saw her own blood smeared on the label.

Raeni shook her head, lashed the helm like it was second nature, and approached. The wooden soles of the commodore's boots knocked against the deck and sent a shiver down Bryony's spine. She took another swig to quiet her fears.

"I see you've raided the galley, medic. Does Rose know?"

Bryony shook her head but clung to the bottle defiantly.

"You know this means you have to be punished, don't you?"

Bryony nodded. Scouring duty would be a relief to her. She wouldn't have to talk to anyone, or look at anyone, or think at all. Just clean. Clean until it shines.

Raeni went on. "That's a fairly egregious crime you've done there. You know that, don't you?"

Bryony did not respond.

"We take our rum very seriously here." Raeni stood over her now, hands on her hips, glaring down. "The crew will not be happy, so I believe your punishment will have to be twofold."

Bryony choked back an exhausted sob and took another drink.

Raeni held out her hand. "Give it." Reluctantly, Bryony did as she was told. "Your first punishment is that you have to share this with us." Raeni turned to Andrew, who had stopped playing to better hear the drama unfolding before him. "Don't you think that's fair, Andrew?"

No hesitation. "Absolutely, one hundred percent fair."

"Good. We agree." Raeni sat down on the other side of Bryony and took a swig of rum. Then she passed the bottle to Andrew, who did the same.

They passed the bottle back and forth several more times before Bryony found the courage to speak. "What's going to be my second punishment?"

Raeni chuckled. "It's a surprise. You like surprises?"

Bryony shook her head.

"Good! Then it'll make a perfect punishment." Raeni passed the bottle to Bryony, who took it, shocked she was being offered anything at all.

"Why are you being so nice to me?" she asked. The slur in her own voice surprised her.

"Because you look like you've been through hell." Raeni took the bottle back and held it up to eye level, noting the blood on the label. "And so does this bottle. I do hope whoever belongs to the blood is still among the living."

Bryony opened her hand and saw the lacerations Chuy's cross had made. The sight of them brought the moment back. Fresh fear. Fresh helplessness. Fresh shame. And joining all of them now was an intense feeling of disappointment. She had not found the godhunter. There would be no reasoning with Chuy, no conspiring with him to make the world a better place. It wasn't over at all.

In fact, the godhunter might be sitting beside her right now, sharing a bottle of rum. The commodore would not be as hesitant to kill as Chuy would have been. Although Bryony thought Raeni a kind person overall, there was no denying the ruthlessness she could display when she needed to.

"How'd that happen?" Andrew stared down at Bryony's palm.

Too tired to lie, she answered, "Chuy. He was asleep. I moved his pendant, and he caught my hand and—"

"Say no more." Andrew reached over and took the bottle. "You committed a cardinal sin, Tinctures. Ya don't touch Chuy's cross. Everyone knows that."

"*I* didn't!" Bryony threw her bloody palms up and buried her face in her knees.

"Poor Chuy." Andrew chuckled. "He probably feels like an asshole."

Bryony couldn't believe it. "Poor *Chuy?*"

Raeni echoed Andrew. "Poor Chuy. The boy wouldn't hand that pendant over to save his own life. It's down to instinct at this point. Assuming he's the one you shared the first half of this bottle with, I doubt he even knew what he was doing."

Bryony lifted her head from her knees. "But why? What's so special about a pendant?"

"Plenty to him." Andrew swallowed another mouthful of rum. "His lover made it."

"He has a lover?"

"Not anymore, he doesn't."

"Oh." Bryony bowed her head again. How had she not even considered that the pendant was important to him for another reason? Why did it have to be an angel's sword for it to mean something? And of course he would be curious about her ring. He probably thought it reminded her of someone she'd lost. He probably thought they had a tragedy in common, that she would understand. The thing was she did. She knew what it was to lose someone she loved—multiple someones—but her ring held no memories for her in that respect. Every physical remembrance Bryony had of her family she'd left behind the day she joined the Black Armada.

And now she was crying. She didn't know when she'd started or how long she'd been coughing through her tears like a child at the tail end of a tantrum. She was exhausted, drunk, and feeling utterly wrong. She'd gotten herself into a mess she could never get herself out of. It had started the day she'd picked up that damned sword. Part of her wanted to remove her ring and toss it overboard just to be rid of the thing forever, come what may. But then she thought of the people she had healed already and the ones she might heal in the future.

And Michael.

Then, to Bryony's utter shock, Raeni leaned over and put an arm around her. The commodore didn't say a word, but she didn't need to. It was enough to know she was there, fierce as ever, looking after her crew, which now included Bryony. Defenseless and alone, Bryony couldn't resist resting her head on the commodore's shoulder. Was this what it felt like to have a big sister?

Still on Raeni's hip was her iconic machete. Bryony thought about how easy it would be to grab it by the hilt and run, but every time she pictured it, it all went wrong in her head. If she couldn't even get a pendant from Chuy, who was by all accounts a regular teddy bear, how did she expect to take a machete off the commodore? No, it was better not to try. Ever again. There would be no more hunting for the godhunter. She was done. She was just going to hide her godhood forever, and that was the end of it.

But what if the godhunter found her?

She groaned, and Raeni squeezed her shoulder. "You'll be all right in the morning, girl. Just be kind to your own self tonight, eh? Just be kind." She took another long swig of rum and handed the bottle back to Bryony. Then she got up and returned to her place at the helm. Andrew resumed his playing, leaving Bryony to finish off what little was left in the bottle, and she did.

"Good girl," Raeni said from the helm. "Now get rid of the evidence."

Bryony lazily chucked the bottle overboard and then lay on her back to listen to Andrew play. The stars were bright and numerous—so numerous it was at times difficult to tell where one ended and the other began. Then again, it could have been the rum. Ah, what did it matter? It was beautiful either way.

She stared up at the hazy, glittering night sky and allowed *Dragonfly* to rock her to sleep.

CHAPTER TWENTY

The earliest memory Bryony had of her mother was of one of her performances. She didn't recall which, but she could remember sitting on her knees in the faded, red theater seats, waiting for her mother to emerge. As soon as her mother stepped onto the stage, little Bryony had leapt up and waved her hands to get her attention. Her father had pulled her back into her seat, pressing his finger to his lips with stern eyes.

After the play, Bryony's father took her aside and told her she should never try to talk to her mother during a performance.

"But why not?" Bryony had demanded. "It's just Mom. She's not a stranger."

Her father knelt before her and shook his head. "When she's on stage, she is not your mother. She's a completely different person. She's a stranger."

Bryony had giggled in disbelief.

"It's true." Her father managed to keep a perfectly straight face, as though he were imparting sacred wisdom. "You watch next time. If you're quiet and you hold very still, you'll get to see it happen. She'll walk out on stage, and suddenly . . . Poof!" He opened his closed fists and wiggled his fingers in a playful flourish. "She turns into somebody else."

After the play, they went backstage to see her mother, and little Bryony had looked at the woman in awe. She clung to the dress her mother wore that night and imagined it held some mystical property. She thought whoever wore those dresses—the ones her mother put on only for stage performances—would gain her mother's superpowers. That person would have the ability to become someone else entirely.

Like magic. *Poof!*

Bryony woke in the night with a headache that screamed about all the choices she'd gotten wrong, all the tests she'd failed. It was a fire-and-brimstone preacher, her headache. She could only be glad she hadn't been sick in front of the commodore.

When she finally found the wherewithal to sit up, she realized she was no longer on the quarterdeck. She'd been moved to the forecastle for some unfathomable reason. She'd also been covered so she wouldn't feel the chill. If they were going to go to all the trouble to move and cover her, why hadn't they just taken her to bed? She imagined Andrew throwing her limp body over his shoulder like a sack and walking the length of the ship with her passed out drunk, her arms dangling behind him.

Then a deep voice said, "You're awake," and Bryony understood everything. This was her second punishment, Michael's early morning watch. Only something told her Raeni hadn't meant it as a punishment this time—not really. The commodore knew that Bryony felt closest to her roommate, that she liked him for better or worse, and that his presence would soothe her.

The blanket draped over her body turned out to be his coat, and someone had brought a pillow for her head. She briefly wondered who, but Michael was already kneeling beside her.

"I'm supposed to give you this." He handed her a glass of water, and she took it gratefully. "And I'm supposed to go easy on you because you've had a rough night, they said."

Bryony laughed and then groaned at both her headache and the memories that resurfaced when she thought back over the last several hours. "Please don't ask."

"I won't."

He may well have already been told what had happened. But Bryony didn't want to recount it either way, even in part, and she was grateful that Michael didn't push the subject. She sat like a rag doll, spent and dejected, and sipped her water gloomily. She wanted to scream, but she couldn't. She wanted to cry, but she didn't dare. She wanted to curl up and disappear, but she hadn't been so lucky as to find whichever angel's sword gave one the power of invisibility. All she could do was rebel quietly, in her own head, and imagine what she would say to Shakespeare that afternoon.

Michael stood and lifted his lantern high. Then he covered it and returned to her side, gazing down at her with a concerned expression. "Will you be all right?"

Good question. Would she? She honestly didn't know. Hope and despair had taken turns beating her up, and she didn't want to think about her chances anymore. Now it was guilt's turn. Although guilt seemed to be a regular customer lately, and she thought it took more than its fair share. She heaved a deep, shuddering sigh and muttered, "I'm a terrible person."

"I don't think you are."

"You don't really know me. I don't even really know me. I'm not even a person anymore. I'm just a composite of various fakes."

Nothing mattered now. Nothing. All the failures in Bryony's life seemed to culminate in this one. It had hit her perhaps harder than it should have. After all, she'd ruled out Chuy's pendant as a possible death sword, and despite having fumbled her way through it, everyone seemed to buy her version of the story. So why was she so mortified?

Michael sat down beside her. "The first thing you did when you joined the Black Armada was save a woman's life."

That was true, but her reasons behind it were false. Her motive was deceit. "Terrible people save lives all the time as long as it benefits them."

But Michael would not be deterred. "The second thing you did . . ." He hesitated. "The second thing was to treat me like a human being."

She looked up at him like he'd just spoken nonsense. "But that's just common decency!"

"So we've gone from terrible to decent." He grinned. "At least we're heading in the right direction."

Bryony took several frustrated drinks from her glass of water, thinking how much more satisfying it was to angrily drink rum. She wanted to tell him everything—just spill it all on the forecastle deck and let him be the judge—but she couldn't. So she picked out little pieces, small bites she could feed him to make him understand. "Back home, I was surrounded by people who made me feel very important, even though I wasn't. I pretended to be better than I was because I wanted them to love me. I could have just told them the truth, but I never did. Every choice I made was selfish, and I'm just beginning to see that. I have not made one unselfish decision."

"Selfish? Now we've gone back a step. I think you're confused about the rules of this game."

She laughed bitterly. "It's not a real game unless we're on opposite sides."

"Why not?" He shrugged. "Fine. I'll play this." He mimed laying down a card. "We're all selfish from time to time. It's normal."

"No, it isn't." She refused to play along. "Not like this. You . . . You're a good person. Look at you. You're what a good person looks like, not me. I only wish I could be as good as you one day."

"I was just thinking the same about you."

"See that's what I've been trying to tell you. You don't know me, Michael. No one does. I made you believe in a fake person, a fictional person. You don't know anything about the real me."

"I'd like to, though." He wrinkled his forehead and frowned in thought. "What if you told me one true thing about you right now? It doesn't have to be profound, just something small. Then I'll know you a little better. We can start like that. You can just tell me one thing at a time, and eventually, I'll know you well enough that you might believe me when I tell you you're a good person." He scooted closer to her, waiting. "One true thing. You choose."

Bryony couldn't stand his compassion. Not now. Not when she could clearly see how very much she did not deserve it. She was trying to tell him she was a fraud, but he wasn't getting it, and he was going to continue not getting it forever. He would believe in her right up until the moment she betrayed him, right up until she did something unforgivable. But he was still waiting for her answer, and she couldn't help thinking of what she could possibly tell him about herself.

One true thing.

She tried to remember what kind of person she'd been before she found the sword in the graveyard. Who was she really? She thought about the emptiness she'd felt as a teenager, the loneliness, the waiting to die. She remembered endless days of wondering why the universe had chosen to spare her when her mother was so much stronger. Her father was so much wiser. Her brother was younger and more clever than she was. She'd felt like she was the last dregs of her family, not even good enough for death to consume.

Was that who she was—that pathetic, self-pitying child? She bowed her head and let her own tears fall into her glass of water. "I should have died with my baby brother."

It took Bryony a moment to feel Michael's heavy hands on her shoulders. She looked up to see him staring down at her with eyes that spoke volumes. They were troubled, hurt, full of questions he was too afraid to ask. He shook his head. "No, you don't mean that. Please don't mean that."

Gently, he took her glass from her and set it on the deck beside them. Then he guided her in and up until she sat on one of his crossed legs and was elevated enough for a more comfortable embrace. And he embraced her. He drew his arms around her, enclosed her in the shelter of his massive body, and let her lean her head against his chest. She felt wholly hidden from the world, the sky, the stars. He was a quiet, dark place where she could grieve without being watched, where she could let her own weaknesses overtake her for a little while. He was rest, and he was safety.

The deep draw of each breath he took soothed her until her tears stopped of their own accord. The beating of his heart was a drum whose rhythm reminded her of her own humanity. He held her, and he spoke to her, and she felt the low tone of his voice vibrate all through her body.

"Bryony." Her name sounded good in his voice. When he said it, she almost loved the sound of it, even though she had loathed it as a child. "Let's change the rules. I'll tell you what I know about you so far, and you can correct me if I'm wrong. First, I know you look after a crow. A wild crow befriended you, and you feed him and care for him, and he follows you everywhere. So I think, probably, you are kind to other animals too. Am I wrong?"

She did not correct him.

"And second, you saw me—really saw me—when no one else did. You saw that I was alone, that I needed a friend, and you befriended me. So I think, probably, you are kind to other people too. Am I wrong?"

Again, she could not correct him.

"That's what I thought." He drew his long fingers through the ends of her hair, and she wondered whether she was meant to feel it. Every time she shifted in his arms, his heartbeat quickened. And the way he held her—almost like he treasured her. She didn't know whether to feel overjoyed or sorry for him. "Maybe I can't convince you that you're a good person," he said. "But you're a kind person. You can't argue with that. And you should be here." He held her tighter and bowed over her. "You should be here."

He meant she should be *here* among the living—of course that's what he meant. But part of her thought maybe, just maybe, he meant she should be *here* in his arms, resting her head against his chest, listening to his resonant voice. And she wanted so badly to believe it.

After hiding in his embrace for what she was certain was far too long, she remembered why they were on the forecastle to begin with. "Don't you need to hold up your lantern soon?"

He didn't move. He didn't slide her off his lap and set her back on the cool deck. Instead, he said, "Never mind about that for now," and let her stay where she was, warm and sheltered. So she wrapped her arms around his ribcage and clung to the folds in his shirt. She embraced him back, and she knew it was more than okay. He cared for her—really, honestly cared—because she was kind, and she . . . loved him.

She closed her eyes, focused on the drumbeat of his heart, and finally admitted it to herself. She'd fallen hard for him. It was so much more than a little crush. She loved him. She didn't dare say it aloud, so she said it with her arms, the tightness of her embrace and the way she pressed her fists into his back.

I love you.

I love you.

I love you.

And she hoped, deep down, he could hear her loud and clear.

CHAPTER TWENTY-ONE

Bryony dangled her feet off the foretop and watched seabirds circle over *Dragonfly*. The sun was warm and the wind pleasantly cool. Below her the sea yawned, wide and rolling. She got goosebumps watching the world from her high perch. Each boat surrounding them was a little island in the vast, primordial ocean, and they were all at its mercy. She'd learned that hard lesson during her first squall. It had reminded her of the first time she'd experienced an earthquake.

She'd been sixteen at the time, standing in the shower. The once solid ground jolted and rocked her back and forth. She'd run from the shower wearing only a towel, looking for a safe place to wait it out, but by the time she found one, the quake was over. After that, Bryony trusted nothing. She had renewed respect for the steadiness of each surface upon which she walked. The earth was more liquid than solid, it turned out, and on any given day, a distant force could send ripples all through it, demolishing every structure, animal, and human who dared trust it too much.

But the sea never pretended to be trustworthy. It told you straight away that it was changing, shifting, dangerous. It could bear you aloft or swallow you whole, and there was nothing anyone could do to stop it. Bryony almost preferred that kind of blatant brutality. At least she knew where she stood. What had Raeni called its angel? Rahab. The dead angel.

Usually, it felt good to hate them, the angels. It gave her somewhere to keep her blind rage at the unfairness of it all—the violence, disease, rot and disintegration, an entire system that ate itself to survive. It was so much easier to lay it all on the shoulders of angels. Lately, though, her rage seemed to have taken a back seat to something else.

Michael moved across the deck, instruments in hand, and knelt at the bulwarks to take his noon measurements. Bryony watched him, this time without the blinders and denial. She couldn't help smiling. He was beautiful, and she loved him. It didn't matter that it would be a one-sided relationship. She was good at one-sided relationships. She'd been in one with her congregation for the last ten years of her life. Michael was celibate, but Bryony didn't care. She would be satisfied with holding his hand from time to time, resting occasionally in his arms, listening to his incomparable voice. And he would never know how deeply, how unequivocally she loved him.

Shakespeare circled overhead, but Bryony did not put an arm out for him, so he landed on the yard just above her.

"Well?" He paced. "How did it go? I assume the captain of *Papillon* wasn't the godhunter since I'm not seeing any kind of funeral at sea for either of you."

Bryony wrinkled her nose. "His pendant is just a pendant. I don't know whether he's the godhunter or whether it could possibly be someone else aboard the scout ship, and frankly, I don't care."

Shakespeare shook his head. "Come now. Let's not get so discouraged after every little failure. If it must be a game of ruling things out, then that's what we'll do. We'll find that death sword the hard way and with it the godhunter. Then you'll never have to worry again."

"I'm not worried." Bryony swung her legs as she watched Michael walk back to his cabin to adjust and record his findings. "It doesn't matter who the godhunter is. I'm not looking anymore."

"What?" Shakespeare flicked his wings angrily and hopped closer to her. "You're giving up?"

Bryony watched Michael until he closed the cabin door behind him, and then she leaned against the mast with a long, happy sigh. "I think so. I don't want to be a god anymore. I want to be a librarian."

"You mean a pirate."

"Eh." She shrugged. "Six of one, half-dozen the other."

"I don't believe this." He flew down, landed on her bent knee, and stared into her eyes. "You'll die. You know that, don't you? When the last of your worshipers dies, you will die with them."

She frowned. She didn't understand why any of this was so important to a bird. "That's still a longer life than most people get, isn't it? So what if it isn't forever? Maybe I don't want immortality. Maybe I want to be allowed to die one day like everyone else."

"That's . . ." Shakespeare began to nervously shift from one foot to the other. "You can't just do that. What will become of me?"

"Nothing, silly. You're a crow. I hate to break this to you, but your lifespan will probably be shorter than mine, even if I stop growing my congregation. You'll be long gone by the time I finally die. Hey, how old are you anyway? I never asked."

"I don't keep track," Shakespeare grumbled. He flew back to the yard and then onto the foretop. Then he bounded up Bryony's knee, leapt onto her shoulder, and flew back to the yard again. He was scared, obviously. She almost felt bad for him, but his fear was unfounded.

"I'll still take care of you. I'll keep feeding you. You can stay with me for the rest of your life if you want. Or you can go back to being a wild crow, find a lady crow, make little crow babies." She chuckled at the thought of Shakespeare endlessly shoving food into those adorable, gaping maws.

"So what'll you do with the ring then? Do you plan to give it to someone else?" The bird's distress was growing by the minute. "Or are you going to just throw it away?"

She held up her hand to examine the ring she had worn for so many years. "No, I think I'll keep it. I'll use it to benefit the armada. They're doing good work. Did you know they distribute medical texts? Strategically, I can save more lives by saving theirs. It's so much better than selfishly sucking up worship, don't you think?"

"You'll go through withdrawal as your congregation shrinks. Have you ever even seen what that looks like? You're addicted to worship just like every god who ever lived." He was getting angry now, but that just made Bryony more resistant to his advice. "You'll suffer, Bryony."

"I'm suffering now." She glared at him. "This isn't who I am at all. How much of myself do you expect me to give up for this . . . this bad habit? I swear I don't even recognize myself anymore. Do you? Does this look like me to you? Am I the type of person who goes around killing people just because I'm worried they *might* kill me?"

"*Might? Might?* This isn't a matter of *if* but *when*. Godhunters are godhunters. That's literally all they do."

"Sure." She stared down at her feet. "But what if I'm not a god anymore?"

"And how are you going to manage that?"

She chewed her cheek in thought. "I'm . . . not sure."

"Because it isn't possible, Bryony. You have a power right now that no one else has. No one! And it's a good power, and you're a good god. Don't do this to your congregation."

"Do what?" Bryony stood abruptly, causing Shakespeare to flutter back. "Make my own choices for once? Give myself something to look forward to? At what point do I get to have anything at all in this divine, immortal life? At what point do I get to have a real job, make new friends, see new places, maybe even fall in love?"

"Maybe even . . ." Shakespeare cocked his head at her. "Oh, that's what this is, isn't it? It's the giant. It's that goddamned, sentimental, nauseating roommate of yours. You think you've got something going with him, do you?"

"No," she lied.

"You do! You think you're going to live happily ever after with him. You think the two of you are going to go traipsing around the world together, spreading knowledge and books and all, making lots of gigantic babies—"

"Stop that!"

"Two can play, Bryony."

She shushed him and spoke through her teeth. "I can't believe you. You're being so . . . so totally heartless right now. And you're completely wrong."

"Am I? Fine. I'll wait to hear you explain away your beet-red face then. Let's hear it. Why do you blush every time I mention the giant?"

"He has a name."

"And I bet you turn even redder when I say it."

This was getting out of hand. Bryony decided to put an immediate stop to it. "Fine! You win. I like Michael. He's kind, empathetic, and smart. And sure, okay, I think he's handsome. But he's also one hundred percent celibate and not in the market for a girlfriend. I know I'm going nowhere with him. I'm not fooling myself about that. This is not about him. Don't you get it? This is about me. This is about the kind of person I want to be."

Shakespeare took a deep breath and let his next words stab her deep. "But you aren't a person at all, Bryony. You aren't any kind of a person. You're a god, and you always, always will be, no matter how much you pretend otherwise."

Bryony sank back onto her heels and stared down through the cracks in the foretop. Maybe Shakespeare was right. Maybe she couldn't just choose who she wanted to be. Maybe she couldn't decide to stop being a god any more than he could decide to stop being a crow.

Shakespeare broke through her newly downtrodden thoughts. "Look. I don't mean to hurt you. I've just been around, you know? Gods don't just stop being gods. And godhunters never, ever stop hunting. The day you stop being a god is the day you die at the hand of a hunter. Please, I just don't want to lose you."

Bryony picked at a loose thread on her sleeve and imagined Michael's needle pushing it through the cloth, making it right again. "It's not fair," she muttered.

"I know it isn't." Shakespeare hopped closer and pecked her gently to get her attention. "I'm sorry it had to be you. I'm sorry there are hunters out there who kill indiscriminately, without even considering whether a god is good or bad. I'm sorry you're the only god who knows about the death sword and the hunter who wields it. And I'm sorry you're the only one who can stop it. But you aren't alone. There are other gods out there—good gods who will soon meet their end if you don't fight for them right now."

Bryony bowed her head. Shakespeare must have taken it as a concession because his tone grew lighter, and he stopped pacing. But he was wrong. Far from concession, Bryony's silence was her finally questioning whether Shakespeare really knew as much as she'd always assumed he did. To her, he'd been a wise creature. Something about him always led her to believe that he knew what he was talking about, that she would be stupid to question his advice. He seemed to have been right about everything until now.

But Bryony was feeling unusually mutinous. In the armada, she'd experienced more than she ever thought possible—real friendship, passion for a cause, love—and she finally understood that the life she'd been fighting for all this time wasn't really the life she wanted. The feeling she got from worship was addictive, fantastic, pure bliss, but when Michael held her in his arms, it was something else entirely. If worship was a pleasant dream, falling in love had been like waking up to find her real life was even better.

Shakespeare was busy making plans. He was going to search *Papillon* stem to stern for the death sword. He thought Bryony's idea that the fastest ship could be an equally plausible base for the godhunter made sense. "And you keep looking here," he said. "Maybe try unlikely places. That gun has me thinking the death sword might not be hidden in plain sight after all. It could be in the chain locker or the engine room. Search every inch of this ship. We'll find it. I think it's time to finally make a real effort to get your hands on the commodore's machete. And stay away from the giant. He's just a distraction."

That did it. Bryony shot to her feet and swept Shakespeare from the foretop. He fluttered in the air for a moment, stunned. Then he cawed and flapped away from her. Infuriated, she screamed after him, "I don't take orders from birds!"

Screaming was not the smart thing to do, Bryony realized when she looked down to see so many faces staring up at her. One of them was Andrew, who shielded his eyes to better see the madwoman fighting with a crow.

Bryony scrambled to think of how she could regain control of the story. "Uh . . ." She waved down at Andrew and called to him. "Always demanding food, even though I just fed him! Greedy bird!" Hopefully, that was enough. Hopefully, they hadn't heard any more than the last sentence she'd screamed at her faithful companion.

Andrew shook his head. "You're an odd one, Tinctures, no doubt about it! Come on down now! You're needed!"

She made her way down the ratlines while he waited for her. She'd become quite adept at scaling and descending them, and it took her half the time it used to.

When she finally dropped to the deck and removed her harness, Andrew said, "Let's go, let's go. Chuy's asked to see you."

Bryony stopped in her tracks. "Chuy? Oh, tell him I'm—" She meant to make an excuse, but Andrew grabbed her by the wrist and pulled her after him.

"Commodore's orders. You don't have a choice."

Chapter Twenty-Two

The mere thought of seeing Chuy again made Bryony break out in a cold sweat. "But why?" she asked, stumbling after Andrew, uselessly hoping this was all just a cruel prank. "He doesn't really want to see me, does he?"

"Sure he does. And you two have got to make good, ASAP. The commodore wants unity in the armada. We're loyal to each other, and we can't have squabbles among us." He said the last bit in Raeni's accent. It was a good imitation, Bryony thought. "No infighting," Andrew concluded.

"Except with Michael." Clearly, Bryony was still feeling mutinous.

"What?"

"Except with Michael. Nobody has to make good with him. No unity required. He's the exception, right?"

Andrew let her descend the companionway first. "Look, I think it's great you get along with your roommate. That guy's needed someone in his corner for a long time now. But there are things about him you still don't know. People who know him better are uncomfortable around him for good reason. Try not to judge us too harshly."

"What don't I know about him?" She'd descended the companionway and stalled there. She didn't want to see Chuy, and she was happy to carry on this disagreement just to put it off a few minutes more.

Andrew bit his upper lip, turning his mustache into a row of little spikes. "See, it isn't really my place to say. Let's just say he's not like the rest of us. He's . . . not normal."

Bryony rolled her eyes. "Yeah, okay. But neither am I, and you all took to me pretty quickly. You should be used to Michael by now."

Andrew laughed and patted the top of her head. "You're not as weird as you think you are, Tinctures. We like you. Let's leave it at that, okay? Michael can fend for himself. He's good at what he does, and he's earned the crew's respect over the years. We don't adore him, but we work alongside him, and we all get along."

He started down the hall, and Bryony groaned as she followed. The ship's hospital was only steps away. Her heart pounded in anticipation. She wondered why the idea of seeing Chuy frightened her so much, why she had frozen so completely when he woke that night. She knew she needed to apologize, but she couldn't think of how. *I'm sorry I tricked you? I'm sorry I tried to steal your very important pendant when I thought it was a death sword?*

No, there was no way to apologize for what she'd done without admitting to it. So when she finally saw Chuy lying in his hospital bunk, looking positively miserable, all she could do was bite her tongue.

He reached out his hand. She took it automatically, and he turned her palm over to see the marks he had left in his anger. He closed his eyes to them, took a deep breath, and said, "I am so, so, so sorry. Please forgive me."

Andrew pulled up a stool for Bryony and left the two of them alone. Bryony tugged her hand back and sat down. She had no idea what to say in response, so she said nothing at all.

"I, uh . . . I don't usually drink." Chuy sat propped up on an excessive pile of pillows and shakily ran his fingers through his hair. "It's been a while anyway. Seem to have lost my tolerance for the stuff."

Bryony bowed her head, ashamed that she knew as much already and had taken advantage of it.

"Anyway, it's not an excuse," Chuy said. "I know that. It's not new either, so . . . I mean don't feel like it was anything you did because it wasn't." He hesitated and grimaced. Bryony got the impression whatever he was about to say was not easy for him. "I stopped drinking some years ago, and . . . Let's just say there was a good reason for it." His smile was a sad shadow of the one Bryony was familiar with.

In the quiet that followed, she finally realized what he was trying to say to her. Chuy was an alcoholic. That was why *Papillon* had the "wholesome" culture that so annoyed Shakespeare. Chuy's crew chose not to make his struggle any harder than it had to be. They cared about him. They respected his hard-won sobriety, and Bryony had just violated it.

She forced herself to look him in the eyes. "I'm sorry. I didn't know."

"I didn't tell you. How could you have?" He was kind, but he shouldn't have been. He should have admonished her. He should have taught her a lesson. She knew better.

She *knew* better. Her own father had struggled, and Bryony had seen how hard it was for him. She recalled the first time he'd caught her trying on one of her mother's costume dresses. He'd been drinking, and his anger was palpable. "*What are you doing?*" He had shouted the question at her, and she'd run from him because he seemed like a stranger to her. In that moment, he was not her father anymore.

Bryony suddenly understood why Chuy's outburst had sent her into as deep a depression as it had. His question had echoed her father's, and an old fear had boiled up inside her until she felt small again—young, helpless, and alone.

"Listen." Chuy leaned out to take her hand again, and she let him. "I'm not telling you this to make you feel worse. It's my fault, not yours. You didn't do anything wrong."

But she had done something wrong, and she knew it. She hadn't even considered his reasons for sobriety, and she should have. She was no stranger to the effect alcohol could have on a grieving man, especially one who was prone to need it. She'd been so worried about her own safety she hadn't even considered his.

Chuy turned her hand over and looked again at the marks he had made. "I swear to you it will never, ever happen again."

Bryony forced herself to smile at him, despite how guilty she felt. He needed to see her smile. "You were so nice to me the day I first met you." She glanced down at her lap. "I think that's what surprised me when you woke up. It wasn't you. I know it wasn't you." She decided to echo Michael's words to her. "Because you're a good person. You're kind."

She glanced up to see Chuy smiling back at her. "I'm glad you still think so." He lay back and heaved a deep, relieved sigh. "I was worried you hated me now."

"Oh, no, I never would," she said, and she meant it.

That evening, Rose enlisted Bryony's help in the galley, and Bryony told her she planned to eat dinner with Chuy. She wanted to keep him company, to show him she trusted and liked him. He needed evidence that he hadn't destroyed their friendship. She felt she owed him that much at least.

"You like that boy, don't you?" Rose winked. She was chopping onions and blinking back tears, but she made it look like she hadn't even noticed them. "It's okay if you do. I won't tell. He's a cutie, isn't he? I also happen to know he's single."

"What makes you think I like him?" Bryony laughed nervously and began peeling another potato.

Rose pointed at her with the tip of her overlong knife, and Bryony did her best not to take a step back. "You spent the evening with him, didn't you? And you stole my rum to do it."

It took Bryony a moment to find her tongue. Either Raeni or Andrew must have enlightened Rose. "I . . . Yeah, I'm sorry about that. I just wanted to cheer him up."

Rose cackled. "Indeed. You're lucky that bottle wasn't the last of it, or I'd have your head on this here platter." With the tip of her knife, she tapped the plate on which she'd piled the diced onions. The knife seemed to be her favorite instrument of gesticulation, and Bryony was glad she'd already tested it and found it was no death sword.

"Sorry." Bryony repeated her apology and added her potato to the pile to be diced.

"It's fine, it's fine. You can make it up to me with details. What do you like best about him? When did you first feel that flutter in your heart? How do you plan to seduce him? Now, you should know you're not really his type. He usually goes for older men, but I've seen him with a woman before, so it's not unthinkable."

Bryony cleared her throat and tried to keep her voice playful. "I thought I was meant to be having an affair with my roommate."

Rose threw her head back and laughed. "That was a good one, wasn't it? You should have seen your face!"

So it was funny, was it? Unthinkable even. A joke. Bryony did her best not to scowl. Instead, she laughed along and violently gouged her peeler into another potato.

Rose went on. "I hear tell you were fond of Chuy from day one. Is that true?"

"It is." Bryony decided to play along rather than correct Rose's misapprehension. It was better than losing her temper, which was quickly becoming the only other option Bryony could stomach. "He was so welcoming. And I love his tattoos."

Rose nodded. "They're something else, aren't they?"

"He told me all about them last night, and he showed me some of the hidden ones."

"Oh, did he?" Rose was so delighted she stopped chopping onions. "Do you think he likes you back? Oh, I hope he does! He's never gotten over the last one, you know? We've all wanted to see him fall for someone nice for a long time now."

Convincing Rose she had developed something of a high school crush on Chuy was so easy Bryony almost felt guilty. Almost. Each time she felt a twinge of shame, she reminded herself of the way Rose laughed at the idea of anyone falling for Michael. Plus, Bryony couldn't resist seizing the opportunity for information. "Do people really have romantic relationships in the Black Armada? I would have thought it was frowned upon."

"Are you kidding?" Rose picked up her knife again. "We're here for life, kid. If we didn't allow ourselves some companionship, we'd all go mad."

"Really?" This was certainly new.

Rose nodded. "Absolutely. The tangled web of relationships aboard *Dragonfly* alone would spin your head." She laughed again. "I know 'em all if you ever want to be briefed. For us, there's just one rule."

"What's that?"

"Don't get knocked up. Or do your best not to anyway. Chuy's parents obviously failed, but they were lucky we happened to have the space for a wee 'un at the time. That and the old commodore was a softy."

"Chuy was born into the Black Armada?"

"Yep."

So Rose proceeded to tell Bryony the story of Chuy's parents. It was long and sordid and full of inconsistencies. As long as she didn't take it as absolute truth, Bryony was well and truly entertained.

When dinner was prepared, Bryony took Chuy's meal to the hospital and sat beside him to eat. He was glad for the company. The hospital had been isolating, and Chuy was not a person who did well in isolation. He needed people. Bryony could have guessed he was an extrovert the day she met him. He was so easy to talk to.

She told him all about Rose's theory, and he laughed and laughed. "*Dragonfly*'s cook is always looking for new drama," he said. "Can't fault her, though. The galley's not the most exciting place on the ship."

"Do you think we should correct her?" Bryony asked.

Chuy grinned. "Let's not. It's more fun that way. We'll see how far the rumor gets. When the commodore comes to give us *the talk*, we'll know it got all the way 'round the ship."

It was a good idea, Bryony thought. Served them right. "Rose originally suggested I was having an affair with Michael—she seemed to think it was funny—so people might not believe her this time around either."

"Michael, eh?" Chuy swallowed an unusually large bite and frowned. "Poor guy. He's the butt of too many of their jokes."

"Right?" *Thank god!* Someone who understood, finally. "Why do they treat him that way? Do you know? Is it just because he looks different?"

Chuy shrugged. "Could be part of it. He also keeps to himself usually, so they might be put off by that. Michael is . . . complicated. Gotta say, I didn't believe it when they first told me the commodore had ya rooming with him. Still trying to figure out what her goal was there."

"Michael seemed to think it was because no one else wanted to."

"True." He sucked his fingers clean and took several gulps of water before he continued. "But the commodore doesn't really take into account what people do or do not want when she gives orders." He laughed. "If she'd told Rose to room with Michael, Rose would damn well room with him."

Bryony grimaced at the thought of Rose in the captain's quarters, grumbling, pouting, hating it the whole time. "I think that would have crushed him," she said. "He does notice, you know. People may think he doesn't, but he does."

"Oh, they know he does. They just don't care."

"But what did he do to make them hate him so much?" She could hear her voice go up in pitch. "Sure, he's got the captain's quarters, but he can't help that. He's a good navigator, and he never complains about having what I'm certain is the worst watch in the entire schedule. He's celibate, right? So he didn't go breaking anyone's heart or stealing anyone's lover. He's a pacifist, so he hasn't hurt or killed anyone. He's never been anything but kind to me, and I've never seen him treat anyone else worse. I just can't understand it."

Chuy shook his head and smiled at her. "Listen to you. So worried for the Black Armada's giant navigator. I wonder if Raeni meant you as a kind of gift to him, an apology or something. I think the crew's intimidated by him, honestly, so they try to take him down several notches when his back is turned. I'm sure the commodore's aware of it, but there's not a lot she can do. Except, apparently, put you on his team."

Bryony blushed. "I wish I was a better player. So why aren't you trying to take him down several notches?"

Chuy finished what was on his plate and set it in his lap. He seemed to think about what to say a moment before he spoke. "I was born into the armada, so to me, he's just . . . always been there. I remember when he was ten inches shorter." He chuckled and wrinkled his nose at the memory. "But to people who join later, he's a bit of a shock, I guess."

"Well, he shouldn't be." Bryony crossed her arms. "Not any more of a shock than a guy with a hundred tattoos anyway."

Chuy laughed as she took his tray away. "He's lucky to have you for a friend." Then his expression darkened for a moment. He recovered almost instantly, but Bryony hadn't missed it.

"What?" she pressed him. "What's wrong?"

Chuy shook his head. "You were so understanding when you learned my secret. I just hope you're as understanding when you learn his."

Secret? Andrew had told her the crew knew something about Michael she did not. Perhaps something in his past made it difficult for others to accept him. Bryony wondered what it could be. Did it explain his pacifism or celibacy? Chuy seemed confident she would learn it sooner or later. He said *when*, not *if.*

So Bryony tried to prepare herself to learn something troubling about the man she'd only recently begun to admit she loved. She imagined endless possibilities, some of them laughable, some of them too sad to dwell on. But nothing she imagined came close to the truth when she finally learned it. And no amount of fantasizing could have prepared her for it.

CHAPTER TWENTY-THREE

As much as she hated them, Bryony had actually seen only one angel in her life. She'd been ten years old at the time. Her parents and brother were still alive. A rumor had gone around that students in a nearby town were learning physics and biology. Bryony had been fascinated at the mere mention of the sciences. She would climb up into her favorite plum tree and watch the lights of the neighboring town go out one by one, imagining what it would be like to study there one day. At the time, she'd half-believed in the possible benevolence of angels. After all, why would they allow a whole town to disobey them if they weren't at least a little forgiving?

But one night, from the branches of that same tree, ten-year-old Bryony watched an intense brilliance descend. It was disorienting, like spinning wheels of light. It seemed to move in two opposing directions at once. She shielded her eyes and peeked through her fingers, still too young to have developed a healthy fear of the unknown. Scores of enormous eyes blinked all around the wheels like spotlights flashing on and off in regular patterns. Wings like beams of light surrounded the eyes in even stranger patterns. The creature descended quickly, too quickly for Bryony to run inside and ask what it was. And when it hit the neighboring town, it left nothing behind.

Every building on the skyline vanished in a blink of blinding light. All the trees, all the animals, every human being was gone. That brilliant creature had consumed the entire town. It was a merciless evil, and it changed her. She would never look at the skyline and imagine her future again. It was too dangerous.

Later, she learned it was one of the ophanim that had come to annihilate the town, but Bryony didn't really care. An angel was an angel. And this one had given her enough reason to hate them for the rest of her life. Someone in that town might have become a doctor or learned how to prevent disease. Someone in that town might have saved her family, but the ophan had eaten them all.

Bryony spent the evening high on the foretop watching the stars. The sky was clear and lovely, the moon a suspended sliver in the night. She found herself newly amazed every time she looked up to see the Milky Way stretched across the blackness like a scar.

Shakespeare had not come back to pester her, and she was sorry for it. She loved that bird, as much as she disagreed with him. But she had seen his little form fluttering around *Papillon* and later over *Cicada,* so she knew he was all right. He seemed to have taken it upon himself to continue the search for the godhunter alone until she came to her senses. He had no idea just how serious Bryony was when she'd told him she was through.

A cool breeze whistled through the lines, and Bryony closed her eyes to savor it. But a familiar brilliance startled her out of her comfortable doze. It was a brilliance she had only seen once in her life. It was a brilliance that made her heart stutter in her chest and her breath stop for fear. For terror.

That poor little town. Those people. Those poor people.

She opened her eyes and blinked in the light. Above her, descending like a plague, she saw it. Her second angel. She sat bolt upright and clung to the mast. She held her breath like she was underwater. An angel could see her breath—she was sure of it. An angel would know she was there. But did it matter really? If the angel had come to consume the armada, the armada would be consumed and Bryony along with it.

White flare. Where was the white flare? She needed to alert the godhunter, whoever it was, that an angel had come. No one would be expecting this. It hadn't happened in twenty years.

Why hadn't she asked Michael where they kept the flares? But Bryony wasn't really on watch. Who was? And why hadn't they sent up the white flare? Why hadn't any of the other ships? The angel was certainly not hiding itself from any of them. It could surely be seen for miles. Surely.

It wasn't an ophan. It looked completely different, aside from that terrible, all-consuming light. This angel had faces—four of them, facing four directions—all different shades, all different creatures. It had fewer wings, which were shaped more like something belonging to a bat than a beam of light. And its body was more like a beast than a wheel. It moved too slowly for an attack. Angels could move as quick as lightning, unless they wanted to torture you or use you as an example, which they frequently did. Still they dove with raptor speed when they came in for a kill. This one hovered and descended like a fog onto the ship.

Bryony panicked. She unhooked her harness and climbed down the ratlines without it. The harness didn't matter at this point. If she didn't find the white flare to warn the godhunter, they were all as good as dead.

On her way down, she kept glancing back at the angel, who had shrunk its body for some unfathomable reason and was now mere feet from the quarterdeck, where it seemed about to alight. The fact that she could not imagine what the angel was trying to do or what it might want from them only made the situation more terrifying.

From halfway down the ratlines, Bryony watched the angel's light dim and its body transform. Three of its animal faces sank back into its skin until only the forward-facing, human one was left. Two of its wings wrapped around its now human-shaped body like a garment while the other two stretched toward heaven, ready and waiting for flight.

She saw Andrew descend to the main deck, fleeing from the beast, no doubt. If she hadn't felt the same fear, she might have called him a coward as he left his commodore to fend for herself.

Raeni. Bryony wanted to scream for her, to distract the angel and sacrifice herself, but her throat closed and terror overtook her. She recalled her own conclusion that immortal creatures feared death far more than mortals did. It appeared Bryony had caught the same affliction. She couldn't even think straight. Her own heart thundered in her ears, and she was certain she'd begun to hallucinate. She saw Raeni approach the angel, weapon still sheathed at her hip—Raeni's comparably small form, wavering in the now dim, bronze light the angel gave off—Raeni with outstretched arms . . .

Embracing the creature.

Bryony froze at the base of the ratlines. Her feet had touched the rail and she was about to run for help, but she could not believe her eyes. She was not hallucinating at all—she couldn't be. She was completely lucid as she watched the creature bend over her commodore, caress her, and kiss her mouth with its own hideous mouth.

How many cities had that mouth devoured?

Bryony felt sick. Her heart beat too fast. Her limbs trembled with untapped adrenaline. She couldn't focus. She watched, unbelieving, as Raeni and the angel held each other, swayed, and kissed again.

How was this happening? Did Andrew know? Was he going for the white flare right now? But he was nowhere to be seen. He must have gone below, but why? Was Raeni a traitor or a prisoner of this beast? How could she caress it like that? If Bryony hadn't been paralyzed with fear, she might have retched at the sight.

The angel brought its second pair of wings around the commodore, and she was completely hidden in its embrace.

Bryony ducked down in the shadow of the bulwarks and crossed the main deck to the captain's quarters. Slowly, silently, she slipped inside. Michael was asleep, but Bryony didn't hesitate to wake him this time. She shook him violently, and when he shot up, she covered his mouth with her hand.

He stared, wide eyed and horrified. He pulled her hand down and whispered, "What is this?"

Bryony caught her breath and leaned in close. "An angel," she hissed. "An angel on the quarterdeck."

Michael mouthed, *What?*

"And no one's fired the white flare."

Michael's brow furrowed a moment. "What did this angel look like?"

"It's still there." She was frantic. "It has the commodore."

"Seraphim or cherubim?"

Why wasn't he listening? "Does it matter? It's an angel!"

"Bryony . . ."

"Okay, fine. Not ophanim. I'm sure of that. It had like . . . faces."

"How many wings?"

She could not see how this mattered. "Four. Listen, it's up there now. It has the commodore."

"So it's a cherub. And you say other crew saw this angel and did not fire the white flare?"

"Yes! Andrew saw it." Her heart was pounding. How did he not hear her heart pounding? How was he so calm?

"Thank god." Michael sighed and leaned back. He sounded relieved. *Relieved!* And a little annoyed to have been woken. "It's probably just Daniel then."

"*Daniel?*" She tried to physically shake the confusion from her head and failed. "Who the hell is Daniel?"

"Bryony." He took her shaking hands in his and stilled them. "Daniel is an informant. He works with the armada. He won't hurt us."

"He won't . . . He won't . . . What?" She couldn't fathom a friendly angel. She couldn't forget that mouth, that terrible, insatiable mouth.

"He's harmless."

A little well of anger bubbled up in her, and she hissed, "There is no such thing as a harmless angel. Every one of them . . . Every one . . ." She couldn't finish. She couldn't think of any word that matched the horror she felt when she thought of the angel that devoured the little town on the horizon.

"I know this might be hard for you to hear," Michael said, still holding her hands in his. "But not all the angels participated in the massacre. A few even fought against it. Daniel was one of them, and now he's working with us."

Working with us. Bryony tugged her hands away. "So we're just trusting angels now?"

"Not all of them. But we need powerful allies if we're going to fight powerful enemies."

Bryony's shoulders dropped, and her arms went limp. She couldn't believe it. Everything she thought she knew about the armada . . . "So we're just trusting angels now," she repeated. "Unbelievable. We're trusting angels." She began to pace, and her tone grew more sarcastic. "That's fine. That's normal. We're just trusting them now for no reason, and apparently, we're making out with them on the quarterdeck too. That seems normal."

Michael caught her wrist. "What did you say?"

Bryony pulled it away. She was tired of repeating herself. "I told you. He has the commodore. Or she has him. I can't even tell anymore. But they were all over each other—like lovers. Which I'm sure is fine now because we trust angels, right?"

Rage did not belong on Michael's face. Anger was out of place in his voice. But Bryony saw it, and she heard it when he said, "No, it is not fine."

Not a second later, he was on his feet. He strode to the door, his footfalls heavy and furious. He threw it open, and she heard it hit the bulkhead hard. He did not close the door behind him, and Bryony watched it swing with the motion of the ship as Michael's footsteps ascended the stairs to the quarterdeck.

His voice came again, a little more distant, a little more angry. "No!" he shouted. "This is not happening! You are not doing this!"

Bryony edged her way toward the door, and she heard a departure like the wind on the sea. The angel Daniel was gone, leaving Michael and the commodore alone together.

Raeni's voice matched Michael's for passion. "How *dare* you come out 'ere and give me orders."

"There are rules, Raeni, boundaries you do not cross. You know better than this. Daniel knows better than this!"

"I am your commodore! I make di rules! I draw di boundaries!" Raeni was so furious Bryony half expected to hear her draw her machete. But Michael was bigger and stronger, and even though he was a pacifist, Bryony had no doubt about his ability to defend himself.

"No, you don't," he said. "Not these boundaries. These were drawn in the days of Enoch, and you both know better than to cross them."

Bryony backed against the open door and breathed shallow to listen.

Raeni softened but only a little. "Those boundaries were for child-bearing, yeah? That's di crime. That's di sin. But yuh know me, Michael. Yuh know me before I was captain, before I was even Raeni. Yuh were there for my transition. Yuh know I could no more carry a child than you could."

"That's not the point," Michael said. "You'll become the excuse. Others will tell your story and use it to justify their own. You have no idea how angels respond to any hint that they could couple with women again."

"Oh, so yuh sayin' di real problem 'ere is Daniel and I setting a bad example for di other children. Now I 'ave to live my life as though everyone is watching and imitating me, a dat?" Her accent grew thick and heavy in her temper, and she slipped into a language Bryony struggled to understand. "Mi refuse! Mi live my own life di way mi waan tuh! If dem waan tuh imitate mi, a fi dem mistake!"

Michael breathed deep, dousing his own temper. "You won't even consider the consequences?"

"Wah consequence, Michael? Mi naw have no child by him. If yuh only worry 'bout di lesson others will learn, go lecture *dem*. Lef mi alone!" She paused. "Or procreation a jus di excuse? Is taboo yuh real worry? A dat, yeah? Taaaboooo." She drew the word out long and angry. "Fine! Mi a di queen a taboo. Mi shame tree dead. At least I know who I am! Yuh may be content tuh live yuh life alone and unloved, but nuh mi." Her voice cracked, but she quickly took control of it. "Daniel loves me fah who I am, and I intend tuh let 'im. We will not let yuh self-hatred dictate what we do wid we life."

"That's not what this is." Michael's voice was quiet now, subdued compared to Raeni's.

"No? Seems awfully familiar, yeah? Isn't dat what yuh 'fraid of—passing on yuh tainted genes? So yuh won't even allow yuhself fi love. Fine. Go live yuh pitiful life alone. Mi nuh bizniz. Yuh cyaan consign mi tuh yuh hell. Stop! Trying!"

Bryony heard footsteps and quickly ducked back inside, but the footsteps stopped and Raeni spoke again, her voice now calm and measured. "And, Michael, never speak to me 'bout dis again. I don't care who yuh are. I'm not afraid of yuh."

The footsteps continued down the stairs, and soon, Bryony saw Raeni's shape walking away across the main deck. The commodore did not look back.

Bryony ran to her bunk, ashamed somehow. She was afraid Michael would scold her for getting him involved in this mess, but he didn't. Of course he didn't. He slowly made his way back inside and closed the door behind him. His silence was eerie, and Bryony hugged her pillow in response. He did not speak a word to her but walked across the room, dropped onto his own bunk, and rolled away from her.

Then Bryony heard a sound she had not imagined she would ever hear in her lifetime. In the dark, the same giant who had so intimidated her the day he first rose up before her drew one long, trembling breath and buried his face in his bedding. He wept. After all the abuse and isolation the flagship navigator of the Black Armada had endured, it was this that finally broke him.

CHAPTER TWENTY-FOUR

The darkness was kind to Bryony. She felt small and useless. But she remembered how Michael had comforted her when she'd broken in front of him, and she'd be damned if she wasn't going to find the strength to be there for him too. She tiptoed across the captain's quarters until she stood between the table and his bunk. And with one tentative touch, she roused him. He sat up, hastily rubbing his eyes with his sleeves.

"Michael?" she whispered.

He turned to her in the dark, and she saw the silhouette of him against the row of back windows. It reminded her of the day she'd first met him, only this time he wasn't happily reading one of his romances. This time he was heartbroken.

"What is it?" he asked. His effort to hide the tremor in his voice was obvious.

For a moment, Bryony thought it would be better to preserve his dignity and pretend she hadn't noticed his tears. But no, she would not let cowardice get the better of her. Because he had pulled her into his arms, and he had created a safe place for her to hide. She girded her courage and spoke to him. "It's my turn this time." She stepped in and opened her arms to him.

The change in him was instantaneous.

Though he sat on his bunk and she stood before him, he was still a little taller. He bent himself to her and accepted her embrace. He let his forehead come to rest on her shoulder, and she drew her fingers through his hair. It was thick and soft the whole way through, from the dense roots to the gently curled ends. She was certain she'd never felt anything so soft in her life. She wondered briefly if he'd been taking the same saltwater showers she had.

She muttered, "What shampoo do you use?"

And he burst out laughing.

That was all it took. His tears were gone, and he lifted his head again. "I'll share it with you."

She reached back and felt her own ponytail. The salt film was still there, stiffening and thickening each dark strand. "It's crazy. Mine doesn't even compare."

He reached out and touched her hair, though she knew he didn't need to. He'd already run his fingers through it that night on the forecastle, and she was suddenly embarrassed at the state it must have been in. He let his hand come to rest on the back of her neck a moment before withdrawing it again. "I'm sure it's just one of the few ways in which I'm genetically lucky, as opposed to . . ." He gestured to the rest of his body.

Bryony backed away and leaned against the table opposite him. She braced herself with her hands and frowned in thought. Raeni was right about one thing. Michael had sentenced himself to a lifetime of loneliness. But why? If the idea of solitude grieved him so much, why did he insist upon it? She decided to take advantage of the levity. "Is that really why you're celibate? Genetics? Was Raeni telling the truth?"

"So you did hear all that." His expression fell. She regretted her question, but he answered it anyway. "It would be, for lack of a stronger word, irresponsible of me to produce offspring with my particular . . . issues."

His gigantism? That didn't seem right. Perhaps he didn't know. "But your condition won't necessarily be passed down. And on the slim chance it is, it's treatable. We just need more doctors, and the armada is working on that, isn't it? Even you could be treated one day. In fact . . ." She paused, unsure how much she should promise him. "I'm pretty sure I could treat you if you wanted me to." She was thinking of her healing sword, but she didn't dare say it.

Michael sat across from her, stunned beyond speech.

Bryony felt the urge to explain. "Of course, you don't have to be treated if you don't want to, but your continued growth will likely shorten your life. The growth could be stopped. You would just stay the way you are now. You could live a normal life, relatively. And if children with your condition are treated early on—"

"Bryony." He stopped her, and she bit her tongue. Part of her was mortified, but she wanted to help him so badly. He didn't deserve to spend the rest of his life alone.

Without a word, Michael stood and reached over her head to light the lamp behind her. Its soft glow finally illuminated his expression. Then he drew the curtains and sat back down. She was grateful for the light. Now she could see whether the information she shared helped or hurt him. He leaned back into the curtains and crossed his arms. Bryony narrowed her eyes at the position he took. He didn't seem excited or dejected. He didn't give anything away.

But she'd already begun her journey down this path, and she intended to finish what she started. "It's a surgery. I've been reading about it. They used to perform it on people like you before the massacre."

"People like me," he echoed.

"Yes. Giants." She was frustrated. He wasn't hearing her. Surely, this information would be good news. He could stop his growth and live his life like anyone else. He didn't have to fear for himself or any offspring. "I mean gigantism wasn't always the life sentence people think it is. It's usually caused by a benign brain tumor." She tapped the side of her skull. "It's over-stimulating your pituitary gland, causing it to produce too much growth hormone. If you remove or weaken the tumor, your growth could stop."

His mouth dropped open, and he let his arms fall to his sides. She waited for a reaction she could interpret one way or the other, but what she got from him was the saddest smile she'd ever seen. "You think I have a tumor." He laughed, and that, too, was a miserable sound. "You think I have a *tumor*. My god, I could kiss you."

Bryony didn't know what to make of his reaction, but she wasn't ready to give up. "It's the most likely cause. It's rare for your condition to be caused by anything else."

"My *condition*." Michael planted his elbows on his knees, dropped his head into his hands, and groaned. "I thought you were just curious."

The ship listed, and Bryony had to tighten her grip on the edge of the table. This was not going the way she thought it would. She had imagined Michael grinning, hugging her, thanking her, his life forever altered for the better. He could stop worrying, stop isolating himself. He could just live. The crew would see the change in him and welcome him into their odd, little family. He wouldn't have to be alone anymore.

She felt her chin wobble and stifled her own childish disappointment. "Did I do something wrong?"

"No." Michael lifted his head and shook it in earnest. "No, you didn't. I just misunderstood. I thought you were curious, but you were studying to help me. You thought you were going to help me." He laughed another disconsolate laugh.

Bryony glared at him. "Don't underestimate me."

"I'm not. I swear I'm not." He took a deep breath, and Bryony recognized it as preparation. He was about to say something extraordinarily hard. He spoke slowly. "It's just, if you really wanted to learn about me, you were reading the wrong book."

"What book should I have read then?" She threw her hands up, frustrated and confused.

"Let me write some down for you." Michael stood and opened a drawer in the little desk on the starboard side of the cabin. He took out a notebook and pen, and returned to his place on the bunk. Gloomily, he wrote. "These should give you a place to start." When he handed the notebook to Bryony, she was almost afraid to look down.

She read. "*Genesis? Enoch? Numbers?* And what is *The Book of Giants?*"

"*The Book of Giants* might be more difficult to find. Only fragments survived, but we might have something on the Dead Sea Scrolls that discusses it at length. I believe you'll find the others among the religious texts in the cargo hold."

Somewhere in the back of her mind, Bryony heard Andrew's voice saying, *There are things about him you still don't know.* And Chuy had warned her too. Michael had a secret. He was not normal. He was not one of them. He was something else instead. She gulped and clutched the notebook. When she spoke again, her voice was thin and dry. "I don't understand."

"I'll give you a word to look out for. That should make it easier. Here." He placed the pen in her hand and closed her fingers around it. For a moment, he held her hand in both of his like it was the last time he would be allowed to touch her. "Are you ready?" he asked, but Bryony couldn't be sure whether he was asking her or himself. He began to spell it for her. "N-E-P-H . . ." He hesitated, and Bryony wrote down the first part before she forgot it. He swallowed a lump in his throat, and when he finished the word for her, it sounded like he had given up entirely. "I-L-I-M."

Bryony stared at the word she'd just written. The suffix jumped out at her. She'd seen it before—I and M—at the ends of other words she knew, words like *seraphim*, *cherubim*, and *ophanim*. She dropped the notebook and pen and tried to back away from Michael, but the table blocked her path.

"You . . ." She was hyperventilating. She could feel her world grow narrow. "You're an angel?"

"Only half of one." Michael looked pathetic. "My father was an angel."

This . . . This was his secret? This was his condition? An angel! Suddenly, she understood everything—the way the crew avoided him, the way they didn't include him in their everyday lives, why no one wanted to room with him, why some of them even hated him. She herself could barely stand to look at him now.

Try not to judge us too harshly, Andrew had said. He'd been right. She had misjudged them all. They didn't avoid Michael because he was a giant, or a pacifist, or a celibate. They avoided him because he was half angel.

And that mouth—that beautiful, expressive mouth with its broad and dimpled smile—belonged to an angel's child. She pictured the ophan devouring an entire town before her eyes, its mouth a great black hole in the fiery wheel of its body. It was monstrous. They all were. They were everything Bryony had learned to hate and fear. They were her nightmares incarnate.

Michael's entire body was shaking now. His eyes betrayed the shame and grief he must have felt. "Say something," he whispered.

But Bryony did not know what to say. The fact that she had yet to bolt from the room was something she was still coming to grips with. She felt tears roll down her face, though she hadn't known she'd been crying. She knew nothing other than pure, animal fear.

He begged her. "Please, Bryony."

"Angels killed my family." She repeated the refrain that had gotten her into the Black Armada in the first place.

Michael slumped and stilled. He wasn't shaking anymore. Grim acceptance seemed to have weighted down every other emotion he was capable of feeling. "I'll understand if you want to find other sleeping arrangements."

There is no such thing as a harmless angel, Bryony reminded herself. But wasn't that what godhunters believed about gods? Wasn't that exactly the sentiment Bryony wanted to fight against? Didn't she hope to prove she was a benevolent god, a harmless god, a god who didn't have to die because she was willing to learn to be better? Michael had never harmed her. In fact, she had never seen him harm anyone. Why should she not give angels the same benefit of the doubt that she herself hoped to receive from the godhunter? Maybe there was such a thing as a good angel.

Change the world instead.

Bryony bent down and picked up the notebook and pen before it could roll away from her. "If I were to find these books and read them, what would they tell me about the"—she paused to read the word again—"nephilim?"

Michael looked up, something like confusion mixed with hope in his expression. She resumed her place against the table and waited until he was over his shock enough to speak.

He cleared his throat a few too many times before he began. "They are . . . *We* are the hybrid children of angels and women. In the days of Enoch, a host of two hundred angels came to prove they could manage life on this planet better than humans. They were wrong, of course. But they saw women in the flesh for the first time and fell head over heels, I suppose." He shrugged. "I don't know how else to put it. Angels crave after women. They all do. And it's only women they want, no matter what shape they take. No one really knows why, not even the angels. This angelic host—we call them watchers now—took human wives and had children with them."

Bryony held eye contact with Michael, though it took enormous effort to do so. "So you're the child of a watcher?"

"Not me, no." He pinched his lips between his teeth as he considered how to proceed. "The first nephilim and their offspring were notoriously violent and destructive. At least, that's what the stories say. So the watchers were punished—bound and forced to watch as their own children killed each other. All the angels, when they saw what became of the watchers and the miserable fates of their children, vowed never to couple with women again. And most have been true to that vow, with some notable exceptions. My father is one. So, apparently, is Daniel."

Michael sneered when he mentioned his father, and Bryony held her tongue about it. There was real hatred there. She disliked the look of it on his face.

"The nephilim,"—he frowned whenever he said the word, like it hurt him to speak it—"went extinct, and they should have stayed that way. I should not exist."

"But why?" Bryony found herself desperate to know. "What's so bad about you?"

"My *condition*, as you put it, does not end well. I age slowly, but with every year I age, I continue to grow. I'm only half mortal, so while I *will* grow old, I won't die naturally. My kind used to take poison or drown themselves if no one murdered them before their lives became unbearable. You know the story of David and Goliath, don't you? Well, from our perspective, David just saved Goliath the trouble."

Michael studied Bryony's expression like it held all the secrets of the universe and he could not read them. He went on. "It doesn't end there. After we die, we become what you call demons. We're neither of heaven nor of earth, forever stretched between two worlds. I've read that our ghosts, when not enslaved, continually fling themselves against the gates of heaven, only to fall back to earth in a never-ending, hellish cycle. Our own nature condemns us, and we can do nothing to change it. There's no salvation in store, no treatment, no hope. That question was already asked and answered in the days of Enoch."

Bryony ran her finger along the spine of the notebook Michael had handed her. So he would grow taller until he died, and he would age until he died—until he took his own life. And then he would become a demon, lost and tormented to the end of time. That was his condition. It wasn't medical at all. It wasn't a disease or a tumor, and there really was nothing Bryony could do for him, not even with the healing sword.

"Okay." She frowned. "That explains . . . a lot. You don't want your children to share your fate."

"And they won't if I don't have any." He smiled again, but there was no dimple to be found, and Bryony hated its absence.

"And you won't even allow yourself to—I don't know—go on a date, just in case?"

"Neither nephilim nor angels are capable of loving in halves, my father in particular. It's not just about procreation. That's what Raeni doesn't understand. Love makes us into monsters. Asmodeus himself killed seven innocent men over the love of one girl, and he was already a ghost by that time."

"Asmodeus." The name rang a bell. "Who is that?"

"A nephil, the son of a watcher. They call him the demon king, though he famously spent years enslaved to King Solomon. They say by the time he died, he stood so tall one wing touched heaven and the other dragged upon the earth. I'm sure that's somewhat of an exaggeration . . . I hope."

But Bryony clung to the entirely wrong detail. "Wings?"

"Some of us have them. They're quite flashy." Michael's smile was less mournful now. He was warming to the conversation. She had not run from him. That alone seemed to give him some hope, and hope looked magnificent on him. "But as you can probably predict, Raeni is in for an unpleasant surprise should she ever attempt to break it off with Daniel. I did try to tell her."

Over the course of their conversation, Bryony's heart had begun to slow. Her palms were less sweaty, and she stopped hyperventilating. Somehow, he was still Michael, angel or no. And once again, she began to feel a twinge of righteous indignation on his behalf. "So you spend all your spare time reading love stories, and you can never have one of your own?"

He coughed to stifle an awkward laugh. "That's about the shape of it. Ah, Bryony, if only you knew how much I wish it was just a tumor."

CHAPTER TWENTY-FIVE

B ryony sat beside Michael on the edge of his long bunk, the row of midnight curtains at her back, and felt a puff of pride. She should have been terrified. She should have run screaming, but she'd seen a cherub and had not panicked . . . much. And now she sat beside a half angel, and she wasn't even worried. He would not harm her. He was just Michael.

She glanced down to see his hand grip the edge of the mattress, and she slid her own hand closer. Then she lifted her little finger and rested it atop his.

He looked down at her.

"Is this still okay?" she asked.

"Yes."

She laid her hand over the back of his and interlaced their fingers. "And a hug is still okay?"

He nodded.

She thought a moment. Then his situation was not so dire. He could have some kind of companionship. "So you don't have to be totally alone."

He knit his brow. "What do you mean?"

"You just have to find a partner you trust."

"Bryony . . ." His tone was a partial admonishment, but she also saw the way he smiled at the thought.

His smile encouraged her to push on. "What about a kiss? You said earlier you could kiss me, and I know it's just a thing people say, but now I'm wondering, could you? Would a kiss be okay?"

He shook his head, frowning.

"Oh." Bryony sighed. She turned his hand around and examined his palm as though it were not at all attached to the person watching her. She wanted so badly to lean down and plant a kiss on the palm of his hand. "What if it wasn't on your mouth? I heard there are parts of the world where people kiss each other just as a greeting. Here and here." She touched both of her cheeks. "Would that be okay?"

"If I met someone in those parts of the world, and they wanted to greet me that way, it would be okay." His fingers relaxed in her hand, but he did not take his eyes off the place where his skin met hers.

"But it wouldn't be okay where we are?" she asked.

"No, not here."

"That seems weird to me." His shin was so close to her knee. She resisted the urge to scoot nearer to him and rest her leg against his. Her own body, it seemed, did not care that he was part monster. "So if it was you and I, and we were in France, let's say, and you wanted to greet me—"

He sighed heavily. "Bryony, what are you trying to do here?"

"I'm trying to figure out where you've drawn your lines and why. Maybe you could have a chaste romance if it was with someone you trusted. So just as a greeting, if we were in France, a kiss on the cheek would be okay?"

"But we are not in France."

"If we were, though?"

"No." Michael frowned. "It wouldn't be a good idea."

"But you just said—"

"Let me clarify." He held up a hand. "It would not be a good idea if the person I was greeting was you."

She dropped his other hand. "So just . . . not me." Anger crept up from her stomach and colored her voice. "You would trust literally anyone other than me." She felt like slamming a door, but she didn't have one handy.

"That's not what I mean." He turned to her, his eyes struggling to read her.

"What do you mean then?"

"It isn't *you* I don't trust." He looked away. "It wouldn't be a good idea with you because . . ." Every muscle in his face tensed and then relaxed. He had lost the game Bryony didn't even realize they were playing, and she could clearly see the moment of his total and complete surrender. "Because I seem to have . . ." He closed his eyes. "Somewhere along the way . . . At some point . . . I seem to have fallen in love with you." He added, "Just a little," as though that could somehow temper his confession.

"Oh," she muttered, too shocked to say more. This was an unexpected complication, but it shouldn't have been. The way he looked at her every time he held her hand. The way he talked to her. It wasn't that he didn't trust her to respect his boundaries. He didn't trust himself to respect them with her. She'd thought there might be a chance he was attracted to her—maybe he'd developed a crush like she had—but apparently, it was love. He knew it, and he'd already told her, *Neither nephilim nor angels are capable of loving in halves . . .* She began to see where he was coming from. "When?" she asked.

He looked up from straightening his sleeves. "What?" That clearly wasn't the question he was expecting.

But Bryony's head was swimming. How long had he loved her? How many of his little kindnesses meant something so much more? She'd never been loved like that before, so of course she hadn't recognized it. "When did you fall in love with me?"

He took a deep breath and massaged his brow. "I suppose it was when you first surprised me by asking what I was reading. And again when you wanted to eat breakfast with me." He turned his eyes to her, and she felt the weight behind his confession. "And again when you found out the sun was a star." He smiled at the memory. "After I dove for the anchor and you were angry on my behalf. And on watch when you accidentally held my hand. And during the squall." He looked down at his lap. "And again when you tried to talk me into a kiss, and instead somehow, you got me to admit that I loved you."

Bryony was stunned speechless.

Michael's voice was small and quiet. "So you see why it wouldn't be a good idea with you, even as a greeting."

She bit her lower lip in thought. "That is a problem," she said. "Because I also seem to have, somewhere along the way, fallen in love with you." She added, "Just a little," to keep things manageable.

The shock on his face was something to see, but his question was different from hers. "Why?"

She shrugged. "I think at first it was your smile. And then it was everything else."

The corners of his mouth drew up and immediately down again as he tried to smother the very expression that had gotten him into this mess in the first place. "I see. The commodore has a lot to answer for, it turns out."

"I don't think it would have made any difference if she'd assigned me another bunk." Bryony stood and began to pace the cabin. "You're beautiful, and you're kind, and I was bound to notice you eventually."

Michael went completely red in the cheeks, and the sight of him blushing over her compliment was all the motivation Bryony needed to say what she'd been wanting to say all along.

"What if Raeni was right, though? What if you're being unnecessarily strict with yourself?" She stood across from him again and leaned back on the table, hands on her hips in fierce determination. "Think about it for a second. If you found someone who would never ask you to have a child with them, who would never ask you to kill seven innocent men." She laughed at the absurdity of the idea that Michael could kill anyone.

"If you found someone who promised to be exactly as discreet as you needed for as long as you needed, then what would your problem be?"

He sat straight and tall and still. He was thinking, really thinking about it. Bryony could hardly believe it. "My only problem then would be the strength of my attachment, I suppose."

"Why?"

"When angels and their offspring fall in love, there's rarely a happy ending. Obsession, jealousy, single-minded devotion. Every angel was built for worship—that's what they excel at—but romance is different. Romance is a relationship of equals, and angels can't handle it. It drives them to madness."

Bryony wrinkled her nose. "But there's no reason to believe that'll be what happens to you. I mean so far you've been perfectly sensible."

He chuckled darkly. "So far."

"Okay. So how do you prevent an angel from going mad with love?" She couldn't help rolling her eyes at that. It seemed so incredibly unlikely that Michael, of all people, would lose his mind over anyone let alone her.

His expression was dead serious. "You limit the depth of the relationship."

"So we just keep things . . . shallow?"

"Casual," he corrected.

"I see." She chewed her cheek in thought. "And that's what you've been trying to do with me?"

He nodded.

"And a kiss on the cheek isn't casual."

Michael smiled his broad, beautiful smile. "Not if it's you."

"That's hardly fair." She crossed her arms and pouted. "That's where my favorite part of your smile is."

"Your favorite part?" He was confused but still smiling, so Bryony stepped in and traced the dimple on the left side of his mouth.

"There," she said. "It creases when you smile. I like it."

She let her hand drop, but he caught it before she could return to her place at the table. With his other hand he touched the part of his cheek she had just traced. "Here?" he asked.

She nodded. Her heart pounded in her chest. She'd never been so bold as this. She was afraid she might have taken things too far, made a fool of herself, or even embarrassed him.

But Michael just tilted his head down to her and said, "Okay."

"I'm sorry?"

"It's okay." He pointed to his cheek again. "Just as a greeting."

She tried not to scream for unadulterated joy. *This is happening. Unbelievable.* Her heart, her lungs, her limbs all shared the same sensation of far too much life.

She stepped between his legs, let her knees come to rest on the mattress, and kissed the place on his cheek that creased when he smiled. His face was hot from blushing, almost uncomfortably so. She lingered as his hands came to rest on her shoulders. He trembled when he touched her.

She pulled back, hating every second of her retreat, and looked him in the eyes. They were full of worry, but something else too. "Was that not casual enough?" she asked.

"Oh, Bryony." He smiled a fleeting smile and shook his head. "It's too late for that. It's been too late for a long time." He took one hand from her shoulders and let his index finger come to rest on her lips. For a moment, she didn't understand what he was doing. And then she did.

He was asking permission.

She whispered, "It's okay." And he kissed her.

He sat on his bunk, and she stood on her toes, and he kissed her and kissed her. She leaned closer. He closed his eyes. He brought both hands to her back and pulled her gently, earnestly toward him. She laid her palms flat against his chest like she had in the squall, but this time she did not push away. She drank in his racing heart, the rise and fall of every fevered breath he took.

Michael's kisses were surprisingly tender. Bryony had expected a hard and eager mouth, but his wasn't. Instead, he expressed the intensity of his desire with his hands. He dragged one hand down her back and let his middle finger trace the entire length of her spine. He touched her differently than she'd been taught to expect of a man. He seemed to linger on her bones—her hips, her shoulder blades, her wrists—and pass over her softer curves with a gentleness that made her shiver. Nothing in her life had prepared her for the way Michael explored the shape of her.

He slid back on his bunk, and Bryony followed him, walking on her knees to keep her height. He rested against the curtains. She straddled his leg, and he supported her while she kissed his throat and memorized the topography of his body with her hands. The way he responded to her touch made it undeniably clear that his celibacy was never about a lack of desire. Each long, deep breath he drew was a deliberate measure of restraint, and every time he exhaled, Bryony felt him waver.

Then, just for a moment, he held her back. He gripped her upper arms and caught his breath. His stare was intense and needy, and she loved it. "So what do we do now?" he asked. He was lost, utterly.

Bryony reached past his shoulders and curled her fingers into the ends of his hair. "We trust each other."

That must have been the right answer because he sat up, hugged her, and kissed the place where her neck met her collarbone over and over. He crept closer to her shoulder with each kiss, and she unbuttoned her blouse partway to bare it for him. She slid her hands under his shirt and around his waist to caress the small of his back. His skin was smooth and exceptionally warm. She wondered briefly whether it was the angel in him that made him grow hotter by degrees each time she touched him but pushed the thought aside. She focused, instead, on finding the places he liked to be touched best, and she sent him every wish, every dream she ever had through the tips of her fingers.

He paused again to catch his breath, to cool the space between them. "I love you." His mouth was still close enough that she could feel the hum of the words on her skin.

"Just a little." She amended it for him.

He shook his head. "That was a lie. Didn't I warn you? Nephilim can't love in halves."

"Good," she said, "because I lied, too, when I said *just a little.*"

He worried at a lock of her hair, winding it between his fingers. "This will end badly."

"No, it won't. Don't say that." She kissed his mouth again so he could not say more. In a short space of time, his body had become so familiar to her. The way he moved, the way he wanted her. The shape of him and the heat of him. He was happy, laughing in disbelief between each deluge of affection. Because of her, he was happy, and she intended to protect the hope she saw in him for as long as she could. He would not be alone again. He would not hate or doubt himself. She would love him enough, believe in him enough for both of them.

But no amount of bliss can last forever, and long after Bryony had lost all sense of how much time had passed, she heard a bell ring on the quarterdeck above.

Michael sat bolt upright at the sound. "The watch!" He lifted her off his lap like she weighed nothing and set her down on the bunk beside him. "I'm late for the watch."

It was midnight, and they'd both forgotten his terrible, early morning watch. He quickly tucked in his shirt and ran his hands through his hair.

"The commodore should expect you to be late after all the things she said to you," Bryony reminded him. "They won't be suspicious."

"I am never late," he said, pulling his coat over his shoulders.

"I'll join you," Bryony offered.

He turned to her and appeared to consider it. "We can't let them know." He was so worried it pained her.

"I swear to keep my hands off you." She grinned. "Mostly."

"Okay," he breathed. He stood over her, hesitating, and stared down with a look that was pure hunger. Then he said, "Just one more," and lifted her into his arms. He supported the backs of her thighs with one arm and kissed her again like it was the last chance he would get. "I love you. I love you." He couldn't stop saying it. "So much. Please don't ever go."

"I won't." She laughed, only a little troubled by his intensity. "I love you too. We'll make this work. You'll see. It'll be good."

He let her slide down until her feet touched the floor, and he took a deep, calming breath. "It'll be good," he repeated. "Yes." Then he opened the door and strode out into the night.

Chapter Twenty-Six

While Michael joined the watch, Bryony thought to get him coffee. It was, after all, partly her fault he was late. And she remembered he had gotten it for her, despite the obvious challenge it posed to him.

Rose was still in the galley, smoking a long tobacco pipe. "Coffee, eh?" She grabbed the makings and handed them to Bryony. "Michael likes it strong with cream."

"I know." Bryony grinned at her and filled the kettle. Every few seconds, her thoughts wandered back to the captain's quarters, where his hand had traced the curve of her spine, where he had pulled her in and kissed her with that beautiful, expressive mouth. She could still feel the heat of his touch and blushed at the memory.

Rose, unfortunately, noticed. "Oooh, you've been with your man, haven't you? Did you finally confess to him?"

She meant Chuy of course. Bryony nodded, still thinking of Michael. Why correct her when she would only ridicule the truth?

"So it went well, I assume?"

"Yes." It felt good to share, even if the story was one character off. It felt like friendship. She leaned in and whispered, "He kissed me."

"A win!" Rose bit her pipe and held out her hand for a high five. Bryony obliged her. "Do share. How was it? Was he shy? I always thought that boy would be a shy one."

Bryony poured grounds into the coffee press, eyeballed it, and then added more. "He was shy at first."

Rose leaned her elbows on the countertop and readied herself for a story.

"Uh . . ." Bryony thought about how much to share as she poured the now steaming water into the press. She didn't want to disappoint, but at the same time, she loved that there were things only she and Michael knew. "He was gentler than I expected, but still . . ." She laughed, more than a little self-conscious about the color creeping into her face. "He's good with his hands."

"My, my." Rose took a long puff off her pipe. "And when do you plan to see him again?"

Bryony smiled. "Soon." She poured two coffees and added cream to Michael's and sugar to her own. "But we're trying to keep it quiet for now."

Rose winked. "Just between us then." How long that would last, Bryony could only hazard a guess.

She carried the coffee to Michael, who sat against the rail, deep in thought. His entire body, expression and posture, changed the instant he saw her. He smiled when he took the cup from her, and she recognized that smile as the one he had given her—just her and no one else—time and again since the day he met her. Now she understood how he'd loved her and how the smile she adored was the only way he'd been able to tell her.

She leaned back against the bulwarks and sipped her coffee while he lifted his lantern on cue. Then he joined her, and in the narrow space between them, Michael took her hand. He drew his thumb over the bones of her wrist and the back of her hand like he was playing a delicate musical instrument. She cradled her coffee to her chest to keep from throwing herself into his arms.

"Temptress," she hissed at him.

He chuckled but continued stroking her hand.

Bryony found it increasingly difficult to casually sip her coffee without at least leaning her head against his arm. But when she heard footsteps approach, she was grateful for her own fortitude. She tried to pull her hand away, but Michael held her fast. She set her coffee on the rail and leaned forward to glance around him and see who belonged to the footsteps. She needn't have bothered, though. She would know the sound of those boots anywhere.

It was the commodore.

Oh god, it was the commodore. Bryony looked to Michael, failing to understand why he wouldn't let go of her. He just squared his shoulders and intertwined his fingers with hers.

Raeni stood before them, crossed her arms, and frowned. "Michael, about earlier. I stand by everything I said to you, but . . ." She sighed. "I might have gone a little easier."

"No, Commodore," Michael said, and Raeni narrowed her eyes at him. "You were right, and I was wrong." He squeezed Bryony's hand. "I was wrong about everything."

That was when Raeni finally looked down. Her eyes grew wide when she saw the way Michael held Bryony's hand. Bryony had no idea what to expect from her. For some reason, Michael trusted his commodore and wanted to tell her the truth, and Bryony didn't understand it. But then she herself had been desperate to share something with Rose, so maybe he was feeling the same.

"I knew it," Raeni growled. Then, grinning, "I knew it! I knew you'd crack, Michael, you bastard! I knew you would eventually." Raeni held out her hand to Bryony, and Bryony took it automatically. "I just want to shake the hand of the woman who managed to melt the coldest heart in the Black Armada. Well done, medic!" She turned back to Michael whose grip communicated to Bryony exactly how terrifying this was for him. "You know the crew will never let you hear the end of it."

"Which is why I'm hoping for discretion," Michael said, lowering his voice.

"Of course." Raeni could not stop grinning. She'd won, and she knew it. "And now you'll get off my back about Daniel?"

"I would not have the right to criticize."

Raeni cackled. "I'll look forward to our double date then."

Bryony knew the commodore was only kidding, but she couldn't help scowling at the thought of such close proximity to an angel. She'd managed to overcome her fear where Michael was concerned primarily because he had been wronged by the angels too, in his own way. But Daniel was another story, and his many faces repulsed her.

Raeni leaned in and took hold of Bryony's chin. "Don't you go breaking his heart now." Then she stood back and addressed them both. "And no babies. There's no more room." She pointed back and forth between them and then lingered on Bryony. "I'm sure you know how to prevent such a catastrophe, medic. I am not nearly as certain that he does, if you catch my drift." She rolled her eyes. "Celibacy, indeed."

Bryony nodded, even as she made a mental note to grab all the books on human sexuality and reproduction she'd passed over in the cargo hold.

Michael massaged his brow and groaned.

The commodore was like an overexcited mother, laughing and scolding in turns. "Let me know when you're ready to go live. Until then . . ." She shrugged.

"Until then, everyone thinks I'm dating Chuy," Bryony said, certain it would get around to the commodore eventually.

"Ha!" Raeni laughed again. "Rose's doing, no doubt, lord love her. Is Chuy aware of his pretend affair with you?"

Bryony nodded.

"Good. It'll get everyone off his back too. These people are relentless, I tell you, bored out of their minds. Well, they were always going to pair the new recruit with someone. You're lucky it was Chuy." She chuckled. "So is he." She lifted both her arms high in what looked like an exhilarating stretch and yawned. "Well, mi aff tuh bed. You children behave now." As she marched away, Bryony heard one last triumphant, "I knew it!"

Michael sank to the deck and rested his head on his knees. "I do not have *the coldest heart in the Black Armada.*"

"She had to get a jibe in somehow." Bryony stood beside him and let her hand come to rest on the back of his head. "Don't take it too seriously. You aren't cold just because you're celibate. You made a choice you felt was the right one, and you stuck with it." She quickly added, "And that doesn't have to change with me if you don't want it to," realizing he might have needed to hear it from her. "We'll figure all this out together, just us. We'll take our time."

"You"—Michael took her hand from his head and pressed it to his cheek—"are exactly what angels *should* have been."

The midnight-to-four watch was unreasonably pleasant. Michael and Bryony sipped coffee and watched the bioluminescence, which had returned even brighter than it was before. "We're heading south," Michael said. "So we'll be seeing a lot more of it."

They spotted several falling stars too. It was like the sky and sea had conspired to put on a show just for them. Once, when Bryony pointed out a particularly bright falling star, Michael spoke under his breath. "They say those are the souls of the nephilim falling back to earth after hurling themselves at the gates of Heaven."

Bryony sulked. "Don't ruin falling stars for me."

He laughed. "Really, they're meteors—huge chunks of rock from space, burning up in Earth's atmosphere."

"That's much better."

As the night wore on, Bryony began to fade. She slumped against the bulwarks and dozed off repeatedly before jerking awake again.

"You don't have to stay." Michael crouched down beside her. "Go on to bed. I'll be there soon. Just a couple hours." He helped her to her feet and then looked around to see if anyone was watching. When he determined the coast was clear, he bent down to kiss her forehead. "I love you," he whispered.

"You don't have to keep saying it." She smiled up at him.

"Yes, I do. I waited too long, and I have to make up for it now."

She laughed and shrugged. "Your rules." Then she yawned and left him.

The captain's quarters were dark and quiet. Bryony thought of all the times she had gone to sleep alone in her own little alcove while Michael was out on watch. Now it felt wrong. The room was lonely without him.

She crossed the floor to his bunk and crawled over it to open the curtains. A little moonlight shone in and drew long shadows over his rumpled bedclothes. She gathered them to her face, breathed in his scent, and then gave in and lay down among them. *Just for a little while*, she told herself. *Just to feel him close, one more time.* But she stayed. She gazed out the windows at the trail of bioluminescence swirling behind *Dragonfly* and fell asleep with her head on his pillows and her arms full of his blankets.

She woke to a touch and turned to find a pair of long legs in soft, hand-sewn sleepwear standing before her. Both her feet hung off the edge of the bunk. She was sprawled diagonally across the mattress, and she had gathered all the blankets in her arms, leaving none for cover or warmth. Somehow, she'd managed to take up the entirety of the giant's bed with her own little body. She quickly pulled her arms and legs in and started to sit up. "Sorry," she muttered.

"You don't have to move if you don't want to." Michael stood over her, his hair still damp from a shower. He wore a towel draped over his shoulders but no shirt, which Bryony completely failed to disregard. "I don't mind," he assured her, grinning at her notice.

She lay back down, and he climbed over her to stretch lengthwise against the windows. He faced her, and she curled into him. Then he reached out and caressed her cheek with the backs of his fingers. The gentleness, the warmth, the quiet sea and swaying ship was so much like *home*, Bryony could hardly recall her own farmhouse. Was this what it felt like to wake up beside someone you loved, knowing they were there to stay?

"We should get some sleep," Michael said.

Bryony nodded. "Especially you."

"I don't want to close my eyes." He tucked her hair behind her ear. "When I wake, will all this have been a dream? It feels like a dream. It can't be real. I just keep waiting for the bottom to drop out."

He traced the line of her lips with his thumb. Then he slid closer and kissed her. His kiss was heavy, hungry, uneasy. His hand moved to her waist, her hips. The tips of his fingers were five points of pressure on her skin. He rolled into her, hovered over her, brought his mouth to the hinge of her jaw and her throat and the dip of her shoulders. The pressure from his fingers increased, his kisses intensified, and his skin grew hot with need.

But behind every touch thrummed the combined frequencies of urgency and fear. Bryony squeezed his arms and stilled him. "Breathe a minute," she said, and he did. "I'm not going anywhere."

He let his head fall to her chest and lingered there, as though listening for her heart. "The commodore was right about one thing," he murmured. "I have no idea what I'm doing."

Bryony laughed. "You could have fooled me."

He blushed so deeply she thought she could feel it through her shirt. "That's not what I mean." He lingered a moment and then forced himself to withdraw. "You mentioned a chaste romance before. I thought that could be a good place to start, but I . . . I mean what does that look like to you?"

"I'm not sure." She shrugged. "I've never had one before."

The flicker of an expression crossed his face, and it was one she hadn't yet seen on him. "So you usually prefer to move more quickly than this," he said.

She propped herself up on an elbow and studied him. "What do you mean?"

"In your . . . previous relationships." The words seemed hard for him to say.

"Michael. Are you feeling jealous?"

"Only if you loved them." He clenched his jaw a moment. "And if . . . If this is not enough for you . . ."

So that was the expression she had seen—a wavering mix of insecurity and jealousy. She could tell he was fighting it but failing. And she hated to see him squirm, so she put a stop to the misunderstanding. "I meant that I'd never had a real relationship before this, chaste or otherwise."

His relief was palpable. "Neither have I. It feels like deep diving, what we're doing—like I know the last breath I took isn't enough, but I can't stop sinking." He sat up, and Bryony followed him. "I'm terrified, and you're telling me I can breathe. All I have to do is breathe. I want to believe you, but how can it be true when everything I know and every fiber of my body is telling me I'll drown?"

"Okay." Bryony sat cross-legged and studied the giant sitting opposite her. She'd never seen him so distressed. "This is what you warned me about when you said nephilim couldn't love in halves, right? It doesn't even start small, does it? It's all of a sudden, and it's overwhelming."

He hesitated, ashamed, but eventually nodded. "I'm sorry."

She put both her hands up to quiet him. "No, it's all right. It's your nature. We just have to figure out what you need to feel safe. We have to find you a scuba mask," she concluded, proud she was able to complete his metaphor.

"But you must be so tired. I should have let you sleep." He reached out and held her hand, stroking her wrist like he had before, and she realized his little fixations were all part of the only way he knew how to love.

"I'll live." She crawled closer to him and let him enfold her in his long arms. In the dark, they leaned back alongside the windows together. Bryony looked out and saw a ribbon of purple separating the sea from the sky. Dawn. "Let's start with the illness and then see if we can think of a cure. First, tell me how an angel goes mad with love."

Chapter Twenty-Seven

"The best example I can think of is my father," Michael said.

Bryony sat between his legs and leaned back against him. He toyed with her hair absentmindedly. In the row of windows beside them, the sun slowly emerged from the horizon.

She was surprised how quickly they'd both become comfortable with intimacy. Only days ago, his body was a boundary she dared not come near. He was so breakable, such a carefully balanced person. She realized she'd been afraid to get too close to him, to learn too much, to change him. Now he was changing. She'd broken through his boundaries and taken hold of his heart, and his world shifted under his feet like an earthquake. All it took was a kiss on the cheek. He hadn't been wrong about that.

"My father worshiped the Ancient of Days like most angels, but in him, worship . . . mutated. He let romance creep in—a love of equals—and with it came jealousy, obsession, anguish. It's so absurd if you think about it. My father fell in love with a god he'd neither seen nor heard. Two kinds of love coexisted in the same heart for the same being, and . . . Well, they're diametrically opposed, aren't they? The dissonance broke him. It ripped a hole in him, and he's spent every day of his existence since trying to fill the emptiness, consequences be damned."

"And what were the consequences?" Bryony tipped her head back to see him looking down at her.

"Me." He smiled sadly. "I'm far from the only child he sired, but I'm most certainly the youngest and the only one left alive. For millennia, he seemed to have conquered his addiction, but I guess the massacre shook him to his core. So he found another woman to worship, love, and devour—my mother."

Bryony turned to face him. His jaw was clenched, and he gripped his own knees with whitened knuckles. He was angry. She tried to keep him on track. "Do you think there's any way he could have prevented his madness?"

"Possibly"—Michael shrugged his broad shoulders and, oblivious, utterly crushed Bryony's heart—"had he not been fool enough to fall in love with a god."

She did her best to hide her hurt, painfully aware that her expression was in the spotlight of the rising sun. "But the nephilim and other angels—you said the same thing happens to them. Did they all fall in love with their god too?"

"No. They let worship slip into their romantic relationships. Different path, same results."

"So, as long as you don't mix the two, you'll be fine?" Bryony began to hope again.

"That's the theory."

She sat up on her knees and clapped her hands. "That's great! That's so easy. Just don't put me on a pedestal, and we'll be good. I'm far from perfect. Look." She held out a lock of her hair. "Not clean. Not soft. I could really use a shower. And my eyesight is not amazing. I should probably get glasses. I'm not nearly as fit as I ought to be." She thought a moment. "Oh, and this." She pulled off her sock and stretched a foot out in front of him. "Those two toes look weird, don't they? I think there's something wrong with them, but my father said I got them from my mother. Still maybe there was something wrong with her toes, and I just inherited it."

Michael laughed at her, but she didn't mind as long as he was laughing. He took her hands and kissed them. "It was a good thought, but I don't think it'll work like that. Those aren't flaws to me. They're just . . . you."

"That's not fair." She folded her arms and knit her brow. "I'm nothing special. How can I convince you of that?" She stared at the beams above them. "No one should worship me," she said, and she meant it. "I'm just a person, a nobody, a kid who used to get mad when her little brother trampled the pretend horse stables she made out of twigs. I threw tantrums. I refused to bathe. I stuffed an old T-shirt in my underwear when I got my first period and then tried to burn it in the yard. How could you worship that?"

She was blushing furiously, but she forced herself to go on. "I accidentally killed a baby bird once while trying to save it, and that devastated me for years. When I was fifteen, I tried to seduce a boy in class by reading him terrible poetry I'd written. It was so bad, Michael, you should have seen it. He laughed at me, and I never wrote poetry again. I can't sing to save my life. I like horror stories and skeletons and dried up old mummies, and I used to look at pictures of dead things for fun. I hung out in graveyards and talked to tombstones because I was ridiculously lonely and scared, and somehow it made me feel better to think of the ghosts as my friends. Imaginary friends! I had imaginary friends when I was twenty. How could anyone worship that? But that's who I am, so we should be fine, right?"

She stopped ranting because of the way he smiled down at her. His dimple was deep, and his eyes were laughing. He loved her so much, and every stupid detail she told him about her life only made him love her more. He reached out and pulled her into his arms, and she gave up. He kissed the top of her head and said, "That settles it. We have a plan in place. Every time I begin to think too highly of you, you'll simply have to write a poem and sing it to me."

"You think you're kidding, but I'm telling you it was bad."

He squeezed her tighter and then let her go. "I don't think I'll become my father with you. But if this works . . . If we work, it'll be because of you—because of how honest and grounded you are—and not because I'm not infected with his disease."

Honest. She cringed at the word.

By now, the sun flooded through the windows in the captain's quarters, painting everything gold and orange. Michael's reaction to her confessions made Bryony feel braver. She wanted to know everything about the man who loved her, and one question had been shadowing her thoughts since he'd first told her he was half angel. "You said curiosity was okay, so . . . can I ask you a personal question?"

He nodded.

"Was your father an archangel?"

Michael hesitated. The subject was clearly a tender one. "He was."

"Were you . . ." Bryony took a deep breath, swallowed her fear, and asked, "Were you named for him?"

Michael went still, his face expressionless and cold. Had she finally found the line and crossed it? When he spoke, his voice was so subdued, she actually believed she had. "You have to understand," he said, "how much I hated my father. I hated him for giving life to a soul that could only ever be damned. I wanted to hurt him, even as a child. I chose my own name. That was the only power I had over him. So I named myself after the angel who conquered and rose above him to remind him of what he'd lost."

Bryony whispered the name *Michael* before she realized she'd done it. So it was true he was named for the archangel Michael, but Michael was not his father. Then it began to dawn on her. "But Michael is usually depicted conquering . . ." Suddenly, her mouth went dry. Her heart began to race, and she had to remind herself to breathe. "The angel he conquered was . . ." She couldn't speak it. She wanted Michael to cut in, correct her, tell her she'd gotten it all wrong. She'd misunderstood—she had to have. "Surely you don't mean . . ." She forced a nervous laugh. She still couldn't say it aloud, but she didn't have to.

Michael said it for her. "Samael."

She caught her breath and scrambled away from him. The Angel of Death. The Angel of Death was his father. Samael, the first satan, original wielder of the death sword. Bryony gasped and stood and backed away from Michael. She could no longer hide her horror. Her mind clambered for any sliver of hope to grab hold of. "But you didn't know him," she said, desperate. "You never met him, right?"

"I met him once." His expression was anger mixed with pure heartache. "But he didn't know me, and he left me with nothing." So there was still hope. He did not have the death sword after all. He couldn't have it. But then Michael spoke again. "The only thing I ever got from my father I had to steal from him," and all hope was stamped out.

Bryony covered her mouth with her hands.

Michael stared at her, confusion creeping into his expression. Disbelief and panic flickered in his eyes. Then Bryony saw him begin to understand, and his whole demeanor shifted into a terrible acceptance. His shoulders slumped. He bowed his head. He had been waiting for the bottom to drop out, and this was it, his expectations met. Bryony had not surprised him in the end. She would be a scar on his life just like everyone else. She tripped over her own feet trying to back away from him. She couldn't see through her horror, through the tears welling in her eyes.

Without meaning to, Bryony Moss had succeeded in her first objective. She had found the godhunter.

She backed into the door and struggled to find the handle. She couldn't take her eyes off the giant sitting across the room, watching her in agony. The corners of his beautiful mouth turned down, and she saw the light in him extinguish. Her thoughts kept running over one roaring, persistent detail. She had not found the sword. He still had it. She'd been a fool to stop looking. And though Michael's silence was devastating, Bryony had no words of comfort. *This will end badly*, he had said, and he'd been right. He'd been right all along.

She flung the door open and ran from him, but there was nowhere to go, no corner to hide in. She was trapped on a ship with a real godhunter, and he had the death sword in his possession. All she had was a healing sword, and everyone knew you could not heal death. Death was death. It was neither illness nor injury. It was the end of both those things, and the end of everything else too.

Bryony clawed her way up the ratlines without a harness. She spoke to no one, made eye contact with no one. She just climbed to the only place she felt safe. Then she curled into a ball, wrapped her arms around the mast, and wept. Nothing would be okay ever again. She would either have to kill the only man she'd ever loved or let him kill her. She saw no other options. How could she change the world when the one person who made her believe it possible was not who she thought him to be?

A godhunter is cold.

A godhunter is merciless.

A godhunter is methodical and efficient.

That was the wisdom she'd been taught, even as a child. It was uncontested truth. And now she'd given the godhunter, the son of the Angel of Death, a broken heart to add to the list. Bryony was as good as dead.

Above her, she heard the caw of a crow, and she glanced up to see Shakespeare sitting atop the highest yard, looking down on her with one beady eye. She didn't greet him. She put her head back down and wallowed. Shakespeare flew down to her.

The ticking of his claws as he paced the foretop reminded her of home, of putting her hair up at her mother's old vanity while Shakespeare yammered on about dinner. He always tried to comfort her when her spirits were down, and despite the way she'd treated him the last time they spoke, the bird continued the tradition.

"You should know I'm still looking for the godhunter on your behalf. And I decided you're right." He sighed. "You shouldn't have to hurt anyone until you have no other option. So I'll just keep looking, and you can take your time, enjoy the trip, soak up some rays."

She groaned.

Shakespeare kept talking. "Anyway, it should please you to know I'm reasonably sure it's no one on *Papillon*. I've been in every nook and cranny on that boat, and there's not a death sword to be found. Next I'm heading over to another little cutter called *Locust*—as if *Black Armada* wasn't ominous enough. I'm going to go through every ship, one at a time. No more targeted searches for me. Those haven't been helpful at all, have they? So cheer up. It's probably not even someone you know."

Bryony lifted her head and Shakespeare hopped back in shock. "What's got you all red and puffy?" he asked.

She let a thin whine escape her throat and dropped her head again. "You can stop looking for the godhunter, Shakespeare."

"Don't be silly," he said. "It'll still be helpful to know, even if you don't plan to strike right away. We'll just get the information we need for your own safety, and then we'll sit on it." He chuckled and added, "Like an egg."

Bryony did not laugh. "You can stop looking for the godhunter because I know who it is."

The bird was quiet for a moment. Then he hopped closer and whispered, "Is it the commodore after all?"

Bryony rolled onto her back and dropped an arm over her eyes. "It's Michael."

"No!" Shakespeare sounded like Rose hearing juicy gossip for the first time. "The navigator? But I thought you already tested everything he has. Did you find the sword?"

"No." She wanted to disappear, just roll off the foretop and vanish in the air.

"Well, then don't be so sure." Shakespeare picked at her hair reassuringly. "You were so certain it was the captain of *Papillon*, and you turned out to be wrong. Maybe you're wrong about this too."

"Michael is half angel, and his father is Samael."

The silence the crow allowed to fall said all he needed to say. A coincidence like that left no real room for doubt. When Shakespeare finally spoke, his voice was gentle and sympathetic. "I'm so sorry, Bryony. I know you were fond of him."

She sat up and rubbed her tears away with the sleeve of her blouse. "It's so much worse than that. You were right, stupid bird. You're always right about everything. I got attached." Fresh tears rolled down her cheeks, and she couldn't rub them away fast enough. "I love him."

"Oh, no." Shakespeare hopped onto her shoulder and cuddled up under her chin. "You poor thing."

"It gets worse." She continued to dry her face with every part of her shirt and realized she would have to change it before breakfast. "He loves me too. And I made him believe we could be happy, and now I have to break his heart and murder him with his own sword." She wailed, and Shakespeare did his best to comfort her with his little bird body.

"That is pretty bad," he said. "But there may be a silver lining."

"What could possibly be good about this?" she snapped, but he just hopped to her other shoulder.

"Well, does he know you're a god?"

She thought about it. "No." He didn't. Michael didn't know she was a god. Why had she even run from him? She wasn't in danger. She had panicked and behaved like an absolute fool. But the primal terror of being so close to death stole all her ability to reason.

"That's excellent." Shakespeare's voice had a tinge of glee he hadn't quite managed to disguise. "The godhunter loves and trusts you, so keep your enemy closer." He flapped his wings excitedly. "Spend more time with him, and find his sword. Use your feminine wiles. I bet you can even steal it while he's sleeping. We couldn't have asked for a better scenario."

Bryony gutted him with her eyes.

He hopped away from her. "I mean aside from all the heartbreak it'll cause, obviously. But people have their hearts broken all the time, and now you're no exception. Better to have loved and lost, eh?"

"You're terrible," she snarled. "And what if I can't kill him? What if you're right about that too? I'm too tenderhearted after all."

Shakespeare cocked his head. "Even a mouse will bite when the cat comes for it. So here's what we do. I've been lurking around the ships, listening. People talk, you know? And word is the angel that visited last night was here to alert the armada to a nearby god. The fleet is on its way to his port now. They say it's just a forgiveness deity, so the god himself shouldn't be a danger to you. All you have to do is join your boyfriend on the hunt."

Bryony recoiled in horror. "That is perhaps the worst idea you've ever had!"

"It's not, though. It's perfect. You'll see the sword for yourself, and you'll see the godhunter use it. Keep your eyes open no matter what, and you'll find the strength you need to survive. After that, he still won't know what you are, but you will know what he is."

Bryony dug her fingernails into the foretop and swallowed the bile in her throat. "Fine," she said between her teeth. "I'll join him on the hunt." And she climbed down the ratlines, sick, exhausted, and alone.

Chapter Twenty-Eight

The sea was abnormally calm, which troubled Bryony because there wasn't much for her to do on deck. She wanted to stay out of the captain's quarters. Shakespeare may have wanted her to use *feminine wiles*, but she was not ready to confront Michael again. It wasn't that she was frightened or worried about his anger, but she could not bear to see the pure defeat on his face. And she wasn't confident she had the strength to undo the damage she'd done.

At breakfast, she went to the mess hall expecting to eat with the rest of the crew, but Rose pushed a tray with two plates at her. "Go spend some time with your man, will you? He's been moping all morning, and he could use some company." For a moment, Bryony panicked. If Rose knew, everyone knew. But then she saw the relatively normal amount of food on both plates and realized Rose meant for her to eat with Chuy. Her *man*.

The ship's hospital desperately needed more natural light, better furniture, and more attractive décor. Bryony felt a twinge of guilt that Chuy had spent so much time in such an uninspiring room "recuperating" from an injury he no longer had. So she told him he was well enough to return to *Papillon* at their next anchorage. Then she sat with him and ate while they discussed all the goings on aboard *Dragonfly*. It was good to talk to him again. He usually managed to make her feel better about things, but he must have noticed his charms weren't quite hitting the mark on this particular occasion.

He swallowed a mouthful of fried potatoes and said, "What's eating at you today?"

Bryony started to say, *Nothing,* but thought better of it. If she had one friend in the Black Armada, it was Chuy, and right now, she needed to talk to a friend. "This morning, I learned Michael's secret." She heaved an uncomfortable sigh. "And I was not as understanding as I should have been."

"Oh? What secret is that?" Chuy waited, grinning. He wasn't going to be tricked into giving anything away.

"I know his father was an angel." Bryony gripped her fork a little tighter. "And I know which angel it was, too."

Chuy nodded. "Right."

"I panicked. I don't know what came over me. I just . . . lost it. I mean why did it have to be the Angel of Death? Any other angel, I think I could have handled." She thought and corrected herself. "Except an ophan. I don't think I'll ever be totally okay with them."

"Then you're in luck. Samael is famously one of the seraphim." Chuy smiled, stabbed at his egg, and broke the yolk. "Most people don't even count him among the worst anymore, you know. None of his host took part in the massacre."

"Samael is a massacre all on his own."

He swirled the rest of his potatoes in his egg yolk. "Fair point." He took another bite and washed it down with tea. "But I feel for Michael. Ya can't help who your father is."

Bryony sipped her glass of orange juice—she was not about to drink more coffee after the night she'd had—and countered, "You can help what you steal from your father, though."

"Ah, so you know pretty much everything then." He paused, clearly considering whether to say more or keep it to himself. "Did he tell you why he stole his father's sword?"

She shrugged. "To kill gods?"

"Nah." He laughed. "That's just an added perk."

Bryony took a quick gulp of orange juice to hide the scowl that crossed her face.

Chuy sat up a little straighter. "Look, I'm gonna tell you something I probably shouldn't because I trust you, and I like Michael. I don't want him to lose his only friend aboard *Dragonfly* just 'cause she thinks he's as bloodthirsty as his father."

She started to protest but caught herself. Any contradiction would have been a lie.

Chuy went on. "See, the Angel of Death's sword is the only weapon in the known universe that can annihilate an immortal soul. Sure, it kills off the flesh if that's what it's aimed at. But it can also kill things that won't die any other way."

"Souls?" Bryony frowned at the thought.

"Damned souls." Chuy looked at her meaningfully.

And suddenly, she understood. Michael had taken the sword in order to annihilate his own immortal soul when he died. It wasn't spite or bloodlust. It was despair. It was, to him, the only way out. Bryony let her fork fall to her plate. The mere idea of another bite made her feel sick. The stress of the last twenty-four hours was finally honing in on her stomach. "Why does he use it to kill gods then?"

Now it was Chuy's turn to shrug. "Why not? They're pests."

"Even the harmless ones?" Bryony was finding it harder and harder to hear so much hatred from her friend.

Chuy spoke with a mouth full of bread. "No such thing." He swallowed. "They're as bad as angels. They keep people ignorant and superstitious. They make entire congregations dependent on them. No one ever learns anything. No one can fend for themselves. Whole communities lose their sense of self, their culture, all so gods can eat up worship like it's too much frosting on a cake. Gluttons, that's what they are. They take more than their share, and they give nothing in return."

Nothing? Bryony clenched her teeth. She gave something, didn't she? She gave healing to her congregation. But what if Chuy wasn't all wrong? What if she had somehow kept her congregation from seeking out new information? What if she'd made them dependent on her and then just left them to fend for themselves? Was it possible she was not a harmless god at all? Was it possible she was even malignant to her community?

"I'm sorry, Chuy." She stood quickly and left her half-eaten breakfast beside him. "I'm suddenly not feeling so well."

She needed fresh air. She went topside and dragged herself to the quarterdeck where Dara was at the helm, lazily reading a book. Bryony slumped against the rail and groaned.

"You okay?" Dara asked.

Bryony waved a hand dismissively. "Way too much coffee last night. Way too much stress this morning. Not nearly enough sleep. But I'll be fine." She hoped it was true even as she said it.

"You want to take the wheel for a while?"

Bryony straightened up. "Really?"

"Sure." Dara smiled a crooked smile. "I find it meditative. It works wonders on the nerves. And it'll still your stomach if you're feeling a touch nauseated. Here." She offered Bryony the wheel and showed her how to hold her heading. "Try not to stare at the compass too much. It'll drive you crazy and make your headache worse. Just find something on the horizon and lock on to it. Check the compass every once in a while to make sure you're still on track. Got it?"

Bryony nodded enthusiastically. The enormous, wooden wheel seemed incredibly powerful to her. She felt the sea tug at the ship's rudder as though they were locked in a struggle—she and the primordial deep—and with the wheel in her hands, she actually stood a chance. "This is so cool," she said over her shoulder.

Dara stood behind her, leaning against the bulwarks, ankles crossed and a book in hand. "Perfect. It'll free me up to get more reading in." She grinned.

They took turns at the helm over the next few hours. On her off hour, Bryony read a little of Dara's book—a biography about someone named

Nikola Tesla—and what parts of it she could understand fascinated her. She supposed they were all lucky the angels had allowed them to keep electricity. For now.

The day wore on beautifully, and Bryony nearly forgot her most recent troubles. Her head cleared and her stomach calmed. The sea breeze was good for her spirits. So by the time the commodore came marching up the stairs, Bryony was almost ready for her.

"Medic!" Raeni shouted, pointing an accusatory finger at Bryony. "What did you do to my navigator?"

Dara looked up with mild indifference, and then went back to her book. Bryony only wished she had that kind of composure. Raeni drew her machete and continued toward Bryony, who stood behind the wheel, willing it to make itself into a better shield.

"You broke him," Raeni said, wagging her machete. "He missed the noon reading, and he never misses the noon reading." Now she was close enough to lower her voice to a menacing hiss. "I told yuh not to break his heart."

Bryony protested. "I didn't do anything."

"The hell you didn't." Now Raeni was less than three feet away and could easily close the distance between them with her weapon alone. "I need my navigator functional, especially now. And you are going to go right now and fix what you broke."

Fix the godhunter? Bryony tried not to shiver at the thought. The godhunter needed to be functional, especially now, for the hunt he was due to go on. Soon. She gritted her teeth and left the helm. "Fine, I'll talk to him. But he's being oversensitive," she lied.

Raeni rolled her eyes. "Michael? Oversensitive? I don't think so. Just take care of it, medic. And, Dara, back to your post."

Dara stood at attention. "Yes, Commodore."

"Yes, Commodore," Bryony echoed, her voice subdued. And she headed down to the captain's quarters.

Michael *was* broken. There was simply no other way to describe it. Bryony had expected to find him curled up in bed, buried in blankets, sulking. But he wasn't. He was, in fact, in the exact same position he had been in when she'd left him. She squinted, taking in the room, the daylight, and the statue of a man sitting at the back. He hadn't moved. He hadn't even moved.

Slowly, his eyes turned toward her, and she saw his chest rise and fall at a slightly quicker pace, so she knew he noticed her. This was bad, but she didn't want to let on how bad she thought it was or how unusual. She worried that he'd been right about his inability to handle the ups and downs of a real romance. But if she scolded or shamed him about this breakdown, wouldn't that just make things worse? Wouldn't he feel even more alone, more abnormal, more isolated?

She got a shirt from his locker and brought it to him. Numbly, he took it from her and slipped his arms through the sleeves. She sat next to him, noting the difference in their size, their strength. If he took hold of her now, she would not be able to escape, no matter how much kicking and biting she did. Seated beside him, the top of her head didn't even rise above his shoulder. The godhunter. Oh, why did it have to be him?

What could she say to him? *I'm sorry I ran from you. It's just that I'm a god, so finding out you were the godhunter really threw me for a loop, you know?*

He doesn't know, she reminded herself. She cleared her throat and tried to speak above a hoarse whisper several times before she actually managed it. "That was not the right reaction on my part," she said. "And I'm sorry."

He continued to stare straight ahead. "You're afraid of me," he muttered.

True. So how does one counter the truth? "It's not what you think."

He let his head drop. "Please don't lie to me."

"I won't." She turned to him but hesitated to take his hand. "I won't lie." She was determined to find a truth she could share with him, somewhere deep inside her, deeper than her godhood, deeper than her immortality, as deep as the person she used to be. Formative.

"I have a . . . complicated relationship with death." Something true. "It fascinated me most of my life. It was peace, an end to all the worry and fear. I watched my brother suffer for weeks before he died, and his death was the end of his suffering." She paused to pull herself together. Just thinking about her little brother still cut her too deep. The relief she'd felt when she looked down at his face—still and quiet at last—and the shame that followed that relief was something she could never quite manage to forget, no matter how hard she tried.

"But then he was gone." She wound a twisted piece of her shirt too tightly around her thumb and watched the blood drain from it. "He was just gone, and I didn't have a brother anymore. That was when I understood, on a visceral level, the way death takes. It takes suffering and pain, but it takes everything else too. All the joy, the warmth. The music of his little voice was gone, and in its place was emptiness, a blank space where my brother used to be. And then I started to forget him."

Michael finally looked down at her, so much hurt in his eyes. "I'm so sorry, Bryony."

She acknowledged his sympathy with a nod. "It hit hardest when I thought I saw him out of the corner of my eye. Or I heard his voice calling my name, and I had to remind myself that, no, it isn't him. He's gone—really, truly gone."

Michael's hand twitched, and she knew he wanted to hold her but didn't dare. "I know the way death takes," he said. "And, yes, my father is the same. His appetite is never sated, and he's taken so much from so many people, myself included. I'm afraid of him too. So I think I understand why you ran." He turned his body toward her, and the flicker of hope in his eyes made her want to cry. "But I am not my father. I'm not the Angel of Death."

"You just bring me one step closer." She meant one step closer to death itself rather than its angel, but she didn't say so.

His shoulders dropped, and he looked away. "So what does this mean? Are we through? Are we breaking up?"

"I don't know. I don't think so." She sighed. "I just need a little time to think." She turned to him and forced herself to look up into his black eyes. "Try to imagine what it would be like if you learned something about me that changed the way you saw me. Something big. And you had to rethink your whole relationship with me, which meant rethinking your identity, your history, and your future."

"I would need some time too." He smiled a dispirited smile and nodded. "I'll try to give you the space you need. Just . . ." His voice cracked. "I don't want to lose you. For the first time in my life, I believed I could have something real with someone real. It wasn't a dream or a fiction. It was you, and . . ." He gulped. "I love you, no matter what you decide. I can't seem to stop."

She smiled up at him.

He leaned in. Bryony thought he meant to embrace her, but she never got the chance to find out. He aborted the gesture abruptly when her body reacted in the worst possible way—she flinched. And she saw his heart break all over again.

Michael stood. He towered over her as he buttoned his shirt and smoothed out the wrinkles. "Thank you for the talk. I'm sorry I made it necessary." He was cold, angry. "Tell the commodore I no longer intend to shirk my duties." Then he gathered his instruments and left.

Chapter Twenty-Nine

S hakespeare wanted Bryony to keep Michael close in order to find and steal his sword, but Bryony wanted to keep him close for her own reasons. She just had to overcome the god in her that reacted so strongly to the hunter in him. She had to find a way to recognize him as Michael and not just the godhunter.

At some point, she realized how little sleep she'd allowed herself over the last twenty-four hours. She showered, dressed in jogging shorts and a T-shirt, and crashed in her own bunk. She slept deep, recalling no dreams or nightmares. By the time she finally woke again, it was dinner.

She ate in the mess hall but didn't participate in the crew's conversations. Instead, she spent the time remembering each kindness the godhunter had shown her over the last several days. And the memory that sang louder than all the others was that of Michael holding her after she'd betrayed Chuy. He had told her she was a good person, and when she hadn't believed him, he'd done his best to convince her. He made her believe in her own goodness. He gave that gift to her.

Maybe she just needed to do something like that for him. He was hurting, probably feeling ashamed of his lineage. He knew she was afraid of him, but she only feared the godhunter, and Michael was so much more than that. She wished she could tell him everything, but she knew it would backfire if she did. If he was hurt because she was afraid of him, she would just have to convince him she wasn't. And she would have to convince herself too.

She helped Rose clean up after dinner, played cards with her for a while, and then helped her prep for breakfast. Rose wanted to hear about her relationship with Chuy, so Bryony told her they were taking things slow.

"Good," Rose said. "Kids these days all move too fast if you ask me."

But *kids these days* had no idea how much of their lives they had left to spend together. Slow wasn't always an option. Life was short for most people, shorter than it had been in the past. Bryony didn't argue the point with Rose but quietly resolved to overcome her own trepidation. She had somehow survived her entire family, and she'd be damned if she was going to waste it on fear.

At midnight, Bryony brought coffee to Michael on the forecastle. She tried not to let her hands shake as she did. She would join him on his watch, she'd decided. Only good things had happened between them on his watches, so she felt optimistic about this one.

It didn't start well.

Michael stood at the bulwarks, looking out over the sea, deep in thought. When Bryony approached with two mugs, he didn't even acknowledge her. She assumed he was angry, so she just handed him his coffee. But he must not have noticed her at all because he started at the gesture. She jumped in turn and dropped a mug overboard. It hit the water with a splash and quickly sank into inky blackness.

"Oh!" Bryony watched after it. "That was yours. You can have mine if you want." She handed him her own coffee. It wasn't his preference, but it was something, and he took it with a weak smile.

"You don't have to stay," he said.

"I know."

The wind kicked up around them, curling the tops of each wave into gentle whitecaps. Faded bioluminescence made its presence known but did not put on the same spectacular show it had on previous nights.

Bryony had spent most of the day trying to think of what she could say to heal Michael's hurt, but nothing useful came to mind. She'd hoped that if she just built up her courage and forced herself to face him, the words would come to her. They did not, but something else did.

The way his mug had tumbled out of her hands and slipped so easily, so quickly into the depths alarmed her. In an instant, she tasted the danger just being at sea posed, even in calm waters. Here she stood on a little, floating island made of wood, at the mercy of a godhunter who didn't even have to draw his sword. He could just as easily throw her overboard, and she would be lost to the sea. If he needed to see that her trust was stronger than her fear, she knew exactly how to show him.

"I remember," she said, "after the squall, you told me I'd always be safe with you."

"Because it's true." He narrowed his eyes like a teacher who was certain his student was up to no good but had yet to work out exactly how. "Where are you going with this?"

She placed both her hands on the rail, took a deep breath, and hoisted her whole body up in one smooth movement. It was easier than she expected, and she allowed herself to feel some pride that her morning ratline regime had improved her upper-body strength significantly.

Michael reacted quickly. "What are you doing?" He set his coffee on the deck as Bryony drew one foot and then the other onto the rail. "Bryony?"

"Trusting you." She crouched and gripped the rail with her hands. "I'm not afraid." Then she told herself how unbelievably reckless this was, countered her own good sense, and rose to her feet.

Michael didn't let her get all the way to standing before his arms were around her. "What are you doing?" he repeated, louder this time. "This is not safe."

"Yes, it is." She stood more than a head higher than him now. His arms were around her waist, and she looked down at him. "It's safe because you're here. Because I'm with you, I'm not afraid. I shouldn't have let your father scare me away from you. It was wrong. *I* was wrong."

He held her tighter. "This is an overdramatic way of telling me, don't you think?"

"My mother was an actress." She shrugged and turned her face to the sky. "Drama is in the blood. And I had to prove it to you. Words were not enough." The stars shone crisp and bright. The wind tangled her hair, chilled her skin, and thrilled her to her core. She was alive. For now, she was alive, and that was all that mattered. She leaned back and let her arms dangle behind her as Michael held her. His forearms supported her back like the branches of her favorite plum tree. She stared up and imagined falling petals on her face. Falling stars all around her. She imagined falling, and it was exhilarating.

"Okay, okay." Michael pulled her in. "I believe you." He laughed, and there was no melancholy in his laugh. It had worked. "I believe you."

Bryony slipped her arms around his neck and said the words she didn't even know were sticking in her throat. "I don't want us to be through. We're just getting to know each other. I panicked like an idiot, but I refuse to give up on us so easily. If you could just . . ." Her voice quieted to a whisper. "Please don't give up on me."

"My god, Bryony, what made you think that was even on the table?"

"This morning you were angry with me, and I was sure I'd ruined everything." She crouched down until she could sit on the rail with her back to the sea. Never once did Michael let go of her.

"I was angry with Samael." He bent down to hug her tight, and she arched her back to meet him. "I couldn't blame you for feeling uneasy. I was certain you'd run the moment you found out *what* I was let alone *who*. You stayed so much longer than I thought anyone would."

"I'm still here," she said, and she was. She could hardly believe it herself. She'd gone looking to kill a godhunter and wound up falling hard for him instead.

Michael studied her face and shook his head. "You're so beautiful right now." He curled his fingers around the sides of her ribcage. His thumbs rested just below the line of her breasts, and she blushed at his touch, wondering if he even realized how intimate it was.

Darkness was on their side, so Bryony reached up to caress his cheek before slipping her hand behind his neck and drawing him close. He bent a little, and she kissed the corner of his mouth. It was gentle, sweet, and quick enough to evade the detection of anyone who might have glanced their way.

Michael didn't let it end there. He stepped closer, supported her back and shoulder with one arm like a dancer, and dipped her over the yawning sea. He leaned over her and kissed her fully, unashamedly on the mouth. They'd been lovers for years—that's what it felt like. They moved together so naturally, so easily. The way he read her body, knew her so well when he'd only just begun to explore her, astounded her. It should have been awkward and clumsy, but it wasn't—he wasn't. It was as though he'd been imagining this kiss, practicing it in his dreams for years. And maybe he had. Maybe Bryony wasn't just falling in love with someone for the first time in her life. Maybe she was making his dreams come true too.

But he was being careless, and she tapped him on the shoulder. He pulled back and cocked his head. "The crew," she whispered. "Discretion, remember?"

"Right." He sighed and brought her back to a seated position. Then he crouched down and picked up his lantern. "It's about that time anyway."

And just when Bryony was certain he couldn't possibly shock her more, he lifted the lantern, took her chin between his thumb and forefinger, and kissed her mouth again. He had put a spotlight behind them and continued as though no one else were even on the ship with them.

"What are you doing?" Bryony managed to ask between kisses.

He grinned at her. "Going live."

The following day was more of a gauntlet than Bryony had expected. Rose didn't even speak to her, which was more than a little unnerving. Once, Bryony heard her mutter under her breath, "Greedy, that's what it is." Apparently, Rose thought that she'd taken more than one lover aboard *Dragonfly*, maybe even that she was cheating on Chuy. The idea was laughable. Bryony tried to imagine herself as some kind of playgirl and couldn't keep from snickering at the thought.

She brought breakfast to Chuy and prepared herself to hear from him.

He snatched the tray from her and snarled, "How could you? I thought our relationship meant something. I thought we'd last."

Bryony laughed, relieved when she realized he was only teasing her. She sat down beside him and buttered her toast. "I thought we had an open relationship. Did we not? Oops."

He chuckled. "Figured ya might've been a bit more serious with Michael than you were letting on, but I didn't want to pry."

"It was important to him that we keep it quiet at first. I honestly had no idea he was going to just"—last night's kiss flashed through her mind, and she blushed—"do that."

"Keeping it quiet wasn't a bad instinct." Chuy stuffed a forkful of breakfast into his mouth. "He's always been dogged in his belief that no kind of angel, himself included, should ever be allowed a relationship like the one you two have gotten yourselves into. He'll get some grief for his hypocrisy." He pointed his fork at Bryony. "And you should be ready to join him in social purgatory. The crew already doesn't know what to make of ya. It's only gonna get worse from here on out."

Bryony frowned. "So what do *you* make of me?"

Chuy arched an eyebrow. "I think you're the best thing that's ever happened to Michael and maybe the best thing that ever will. Course I think you're both inviting catastrophe, but I'd be a hypocrite if I disrespected your decision to do so. And who knows?" He shrugged. "Ya might be okay. Worth the risk either way." He looked at her meaningfully, and she remembered the pendant that meant so much to him. A lover had made it and given it to him, and he seemed to subsist on that memory alone.

He lifted his glass of orange juice. "To risk."

She did the same. "To changing the world."

"Perfect." He drank to that.

Bryony quickly learned who her friends were, or rather who Michael's friends were among the crew. Those who most disliked their navigator wouldn't make eye contact with her. Even Andrew, when he passed, did not acknowledge her beyond a cursory nod. She huffed and found Dara on the quarterdeck.

"Please tell me you have something for me to do," she begged. "Rose doesn't want me in the galley, and I can't spend the entire day reading."

Dara didn't hesitate. "Sure thing. I'll give you a list of books. Find them, pack them in the small crates, and bring them up here. Does that sound doable?"

"Yeah, sure. I can do that." For that, Bryony would have to rely on her upper-body strength again, which pleased her.

Dara went for a notebook and pen while Bryony waited on the main deck. The day was windy, and *Dragonfly* clipped along at a pleasant pace. The sun was warm and high in the sky. In the distance,

Shakespeare circled one of the other boats, and Bryony was glad for his absence. She didn't want to hear him praise her for keeping her enemies close or whatever scheme he decided she had up her sleeve.

Michael crossed the deck toward the captain's quarters, having just taken his noon reading. As soon as he spotted Bryony, he changed course and headed her way. "How are you? How was breakfast? I missed you." He said it all at once and dropped to one knee to hug her. On his knee, he was only a little taller than her, so she could drape her arms over his shoulders and kiss his cheek.

"Good." She smiled. "It was good. You should know you have a friend in Chuy."

Michael cocked his head. "Chuy?"

"He's one of the few still talking to me. He wishes you well, and he's defended you every step of the way. I thought you'd like to know. If you're ever besieged by vigilantes again, he'll probably have your back."

"I'd expect nothing less of Chuy. He's always been kind, but . . ." Michael rocked back onto his heel, and she saw the hinge of his jaw work in frustration. "Are you telling me the rest of the crew is punishing you? This is not your fault."

"I mean it partly is, isn't it?" She frowned at him. "Give me a little credit at least."

He grinned, took her hand, and stroked the back of her wrist in his characteristic way. "I give you all the credit and none of the fault."

Dara approached, her notebook in hand. "Take the deal, medic. You won't get better from the likes of him." She smiled, and Bryony nearly laughed aloud in relief. Dara was teasing him—good-naturedly if Bryony read her right. As it stood, Bryony counted the commodore, Chuy, and now Dara among the crew members who would still talk to her. She honestly didn't know where Andrew stood, but she wasn't holding out much hope for him.

Michael rose and turned to Dara. "Do you know anything about why she's been ostracized? Is the crew trying to punish her because of me?"

Dara handed the notebook to Bryony. "I'm not privy to their little games, no. I'd guess it's because of you, although I'm not sure what they think they'll accomplish. If she loves you, she loves you." She was blunt. Bryony liked her more and more.

"I'm sorry," Michael said to Bryony. "I didn't know they'd behave this way."

Dara rolled her eyes at him. "Of course you did. If you didn't, you're unforgivably naïve. You're half angel, Michael, so they have to half hate you. And now they have to half hate her too. It's the nature of bigotry."

"It's okay," Bryony cut in. "I don't care. I'm glad we went live." She smiled to reassure him. "They can think whatever they like."

"There's a girl." Dara clapped her on the shoulder. "Don't let anyone control you, ever. Not even him." She shot a glance at Michael, and he actually shrank from it. Dara laughed like a cartoon villain. "Let's stock the boats now, shall we? We're due to make the bay tonight, and we have a god to kill."

With that, all the warmth and camaraderie Bryony had just begun to feel faded away like bioluminescence in the wake of *Dragonfly*. The hunt was less than twelve hours away.

Chapter Thirty

Bryony Moss was not a patient woman to begin with. Being made to wait for something terrible was a special kind of hell. She would have liked to nap through it, but she couldn't sleep. She tried to study, but she found it impossible to focus. She just sat on her bunk, kicking her heels against the drawers below it, picking up first one book and then another in an effort to get her mind off the coming hunt. But there was nothing for it.

Michael laid his novel face down on his mattress. "You're worried about something."

She considered denying it but thought better of it. "You're going ashore, aren't you?"

"Did Dara tell you that?" He honestly didn't know. Michael still had no idea that Bryony had identified him as the godhunter. She wanted to keep him in the dark as long as possible, but she couldn't resist one last Hail Mary.

"You're wearing shoes," she said. He was. They were dark leather, laced up, worn but fine. His shoes were reason enough for her to have guessed he intended to go ashore. He'd told her he rarely wore them for any other reason. "Please don't go."

He laughed a bewildered laugh. "Why?"

She fidgeted, wringing her bedding like a galley washcloth. "Just don't."

"I won't be long, you know. I'll be back before dawn." Now he sounded worried. *Good.*

"Please just trust me," she begged. "Don't go ashore tonight. Please stay."

He shook his head, still perplexed by her sudden, seemingly meaningless request. "I have to go ashore, Bryony. It's my job. If I don't do my job, what use am I to the armada?"

"You're the *navigator.*" She stood and paced, feeling far too keyed up to spend another second in her bunk. "That's your job. They need you to navigate and repair their sails, and you don't have to go ashore for that."

"Okay. What's this really about?" He watched her pace the room. "Please, tell me what you're afraid of so I can put you at ease."

"I don't want you to put me at ease!" She whirled on him, desperate, furious. "I want you to swear to me that you won't go ashore tonight." Oh, why couldn't she just tell him the truth?

She was tearing up, and Michael rose to approach her. "Bryony, it's just for the evening."

She grimaced. "Just for the hunt."

"Oh." He paused his approach and stared down at her. "Dara shouldn't have mentioned that to you. It was bound to make you worry. But I promise it's not what you think it is. It's not dangerous. No one is ever hurt."

Except the god. Bryony realized that Michael thought she was worried for his safety, and maybe she should have been. But a godhunter with the death sword was a thousand times more frightening than a forgiveness deity, and it wasn't Michael's safety she worried about.

"Don't go." Bryony stood as tall as she could and glared up at him with her hands on her hips. It was impossible to feel in any way imposing when she was staring at her opponent's stomach, but she tried. "If you go . . ." *If you go, I'll have to go with you and watch you murder a god. If you go, I'll know without a doubt you're a killer, I'll know what the death sword is, and I'll have no excuse not to take it and use it on you before you can kill again.* "If you go, then don't bother talking to me tomorrow . . . or maybe ever!" The Hail Mary wasn't the time to be timid.

That hurt him. She could see it in the way his mouth twitched. "I really don't understand this," he said. "But I can't abandon the rest of the crew. I promise I'll be back before dawn."

Bryony didn't understand his loyalty. The crew certainly weren't loyal to him. They only tolerated him because he was an angel-deterrent and a godhunter. It was the death sword they were loyal to, not Michael. But Bryony didn't know what more she could say without giving herself away completely. He was forcing her to follow Shakespeare's plan. She threw herself into her bunk, pulled the curtain closed, and screamed like an angry teenager.

She stayed behind her curtain until Michael left the cabin. As soon as he was gone, Bryony knotted her hair into a bun and changed into black pants, black shoes, and a black hoodie. She closed her curtain again—hopefully, Michael would assume she was still sulking or had fallen asleep—and before he returned, she slipped belowdecks and hid in the cargo hold. There she waited until most of the crew were occupied with dinner.

The ship's boats were loaded and ready to launch. Bryony easily found the one Michael would be riding in. It had comparatively less cargo to make room for his long legs. The weather, it seemed, was on her side. Summer rains were warm but still troublesome for a crew that trafficked primarily in books, so every boat was equipped with a black tarp or two to protect them. The tarp in Michael's boat covered a few empty boxes, some fuel cans, and two crates of books. Bryony crawled into the midst of the cargo, between the two crates, and pulled the black, plastic sheet over her head. She hugged her knees and made herself as small as she possibly could. Then she waited, listening to the loud patter of rain on the tarp.

The anchoring of *Dragonfly* and launch of its boats was a raucous affair. Bryony had to grip the crates on either side of her for support as her boat was carried and dropped, jolted and shifted. She heard Michael's low voice coordinating with the rest of the crew. She could tell when she was lowered by the davits, and she felt the boat rock when he stepped off the ladder and boarded with her.

This was the first time she would go ashore since she joined the Black Armada. It was a point of no return, and Bryony shivered to think that her dreaded plan was finally in motion. She closed her eyes and listened. She could feel the catch and pull of every long, powerful stroke of the oars. Michael was alone, so it would be him rowing. She could almost hear the solitude in every breath he took, and she was sure, somehow, she had worsened it. But Michael had chosen to leave her when she'd begged him not to. Maybe he didn't know how serious the situation was, but she'd hoped her fervent request would be enough and it wasn't.

Michael's rowing slowed, and the boat thumped against the dock. The armada had anchored right outside the city this time. Bryony guessed correctly that Michael would not be unloading his own boat but would leave trafficking to the rest of the crew and head immediately out on the hunt. As soon as she heard his even footsteps move away, she emerged. He'd easily beaten the other boats, and Bryony recalled the way he dove down to retrieve the ship's anchor on his own. He was much stronger than the rest of them, undeniably.

The city, called San Diego, was a jungle of high-rises and night life. She could hardly believe there was any such city in the world of the angels. The buildings made a boxy horizon against the night sky, and palm trees lined an illuminated boardwalk along the water. She turned around to see the other boats still rowing toward the docks, their occupants' backs turned to her. This was going to be easier than she'd thought. *Damn it.*

She started down the dock after Michael, occasionally ducking behind a moored boat when she thought he might look back, but he never did. She followed him through a shadowy parking lot toward the street, crouching from car to car until she was almost close enough to touch him. Then he waited under an orange streetlamp, and Bryony breathed shallow.

What was he waiting for? It didn't take long to find out. A black van with darkly tinted windows rolled up under the lamp, and the side door slid open. Michael ducked and folded himself into the back of the van. Bryony cursed. He wasn't going to be on foot after all. She couldn't believe she hadn't expected this. Of course the armada had allies on land. If it ran a successful smuggling ring, it would need third-party middlemen.

She couldn't let Michael get away. Once he was gone, he was gone, and there would be no following him after that. Now was her only chance. So she bolted toward the van, and just as Michael began to slide the door closed, Bryony called out to him.

He froze, his eyes widening in alarm. "What—" He couldn't finish. Bryony pushed past him into the van, crawled over his lap, and sat on the opposite side.

"I'm coming with you," she said. Her heart raced and her hands were shaking, but she tried not to let it show.

The driver turned around at the commotion. "Sir?"

Michael hesitated. "She's one of ours. A new medic." He glared down at her. "She must have stowed away on one of the boats."

"Do you need her taken care of?" the driver asked.

Michael gazed down at his obstinate new girlfriend. His eyes said, *How dare you?* But he shook his head at the driver. "No, I have a schedule to keep. It could be good to have her along anyway, just in case." And he closed the door.

Bryony breathed an enormous sigh of relief before she even realized she'd done it, and Michael shot daggers at her again. He had to slouch to fit in the van, with his knees high and his shoulders drawn in, especially now that Bryony took up part of the back seat with him. He looked incredibly uncomfortable. "What is this?" he asked.

"I know everything," she muttered.

He stared straight ahead. "What do you mean?"

Time to lay all the cards on the table. Well, all but one. "I know you're the godhunter." She watched for his reaction, but he gave her none. "And I know you use your father's sword to do it." That dropped his jaw.

He stared down at her, horrified. "How long have you known?"

"Since you told me who your father was." She forced herself to look him in the eyes. "Word gets around about godhunters. I knew there was one traveling with the armada. I just didn't know who it was until that morning."

He grimaced. "Samael strikes again."

The city lights flew by outside. They had entered the highway, and Bryony realized she could no longer get back to the armada without Michael. She was stuck with him. Now was the time to talk him into turning around.

"I thought you were a pacifist," she whispered so the driver wouldn't hear.

"I am." He looked down at her again and dug his fingernails into his palms. "I don't kill people."

Bryony understood the implication quite clearly. "So gods aren't people?"

"No, they aren't." His voice was firm and sure. "They gave up their humanity when they chose to encourage worship, when they gave up mortality and humility and truth."

Bryony bit her tongue. She wanted to scream at him. How could he? She had given *him* a chance, hadn't she? He admitted he was half angel, and she had given him a goddamned chance. Why couldn't he afford her the same courtesy? She wanted to tell him, to show him that she wasn't evil, that she'd just gotten mixed up in something she didn't fully understand. She tried to be good. She tried to be the best god she could be. But all she could say was, "Why did it have to be you?"

He slouched a little further in his seat to be closer to her. "It didn't have to be me. For a long time, it wasn't. The Black Armada was killing gods long before I joined it. They just had to annihilate every last worshiper to do it. This way only the god has to die."

"But why do gods have to die at all?"

"I'd expect you, of all people, to understand," he said. "Do you know why the angels allow so many gods to exist along the coast?"

She shook her head.

"Because, to angels, the sea smells like death and decay, and they don't want to come anywhere near it."

Rahab. Bryony remembered the way Raeni had spoken of the sea's dead angel, like he was more of a volatile ally than an enemy.

"Angels hate death and all it represents," Michael said. "Impermanence, evolution, chaos. They prefer to deny its existence, and that's tricky to do when you're overwhelmed by the stench of it. That's why the armada values Daniel as highly as we do. He sacrifices so much to help us, although I've recently become convinced he's doing it for other reasons entirely." He rolled his eyes.

So it wasn't just the godhunter that kept the angels from attacking the Black Armada. It was the sea, though Bryony was certain having a death sword aboard didn't hurt. It seemed angels would only brave the coast if they had no other choice. The ophan that devoured the neighboring town must have drawn the short straw.

Michael went on. "Angels allow gods because they help subdue the populations on the coast."

"That's ridiculous." Bryony scoffed. "Gods don't work for angels." But even as she spoke the words, she questioned them.

"Maybe not directly, but they help to thin the herd. Gods encourage ignorance and superstition. People who don't fall in line are often executed by fanatics. The angels don't even have to show up."

"That's not true." Bryony thought of her own sweet congregation, people who just wanted to be healed, who wanted their loved ones to live, who wanted to end the suffering around them. They would never intentionally harm anyone. "Not universally anyway. And what about this god you're going after now? I heard he was a forgiveness deity. What harm does forgiveness do?"

Michael massaged his brow. "I didn't want you involved in this."

"Well, now I'm involved."

She saw his eyes flick to the rearview mirror where the driver glanced back. "All right. You deserve to know if we're going to . . ." He shifted uneasily in his seat. This conversation was clearly not one he was prepared to have in front of an audience. He muttered, "If we're going to continue seeing each other, we shouldn't have secrets between us."

Bryony cringed. She was the liar in their relationship, and he still had no idea.

Michael cleared his throat. "There's been a rash of theft and violence in this area. Our informants have learned it's related to this god. He forgives sins, and the worse the sin, the more gratifying the forgiveness. His worshipers feel like they've been challenged to"—he paused and searched for the right word—"one-up each other, I suppose. When they're forgiven for increasingly horrific acts, they believe they've satiated their god."

"That's . . ." Bryony stared down at her hands. "Okay, that's terrible." She didn't want to be on the godhunter's side on this one. She wanted to prove there was such a thing as a harmless god, and she had thought a forgiveness deity would be the perfect way to do so. "Does he know? The god. Does he know they're doing these things in his name?"

Michael shrugged. "I can ask him. But in the end, does it really matter? He won't give up their worship—he can't—and they'll keep doing what they've always done. It's the nature of the beast. They're addicted to his forgiveness, and he's addicted to their worship."

"But addiction can be treated." She was desperate, grasping for any fraction of hope. "Can't he be helped instead of killed? Why won't you give him a chance? What if he doesn't know what his worshipers are doing? Why does he get punished for what other people do in his name?"

"Bryony, it's not a punishment. It's just an end." He turned to her and reached out to touch her. She flinched, but this time he didn't let it bother him. He cradled her face and stroked her cheek with his thumb. "It's just an end to the cycle. He'll feel no pain. I swear it."

She blinked back the tears welling in her eyes. He wouldn't listen, but she refused to cry in front of him—not again. "That's not the point."

"Isn't it?"

His hand was warm and gentle, and his touch made her feel too small. "What if he doesn't want to die?" Her voice cracked.

"Not many people do," he said. "But death comes for everyone in their time. Right now, he's outlived himself. He should have died years ago, and so many people are dying prematurely because of him."

"But if he doesn't know . . ." *Don't cry. Do not cry.* "Why can't you just *try* to help him?"

Michael bowed over her and wrapped his arms around her. "I'm sorry, Bryony. It's not easy for me either, but you have to trust me. This is better than the alternative."

She let her head settle against his chest and hated herself a little. Shakespeare was right again. She was too tenderhearted. And now she was in love with the enemy, resting in his arms, listening to his heart, enjoying the vibration of his voice against her cheek.

The van rolled to a stop, and Bryony clung to Michael harder. She didn't want to see where they were. She didn't want him to leave the van. Everything was happening too fast, and Bryony couldn't seem to slow it down let alone stop it.

Michael took a deep breath and spread the whole of his hand across her back. "I swear to you," he murmured, "he'll feel no pain, no fear. He won't even know what's coming. His death will be a good one." He let her go, opened the van door, and stepped outside. Then he ducked his head back in and said, "I love you, Bryony. Please don't forget that." He turned to the driver. "Keep her safe for me. Circle the block or something. I'll be right back."

He slid the door closed and started toward the building. It was a large church—a megachurch even—with a full, concave façade and neon lights that lit the whole thing up like a casino. Out front, she saw a blinking sign. It reminded her of the *Open* sign at Martha's Café but huge. It said, *Service in Session,* in giant pink and green letters.

The driver glanced back at Bryony and grinned. He was a middle-aged man with sandy hair and a face like a used-car salesman. "So the hunter went and got himself a girl, did he?"

Bryony frowned. Her whole body was on edge. This was not going the way she wanted it to go. This was going, instead, the way Shakespeare had warned her it would go, and no amount of reasoning or begging on her part seemed to be doing any good. "I won't let that damned bird be right," she grumbled. As soon as Michael went around the side of the building, she slid the van door open.

"Hey now," the driver said. "The hunter wants you to stay here with me."

Bryony rolled her eyes at him. "*The hunter* doesn't get to tell me what to do." And she jumped out of the van and ran toward the church before the driver could even get his seatbelt off.

CHAPTER THIRTY-ONE

B ryony was a small fish swimming against a tide of worshipers. About a third of the congregants in the arena-sized church had chosen to leave a few minutes early, presumably to avoid traffic. Music piped through the speakers in the lobby, and she heard the voice of the god, blessing all of them and wishing them a safe drive home. She finally surrendered to her own aggression and shoved her way past the double doors into the sanctuary. This was no time for courtesy.

Rows of seating sloped down toward the stage, and above her, she saw tiers and boxes. It was more like a theater than a church. All the carpets and the cushions on the seats were a luxurious, deep red. The walls were white and trimmed with gold. The sound system was impressive. Bryony was momentarily envious. All she'd ever had was a tent and a black veil.

She jogged toward the stage, not at all shy about pushing congregants out of her way as she did.

The god himself was an old man with white hair. He wore a brown suit, a white shirt, a blue tie. Everything about him looked nondescript, commonplace. He wore glasses that reflected the spotlight and made it impossible to see his eyes. His hands were spotted and twisted with arthritis—he'd become a god late in life, it seemed—and he failed to notice Bryony until she was climbing the stage right in front of him.

He looked down at her, a little put off, but he recovered quickly and included her in his act. "My daughter!" He opened his arms to welcome her. "What brings you to us this fine evening?"

Bryony straightened her hoodie and turned to see the audience behind her. Their applause unnerved her. "I need forgiveness," she said, turning back to the god.

"What sin have you committed, my daughter?" He spoke as much to the audience as he did to her.

"I, uh . . ." She looked around and saw stillness in the audience. They all waited to hear her. She had to think of something quick. She spoke into the microphone. "I have lied, Your . . . uh . . . Divine Holy Master." She wasn't sure which honorific he preferred, so she decided to go over the top.

The god smiled a sweet but ultimately condescending smile. "Oh, but that's nothing at all, my daughter. Surely it hasn't inspired the urgency with which you've approached us today. Surely your true sin is much more . . . interesting."

That left a foul taste in her mouth, and she was certain her expression reflected as much. So he *was* encouraging his congregants. What if Michael was right after all? What if this god was not redeemable? Well, Bryony was determined to try. She turned and squinted at the audience through the spotlights. "I can't tell you in front of all these people."

"Oh, that's fine, my daughter. Why don't you just whisper it into my ear? Remember, there is no judgment here, only forgiveness."

She approached him. He smelled like aftershave and musky cologne. He was well groomed, his dress shoes polished to a high shine. He barely had to bend his head to hear her confession, and Bryony realized she'd grown used to Michael. The god seemed unusually short, though he was probably an average sized man. She leaned in and whispered, "A godhunter is waiting for you backstage. He has a weapon that can kill you without touching your worshipers, and he plans to do just that as soon as you're finished here. I've come to warn you."

"Is that so?" The god smiled. "And how did you come to know this information, my daughter?"

He doubted her. She whispered to him again. "Because I came here with him. I'm on the crew of the Black Armada, but I don't think it's right, what they're doing. Please, you've got to believe me. Don't go backstage."

The god gently touched her shoulders and then raised his hands slowly into the air. She recognized his theatrics and felt momentarily ashamed of her own. "You are forgiven, my daughter. See your sin float to the heavens and fade away like smoke from a fire. Go and be clean."

The audience went wild, and the band began to play the god out. It was sappy music, Bryony thought, a lot of saxophone and acoustic guitar. She groaned and shook her head. "Look, have you got a car?" He nodded, and she gestured for him to follow her.

She led him straight down center stage and took his hand to help him descend. They left the same way she came in, which would be the last thing Michael would expect. Most gods were careful to limit contact with their congregants to keep the illusion of holiness alive. Now this one waded among them, and all their hands reached out to touch him. He grasped them in turn and blessed them again and again.

"We don't have time for this." Bryony grabbed his hand and began to run. He followed, pushing his crooked glasses back up his nose. They exited the building in a crowd of people. The van still waited outside. "Where's your car?"

The god pointed to a parking lot across the street.

"Okay, see that van? The driver works for the armada. Don't stop for him. Don't even look at him." The crowd that had slowed them down before suddenly became vital camouflage, and they managed to evade the driver's notice. Once in the parking lot, the god pointed out a white Town Car.

"Keys?" Bryony asked.

He took them out of his pocket.

"Good. Let's get out of here."

The first place the forgiveness deity drove to was his own home. He wanted to pack a bag, he said, but Bryony was suspicious of his lack of urgency. The man had money—that much was clear. His home was an opulent, white mansion on the water. She stood in his bedroom and looked out floor-to-ceiling windows at his private beach, an infinity pool, a hot tub, and several water features. She wondered if he made his fortune from tithes alone. He didn't appear to have any other work.

He had several suitcases spread out on his bed and was methodically folding his socks into thirds and lining them up like dominoes.

"So," she said, feeling a little awkward, "what do people call you when you aren't on stage? I mean what was your name before you became a god?"

"Frank." He smiled. "Frank Dolamore. Pleased to meet you." He held out a hand, and she shook it.

"Bryony Moss," she said.

"Well, I'd like to thank you for saving my life, Ms. Moss."

"Yeah, sure." She fidgeted. "No problem." But it was a problem. It was a big problem. Bryony was just beginning to realize that she would never see the crew of the Black Armada again, and if she did, they would be enemies. Michael was certainly lost to her now. And Shakespeare. She swallowed her fear and the knot in her throat. A life was more important, she told herself. A life was the most important thing, and her lost relationships did not compare in value.

"May I ask," Frank was saying, "why you were traveling with the godhunter?"

Bryony groaned and held her head in her hands. "He was my boyfriend, sort of."

"Oh my!" Frank went to a drawer and began removing several exceptionally well-folded, white T-shirts. "Won't he be angry with you for going against his wishes?"

That was just the thing. "I don't think so," she said. "He's never gotten angry with me. Not really."

"A new relationship then." He laid his T-shirts next to his socks. His packing was so slow it drove Bryony to distraction. She wanted to raid his drawers and closets, take half of what he owned, and cram it unfolded and disorganized into his many suitcases. "He will get angry with you one day. But you should know"—he pointed a rolled-up T-shirt at her—"that doesn't mean he doesn't love you."

Bryony laughed. "Did you used to be a marriage counselor or something?"

"No, but I was married fifty-five years. I think that qualifies me to give a little advice."

"Oh, wow." Bryony sat at the foot of his bed. She may as well get comfortable. "I mean congratulations."

Frank waved a dismissive hand. "Little late for that, dear. She's been dead for ages."

"I'm sorry." Bryony chewed her lip. For a moment, she'd forgotten he was a god. He was immortal. Everyone he knew and loved in his mortal life was probably long dead. Here, at last, was someone who might understand her own predicament, someone she could share her truth with. "I'm a god too."

Frank paused his packing for the first time since they'd entered the room. "Well, I'll be damned, kid. You are?"

She shrugged. "Small-town healing god. No one's heard of me really." She smiled bashfully.

He straightened his glasses. "If you don't mind my asking, what on earth are you doing with the Black Armada? And dating a godhunter no less."

"I know, right?" Bryony threw her hands up, finally able to express her frustration to someone who could come close to understanding. "I went looking for him to stop him from killing any more gods. I just didn't know he'd be so . . ." She scrunched up her entire face in thought. There wasn't one word to describe what had drawn her to Michael, why even after she learned he was half angel, even after she realized he was the godhunter, she couldn't manage to turn her heart against him.

"Poor kid." Frank reached across his bed and patted her cheek like she was his granddaughter. "You're young. It's easy to fall in love when you're young."

"Easy is an understatement. He just smiled at me—that's all it took. But he doesn't know I'm a god. What'll he do when he finds out? Kill me? I was hoping to talk him out of killing you just to prove to myself it could be done, but it didn't work. He said . . ." She hesitated. "He said your worshipers do terrible things in your name."

Frank zipped up one suitcase and began filling another. "They do terrible things, yes, but not in my name. They do terrible things because they're terrible people who need forgiveness to be better."

"I . . . I don't think that's how they see it, though?"

He zipped his second suitcase closed before it was entirely full and picked both of them up. "Let's go, kid."

Bryony looked around his room. He'd only really packed socks and underwear, and there were still several empty suitcases lying open on his enormous bed. "Are you sure you have everything you need?"

"Absolutely." He marched back outside his house with more purpose than Bryony was strictly comfortable with.

"And you're sure you have a safe place to go? You know the armada has spies and informants, yes? It shouldn't be a place you would normally go."

"I know exactly where I'm going." He opened his trunk and carefully placed both suitcases inside. Then he opened the passenger door of his Town Car for Bryony, shut her in, and joined her.

Bryony ran her fingers along the stitching in the leather passenger seat. This car was like new, a classic but well maintained. Just how long had Frank Dolamore been a god? She briefly wondered if he'd bought the car new and how many years ago that might have been. Then she compared it to Martha's rusty van. Then she missed Martha, her entire congregation, and her little farmhouse on the outskirts of town.

Maybe it was time to just go home. This whole endeavor was folly anyway. Shakespeare should have known. She'd told him she didn't want to kill anyone. He knew she was too tenderhearted for that kind of violence. Best to just see the forgiveness deity to somewhere safe and leave.

But even as she considered it, her eyes began to well with tears. On *Dragonfly*, for the first time in her life, she'd been part of something real, something meaningful. She'd made friends. There were even people who didn't like her, which had never happened when she was a god. People back home were afraid to express any kind of disapproval. She thought about how she would never see Raeni again, or Chuy, or Dara, or Rose, or Andrew . . . or Michael. She sniffed.

Frank glanced over from the driver's seat. "Take heart, dear," he said, and he smiled. Bryony looked up to see that they were exiting the highway. She recognized the area. They were headed right back to the church.

"Where are you going?" she asked, baffled.

"We'll see if your young man is still at my church, and we'll confront him."

"No!" Was he mad? "What are you thinking? He'll kill you."

Frank gave her that same condescending smile he'd given her on stage. "Forgiveness can be very powerful, dear. You'll see. Your young man just needs to experience real forgiveness."

Bryony's mouth hung open in absolute shock. She couldn't believe it. Frank was driving right back to his death. "Did you not hear me before? He's a godhunter. He has the Angel of Death's sword. He can kill you permanently, and he will."

"Oh, I'm not sure that's true." Frank pulled into the same parking lot they'd left, noting the van still waiting at the entrance. "See? Your young man is waiting for another chance."

"Oh my god! No, he's not! And he's not my *young man*. He's half monster. Look . . . He's not who you think he is!"

Frank opened his door and stepped out. Bryony followed, tugging at his arm, but he just headed for his church like she wasn't even there. "It's like Romeo and Juliet," he said, beaming. "Let's give that old story a better ending, shall we?"

"Why aren't you listening to me?" She still had his arm, and she anchored her heels on the pavement. But as old as he was, Frank was far from weak.

They made gut-wrenchingly quick progress across the street and into the church. Frank dragged Bryony like she was an insufficient anchor for an oversized vessel. He was caught up in his own tide. He kept on smiling and telling her not to worry, telling her she would soon see the real power of forgiveness. She was certain she would not be able to prevent him from marching backstage to find his own executioner. But when Frank finally pushed through the double doors of the sanctuary, Bryony saw that marching backstage wouldn't even be necessary.

Michael sat at the edge of center stage, waiting for them.

Chapter Thirty-Two

B ryony screamed, "Don't do this!" But she couldn't have said which man she was addressing. They were both on a collision course from which they refused to deviate, and neither of them knew how deeply their course affected the girl protesting it. "Why are you doing this? How are you doing this?" Now she was most certainly addressing Frank. "This is your own death, and you know it! You should be too terrified to come this close!"

Michael answered her question. "His addiction is stronger than his fear. Isn't that true, Mr. Dolamore?"

"So you're the infamous godhunter, eh?" Frank approached. Michael stood, and Bryony watched Frank's eyes grow wide when he saw just how impressive the godhunter's stature was. "Oh, my! Forgive me for asking, but how tall are you?"

"More than seven, less than eight." Michael gave his practiced answer with an even more practiced smile. "Maybe. I haven't measured in a while."

Frank gazed up at him and adjusted his glasses. "Well, that's something else, isn't it?"

"It is definitely something else." Michael reached into his coat pocket and pulled out a small, rectangular, wooden box. And from that box, he withdrew a tool Bryony had seen him use a dozen times or more. It was smaller than a pair of standard scissors, and it looked like two brass legs on a hinge. She recalled the way he would walk the device along his charts and record the measurements in his notebook. She'd never thought of the tool as sharp or ominous. She'd never really thought of it at all.

"What is that?" she asked through her teeth.

Frank answered. "Oh, those are dividers, dear. They're used in nautical navigation. That's quite a handsome pair you have there. May I see them?"

Bryony fumed. "Shut up, Frank." Why did she have to wind up protecting a god who seemed so unaccountably eager to die?

Michael smiled a polite, tight-lipped smile. "I'm afraid these are too delicate to be handled by anyone other than me, but I do appreciate the compliment, Mr. Dolamore." He sounded overly formal. Bryony hated it.

She took a deep, purposeful breath and stepped between god and hunter. "I won't let you kill him, Michael. It's wrong. Do you even know why he came back here? To help you. To save you. He wants to forgive you for hunting him. *You.*"

Frank stood behind her, laid his hands on her shoulders, and squeezed.

Michael frowned. "Of course he wants me to accept his forgiveness. He believes that would earn him the worship of a godhunter, and that's never happened before, has it, Mr. Dolamore?"

"No, it has not," Frank answered.

Michael was merciless. "It would make you the most accomplished among all the gods, wouldn't it? You would rise above the rest, maybe even rule them. They would see you as their savior, wouldn't they? A god who can turn godhunters into worshipers."

"That's hardly the point," Frank said, but Bryony could hear in the tone of his voice that he was practically salivating at the idea.

She glared up at Michael. "This is not fair."

"All right." Michael sighed and looked down at her, pained and frustrated. "For you, Bryony, I'll accept this god's forgiveness, but on one condition."

"Wonderful!" Frank clapped his hands behind Bryony, who couldn't even stand to look at him anymore. He had no idea what was going on. He was like a vending machine, consuming sin and spitting out forgiveness like it meant nothing at all. "What is your condition, my son?"

Michael did not look away from Bryony as he spoke. "I want you to tell me the greatest sin you forgave this year. I need to know that mine will be greater."

"Oh, that's easy." The glee in Frank's voice made Bryony cringe. "I heard the confession of a woman who drowned her children, and that of her lover who asked her to do it. That's hard to beat, of course, but a godhunter could surely top it."

Top it? Bryony felt her eyes fill with angry tears. Her cheeks were hot with frustration and shame. In vain, she argued, "He doesn't know what he's doing. He can still be saved. He can learn to do better."

Frank and Michael spoke in unison, both of them imagining she was referring to the other.

Frank said, "Of course he can, my daughter."

And Michael shook his head. "No, he can't."

Bryony sobbed. She'd lost, and she knew it. The forgiveness deity was not redeemable. And if this was what Michael encountered every time he met a god, he would not believe she could be saved either.

Frank said, "Now, my son, I'm ready to hear your confession." And Bryony turned to see him, his arms spread wide to receive Michael's sin.

"Bryony." Michael drew close, and Bryony couldn't help backing away from him. "I have to ask you to close your eyes."

Bryony clenched her teeth and continued to stare at him.

"Please," Michael begged her. "Please close your eyes."

"I will not." She lifted her chin to him in terrified, trembling defiance. "I will watch you do this thing."

Michael looked down at her like he might burst into tears, but he didn't. He just whispered, "I'm so sorry." And then the godhunter drew his sword.

He didn't need to move. He didn't need to lunge with the dividers or even open them. He just bowed his head, and they transformed for him. Before Bryony's eyes, the dividers lengthened, sharpened, and narrowed into a single, semi-translucent blade. It curved like a scimitar and glistened in the lights of the church. Of course he didn't use the death sword the same way Bryony used her ring. It was Samael's sword, she realized, in the hands of his son, and it would honor the lineage of its wielder.

The hunter's body, too, transformed with the sword. In the beginning, the change was subtle, a mirage rising off his skin like heat on a desert highway. It wavered and elongated, growing far above his head and broader than his shoulders, swelling and shrinking with every breath he took. Within seconds, the mirage burst into blinding light, and Bryony saw it for what it was. An angel—a terrible, serpentine angel. It coiled around the hunter's body . . . No, it became him. Bryony could no longer distinguish between the creature and the man. He *was* the seraph, hooded and swaying like a cobra. And she saw six split and flickering tongues bloom from its back like wings of white fire. At the heart of the beast were too many points of light to count—stars all—flickering and blinking like otherworldly eyes.

Bryony tried to move her body, but she was rooted to the spot. She could neither tear her eyes away nor close them now—not even if she wanted to. She tried to speak, but found her tongue lay heavy as a stone in her mouth. Tears spilled down her face. Her whole body began to tremble as she helplessly watched a bead of venom roll down the hunter's blade. She could never have predicted the horror she would encounter when she finally saw the death sword. Samael's weapon was the fang of a giant serpent, dripping and hungry for its prey.

Frank still stood behind her, and Bryony realized he was equally stunned. The seraph advanced, and she held her breath as it reached out to her. She wanted to scream, but she couldn't. The creature wrapped an arm around her and pulled her in. Her head tilted further and further back as she gazed fixedly at the monstrous form rising above her—the swaying, mesmerizing inferno. Her throat closed, and she fought to breathe, sucking in air that tasted like ash and burned like fire. She could no longer see the death sword, but she felt its presence at her back. It took her from herself. It ended everything in its path. It was ruin and decay, the antithesis of life itself.

The seraph held her tighter, and she felt the pressure of its hand at the back of her head. It pressed her face into its fiery breast so she could not see more. She burned, but she was not consumed. She could neither scream, nor fight, nor fear for her life any longer. Only emptiness remained.

Faintly, she heard the voice of Frank Dolamore say, "You are forgiven, my son," before all was silence and darkness, and she lost consciousness in the arms of death itself.

Seraphim are worse than ophanim. That was the first intelligible thought Bryony had upon waking. Then she heard the sound of the highway speeding by. A blinker ticked away in the background, and a radio faintly played something bluesy. Without opening her eyes, Bryony worked out that she was laying across the back seat of the van. Her head was cradled between the steep incline of Michael's lap and his abdomen, and he stroked the hair around her face with one hand like it was the most natural thing in the world—like he hadn't just transformed into a monster before her eyes.

Frank Dolamore was dead. She knew it even as she lay in the lap of his killer. Part of her wanted to cry, but she didn't dare. She didn't want Michael to know she was awake. She was still processing everything she'd seen.

He'd already admitted he was half angel, but now Bryony knew it to her core. She'd seen the creature with her own eyes, breathed in the smoke of it, and been paralyzed by the horror of its physical form. She wondered which was the real Michael, the kind giant or the six-winged, fiery serpent. Perhaps it was neither. Perhaps it was both. Either way, she should have expected this. An angel was an angel. An angel couldn't be anything else.

She feigned sleep the entire drive back to the docks. When they arrived, she let Michael carry her to his boat with one arm and lay her gently on the tarp at his feet. He rowed her back to the flagship, fixed the boat to the davit lines, and climbed the ladder to board. Then Bryony felt the crew hoist the entire boat, with her in it, up and onto the main deck.

"What the devil is this?" said an angry voice. It was Raeni. Bryony kept her eyes closed and didn't move a muscle.

"She stowed away, Commodore," Michael said. "She wanted to go ashore. Don't worry. She knows not to do it again."

"She damn well better. Is the god dead?"

"The forgiveness deity is dead, Commodore." Michael's voice was stiff and robotic. "Everything went smoothly," he lied.

"Lucky for her," Raeni said. "Or I'd have her hanged, and you know I would."

"I know, Commodore. I think she was just curious."

"Well, tell your girlfriend, when she wakes, she'd best make better choices next time. You put the fear of god into her."

"I will, Commodore." He already had.

Raeni marched away from them, saying, "Knew that girl would be trouble somehow."

And then Michael was alone. Bryony felt him lift her into his arms and carry her across the deck. He opened the door to their cabin and laid her down on her bunk. He smoothed her blankets over her and tucked a pillow under her head. When he was finished, Bryony expected to hear him pull her curtain closed and walk away, but he didn't.

He knelt beside her, took her hand in his, and held it to his breast. She felt a warm tear fall onto her forearm. Then another and another. Finally, he spoke. His voice was barely there, but she lay perfectly still in the dark and heard every word he whispered. "Forgive me. Please." He bowed over her, and she felt his breath on the underside of her arm. "I can't imagine life without you anymore. I can't see a future that doesn't have you in it. Please don't let this be the end for us. If you forgive me this, you'll never do wrong in my eyes, I swear it. I love you so much I'm drowning in it. I can't breathe without you. Please."

It felt like a prayer. He stayed kneeling beside her for an hour, at least. But all Bryony saw behind her closed eyelids was the brilliant imprint of the swaying, hooded thing he had become, the venomous blade he carried, and six flickering wings. She still tasted the phantom of smoke in the air, still felt the lingering heat of the seraph in him.

"I love you," he whispered again. "I will always love you. Somehow you've stripped my heart of the ability to feel anything else."

So she'd done it. She'd caught the godhunter—son of the Angel of Death—in her net, and now he would lose himself to her. She imagined the many-eyed creature following her through her world, following her home to her congregation, killing anyone else who loved her.

Every decision Bryony had made until now was the wrong one, and she'd been warned. Even Michael had warned her to limit the depth of their relationship, but she hadn't. She'd stupidly kissed him and adored him and let him love her back. Now that she'd seen the seraph in him with her own eyes, she just wanted to shake him off. But no, he would haunt her for the rest of her days, however few she had left, until he took her life with the same terrible blade that had taken the life of Frank Dolamore.

Michael finally let go of her hand and rose to his feet. She heard him go into the head and wash his face, which she imagined looked rather the worse for wear after weeping for an hour or more. When he opened the door of their cabin to leave, he was met with a flurry of wings. "Go on." She heard him shoo Shakespeare away. "She's asleep now. Go on, bird."

Bryony sat bolt upright and said, "No, let him stay."

Michael turned back to her in silence. No doubt, he wondered how long she'd been awake, but she had no intention of telling him. In the dark, she could just see the questions in his face—his very human face. He opened the door wide for Shakespeare, who hopped in proudly and straight to Bryony's bunk.

"I . . ." Michael started, and then his voice failed him. He breathed his last words to her rather than spoke them. "I have to help set sail." And then he was gone.

Shakespeare hopped onto Bryony's arm, his feet trampling over the same skin where Michael's tears had fallen. "So?" he asked, excited. "How did it go?"

Bryony groaned. "You were right, of course."

He hopped to her shoulder, and Bryony gave him a quick scratch. "And did you see the death sword?"

She nodded.

"Good!" He was thrilled. "Perfect. We're two of four on our objectives. Now you just have to steal the sword and kill the god-hunter."

Bryony felt sick. This was far from perfect. None of this was her plan or her choice. It all felt so unlike her, so alien to who she was. She recalled the way Frank had lost himself to his addiction. He'd seemed like such a kind, thoughtful man when they were at his house, but then that thoughtful man just . . . disappeared. He became something else entirely, something perfectly fine with terrible things being done in his name, as long as it advanced his godhood. It was wrong, and Bryony didn't want to be like him. So she decided, despite everything, to take a last, definitive stand against it.

"No," she said.

Shakespeare fluttered to the foot of her bunk and examined her face from the shadows. "I'm sorry, what?"

"I'm not going through with any of this. I'll just try to escape the armada the first chance I get. They don't know I'm a god, so if they catch me, they'll try to kill me the conventional way and I won't die."

Shakespeare shook his head frantically. "You'll still be hurt. You're just immune to death, not pain or suffering.

"I don't care." She gripped her blankets and stared the bird down. "I'm done. They can hunt me down whenever they find out about me. It's fine. I accept that I won't go on living forever, and maybe I shouldn't. The forgiveness deity was not a good person. What if I'm more like him than I realize? What if I change over the years like he did? Maybe it's in everyone's best interest that I have a limited life."

"Bryony . . ." Shakespeare looked at her like she'd just betrayed him in the worst possible way. "You don't mean that."

"Oh, yes I do. This has already gone too far. I've destroyed a man, and I don't intend to kill him too."

"But, Bryony, he's a godhunter."

She just shook her head. "You don't have to stay with me if you don't want to, but I'm not a killer. I never was. This whole plan was the biggest mistake I ever made."

And that was that. She lay back down and hugged her pillow. She was so exhausted she fell asleep almost instantly while her crow watched on, baffled and appalled.

Chapter Thirty-Three

When Bryony woke the next morning, she was already scream-ing. She didn't recall her nightmare, but she still smelled smoke and felt the heat of fire. Her heart pounded. She couldn't seem to catch her breath. Within seconds, her curtain was pulled aside and Michael crouched down next to her bunk. "Arc you—"

She didn't give him the chance to finish his question. He was here, he was human, and she threw her arms around his neck and tucked her head under his chin. Her world was changing, and it terrified her. But somehow, miraculously, the godhunter was still a safe place to hide.

At first, he froze, clearly shocked she even wanted to touch him. But he quickly recovered and wrapped his arms around her. He murmured, "Okay, okay," as though he had to reassure him-self this was actually happening. Then, to Bryony, he said, "It's okay—you're safe," and kissed the top of her head. She drew her knees in and curled the rest of her body against him.

She hated her dependence on him. Now he was the reason for her nightmares, but he was also the one who made her feel safe when she woke. He'd been making her feel safe since the day she met him, she realized. Even as a seraph, he'd pulled her out of the path of his own weapon and shielded her. He did not want her to die, but one day that could change, even if she managed to escape. The godhunter was called a *hunter* for a reason.

"Promise me . . ." She spoke into his chest without lifting her head. "Promise me he felt no pain."

"I swear it," he said. "Samael's sword delivers only death, and death is always painless. It's everything that comes before it that hurts."

She sat back and looked at him. He didn't look like death incarnate anymore. She couldn't grasp the concept of Michael as the same creature that had caught her up and killed Frank Dolamore without hesitation. He wasn't a monster now. He wasn't a serpentine, white-hot beast with a thousand eyes blinking at his core. No wings like deadly tongues of fire branched from his back. He didn't wield a giant fang dripping with venom. He wasn't a living, breathing nightmare. He was just Michael.

He stood and retrieved a bowl and spoon from his chart table. "Rose brought this for you. She said you skipped dinner—to stow away, I imagine. She also said I deserve whatever's coming to me for stealing Chuy's girl."

Bryony shook her head. "I should never have let that rumor get started. It seemed so harmless at the time."

"It'll die down. Chuy returned to *Papillon* last night, so the crew of *Dragonfly* will soon lose interest in his love life. But Rose was right about one thing. You really should eat something."

"I don't think I can."

"She said this is good for an upset stomach." He dragged the spoon through the stuff and made a face at it. "It looks like some kind of soupy rice pudding, but it smells like cinnamon."

Bryony took the bowl from him. It was warm, and it did indeed smell of cinnamon. She tasted it. It was lightly sweetened and flavored with nutmeg and allspice in addition to the cinnamon. It tasted like a winter morning. "Not bad."

Michael smiled down at her and went back to his table where his own plate sat untouched.

"You waited for me?" Bryony asked.

"Ah." He glanced down at his plate. "Not intentionally. I was also feeling a little"—he stared at the ceiling as he searched for the right words—"under the weather."

"Nervous?"

"*Terrified.*" He laughed a little. "I was terrified. I still am."

"Shouldn't that be my line?" She took another bite of creamy rice.

"Right." He sat on his bunk and massaged his brow, still not touching his breakfast. "Bryony, are we okay?"

She didn't answer him. She honestly didn't know. "What was that I saw last night? Was that the real you? Is that what you really look like?"

He sat up a little straighter. "This is me." He gestured to his very human body. "I'm not some kind of glamour or something."

"But that . . . *thing* that grew out of you . . ."

"That was also me." He bowed his head. "When I draw my father's sword, the seraph in me resonates with it. It's not something I can control. It's just the invisible part of me becoming visible for a moment. It's always been there."

"So it's there now?"

He gulped. "It's always there." He was pink with shame. "I wish you never had to see it."

She set her bowl in her lap and frowned. "Me too."

"You won't have to see it ever again if you don't want to."

"Don't make promises you can't keep." One day, that very shape would come for her, and she wouldn't be able to look away. Michael was her angel of death—not Samael—and he didn't even know it. "You should eat something too." She forced a smile and swallowed another spoonful of rice.

"I can't." He wavered in his place a little, and Bryony saw the swaying serpent in her mind's eye. She wasn't sure she would ever be able to forget it.

She tried to lighten the mood a little. "What would you do if we ever *did* break up? Starve?"

He neither laughed nor answered her, and his silence disturbed her.

"Eat," she commanded him. "We're okay. Just breathe and eat breakfast with me."

"We're okay?" The hope in his face was heartbreaking.

She felt the need to temper it. "For now."

His shoulders fell, and he stared at his knees. "But you know everything about me now. I have no more secrets. You've seen the most monstrous part of me. If we survived this, what could possibly break us?"

She shrugged and tried to sound casual. "You could learn something about me you don't like. Maybe something unforgivable."

He stood, and when he spoke, his voice was as solemn as she'd ever heard it. "At this point, there is nothing I could learn about you that would make me stop loving you. Nothing."

Bryony tried to laugh. "Are you sure about that?"

He nodded. "I've never been more sure of anything in my life."

"Then I guess we're okay." She put a stop to the conversation before she became too tempted to tell him everything. "So eat."

Once she'd eaten breakfast, Bryony took an overlong shower and slept through lunch. When she woke, she found Michael fast asleep on his bunk, tangled in blankets. He looked peaceful finally, all the distress gone from his face. She'd caused so much pain for him in the last two days. All she wanted to do was somehow convince him all their problems had melted away, but she couldn't even manage to convince herself.

She left the captain's quarters feeling sorry she'd even gotten involved with him. He'd been content before he met her. He had a job and a life. Maybe it wasn't perfect, but at least it was relatively peaceful. She made his situation worse, not better. She should have left him to his novels.

They were incapable of breaking his heart. She should never have joined the Black Armada in the first place.

Dragonfly was not her home. Its crew were not her people. And nothing could have proved that more successfully than the look on the commodore's face as she marched across the main deck toward Bryony.

Raeni didn't say a word before she drew her machete and grabbed Bryony by the hair. Bryony was too shocked to scream. She stumbled backward, following the commodore to avoid being dragged. Then Raeni threw her against the mainmast and held her machete to Bryony's stomach.

"You can't die," Raeni said, her fierce temper lifting off her like steam, "but you can be disemboweled. Don't even think about moving, traitor." The commodore had a long line in one hand, which she wound around the mainmast and Bryony's throat. She pulled the line tight and left Bryony to support her own weight or choke. "Oy!" she called to her crew. "Someone fetch the hunter!"

Now. It's happening now. Bryony had thought she had so much more time. She saw Andrew cross the main deck with an oar and begged, "No, no, no, no, no, please." She fought to swallow. "Please don't." Her voice was a choked, desperate thing. She didn't even recognize it.

It was no use. Andrew couldn't even hear her. But before he could strike the door to the captain's quarters, help came from the most unexpected of places. Bryony heard cawing overhead and looked up to see Shakespeare circling, calling attention to the sky. "Flare." She forced the word out, though it hurt when her throat moved against the rope.

"What was that, traitor?" Raeni leaned closer.

Bryony turned her eyes to the sky. "Red flare."

Raeni growled—actually growled—at her and called the crew to action. "SOS, children! All hands!"

Everyone on deck ran to see the flare, trying to figure out which ship it had come from. And while they were occupied, Shakespeare landed on Bryony's head. "Don't worry," he said. "I saw the whole thing, and I have a plan."

"What have you done?" she rasped at him.

"Nothing you can't undo in a matter of seconds if they just get you over there. You can heal him. Tell them that. And get that gun while you're there. It's the only way you'll survive this."

So it was *Ladybird* that fired the red flare. Bryony wished the line against her throat was not so tight. She could have told them it was *Ladybird*, but they figured it out eventually. In the meantime, no one even looked at her. Perhaps they hadn't been told she was a traitor yet. Perhaps they thought she was only being disciplined for insubordination. It was just a delay of the inevitable, though. Bryony knew that. Her time with the Black Armada was over. And maybe her life was over, too, if Shakespeare's new plan didn't work in her favor. So she waited and pressed her back harder into the mast in a vain attempt to minimize the sensation of choking.

"All hands!" The commodore's voice trumpeted over the cacophony. It was only a matter of time before Michael heard her. "Get us to *Ladybird*! Now! Now!"

And then Bryony heard him. Michael's groggy voice questioned the chaos and drew ever nearer. But she was tied to the broad base of the mast with her back to the captain's quarters, and he passed by without seeing her.

Raeni approached him and grasped his arm with one hand. It looked like comfort, that gesture, like she knew she was about to deliver bad news. Her voice sounded, to Bryony, as though it were very far away. "Michael," she said. "You should know Daniel visited early today, in daylight."

"He did?" Michael sounded surprised. "Has that ever happened before?"

"No, which is why I took notice. He gave me urgent news. It seems we missed a god up north."

"But how? And why would he tell us this now?"

"Exactly my thoughts. Then I got the details from him. He said we missed her because she's still just a small-time, healing god, but he warned me not to underestimate her."

Bryony saw Michael tense at that. He was beginning to understand, and she hated it. Tears followed one after the other down pre-worn paths on her cheeks and soaked into the layers of line around her throat.

Raeni let the last blow fall. "We were lucky this time, though. Apparently, we won't even have to turn around to find her."

Michael did turn around, and the look on his face was pure horror. Bryony couldn't stand to see him stare at her as though she were a stranger, as though she had lied to him and crushed him and used him. But it was all true, wasn't it? Michael had repeatedly warned her their relationship would not end well, but there was no way he could have predicted just how bad it would be. He'd thought his own lineage would break them. He hadn't even suspected that Bryony had a secret to hide. How could he? He was too busy worrying about his own inadequacies.

"Is it true? Bryony?" He waited for her answer, but Bryony couldn't make her voice work anymore. Her throat was raw and swelling. All she could do was cry. Michael slowly approached her, and she could see the spreading cracks in everything beautiful she'd managed to give him. When he came close, he looked her up and down and clenched his teeth. "You can't tie her like this," he said to Raeni.

"I can tie the little traitor however I damn well please, hunter."

"She can't speak."

"Do we need her to?"

"I do." Michael circled the mast and began to loosen the lines that bound Bryony.

Raeni rolled her eyes at him. "If she jumps overboard, you're going after her."

"Agreed." Michael let the lines fall, and Bryony took in several deep, hungry breaths. She leaned her head back against the mast and massaged her throat. She could not stop crying. Michael stood over her and looked down with icy resolve. "Is it true? Are you a god?"

This is his job, she reminded herself. *This is who he is.* She nodded. "I'm so sorry." Her voice was still rasping and strained.

"Why did you join the Black Armada?"

She couldn't stand to see the way he looked at her, so she tried to focus on his hands instead. "I heard there was a godhunter aboard, and I feared for my life. So I joined to find and kill him first."

"But why?" He reached out to touch her but thought better of it and withdrew his hand. "We hadn't even heard of you. You weren't in any danger from us."

"It was only a matter of time. I accidentally made missionaries. There was this couple . . ." She sobbed afresh at the memory. It seemed so long ago now. "They had a little dog. It was dying."

"All this over a dog?"

She wailed and sank down the mast until she was crouched low. "It wasn't . . . just a dog to them."

"And when were you planning to kill me?" He was merciless.

She looked up at his face at last, so he could see the truth in her eyes. "I wasn't. I didn't know who the godhunter was, and the more time I spent with everyone, the less I wanted to follow through. And then it was you . . ." She buried her face in her hands. "Why did it have to be you?"

He dropped to one knee before her, and she recalled all the times he'd knelt to hold her in his arms. "You know you can't just walk away from this, don't you?"

She caught her breath. Her own lungs betrayed her. She didn't want him to know how frightened she was, but she couldn't help herself. "Please don't kill me."

"I don't want to, but . . ." His voice wavered. "I don't even know who you are."

Bryony hugged her knees as though they could somehow protect her from the death sword. Her own tears humiliated her, but she forced herself to look him in the eyes again. "Yes, you do."

He shook his head and whispered, "I'm sorry."

So this was how it would end. The godhunter was a godhunter and nothing more than that. Bryony was a god and nothing more than that. They were bound to destroy each other.

The commotion from the crew reached a fever pitch, and Michael turned his head to see what it was about. *Ladybird* had come close enough that Bryony could hear the cries of its crew. "Medic!" they shouted. "We need a medic! Our captain is dying!"

Bryony fortified her resolve. Michael's heart was broken, but so was hers. All she had left was her life. "I can heal him."

Michael turned back to her just as Raeni approached.

"I can heal him," Bryony repeated to both of them. "I swear it. Get me aboard, and he will live."

Chapter Thirty-Four

"You're a con artist." Raeni held her machete in one hand as though she might need it at any moment. "All gods are con artists."

Bryony conceded that. "Maybe that's true to an extent, but I *can* heal people. Commodore, you were dying when I met you. You must have felt it. Your infection was too advanced. You had days at most. Please, you know it's true. I healed you, and I didn't give you a drop of real medicine to do it. Go and check." She gestured frantically to the captain's quarters. "In my briefcase. The tinctures. They're just water with food coloring. They're bullshit, but your recovery wasn't. Ask Rose. Or Chuy. I did the same for them. You have to believe me."

Partway through Bryony's passionate confession, Dara approached. She looked miserable, drained and desperate. "My father," she said, her voice just a sliver of the powerhouse it once was. "You can save him?"

Bryony looked her dead in the eyes. "I swear it. On my life, I swear it."

Raeni shook her head. "Impossible."

But Dara found her voice again. "It isn't, Commodore. Your recovery was nothing short of a miracle, and I demand another. Get the healing god aboard my father's boat, or prepare to execute me where I stand because I won't take another breath in service of the Black Armada."

Bryony saw the exact moment the commodore's will finally broke. Raeni hated executions—Michael hadn't lied about that—and she seemed to have a particular soft spot for Dara. "Andrew!" She called her newest deckhand over. "Get the prisoner to *Ladybird*. She's to heal their captain and come straight back to us. Do you understand? Do not let her go anywhere else, not even overboard."

Raeni squatted in front of Bryony and began winding line around her wrists. She tied off the end and handed a length of it to Andrew, who was apparently meant to lead Bryony around like a dog. "You'd better not be lying about this, traitor," she said.

"I'm not."

Raeni stood. "Dara, go with them. Say goodbye to your father if it comes to that."

Bryony watched Raeni and Dara prepare a boat. Michael stood behind her, and Bryony glanced back only once to see him. His shoulders were hunched. His whole posture looked as though someone had suddenly dropped two-hundred pounds of weight onto his back. In her head, she begged him to give her a chance, to let her explain, to let her live long enough to prove she could do better than Frank Dolamore. But she couldn't say any of it aloud—at least, not yet.

She boarded the boat with Andrew and Dara, and they were all lowered on the davits together. Andrew held the end of Bryony's leash while Dara rowed them toward her father's boat. Her strokes were long and powerful, and she broke a sweat within minutes. The pace she rowed was close to the pace Michael had rowed, although she took several strokes for every one of his. Dara was fighting for her father the only way she could.

Ladybird's hull and masts had been painted black to match the other ships, but its decks were old, graying teak. The crew lowered a swim ladder to Andrew, which was all that was necessary for its relatively low freeboard. Dara climbed up first and explained the situation quickly. Bryony had trouble climbing the ladder with her wrists tied, so Andrew lifted her from the ship's boat while a couple crew members hauled her up by her elbows.

Dara had already gone below by the time Bryony finally set foot on deck. The crew of *Ladybird* was small, about seven or eight Bryony guessed, but none of them stood still long enough for her to count. They were bees in a hive, always moving, working, fretting. Their captain lay dying below, and they had no way to save him.

Bryony descended the companionway with some difficulty, and Andrew followed behind her. Just like when she'd first met the commodore, she found herself suddenly overwhelmed by a powerful smell. Though, this time, it wasn't the scent of infection that hit her like a typhoon. It was the sour stench of vomit, and in such a small space, it overpowered everything. She resisted the urge to bring her hands to her nose and mouth.

The captain was a small man with salt-and-pepper hair and an impressive array of laugh lines Bryony would have loved to see in happier circumstances. He'd been laid out on the settee with nothing but a pillow for his head and a bucket to be sick into. Dara knelt beside him and murmured to him in a language Bryony could not understand. Then the powerful deckhand cried onto his chest and begged him in English to fight. But his color was bad, and when Bryony touched his hands, she felt a familiar chill. Shakespeare had gone too far this time.

"I can't help him while my hands are tied," Bryony said to the crew.

Andrew looked doubtful, but Dara didn't hesitate. She stood and quickly unknotted the lines around Bryony's wrists. "Save him," she pleaded.

Her eagerness gave Bryony the confidence she needed to make her second demand. "I need to be alone with him."

"No can do." Andrew shook his head. "I have my orders."

"Where am I going to go?" Bryony gestured to the only way out. "Just let me have a moment alone with him. Please. He's eaten poison, and he's dying. He has minutes left. I need to focus."

Dara shot one look at Andrew, and he immediately complied. "All right, everyone on deck," he ordered. "Guard the hatches. Guard the companionway. Whoever lets the prisoner escape goes overboard after her."

A brief minute of confusion followed. Everyone in the salon scrambled to climb the companionway as fast as they could. But soon enough, Bryony was left alone with the captain and no bonds on her wrists. She gazed down at him. He looked extraordinarily strong for his size, which reminded her of Dara. And she remembered the way Shakespeare had talked about the culture aboard *Ladybird*. He'd called it a *party boat*, and Bryony got the impression the party was sanctioned by the captain, not in spite of him. This was a man who loved to be alive.

Bryony considered securing the weapon before she healed the captain. That would be the most prudent order of actions, in case the captain came to too quickly. But the man's breathing already rattled. She took his pulse. It was uneven and slow. He really was on the cusp of death. There was nothing for it. Bryony made a fist and dragged her ring along his arm. He bled but just for a moment, and then the cut began to heal.

Now it was Bryony who had seconds left. She made her way forward into the crew's quarters and quickly found the chain locker. She opened the louvered door and groped at the inside wall. She couldn't see a thing, but the gun was right where Shakespeare said it would be, taped to the wall to the right of the door. She ripped it from its place and tore through its plastic bag with her teeth. Then she made her way aft to look for ammunition, but she'd been too slow.

The captain sat on the settee, bright-eyed and looking perfectly healthy. He saw her and stood. She began to protest, but he shushed her and she obeyed. He was in earnest. He held her hands and leaned in close to whisper. "It's already loaded. Here's the safety." He turned a switch on the side of the weapon. "Here's how you put a bullet in the chamber." He shifted the slide for her. "Don't touch the trigger until you're ready to fire." And then he let Bryony take the gun.

"Why are you helping me?" she asked.

He bowed his head. "I heard my daughter. You saved my life. Now I will save yours. I pay my debts."

Bryony could not possibly express enough gratitude to him. She said, "Thank you," in as solemn a tone as she could manage while her heart sent electricity all through her limbs.

"Just swear to me you will not harm my daughter."

She nodded. "I swear it. I only want to get out of this alive."

He smiled a fleeting smile, and Bryony saw the lines on his face come to life just for a moment. "I believe you."

She glanced up at the companionway and hesitated.

"Confidence," the captain said. "It's all that matters."

She squared her shoulders and took a long, deep breath. Then she climbed the companionway and stepped out onto the deck. Andrew came toward her with the line for her wrists. She immediately pointed the gun at his chest.

He froze.

"I don't want to hurt you," she said. "I don't want to hurt anyone. Take me back to *Dragonfly*. Now." She turned to Dara. "Your father is alive and looking quite well."

Dara didn't need to thank her. The expression on her face said everything. Her gratitude was immeasurable. She immediately went below to see her father. Andrew, on the other hand, looked horrified, like he'd just been betrayed by a trusted friend rather than a new recruit he never really warmed to.

Bryony descended the swim ladder first and kept the gun trained on Andrew as he followed. He sat in the ship's boat and wordlessly took up the oars. She stifled the urge to apologize to him. "Just do as I say, and you'll be fine. It's only the godhunter I want. He'll kill me otherwise. Now or later, he'll kill me. Do you understand?"

Andrew nodded.

"Don't tell them I have a gun, and I won't point it at you. Just be quiet."

Again, he nodded, and Bryony felt comfortable enough to lower her weapon. While he rowed, she coiled the line loosely around her own wrists, hoping it was enough to fool anyone looking down on them. The gun, she tucked between her knees.

The ship's boat thumped against *Dragonfly*'s hull, and Andrew waited for his commodore to lower the davit hooks. After he secured them, he and Bryony sat quiet as the dead while they were hauled aboard.

"Success?" Raeni asked when they were high enough to board.

Andrew didn't answer.

"The captain will live," Bryony said. Then she let the line fall from her wrists and pointed the gun at the commodore. "And so will I."

Raeni took several steps backward as Bryony climbed aboard. The decks had been cleared of crew, aside from Michael, and Bryony knew why. They'd all be stunned useless the moment the hunter drew his sword, and he would need to draw it soon. But Michael sat on the steps to the quarterdeck, his head buried in his hands, oblivious to everything around him.

"Hunter!" Raeni called to him. "Eyes on the ball!"

He glanced up from his dispirited stupor, took three seconds to process what he saw, and scrambled to his feet. "Bryony?" His eyes darted back and forth between the gun and Bryony's face. "What are you doing?"

"Clinging to life." She threw his own words back at him, even as her hands shook and her gun wavered. "Changing the world."

He took a step toward her. "Bryony, that's—"

"No!" She trained her weapon on his chest. "You have to listen now. I may have failed to argue for Frank's life, but you have to at least let me try to argue for my own."

The flicker of a smile crossed his face. It was barely perceptible, but Bryony found herself obsessing over what it could mean. Was he laughing at her? Was he proud of her? Was he amused at the ridiculous situation? Bryony glanced at Raeni, who looked far from amused.

She was terrified, and she was livid. The hand closest to her machete clenched and unclenched as she oscillated between fear and rage.

"I don't want to hurt either of you," Bryony assured her. "Please don't make me."

Raeni just growled at her. "Make yuh argument, traitor."

And just like that, Bryony had the floor. Truth be told, she hardly knew what to do with it. She knew she wanted to change Michael's mind about gods, but how? If he believed they were all liars, she certainly hadn't done anything to disprove it.

"I'm a person," she began, and she lowered her weapon a little. "I know you don't think gods are people anymore, but you're wrong. I don't feel any differently now than I did before. There's no single day when I knew I'd become a god. It feels like something that just happened over time, over a series of bad decisions and stupid mistakes. But some things, I think, I got right."

Raeni scoffed and gripped her machete.

"Stop!" Bryony pointed the gun at her commodore. "Don't make me do this. I've never killed anyone before." Her voice broke at that. When she turned back to Michael, she saw that he had shown Raeni his palm, signaling her to stop.

That gesture alone was all the encouragement Bryony needed to continue. "The first creature I healed was a rat. It was paralyzed, and I'd found this . . . this sword in a graveyard. It transformed for me when I picked it up, and I wanted to find out what else it could do." She decided to leave Shakespeare out of the story. He had neither known nor signed on to this plan of hers. She didn't have the right to out him.

"The rat didn't worship me," she said, and she thought she saw Raeni chuckle a little. "Animals don't tend toward it. But what was I supposed to do—refuse to heal humans on the off chance they turned me into a god? I considered telling people about the sword, but I got scared. I thought about what they'd be willing to do to me to get their hands on it. I thought about who might take it and profit off it, healing only those who could afford to pay them. I thought about war and angels, and I chose to keep the sword a secret. The result was that people believed I myself had the power to heal, and they began to thank me with the only resources they had. For many of them, that was just love."

She paused and tried to calm her nerves, slow her heart, quiet the ringing in her ears. Michael stood before her, still as a statue, and listened. She could not tell whether her story affected him at all.

"I faked my own medical knowledge—it's true—but that's the only thing I faked." She addressed Michael here and hoped he would understand. "I didn't pretend to be human for you. I'm not playing the part of Bryony Moss. I still feel fear, loneliness, friendship, and love. I've never been so happy as I was when I began to feel like part of the armada.

"What you all are doing here . . ." She swallowed her own impulse to grieve for what she knew she was losing. "What you're doing is amazing. I only wish I'd known about it sooner. I would have begged for books for my own congregation so they could learn about medicine too—so they could treat their own wounds, prevent infection, recognize illness earlier. I can't be there for them all the time, and if you think I don't love them just because I'm a god, you're wrong. I do love them, and I'm not there for them now, and it's killing me. That should tell you just how desperate I was when I left them to come here and find you"—she paused—"Michael."

Raeni broke in. "After all that, what was it you think you got right, girl?"

She hadn't called Bryony *traitor*, this time. That was something. Maybe this could work after all. Maybe Bryony really could change their minds. "Saving you, for one, and Dara's father, and every member of my congregation who only got sick because the angels enforce ignorance. They're so grateful, my worshipers. You should meet them yourself. I've never known people so grateful to be alive."

Raeni shook her head. "So which one of them convinced you your best course of action was to abandon your community and join the Black Armada?"

Bryony didn't answer because it wasn't a member of her congregation. She knew it, and the little, black crow standing on the deck just a few feet away knew it.

"Bryony." Michael's voice was too gentle. "Who told you there was a godhunter in the armada?"

Bryony opened her mouth to explain that it wasn't her secret to share, but Shakespeare didn't give her a chance. He shouted, "Shoot him already! Shoot the bastard now! He's mortal—he'll die like anyone else! Just shoot or he'll kill you!"

Both Michael and Raeni's mouths fell open. The hunter turned to his commodore and said, "Did you hear that?"

"I sure did," Raeni answered.

Then everything seemed to happen at once. Shakespeare took off, but before he could get far, Raeni's machete found him. She drew the blade and struck the crow with deadly efficiency, bisecting it in one smooth motion.

"No!" Bryony screamed and fired her weapon at the commodore, too late and too far off her mark. She hit nothing and dropped to her knees. Shakespeare lay in two halves on the deck beside her, black feathers still falling around him, his head with his left wing, his feet with his right.

Bryony dropped the gun. Her best friend was dead, and she couldn't find the will to fight anymore. The sound that escaped her throat didn't seem to come from her at all. It was an alien, rasping, low-pitched scream. She screamed until she was hoarse, until she grew faint from the breath it took. She had never known despair like this. She drowned in it. She sank and sank and never seemed to reach the bottom.

And that was when the godhunter finally drew his sword.

Chapter Thirty-Five

Through her tears, Bryony saw the hunter's form shift, dance, and brighten. She saw the sword transform into a serpent's fang, oozing venom—this time, for her—but she couldn't bring herself to move. What a ridiculously hopeful thing she'd been. She went looking for a godhunter, and she found one. What did she think was going to happen?

It will be painless, she reminded herself. *Not like Shakespeare's death.* The crow's little body still lay in two pieces beside her. The hunter's form wavered like a mirage before her eyes, and she bowed her head to him. *Let him take me*, she thought. *Better him than anyone else.* Better he should kill her than another hunter should come for her congregation. This was hardly the worst end she could have asked for.

She laid her hands out flat on the deck before her, showing the hunter her surrender, but she couldn't lift her head to meet his eyes. She bowed before him like she was a worshiper and he was her god, and she saw his fiery feet approach.

Closer.

Closer.

She squeezed her eyes shut and tried to ready herself for the end, but it never came. And when she finally lifted her head to see why the hunter hesitated, she found he had passed her by. He stood over the body of her crow and pointed his sword down at it.

"Get up," he commanded, and Bryony choked on the cruelty of it all. Then he shouted, "Get up!" His voice was thunder, and his body was lightning.

At first, Bryony did not believe her own eyes. She was sure this was all just a vivid nightmare—*god, let it be so.* But the two halves of Shakespeare appeared to be slowly coming together. And growing. And changing. The rest of the bird's feathers fell from his body, turned to dust, and blew away on the wind.

Suddenly, there was a man crouched on the deck without a stitch of clothing. He stood and tilted his chin back, proud and tall. He had long, blond hair and a full, splendid beard with streaks of ginger. His eyes were a striking shade of blue. He reminded Bryony of Andrew, but he was bigger and far more intimidating.

The hunter held his position, his death sword pointed steadily at the heart of the man who used to be Shakespeare.

Raeni—who kept her eyes averted from her terrifying hench-man—backed away and shot a seething look at Bryony. "You brought a *shapeshifter* into my fleet?"

Bryony opened and closed her mouth several times in an attempt to answer, but she couldn't find the words. She wasn't sure she even knew what words were anymore. More and more, she found herself wishing to wake from this nightmare. The hunter answered on her behalf. "I don't think she knew, Commodore." He turned back to the man. "What is your name? And don't lie to me."

The blond man puffed out his chest in a way that was too reminiscent of the crow. "Which name were you hoping for?"

Raeni rolled her eyes.

The hunter brought his sword closer to the man's chest. "The name your companion will be most familiar with. This is for her benefit. I already know who you are."

For a split second the blond man's shoulders fell. He refused to look at Bryony as he answered, "Loki."

"Jesus Christ," Raeni cursed.

The blond man chuckled. "No, just Loki."

"Hunter," Raeni said, "I would like to express how supremely disappointed I'll be if you don't kill him."

"I understand, Commodore." The hunter's seraphic shape wavered in the wind. "I just want him to answer some questions first."

Loki held his position. "It's really better if you don't ask, snake."

"I won't be the one asking," the hunter said. Then he turned back to Bryony. "Ask him whatever you want. He will answer."

Bryony tried to sit up, but her hands seemed glued to the deck. Even in her periphery, the sight of the seraph nearly paralyzed her. It was a wonder Loki could even stand. *Loki* . . . The only family she'd known for the last ten years was a lie. Her world, her identity was collapsing around her. She wasn't sure she was ready to know the truth, but she also understood this was probably her only chance. So many questions bombarded her mind, but she could only manage to give voice to one. "Why?"

Loki shrugged. "I needed someone to kill the godhunter, so I created a god. I'd heard a rumor about an archangel's abandoned sword floating around. Finding and claiming it was the hard part. Once I had it in my possession, making a god was too easy. I searched years for the right person, and when I found you, I planted the sword in your favorite haunt." He chuckled at his own joke.

The serpentine monster hissed at him, its voice crackling like fire. "You needed her to kill the godhunter, why?"

"Before *you* could find and kill *me*."

The laughter that rang out at that was so out of place it caused all of them to turn their undivided attention to Raeni. She was cackling like someone had just told the most amusing joke she'd ever heard. "You?" She gasped and clutched at her sides. "But you aren't even a god. Where are your worshipers, fool?"

"I've had some." Loki looked offended, but Raeni didn't seem to care.

"If you ever did, you certainly don't now. Daniel's known about you for ages. Why do you think we never came for you?"

Loki fumed for a moment. Then he glanced back at Bryony and lost all his defiance. "You can stop being a god?"

"*You* can." Raeni kissed her teeth at him. "You were born a sad, lonely Jötunn, and you're about to die a sad, lonely Jötunn."

"That's"—Loki withdrew a bit—"excessively harsh, don't you think?"

"Not for you. And I bet your poor, abused friend will feel di same when she learns how yuh disguised yourself as Daniel to expose her."

The shock on Loki's face told Bryony the commodore hadn't lied, and somehow, learning this was worse than the rest. Loki had given her the sword and made her into a god before they'd developed a friendship—or what Bryony had thought was a friendship—but this . . . He knew she didn't want to kill the godhunter. He knew how much it would hurt her to choose between her own life and that of the man she'd grown to love. Yet he'd plotted a way to force her to do just that.

Raeni was livid, and her accent thickened. "Do yuh know what they used to call dat, what yuh did to me?" She scowled. "*Assault.* Yuh lucky we found yuh before Daniel did. He would'n be as humane as my hunter. Yuh is a predator and an abuser. And yuh tink I would'n notice? Eh, Jötunn?" Her voice was dripping with hate. "Yuh nuh kiss like an angel."

"Better?" Loki, still at the wrong end of the death sword, somehow managed to quirk a wicked smile.

She spoke through her clenched teeth. "Not even close, yuh selfish, mean, little prick."

Loki shrugged. "I tried."

Raeni took a deep breath and composed herself. "You failed, and now you'll die for it. You're not even a god, but you managed to betray your only friend, and in the process, earn the ire of the world's most dangerous godhunter. How very *you*. All because you hate to do your own dirty work. I thought you were supposed to be clever, but I'm guessing that particular rumor was started by you. Give my regards to Baldr, coward."

Finally satisfied with her verbal lashing, the commodore gave her orders. "Hunter, get rid of him. The world will be better off without him." She walked to where Bryony still knelt on the deck, picked up the gun, and casually chucked it overboard. "I fucking hate guns."

Raeni's tirade was a splash of cold water to Bryony. She woke from her stupor and realized two things. First, for the last ten years of her life, she'd danced like a marionette for a liar and a fake. And second, that same liar was moments away from drawing his last breath. "Wait," she said. "I need to ask him one more question."

The hunter lowered his sword.

With enormous effort, Bryony tore her gaze from the seraph and looked Loki in the eyes. "Why me? Of all the people you could have chosen, what made you pick me? All you ever did was complain that I was too weak, too tenderhearted to follow through. Surely, you could see that from the beginning. So why? How did I get to be so unlucky?"

"Oh, you poor child." Raeni sighed, and Bryony heard real sympathy in that sigh. "Don't you realize why a gentle heart was essential to his plan?"

For the first time since he'd transformed into a man, Loki actually looked ashamed of himself.

"Why?" Bryony asked him.

The hunter lifted his sword again. "Answer her."

Loki bowed his head and looked away. "Tenderhearted people are easier to manipulate." He muttered the confession, and Bryony's heart broke to hear it.

The fang in the hunter's hand oozed venom as though the sword itself salivated, hungry for the life standing before it. And Bryony realized, for all the fear she had of them, she'd never seen an angel truly angry before now. The flames of the seraph grew and brightened to a blinding light in the heat of its rage. "You," it rumbled, "were the only family she had. I don't usually enjoy killing anything, but this, I believe, will be a rare pleasure."

The hunter advanced, and Loki seemed as unable to run from him as Bryony had been the previous night. The brilliance of Samael's son was stunning, literally. No one could move much once their eyes were filled with it. Was that the power of the seraphim or just Samael's line? But there wasn't time to wonder. "Stop!" Bryony fought to stand but found it impossible as long as the seraph was in her field of vision. "Please don't kill him!"

The hunter froze and turned his inhuman head to her.

"Please," she begged. "Just give me this one thing before I die."

Why?" the hunter asked. He seemed genuinely baffled. "To him you're nothing, a disposable tool. Why would you argue for his life after all he's done to you?"

"Because I don't think he was faking everything." She thought of her own relationship with Michael and the crew of *Dragonfly*. She'd conned her way into the armada, but she'd grown to love them anyway. There was nothing fake about it. "There were little moments . . ." She recalled the way Shakespeare would laugh with her at some harmless folly, or how he would accompany her despite the tedium of her routine. And when she was lonely or she felt a pang of grief, that little crow would sit on her shoulder and press a warm wing to her cheek. "There were little moments of truth in his lie. I think he was just scared. Like me."

With that, the white-hot body of the seraph flickered and shrank like a fire without fuel. And suddenly Michael stood before her, carefully placing his deadly dividers back in their wooden box and slipping it into his coat pocket. The relief Bryony felt upon finally seeing his familiar, human shape surprised her. He was Michael again, and his eyes expressed the same warmth and love they had the first time he'd smiled at her. Behind him, Loki stood dumbfounded, his mouth hanging open in mute astonishment.

"Well, Jötunn," Raeni said, "you know how to pick your victims. I'll give that to you. You have no idea how lucky you are. Too bad your merciful friend won't be so lucky."

Loki looked from Michael to Bryony and back again. His expression darkened, and Bryony saw a moment of panic in it. But it wasn't panic for himself—not this time. He was afraid for her. He was ashamed and afraid for his friend. "If she wasn't a god, you wouldn't have to kill her?"

"That's the idea," Raeni said. "But she is a god. You made sure of that."

Every muscle in Loki's body tensed. "I can fix this." He approached Bryony, knelt beside her, and took her hand in his. She saw his human face up close for the first time. His blue eyes and rosy cheeks were cold and unyielding, but the tremor in his voice was real. He caught her ring between his fingers and paused. His stare was piercing, and Bryony thought she could almost see the crow in him. "It's true, I wasn't faking everything. I'll make it right again. I swear it." Then he turned to Michael. "Just a few hours. Give me that much time at least."

When Loki stood, he slipped the ring from Bryony's finger. His body grew and changed, and so did the ring. Wings and feet and feathers and beak. Once again, he became a bird, but he was no crow this time. This time, he was an eagle. In his beak he clutched the shaft of an arrow—the new shape of the healing sword. He flapped his wings, and with every downward stroke, he sent a gale across the deck of *Dragonfly*. He grew even more as he lifted off, and again in the sky, until his body was bigger than any building Bryony had ever seen, and his wingspan blocked out the sun.

Chapter Thirty-Six

L oki was gone before Bryony entirely understood what had taken place. Michael and Raeni, it seemed, were equally baffled.

"What the devil was that?" Raeni said.

Michael shielded his eyes from the sun and watched after the giant bird, which had flown so quickly away from them it hardly seemed a spot in the sky now. "I'm not sure."

Bryony held her hands out and stared at the place where her ring used to be. Ten years she'd worn the archangel's sword on her finger. She felt naked and powerless without it. "He took the sword," she said.

"So it was the ring." Raeni made a sour face. "I should have figured that out sooner. Well, this is about as bad as it gets, hunter. Looks like the fool is going to save you the trouble of killing her by doing it himself."

"How?" Michael looked doubtful.

"He obviously intends to strip her of her godhood, probably either by exposing her lie to her congregation or giving them something else to worship. Both would require the sword. He thinks he's undoing the damage he's done by giving her back her humanity. The trouble, of course, is that no mortal can survive godhood the way a born immortal can. She can't be human ever again. Either she stays a god or she dies."

"That can't be true." Michael looked almost as exhausted as Bryony. The hope he had allowed himself to feel had been repeatedly dashed against a rocky shore, but he could no more give it up than he could give up the air he breathed. "Loki might know another way."

Raeni just sighed. "Loki knows Loki and very little else. The armada, on the other hand, was hunting gods long before you joined. From what I hear, it was a nasty business. They wiped out entire congregations until the gods became mortal. And then they killed the gods too, but they didn't need to. Every single god that lost its congregation began to die immediately after the last worshiper fell. The armada put them down as a kindness. If allowed to die naturally, their deaths were . . . Well, *painful* is an understatement."

"Then turn us around!" Michael shouted in a way Bryony had never heard him shout before. He was desperate, angry, irrational. "Turn us around now, and go after him! He can't be allowed to do this! I'll kill him first! I'll kill his immortal soul before I allow this!"

"Settle down, hunter. You know it's impossible. The shapeshifter is moving at a speed we can't begin to match, especially with the prevailing winds against us. He'll be there before we make our first tack."

Michael choked on his own misery. "No, we have to try! We can't just sit here and do nothing!"

That was when Bryony realized the godhunter would never have killed her. She'd won. She'd changed the hunter's heart. She'd successfully argued for her own life, and now he wanted to fight to save her. Only he couldn't. After all that, she was even more certainly doomed to die.

"We won't do nothing," Raeni said, picking up the lines Bryony had dropped. "We'll wait to see if he succeeds in stripping her godhood. If she shows symptoms, we'll do the kindest thing we can."

"No." Michael's hands were whitened fists at his side.

"Listen. If you love her, you won't let her suffer." Raeni approached Bryony and guided her to sit against the mainmast. She wound the line around Bryony's wrists and secured her to the mast in a much kinder manner than she had before. "Just in case your avian friend has another trick up his sleeve," she said, patting Bryony on the shoulder like they were old friends. "Don't take it personally."

Michael continued to fume. "This is not acceptable. There has to be something we can do."

"There is." Raeni finished her knots and stood. "You just don't want to do it. So we'll wait, and we'll watch. But remember, as she progresses, you're the only one who can release her from her suffering painlessly."

The sky was an uncanny shade of electric blue. One lone, wispy cloud slowly shifted through its repertoire of shapes as it drifted across the expanse. It was an almost comically beautiful day, and it was going to be Bryony's last. She tried to focus on the sun, and the cloud, and the gentle breeze that cooled the sweat still clinging to her face.

Michael sat beside her, wringing his hands. He should have given up, Bryony thought. Everything became so much easier when you just gave up—when you finally accepted that you'd lost, that it was over. She had let go of her hope, and now she was determined to spend her last hours being grateful for every minute she'd been alive. She leaned over as far as she could and rested her head against his arm. "You were going to let me live, weren't you?"

He met her eyes, shocked. "Of course I was. I love you." He brought his arm around her shoulder and tangled his fingers in her hair. "When I first learned you were a god, in that brief moment, I thought it was possible you'd only pretended to love me. Even then, I couldn't bring myself to harm you. I honestly don't think I'm capable."

"I felt the same way. When Shakes—" She stopped abruptly and corrected herself. "When Loki said I had to kill you to save myself, I told him I couldn't. I wanted to quit and run away. I wanted you to come with me. I wanted us to change the world together." She laughed despite everything. "How stupid is that?"

"It's not stupid. We can still try. There has to be a way to save you. I just have to figure out what it is."

Bryony shook her head. "If life has taught me one lesson, it's that sometimes, all you can do is let go."

"Don't say that." It was more a plea than a command. He couldn't let go, she realized, not even if he wanted to. He'd warned her about the obsessive, single-minded devotion of angels and their offspring, but she'd thought it a kind of virtue at the time. She could never have predicted that, one day soon, she would need Michael to steady his heart and help her to die. He took a long, deep breath that shuddered at the end. Bryony couldn't stand to hear him suffer.

"Maybe it'll be fine," she said. Allowing him a little hope for a while longer wouldn't change anything, but it would make their last hours together more pleasant. "Maybe the commodore is wrong."

Michael hung his head and drew his knees to his chest.

Bryony tried again. "We should do something while we wait. Maybe we could read one of your books to help pass the time."

"Which one would you like to read?" He was distant, but at least he was talking about something else.

"The one with the horse on the cover."

"Okay." He pushed himself to his feet and retrieved the book.

They spent the next few hours together reading. Slowly, Michael seemed to relax. He let Bryony read first, and then she asked him to read to her. Her head had begun to throb, and she didn't want him to know just yet.

Every once in a while, he would look up from the book and ask how she was feeling. She always said, "Fine," and changed the subject by questioning him about some plot detail she claimed to have forgotten. She begged him to reread "the good parts" because they made him blush and she loved the sight of color in his cheeks. She laughed, and once, she caught him laughing too, which made her feel like she'd accomplished the impossible. More than becoming a god, joining the Black Armada, finding and neutralizing a godhunter, Bryony was proud of kindling that smile one last time.

She was dying. She could feel it. Her body ached. Every breath she took was painful and not enough. While he was still Shakespeare, Loki had warned her about withdrawal, but Bryony knew what it felt like when worship waned. This was so much worse. This was famine. This was starvation. There was no other way to describe it.

In a daze, she reached up to trace the crease at the corner of Michael's mouth one last time, and he caught her wrist before she withdrew it. He looked down at her, his expression nothing short of pure devastation. "Your skin is like ice." He dropped the book. "No, god damn it." His voice rose in pitch, and his eyes drowned in fear. He wrapped his arms around her and bowed over her as though he could somehow physically protect her from the thing attacking her.

"It's okay," Bryony assured him. She thought of her brother, whose life had ended while he was still a child, and she reminded herself how lucky she'd been to have grown up at all, to have even gotten the chance to fall in love.

"It's not okay." Michael studied her face a moment. Then he stood and paced. "You're suffering, and I'm just letting it happen."

Even as he spoke, the ache Bryony had been trying desperately to ignore exploded, and every nerve in her body began to scream at once. She fought the feeling, smothered it, but it clawed its way to the surface like a buried colony of ants. Her fingers curled unnaturally, and her lungs struggled to take in air.

Michael pulled the wooden box from his pocket and opened it. The brass dividers glinted in the sun as he stared at them. He couldn't seem to bring himself to touch them. "Why am I so weak?"

And Bryony remembered holding a rock over the body of a dying rat. She remembered how she couldn't find the strength to bring it down the way she knew she should, even though it would have been the right thing to do. How much harder must it be for Michael? She couldn't ask him to kill her. She knew it would shatter him forever. He would not be the same person. He would not smile as often or enjoy his favorite books anymore.

He gazed down at her, and his whole body shook. She thought she'd never seen another person look so miserable. He took the dividers from the box and knelt beside her. He opened his mouth to speak, but nothing came out, so he just pulled her into a tight hug. It hurt every muscle in her body, but she didn't cry out.

"I'm so sorry," he whispered to her. "Death is all I can give you. I don't know how to do anything else."

He stood again, dividers in hand, ready to draw his sword. He took three quick, sharp breaths and tightened his grip on the weapon. It did not transform. Bryony was ready, but Michael just stood there, wavering on the spot. Then he hastily put the dividers away. "I can give you something for the pain." His voice was frantic, desperate. "There must be something in the ship's hospital that'll buy us a little more time."

He left her and disappeared down the companionway into the guts of the ship. Bryony imagined him bent at the waist, making his way awkwardly to the ship's tiny hospital, tearing it apart in search of something, anything. But she knew he wouldn't find what he was looking for. There wasn't a painkiller strong enough for this. Still his absence gave her a little relief.

Now that he was gone, she finally allowed herself to cry from the pain. She shook and wept and gasped for air. She was so engulfed in her own suffering she didn't see the shadow approach until it was right on top of her.

"He can't do it, can he?" It was Raeni, and she carried something heavy in her hands. She glanced over both her shoulders. "We'll have to be quick about this." She squatted down before Bryony, who could now see what the commodore brought with her. It was an anchor, a small one, probably a spare for one of the ship's boats. Raeni untied the cords that bound Bryony to the mast and fastened them to the anchor instead.

"You saved my life," the commodore said. "I owe you this at the very least. I know decapitation would be quicker, but you understand why I can't leave a mess, don't you?"

Yes. Michael, Bryony knew, could not cope with seeing the evidence of violence committed against her. It took all the strength she had just to nod.

"Good." Raeni put the anchor in Bryony's lap. Though small, it would sink her quickly enough, and she would simply disappear. Michael would know what had happened, of course, but he would never have to see it or be haunted by a memory of bloodshed.

Raeni carried Bryony to the bulwarks and rested her body along the rail. "I nearly drowned once," she said. "The panic is the worst part. Once you get through that, there's peace. Try to let go, and you'll feel peace before you die. I promise." She took a moment to tenderly stroke Bryony's cheek. "I'm so sorry, Bryony. You deserved better than this."

Bryony barely had time to realize the commodore had just used her given name for the first time before her body hit the water.

Chapter Thirty-Seven

As she sank, Bryony watched the retreating shadow of *Dragonfly*'s hull. The sun seemed to grow smaller and smaller, dimmer and dimmer. Little bubbles tickled her skin as they escaped from her clothing and floated upwards. She clung to the anchor, understanding a quick death to be the gift it was meant to be, but she couldn't stop herself from holding her breath. Her body, it seemed, did not believe in the hopelessness of her situation. Her lungs, already starved of oxygen, burned. In seconds, they would breathe of their own accord, and she would not be able to stop it. She would panic. She would take in water. And then she would be calm and die. She tried to think of the coming calm, even as her mutinous wrists began to struggle with her bonds.

Soon, Bryony's slow suffocation brought the expected hallucinations. It wouldn't be long now. As she stared up, the sun seemed to follow her down, growing bigger and brighter, joining her in the darkening sea. It moved closer and closer until she would have sworn she could see a wavering, elongating shape at its center.

Then she recognized the seraph.

The hunter had followed her down. His sword was drawn, and his flickering wings were six tongues of white fire, piercing the sea with rays of blinding light. Bryony was grateful to him, terrifying though he was, and she hoped he knew it. He would help her to die before she drowned. It would be painless. It would be peaceful. She didn't have to die alone. Her angel of death was with her, delivering the final blow.

But Bryony's lungs didn't wait for him. She breathed in water just as he caught her in his arms. She lurched and struggled as he cut the cord between her wrists and the anchor with his death sword. The last thing she saw was the sword returning to its sheath, fading back into brass dividers, before her world went completely black. The last thing she felt was Michael's long arm tightening around her waist. The last thing she knew was that he would not be giving her the gift of death after all. He was still determined to save her.

The next moments of Bryony's life came to her in flashes of consciousness. Each time she woke, her body violently ejected water from her lungs and stomach. Then the pain would hit. Her muscles ached. Every touch was agony. Even the hairs on her arms seemed to sting. She was weak, retching and gasping until she mercifully lost consciousness again.

Once, she noticed that Michael had pulled her bound wrists over his head like the sleeves of an unworn sweater and carried her on his back. In this way, he kept her head above water. Sometimes a swell washed over them both and Bryony thought she would drown again, but she never did.

She tried to focus on the rhythm of his powerful arms propelling them toward the shore. The way his shoulder blades worked under her body told the story of the force he used, the energy and exertion he put into this journey. He gave everything he had—she could tell that much. He wasn't pacing himself or holding back. He fought the sea for her, and he was winning.

When Bryony woke again, it was because Michael had collapsed beneath her. There was sand under his body. He panted and pushed himself to his knees. He slipped Bryony's arms from around his neck and lifted her as he stood. She was shocked he could lift anything at all the way he coughed and trembled. She wondered how long he'd been swimming. The sun was much closer to the horizon, so it had to have been an hour at least. He staggered, and each time he looked down at Bryony, his hair rained seawater onto her face.

He pressed on. She didn't know where he was going, but she could barely keep hold of her consciousness let alone ask. At some point, she woke to the sound of his deep voice muttering. He adjusted his hold on her body, hoisted her a little higher against his chest, and stumbled on. She listened, and she could hardly believe what he repeated over and over again as he marched relentlessly across the beach.

"I know what to do," he said. "I know what to do. I know what to do." He wasn't talking to her. Instead, he seemed to be steeling himself against his own fear. "I know what to do."

She closed her eyes and let herself drift in and out of consciousness. It was still a struggle to breathe, and it hurt too much to move. She did not appreciate being awake, and each time she passed out was a relief to her.

When Bryony woke again, it was because Michael had laid her body out on a hard, unforgiving surface. Her back arched strangely here, so she forced herself to open her eyes. It was a boulder or some large rock formation upon which he'd placed her. It was far from comfortable, and Bryony felt a touch of anger at being made to die on such a disagreeable surface when there had been soft, warm sand where he'd first crawled from the sea.

Michael knelt beside the rock, his hands spread flat against it, his head bowed. His voice continued its quiet repetition, but the words he spoke had changed. Bryony was all but certain he'd finally gone mad, and she felt a pang of regret that she'd managed to destroy such a beautiful person. She'd truly never met anyone like him. There was a paradoxical quality in him and in the way he interacted with the world. He was slow to anger and quick to love. He was gentle but powerful. He had a childlike enthusiasm for everything he enjoyed, though the pain of isolation had aged his heart. He was an open book, and yet somehow, there was still such mystery about him.

How could she not have fallen in love with him? How had no one else in the Black Armada fallen deeply in love with the man shortly after meeting him? It didn't make sense. Nothing about this made sense. And more than anything, the fact that her agony had suddenly begun to ebb did not make sense.

She could wiggle her fingers and toes. Her breaths came easier. She no longer felt surging waves of pain. She propped herself onto her elbows and looked out toward the sea. They were still on the beach. She could hear the sound of crashing waves, and she saw dry sand all around them. The sun-kissed horizon painted every feathery cloud a deep shade of pink. Michael knelt beside her, his fingers still spread wide against the stone. And Bryony finally heard the words he spoke.

> *Oh, god, I beg you change my fate.*
> *Give me a love to remember,*
> *So on the day I finally meet my end,*
> *I'll not fling my soul against the gates of heaven,*
> *But be content to roam the earth,*
> *Where my home and my happiness lie.*

Bryony sat up and stared down at him. Her belly filled with warmth, and her every fiber sang for joy as Michael repeated the prayer. She would have wondered which god he prayed to, but her own body gave her the answer. He worshiped her, and his worship overwhelmed her need. It filled and strengthened her and made her feel invincible. It was unlike any rite she'd experienced before.

It seemed Michael had chosen to sacrifice his own sanity, to plunge their relationship into the depths to save her. He would become a congregation of one, sustaining his god with his devotion alone. He knew what this meant for him—he knew what it had meant for his father—and Bryony couldn't stand it. She grabbed his wrist, and he looked up to see her staring down at him.

He gasped, and hope blossomed in his expression. "It's working!"

"What are you doing?" Bryony demanded, though she already knew the answer.

"Ritualizing this moment." Michael patted the stone under Bryony. "This is my altar." He gestured to the beach around him. "This is my church." Then he stood and enfolded both her hands in his. "And this is my god."

Bryony sat up and frantically shook her head. "No, no, no. You do not sacrifice yourself for me. This is not how we work. Do you understand? I don't want this."

"I'm not sacrificing anything," he said.

"But your father—"

"My father's mistake was allowing both kinds of love into his heart at once. I'll do better."

She stifled a sob. "But I don't want to be your god." The thought of giving him up, losing him to worship, was enough to completely counter her high. "I want to be your partner. I want to love and kiss you, argue and lose to you, laugh and cry with you. I want to spend my days wondering how I was lucky enough to find real romance with the most astonishing person I've ever met."

She watched as the corners of Michael's mouth turned down and then broadened into the widest, most magnificent smile she'd ever seen him wear. He leaned into the stone and stepped between her legs. He curled his fingers around the backs of her knees and tugged her closer.

Then he touched his forehead to hers and breathed her in before kissing her.

Nothing had changed. His mouth was gentle, and his hands were hungry. He slid his fingers from the backs of her knees, over her thighs and around her hips. "I'll always love you like this. I swear it. I'll lock the worship away in the darkest corner of my heart. I'll keep it locked away until you need it. I can do this. I am more than my father's son." He held her face in his hands and swore it again with his eyes. "We'll be partners, friends, and we'll be lovers, if that's okay with you."

"It's okay." She laughed in disbelief. "It's so much more than okay." She threw her arms around his neck, and he lifted her from the stone. He held her tight and sank down with her to the sand. She clung to him with her arms and legs as he bowed over her and kissed every dip and corner in her cheeks, her throat, her shoulders.

It didn't seem real, this moment. Bryony wondered whether she might have drowned after all, and this was some final, cruel trick her dying mind played on her. But Michael's body was warm and solid. He was still soaking wet, and she felt the grit of sand when she slipped her hands beneath the hem of his shirt and tucked the tips of her fingers under his belt.

"How are you even real?" she murmured.

He answered by pulling her closer and kissing just below her ear. His hair painted her cheek with seawater, and his fingers tightened around her waist.

"Michael . . ." she began but stopped short when she felt his tongue on her skin. He was allowing himself so much more than he ever had. Because he trusted her, she realized. She felt the rising heat of the seraph in him as he tasted her for the first time, the growing need in his very human flesh as his abdomen tensed under her hands, the way his hips subtly tilted to meet her before he caught himself and quickly drew back again. He was fire and want and perfect restraint all at once. He was an angel and a man, and he had somehow changed her entire worldview in the space of a few days. "How is any of this possible?" she whispered.

"I don't know." He leaned back to look at her. "Somehow you've reinvented me. Things I thought were impossible seem so easy now, and I love it. I love you. As long as my worship is enough—"

"*Enough?*" She gripped his shoulders and laughed. "You have no idea, do you? I've never been so . . . You're more than my entire congregation put together."

He let his head fall back and sighed. "So I inherited something useful from my father after all."

Bryony took the opportunity to rise up and kiss the feather-soft skin of his throat. She lingered there until she felt his pulse quicken against her lips, until she was full to bursting with desire for him. Then she forced herself to slip from his lap. "I should thank him for it someday." She leaned back against the boulder and caught her breath. "When I meet him."

"Don't even joke about that." He chuckled and joined her, his knees tucked to his chest, his back to the altar he had chosen. "He's still the Angel of Death."

"*You* were my death," Bryony reminded him. "But I faced you. You were terrifying, but I fell in love with you. Now you'll be my constant companion, and I couldn't be happier. Like I said, I have a complicated relationship with death."

"*Constant companion,*" he repeated. "I like that." He slouched against the boulder and held her hand. "So what do we do now?"

She interlaced her fingers with his and stared up at the reddening sky. "I don't know. You're the one who reads romances." She teased him. "Surely you have some ideas."

"No, no." He laughed and blushed. "I meant now that we've effectively quit our jobs." He glanced around the boulder at the sea. "The armada has gone. They left us alive at least, but we have nothing. We'll have to start walking until we find a place to stay."

Bryony glanced down at his bare feet. "Oh, you don't have shoes. And all your clothes were aboard. And your books."

"We'll figure something out." He squeezed her hand. "You'd be surprised how little you need to get along in the world. I spent a good portion of my life with just the clothes on my back."

Of course. She'd almost forgotten who he was, that his father was an angel who destroyed his mother and abandoned him. He must have been so lost the day he joined the Black Armada. They might have been his first real family, and he'd just given them up for her. She shook the thought from her head. "You probably had shoes at least."

He buried his feet in the sand. "I'll be okay."

She wondered how far they would have to walk before they found a town, a meal, a place to stay. His feet would be worn raw. She cringed, anticipating the infections. "I wish I still had the healing sword."

Michael stood and helped her to her feet. "That sword belonged to Raphael. I'm sure of it. He's the Angel of Healing. I can't help but wonder how Loki got his hands on it. What happened to Raphael?"

They began trudging along the beach, hand in hand, away from the shore. "Maybe that should be the next thing we do," Bryony said, "in our quest to change the world. Maybe we should find out what happened to Raphael."

Michael grinned down at her. "That sounds like a good plan."

She kicked sand as she walked. "All my plans are good plans."

Michael burst out laughing, and Bryony's chest ached with joy to see him back to his old self again. They would be all right, she decided. Nothing else mattered in the end. They had each other, and their worlds overlapped in the most magnificent way. He took small steps to keep pace with her, and sometimes she jogged to keep pace with him, but they were always side by side.

When they finally came to a highway, Michael turned to her and said, "You know I'll likely beg you to marry me one day, don't you?"

"No, Michael." She smiled and brought the palm of his hand to her lips. His skin still tasted of salt. "You won't have to beg for that."

Acknowledgements

Foremost, I have to thank my first reader, editor, supporter, and muse. Stephen, I doubt I would have been able to write this series without you. I'm sure you already know that, but I should put it in writing so you can use it against me later. Thank you for everything.

One of my biggest challenges in writing Godhunter was finding a balance between authenticity and understandability for the Jamaican Patois. Andre Cuffe of https://chatpatwah.com was generous enough to advise me. His YouTube channel and audiobook were invaluable, and his willingness to look at my work and offer his opinion was far more help than I could have hoped for.

I'd also like to thank my cover artist, Laura Barrett. I took a chance and reached out to an artist who was well established and knew nothing about me, and I was thrilled when she responded and expressed interest in creating a cover for me. Working with Laura was such a delight, and seeing *Godhunter*'s cover come to life was the highlight of my year. I can't recommend her enough.

Lastly, to the beta readers and teachers who inspired and encouraged me throughout my life: you helped a timid girl to believe in herself just enough to give it a go. Thank you.

A Tyranny of Angels

Book 1: Godhunter

Book 2: Speak of the Devil

Book 3: The Evolution of Angels

https://www.isobellynn.com